"Miss Moorehouse, may I inquire as to what you are doing skulking behind my curtain?"

A guilty flush seared upward from her toes. "I wasn't spying. I was . . . watching for my opportunity to leave your chamber." Which was true. Really, if the man didn't want women looking at him, he shouldn't remove his clothes—ever.

"Are you armed?" he asked.

"Certainly not."

He stepped closer, until mere inches separated them. She drew in a sharp breath as the warmth of his body surrounded her, inundating her senses. A drop of water dripped from his wet hair, landing on her collarbone.

Dear God, it was nearly impossible to breathe, to think, with him so close—that somehow had little to do with his arm pressing against her and the cool blade touching her neck and everything to do with the fact that no more than a thin robe stood between his nakedness and her hands . . .

By Jacquie D'Alessandro

SLEEPLESS AT MIDNIGHT
NEVER A LADY
NOT QUITE A GENTLEMAN
LOVE AND THE SINGLE HEIRESS
WHO WILL TAKE THIS MAN?

Jacquie D'Alessandro

Sleepless at Midnight

AVON BOOKS

An Imprint of HarperCollinsPublishers

This is a work of fiction. Names, characters, places, and incidents are products of the author's imagination or are used fictitiously and are not to be construed as real. Any resemblance to actual events, locales, organizations, or persons, living or dead, is entirely coincidental.

AVON BOOKS
An Imprint of HarperCollins*Publishers*
10 East 53rd Street
New York, New York 10022–5299

First Avon Books paperback printing: July 2007

Avon Trademark Reg. U.S. Pat. Off. and in Other Countries, Marca Registrada, Hecho en U.S.A.
HarperCollins® is a registered trademark of HarperCollins Publishers.

Printed in the U.S.A.

10 9 8 7 6 5 4 3 2 1

This book is dedicated with my deepest affection and admiration to two extraordinary women it was my honor and pleasure to know for what, sadly, turned out to be far too short a time. To LuAnn Stanaland and Diane Cegalis—your faith and courage will never cease to inspire me and everyone who loved you. I was blessed to be your friend, and neither of you will ever be forgotten. You will always live in our hearts.

And as always, to my wonderful, encouraging husband, Joe. You bring sunshine even when it's pouring rain. And to my fantastic, beautiful son, Christopher, aka Sunshine, Junior. Love you—FEAE

Acknowledgments

I would like to thank the following people for their invaluable help and support:

My editor, Erika Tsang, for loving the idea of this book and her help in bringing it to life.

Liate Stehlik, Carrie Feron, Debbie Stier, Pam Spengler-Jaffee, Brian Grogan, Mike Spradlin, Adrienne DiPietro, Mark Gustafson, Rhonda Rose, Carla Parker, Tom Egner, and all the wonderful people at Avon/HarperCollins for their kindness, cheerleading, and for helping make my dreams come true.

My agent, Damaris Rowland, for her faith and wisdom, as well as Steven Axelrod and Lori Antonson.

Jenni Grizzle and Wendy Etherington for keeping me going and always being up for lobster, champagne, chocolate, and cheesecake. And to Stephanie Bond and Rita Herron for joining the party. Here's to good health!

Thanks also to Sue Grimshaw—for both your support and waking up so early to watch my interview—and Kathy Baker, bookseller extraordinaire. And as always to Kay and Jim Johnson, Kathy and Dick Guse, Lea and Art D'Alessandro, and Michelle, Steve, and Lindsey Grossman.

A cyber hug to my Looney Loopies Connie Brockway,

Marsha Canham, Virginia Henley, Jill Gregory, Sandy Hingston, Julia London, Kathleen Givens, Sherri Browning, and Julie Ortolon, and also to the Temptresses.

To my wonderful new friends with whom I shared the Levy Bus Tour—thank you for a fantastic experience: Pam Nelson, Justine Willis, Kathleen Koelbl, Krystal Nelson, Janet Krey, Emily Hixon, Devar Spight, Susan Andersen, Mary Balogh, Allison Brennan, Pamela Britton, Wendy Corsi-Staub, Gemma Halliday, Candice Hern, Sabrina Jeffries, Susan Kearney, Marjorie Liu, Brenda Novak, Karen Rose, and Gena Showalter. And my gratitude to everyone at HarperCollins for the opportunity to participate in the event.

A very special thank you to the members of Georgia Romance Writers and Romance Writers of America.

And finally, thank you to all the wonderful readers who have taken the time to write to me. I love hearing from you!

Chapter 1

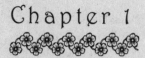

$\mathcal{A}$ chill of unease snaked down Matthew Devenport's spine and he stilled his shovel to scan the darkened cemetery. All his senses on alert, he strained his ears yet only heard the chirping of crickets and the rustling of leaves from the unseasonably cool breeze heavily scented with the threat of rain.

Clouds obscured the moon, enveloping him in shadows, which served his purpose well, but also made it impossible to discern if someone lurked nearby—a realization that did nothing to stop the unsettling quickening of his heartbeat.

He glanced around again, then forced himself to relax. Bloody hell, why this sudden attack of nerves? Nothing appeared amiss. Yet he couldn't shake the eerie sensation that had plagued him since leaving the house at midnight—that someone was following him. Watching him.

An owl hooted, and his pulse jumped, and he pressed his lips together in annoyance at allowing the atmosphere to spook him. He'd made these secret sojourns for months and was well accustomed to the eerie sounds that rose from the darkened forest. Still, he reached down and closed his fingers over the cool metal hilt of the knife tucked in his boot. He didn't relish the thought of using the weapon, but he would if he had to. He hadn't come this far, persevered this long, to have anyone threaten his search.

Search? The word mocked him, and he swallowed the bitter sound that rose in his throat as he jabbed his shovel into the hard ground. This was more than a search. Over the course of the past year, these damned ventures into the night had become more of a quest. An obsession that robbed him of not only sleep, but of his peace of mind. *Soon . . . it will all be over soon.*

One way or another.

Lifting a heavy shovelful of dirt, he tossed it aside, his tired muscles straining with effort. How many more holes could he dig? How many more sleepless nights could he endure? Even during the day, when he didn't search for fear of being discovered, his task haunted him. For he now had less than a month left to keep his pledge. And honor, his integrity, demanded that he do so. He'd once compromised both, and as he was still paying the consequences for that folly, he refused to make that same mistake again.

Yes, so much better to make other *mistakes,* his inner voice sneered.

Such as these nightly journeys into the dark.

But now, after trying for so long yet failing, there was no denying his greatest enemy.

Time.

His time was almost up.

He flung several more shovelfuls of dirt, then paused to swipe his sweaty brow with the back of his hand. Perspiration trickled down his aching back, and he blew out a disgusted breath, frustrated by the fact that as much as he hated this endless searching, he ironically hated even more the fact that his house was now filled with guests, thus allowing him less time to continue the search. They'd arrived en masse earlier this evening and he'd forced himself to endure their company over dinner, an interminable meal he'd thought would never end.

Damn it, he didn't want guests. Didn't want people invading his home. His privacy. Yet what choice did he have? He needed a bride and needed one quick. And by God, he'd do whatever he had to in order to get one. He paused, his gaze lingering on the hole he'd just dug, and his fingers tightened on the rough wooden handle of the shovel. Yes, he'd do whatever he had to.

As was necessary with so many other facets of his life, he shoved aside his own desires and focused on what needed to be done. There were choices to be made, life-altering choices, and as much as he didn't wish to make them, he could delay no longer. And as much as he didn't relish the interruption of playing host, if he'd left the estate and traveled to London instead of inviting guests here to Kent, he'd have lost even more time.

A flash of lightning followed by an ominous growl of thunder interrupted his dark thoughts. Several raindrops splashed against the back of his neck. Seconds later it seemed as if the heavens were ripped asunder. A deluge of water spewed from the sky, stabbing his skin like chilled needles. He was sorely tempted to head back to the house, to abandon his task, but instead he lifted his face and closed his eyes, basking in the sting of the cold spray that made him feel, if only for a few moments, as if he were cleansed of the onerous chore that possessed him.

Lightning flashed again, streaking across the darkened sky, and he opened his eyes. For several seconds the

Devenport family tombstones dating back centuries were illuminated in sharp, rain-soaked relief. Matthew blinked against the sudden brightness, then froze as his gaze riveted on a man. A man making his way in an unmistakably furtive manner across the back boundary of the cemetery. A man he instantly recognized.

Bloody hell, what was Tom Willstone doing skulking about on private property in the middle of the night? Had the village blacksmith seen him? Had it been Tom's prying eyes he'd felt boring into him? Not that he wasn't perfectly within his rights to dig holes on his own estate, but given the nature of his task, Matthew had no desire to be observed. Observation would only lead to speculation, and speculation to endless questions—none of which he would, or could, answer.

Another bolt of lightning flashed and he saw Tom disappear among the soaring elms and shrubbery that marked the property line separating Langston Manor and the path leading to the village of Upper Fladersham. He didn't know what Tom was doing or what he might have seen, but he needed to find out. Which would require a trip to the village.

His stomach cramped at the mere thought. He hadn't been to the village in nearly twenty years. Not since—

He sliced off the thought, refusing to allow the painful memories to swallow him. He didn't have to go to the village himself. He'd simply do what he'd been doing for the past two decades and send someone in his stead. Luckily, Daniel was one of his house party guests. His best friend would make the trip for him.

His guests . . . Daniel—his one trusted male friend, and several other male acquaintances. And a seeming gaggle of young women, all of whom appeared to be duplicates of each other, blending into a single mass of chattering femininity so as to be indistinguishable. And then there were the chaperones—a marriage-minded mama and an equally marriage-minded aunt—who eyed him with the avarice of vultures contemplating a fresh carcass. If those fine protectors of virtue knew the truth of his life, his circumstances, surely they wouldn't be so anxious to foist their charges in his direction.

A humorless sound escaped him, swallowed up by the rain and thunder. But then again, perhaps it wouldn't matter. After all, a great deal could be overlooked when a title such as Marchioness Langston was the prize.

He fought a grimace at the mere thought of the society gems he'd invited into his home. They all seemed so . . . ordinary. So typical of women of his class—ornamental, hothouse flowers who chatted about inane subjects and could wax poetic about the weather and fashion for *hours*. While each of his female guests possessed the necessary traits he required, none had stood out to him.

Well, except for the one who'd sat at the opposite end of the dining room table from him. Lady Wingate's younger sister, whom she'd insisted accompany her to his house party. The one with the spectacles that kept sliding down her nose. What was the chit's name? He shook his head, unable to recall.

Indeed, the only reason she'd stood out was because he happened to glance in her direction after the soup was served. She leaned over her bowl, presumably to enjoy the aroma. When she raised her head, her spectacle lenses were completely fogged over from the soup's steam. An unexpected laugh had risen in his throat at the sight, one born of empathy, as the very same thing frequently happened to him whenever he wore his reading spectacles and sipped from his teacup. He imagined her blinking furiously behind the opaque lenses, and his lips had twitched with amusement. Seconds later her lenses cleared and their gazes met. Something flickered in her eyes, yet before he could attempt to decipher it, she looked away and his attention was quickly claimed by another guest.

Ah yes, his guests, all of whom were fast asleep, cozily nestled in their beds. Their warm, dry beds. Lucky devils.

He blinked the rain from his eyes then ruthlessly shoved aside his pang of envy and again stabbed his shovel into the ground.

"I hereby call our meeting to order."

A thrill ran through Sarah Moorehouse at the softly spoken words she'd waited so long to utter. She stood near the marble fireplace in her guest bedchamber at Lord Langston's country estate, the warmth from the low burning fire in the grate seeping through her thin cotton robe and night rail. Eerie shadows flickered in the room, made all the more menacing by the flashes of lightning, rumbles of thunder, and rain lashing against the darkened windows.

It was the perfect night to talk about monsters.

And murder.

She slowly approached the bed, her gaze touching on the three women perched like pigeons on a branch upon the oversized mattress, their stark white nightclothes appearing to glow in the dancing light. Lady Emily Stapleford and Lady Julianne Bradley both looked at her through wide, expectant eyes, their arms wrapped around their updrawn knees. Sarah had had her doubts that the sheltered young women would follow through with the plan to sneak from their quarters and gather here for this clandestine meeting, but they'd arrived at exactly one A.M., clearly eager for the proceedings to begin.

Sarah's gaze shifted to her older sister, Carolyn. By virtue of her marriage ten years earlier, Carolyn had been elevated from a mere physician's daughter to Viscountess Wingate. And by virtue of her beloved husband's death three years ago, had been deflated into a heartbroken, grieving widow, her soul so shattered Sarah had wondered if she'd ever get her sister back. The sparkle now glowing in Carolyn's blue eyes was worth any scandal their activities might cause, and Sarah was deeply thankful that despite her loss, Carolyn was now making an effort to rejoin life.

After settling herself on the counterpane so the four women formed a small circle, Sarah pushed her spectacles higher on her nose, lifted her chin and said in a serious tone befitting the occasion, "I'll begin by asking a question which, given the nature of our discussion, has surely occurred to all of us: Do you think Dr. Frankenstein was merely a figment of Mary Shelley's imagination—or do you believe it's possible there really was a mad scientist who dug up graves and stole body parts to create a living monster?"

Emily, the most daring of Sarah's companions whispered, "*Was* a mad scientist? Perhaps he still exists. And is continuing with his work. Perhaps Mary Shelley knew him, worked for him, before she embarked on her scandalous affair with the married Percy."

Sarah looked at the beautiful Lady Emily, whom she'd befriended five years earlier through her sister. She'd taken an immediate liking to the energetic Emily, whose green eyes often twinkled with mischief and whose imagination matched Sarah's own. At one and twenty, Emily was the eldest of Lord and Lady Fenstraw's six children. Thanks to her family's recent reversal of fortunes due to her father's unfortunate penchant for unwise investments and expensive mistresses, Emily had no choice but to marry well.

Sadly, Sarah's observations of the ton had shown her that Emily's father was not the only gentleman of his class whose profligate tendencies and lack of business acumen had thrust their families into such dire financial circumstances. And had further shown that even a beautiful girl such as Emily was rendered less attractive by the lack of a dowry. Which of course meant that for someone like her—plain *and* lacking a fortune *and* who'd reached the advanced age of six and twenty—spinsterhood was a foregone conclusion. Which was quite agreeable to her, as her observations had also led her to conclude that men were far more trouble than they were worth.

Clearing her throat, Sarah said, "Do mad scientists such as Dr. Frankenstein truly exist . . . a perfect question to begin our discussion of Shelley's book."

Julianne, the only daughter of the Earl and Countess of Gatesbourne, one of England's wealthiest families, cleared her throat then said, "If Mama even *suspected* I'd read *that* book, she'd succumb to the vapors."

Sarah turned toward Julianne, noting her deep blush. Sarah knew that some people found the beautiful blond heiress cool and aloof; indeed, she herself had thought as much when they first met several years ago. But she had quickly realized that rather than aloof, Julianne was merely painfully shy. She meekly deferred to her overbearing mother, yet Sarah suspected that beneath Julianne's perfectly poised, reserved exterior lurked an adventurous spirit that longed for something more titillating than a stroll through Hyde Park under the close watch of her chaperone—and Sarah was determined to bring that spirit into the open so it could soar.

She barely refrained from allowing her outspoken nature to overtake her and state that a good dose of the vapors would do Julianne's dour-faced, sharp-eyed mother some good. Instead she said, "By calling ourselves the Ladies Literary Society of London, a name that implies we read and discuss the works of Shakespeare while we're actually reading what we want, we should be safe enough. And since *The Modern Prometheus*—or *Frankenstein*, if you prefer—is, in spite of the scandals surrounding it, considered a literary work, no one can accuse us of lying." Her lips curved upward. "Those very scandals being the exact reason I chose it for our first book."

"I have to admit, this is the most fun I've had in a long time," said Carolyn with an enthusiasm that defied her usual sedate manner, filling Sarah with hope that her idea to draw her sister further from her self-imposed shell was working. Already she could sense the change in her two friends as well. This small act of defiance in reading a scandalous book by a woman who'd had an affair with a married man and bore him two children before they'd finally married marked Julianne's first timid steps from her mother's tight control, and was proving a much needed diversion for Emily from her family's financial problems.

"A very fun venture," Sarah said with a nod. "I think we can all agree that Mary Shelley possesses a vivid and formidable imagination."

"I can see why it was at first believed that the book was written by a man," Emily murmured. "Who would suspect that a woman could conceive such a chilling tale?"

"That is just one of the many unfair aspects of today's society," Sarah said, touching upon a subject close to her heart. "Women are constantly underestimated. A grave error in my opinion."

"An error, perhaps," Carolyn said, "but it is the way of things."

Emily nodded. "And the people who constantly underestimate us are men."

"Precisely," said Sarah, shoving up her spectacles. "Which simply proves one of my pet theories: there is no creature on this earth more vexing than a man."

"Are you speaking of any man in particular," asked Carolyn, her voice laced with amusement, "or simply in general terms?"

"General terms. You know how I enjoy observing human nature, and based on my detailed observations, I've deduced that the vast majority of men can be effectively summed up in one word."

"A word other than vexing?" asked Julianne.

"Yes." Sarah raised her brows and paused expectantly, like a teacher waiting for her pupils to answer a query. When no one ventured a guess, she prompted, "Men are . . . ?"

"Enigmatic?" said Carolyn.

"Er, manly?" suggested Emily.

"Um, hairy?" said Julianne.

"Nincompoops," stated Sarah with an emphatic nod that sent her glasses sliding once again. "Nearly without exception. Young or old, they believe that women are nothing save brainless ornaments to be either ignored or just trotted out and then tolerated with gritted teeth. Patted upon the head, then sent back to whichever corner he plucked her from whilst he resumes his brandy drinking or flirting."

"I wasn't aware you'd that much experience with gentlemen," Carolyn said mildly.

"One can draw conclusions from observations. I've no need to jump into a fire to know it would burn." Still, warmth flushed Sarah's cheeks. In truth, she had very little direct experience with men, as their gazes always seemed to skip right over her to land upon someone more attractive. Being of a pragmatic nature and fully aware of the limitations of her appearance, she'd ceased to be hurt by such goings-on long ago. And being nearly invisible to men had afforded her many hours to observe their behavior while she sat in the corners at the numerous soirees she'd attended in recent months with Carolyn—all in her attempt to encourage her sister to step out of her mourning. And based upon those observations, Sarah felt fully confident and justified in her opinion.

Nincompoops.

"If your theory is to hold true," Carolyn said, "then clearly gentlemen believe women are also good for flirting." Her eyes crinkled at the corners, but Sarah caught the flicker of sadness in their depths. "Or are they flirting with the potted palms?"

Guilt pricked Sarah for her unguarded words, and she plucked at the ribbon tied at the end of her long braid, from which unruly curls sprang. Carolyn's husband, Edward, had been a paragon amongst men—devoted, loving, and loyal. Not at all a nincompoop. Yet, more than anyone else, Carolyn was certainly accustomed to her outspoken nature.

"They only flirt with the potted palms after imbibing too much brandy. Which happens with shocking frequency. But I only mention nincompoops as we are speaking about our book selection, and as far as I am concerned, Victor Frankenstein was a nincompoop."

"I absolutely agree," said Julianne with a vigorous nod, her usual reserve temporarily forgotten, as it often was when the four of them were together. "All the bad things that happened in the story, all the murders and tragic deaths, were his fault."

"But Victor didn't kill anyone," Emily said, scooting closer. "The monster was responsible."

"Yes, but Victor created the monster," pointed out Carolyn.

"And then utterly rejected him." Sarah pressed her palms together, vividly recalling her dislike for the scientist and her deep sympathy for the grotesque being he created. "Victor discarded that poor creature as if he were yesterday's trash, running away from him, leaving him with *nothing*. No knowledge of life or of how to survive. He created him, then showed him not even a moment of human decency. Simply because he was hideous. It certainly wasn't the monster's fault he was so. Not everyone is beautiful." She gave a philosophical shrug and forced back the suspicion that her empathy for the monster perhaps reflected a bit too closely some of her own personal struggles.

"The monster was worse than merely 'not beautiful,'" Julianne pointed out. "He was wretched and huge and hideous. Very frightening."

"Still, even if no one else could have found it in their hearts to treat him decently, surely Victor, his creator, should have extended some tiny crumb of kindness to him," Sarah insisted. "The monster didn't turn harsh and cruel until after he finally realized that he would never be accepted. By anyone. How different his life would have been if just one person had been kind to him."

"I agree," said Carolyn. "He was such a tragic figure. If Victor had treated him with decency, I think others would have followed suit."

"But Victor suffered greatly for his sins as well," said Julianne. "The monster killed his brother, his best friend, and his wife. I found I had sympathy for both Frankenstein and his monster."

Sarah pursed her lips. "I must admit my curiosity was piqued by the fact that other than vague references to visiting charnel houses and digging about in graveyards for bodies, Shelley was very evasive on how the creature was actually made and came to life. Makes me wonder if such a thing is really possible." She glanced toward the window where the rain slashed and lightning flashed. "You realize that the monster was created during a storm just like this."

"Do not even consider such a thing," Julianne said with a visible shudder. "Don't forget, it was Victor's obsession with knowledge and learning that led to his downfall."

"There is nothing wrong with the pursuit of knowledge," Sarah protested.

"I suspect Victor Frankenstein, and his monster, would disagree with you," said Carolyn.

"Personally, I think Victor's downfall was creating a creature that was so repulsive," said Emily. "Surely he could see that it was hideous before he brought it to life. I may not be a scientist, but if *I* were going to create a man, I would set my sights on fashioning the *perfect* man. Certainly not one a person couldn't bear to gaze upon. And definitely not one who would resort to murder."

"The Perfect Man . . ." mused Julianne, tapping her finger to her chin. "Do you think such a thing exists?"

Sarah glanced at Carolyn. Saw the shadow of sadness

that clouded her sister's eyes. And could almost hear her thinking, *I know he does. I was married to him.*

Emily sighed. "I'd like to think so, but I cannot say as I've ever met him."

"Nor have I," said Sarah. "And over the past few months, we've certainly had the opportunity to observe the best society has to offer. Not a perfect man in the entire bunch."

"Not even a near perfect specimen," Julianne concurred with a sigh.

"Well, I find that unacceptable," Sarah said, sitting up straighter. "Therefore, in the spirit of our reading of *The Modern Prometheus,* I propose that we do what Victor Frankenstein failed to do." She leaned forward and paused, excitement humming through her, the silence broken only by the ominous rumble of thunder and the violent splatter of rain against the windows. Lightning flashed, illuminating the trio of questioning gazes locked upon her.

"I propose," Sarah said in a low voice, "that we create the Perfect Man."

Chapter 2

Sarah's announcement was met with slack-jawed silence.

Finally Emily cleared her throat. "Create our own man? Are you daft? If you think I'm going to skulk about in charnel houses and graveyards in search of bodies—"

"Good heavens, Emily, your imagination is almost as grisly as Mary Shelley's," said Sarah. "Besides, I'm not convinced it is actually scientifically possible to reanimate dead objects such as Frankenstein did."

"Thank goodness for that," Julianne murmured.

"I meant that we should create our man in the figurative, as opposed to the literal, sense. Decide what would constitute the Perfect Man. Make a list of the physical qualities and personality traits."

"I see," said Carolyn, nodding. "But why stop there? I propose that we actually build him. Not as a monster, but more like a . . . life-size doll."

"Oh, yes!" said Emily in an excited whisper. "One we can prop in a chair, who will sit in the drawing room with us—"

"And discuss fashion without complaint," broke in Julianne with a giggle. "For hours on end."

Caught up in the enthusiasm for the project, especially

as it had clearly captured Carolyn's interest, Sarah rose
and crossed to the escritoire set in the corner near the fireplace. After sitting, she pulled a piece of vellum and the
pen toward her and began making a list.

"So the Perfect Man is one who will sit and talk to us,"
she repeated as she wrote.

"Not just talk to us," Carolyn said, "but *listen* to us."

"And not just listen," stressed Emily, "but he must ac-
tively seek out our opinions."

"Of course," agreed Sarah, dipping her pen tip into the
inkwell again. "Because he will recognize that we are intelligent and have worthwhile things to say. What else?"

"He must be kind," said Carolyn. "Patient. Generous.
Honest. And honorable."

"Witty, intelligent, and a superb—and tireless—
dancer," added Emily.

Julianne heaved out a dreamy sigh. "The Perfect Man
must be knee-weakening handsome, wildly romantic, and
stunningly passionate."

Sarah blinked behind her glasses and shifted her gaze
toward the bed where Julianne stared toward the window
with a faraway look in her eyes. "*Stunningly* passionate?"

Julianne turned toward her and nodded, her expression serious. "Oh, yes. The sort of man who can sweep a
woman off her feet."

"Literally or figuratively?"

"Both. The Perfect Man must make your insides flutter
from a mere look."

"Perhaps that flutter means you've merely eaten some
bad cheese," Sarah said dryly. Good heavens, after seeing
the suffering Carolyn had endured after Edward's death,
she harbored no desire for any sort of grand passion. She'd
simply devote her energies to her books and flowers and

pets and sketches, thank you very much. Besides, she was not at all the sort of woman to inspire passion in a man.

Although sometimes she couldn't help but wonder . . . what would it feel like to possess the sort of beauty that *would* inspire such feelings? What would it feel like to love a man that much? To be loved so much in return? To be desired that much?

Her useless thoughts were cut off when Julianne shot her a stern look and pointed toward her vellum. "'Make your insides flutter.' Write it down."

"Fine," Sarah mumbled, and wrote it down. After she did so, she looked up. "Anything else?"

Carolyn cleared her throat. "He should also be a, um, good kisser." She cleared her throat again. "Of course, that might already be covered under 'stunningly passionate.'"

Sarah added good kisser to her list and frowned at the heat that suddenly rose in her cheeks. "Is that all?"

"I think he should enjoy visiting the shops," said Emily. "And be tall and strong."

"Oh, yes," said Julianne. "With broad shoulders and lots of lovely muscles."

"He sounds like a pack mule," Sarah said, her pen flying across the vellum.

"Thick hair," added Carolyn, her voice sounding wistful to Sarah's ears. "Thick, wavy hair."

"And lovely, full lips," said Emily with a giggle. "All the better for kissing, you know."

Sarah added it to her list, shoving aside the useless thought of kissing a man, full-lipped or otherwise. Still, that didn't stop moments of longing from sneaking up on her. . .

With a brusque shake of her head to clear the image of lovely male lips that would never touch hers, she asked,

"Anything else?" When no more suggestions came forth, she looked over her list then said, "According to the Ladies Literary Society of London, the Perfect Man is a kind, patient, generous, honest, honorable, witty, intelligent, handsome, romantic, stunningly passionate, make-your-insides-flutter, full-lipped, good kisser who can dance, shop, listen, and solicit our opinions, all tirelessly and without complaint."

"Oh, yes, he does indeed sound perfect," said Emily with an approving nod.

"But what about you, Sarah?" asked Carolyn. "You didn't add any qualities to the list."

"No, but I believe you covered everything," she said.

"Surely there must be *something* else you think is necessary for the Perfect Man," said Julianne.

Sarah considered for several seconds, then nodded. "Now that you mention it . . . I think he should wear glasses."

"Glasses?" echoed three doubt-filled voices from the bed.

"Yes. And since I am so fond of horticulture, he should like flowers. And the garden. And digging in the dirt. And pulling weeds. All tirelessly and without complaint."

"I can't imagine a gentleman of the ton pulling weeds, and it's not quite as exciting as being a good kisser," said Emily with an impish grin, "but handy, I suppose, if you're strolling through the garden and have run out of conversation."

Sarah added her requirements to the list then set down her pen and turned toward her partners in crime, or rather, the Ladies Literary Society of London.

"Since it was your idea, Carolyn, how do you propose we make this life-size doll?"

Her sister frowned and tapped her finger to her chin.

"Let's see . . . we shall need some gentleman's clothing. Breeches, a shirt, cravat, some boots."

"Yes, and then we can stuff them," said Julianne, her eyes shining in the firelight. "Like a pillow."

"Form his head from a roundly stuffed pillow case," added Emily. "Since Sarah's the only one of us who can draw worth a whit, she can sketch his face on the material. I vote for blue eyes."

"I prefer brown eyes," said Julianne.

"Green," voted Carolyn, not surprising Sarah with her choice, as Edward had possessed green eyes.

"In that case, in order to satisfy everyone, he shall have hazel eyes," decreed Sarah, then she grinned. "Which just happen to be *my* favorite. Now, our gentleman needs a name." She pursed her lips, then smiled. "How about Franklin N. Stein?"

Everyone laughed and agreed. Then Julianne asked, "How are we going to procure a set of gentleman's clothing? Purchase the items in the village?"

"Completely boring," Sarah scoffed. Her lips curved upward. "I suggest a scavenger hunt. The gentlemen attending the house party will be occupied during the day with riding and shooting and billiards. We'll each simply pick a gentleman, nip up to his bedchamber when he isn't about, relieve him of our assigned article of clothing, and *voilà*! Franklin N. Stein is born."

"We can't *steal* things," Julianne said, sounding aghast.

Sarah waved away her concern with a flick of the wrist. "It's not stealing—we're simply *borrowing* the items. We'll dismantle Franklin before the house party ends and return the items to the gentlemen in question."

Julianne worried her bottom lip between her teeth. "But what if we're caught?"

"You'll go to the gallows," Emily said with a perfectly straight face. "So you'd best be careful."

Even in the dim light, Sarah saw Julianne's face pale. "You won't go to the gallows," she assured her friend, shooting Emily a quelling look. "But you'd die of embarrassment and your mother would faint dead away so you'd best not be caught."

Julianne chewed some more on her lip, then jerked her head once in a tight nod. "All right, I'll do it."

"Finally," said Emily. "A bit of real excitement." She bounced up and down several times and rubbed her hands together. "Who shall pinch what and from whom?"

"Hmmm . . . let's base it on which article of clothing seems to mean the most to each gentleman," Sarah suggested. "What about boots?"

"I suggest Lord Berwick for the boots," said Julianne. "Not only does he walk with an air of great confidence, but he clearly takes pride in his footwear. We partnered in the quadrille several weeks ago at Lady Pomperlay's soiree, and when I admired his Hessians, he waxed poetic about their fine leather for the next five minutes."

"Excellent suggestion," said Sarah. "You're in charge of procuring Lord Berwick's boots, Julianne. But don't relieve him of that particular pair, as he's certain to notice their absence. What about the cravat?"

"Lord Thurston is proud of his intricate neckwear," said Emily. "And with good reason—I've never seen a gentleman with more beautifully tied knots, and 'tis admirable when a man takes pride in his appearance. I'll pinch one from him. Shouldn't be too difficult. I've had plenty of practice taking back things my annoying younger siblings have stolen from me."

"I thought we said this isn't stealing," Julianne said in a worried tone.

"It isn't," Sarah assured in a soothing voice. She turned to Carolyn. "That leaves you and me, and a shirt and breeches. Seeing as how breeches seem more . . . personal, and you've been married and are therefore more familiar with things of a, um, personal male nature, I think you should get the breeches."

"Very well," Carolyn said calmly, as if Sarah had just suggested she pour another cup of tea. "Of the gentlemen remaining in the house party, I believe I shall borrow a pair from Lord Surbrooke. His taste is impeccable and his clothing is always perfectly tailored."

"Not to mention that he fills out his breeches very nicely," Emily said with a mischievous grin.

Sarah watched as her sister and two friends glanced at each other, then burst into smothered laughter. She joined in, delighted to hear Carolyn laugh, but annoyed at herself for not noticing how Lord Surbrooke apparently filled out his breeches. She was normally very observant. She made a mental note to look at him more closely at her first opportunity.

"I think the shirt should come from our host, Lord Langston," said Julianne. "I noticed at dinner this evening that of all the gentlemen, his shirt was the whitest and looked the most crisp."

"Plus he has very broad shoulders," Emily chimed in with her impish grin in place.

"Lord Langston it is," said Carolyn. She looked at Sarah. "Your assignment is to procure a shirt from our host."

Sarah pressed her lips together to keep from grimacing. Ah, yes, their host. Who, in the course of mere seconds during dinner this evening, had noted her soup-fogged spectacles, laughed at her, then instantly dismissed her. Oh, he hadn't laughed outright, but she'd seen his lips twitch. Then the all-too familiar way he had quickly averted his attention to someone else—a very attractive female someone else. The way other gentlemen's attention always quickly veered away from her. It had ceased to bother her long ago, yet with Lord Langston, for the tiniest fraction of an instant, she'd thought he meant to speak to her. Ridiculously believed he might be laughing *with* her rather than *at* her. Which is why she'd felt the sting of his dismissal more strongly than she'd wanted to.

She'd observed enough men like him to know his sort all too well. She had no doubt that Matthew Devenport, who'd inherited the title Marquess Langston upon his father's death last year, was merely another handsome, wealthy peer spoiled by too much money, too much free time, too much pleasure seeking, and too many fawning women. And certainly a man of his striking dark good looks had to be accustomed to fawning women. Indeed, it was fortunate she was immune to such superficial attributes as a handsome face lest she'd be tempted to simply stare at the man.

She'd known her invitation to his house party was Carolyn's doing. Although Carolyn was officially her chaperone—heaven knew she didn't require one—Sarah knew she was more her sister's traveling companion. If the only way to get Carolyn back out into the world was to accompany her there, then by God, she'd go to the ends of the earth if necessary.

Still, she suspected there was more to this house party than a simple gathering of friends. She'd heard whispers that the eligible Lord Langston—holder of one of the oldest and most venerable titles in England— might be looking for a wife. Of course, that could have merely been wishful thinking on the part of the young women she'd overheard talking about it at a musicale last week. Yet, if it were true, from his perspective either Julianne, Emily, or Carolyn would be perfect candidates. She strongly suspected he'd invited them to look them over. Humph. As if they were horseflesh to be inspected.

She'd been tempted to tell her sister and friends of the rumor, but hadn't wanted to say anything that might discourage Carolyn from attending the house party. Especially now that her sister was making such strides in rejoining society and emerging from her mourning—accepting Lord Langston's invitation being the largest and most significant step thus far. It was, after all, only a rumor. If Lord Langston was indeed looking for a bride, Carolyn was out of the question as a prospective candidate. Her sister had confessed to her that she had no intention of ever marrying again. That she would only marry for love, and could never love another man as she'd loved Edward. Of course, Lord Langston wasn't privy to that information, but Sarah had every confidence that Carolyn would make certain he knew should the need arise.

Of course both Emily and Julianne were both eligible bride candidates. Therefore, she intended to keep a sharp eye on Lord too-handsome-for-his-own-good Langston to determine if his character rendered him good enough for either of her friends. Unfortunately, based on what she'd seen of him thus far, he fell firmly into the nincompoop category.

And now she had to pilfer—or rather borrow—a shirt from her dismissive host. A tiny smile pulled at the corners of her mouth. It might actually be fun to get the best of him. Take something of his—temporarily, of course—

without his knowledge. A chortle tickled her throat. *Laugh at me, will you, Lord Langston? Well, you're nothing but another of those spoiled nincompoops. And I shall have the last laugh upon you.*

Pushing her glasses back into place, Sarah said to her companions, "We all have our assignments. I call this first meeting of the Ladies Literary Society of London adjourned and move that we reconvene here at one A.M. tomorrow to begin work on Mr. Franklin N. Stein."

"Hear, hear," said Emily, raising an imaginary glass in toast.

Quick good-nights were said all around, then they slipped from Sarah's room to make their way stealthily down the corridor to their own bedchambers.

After closing the door behind them, Sarah leaned against the oak panel. Her gaze fell upon the list she'd left on the antique escritoire, and pushing off from the door, she walked toward the small desk. After picking up the pen, she slowly dipped the nib into the inkwell and added her last requirements to the Perfect Man list. The most important requirements. The ones she hadn't been able to bring herself to say in front of the others. For although she was among her closest confidants, some things were still difficult to admit. To anyone.

When she finished writing, she set down the pen and looked at her words. *Does not judge people by their looks. Can discern beauty beneath that which is plain. Does not look through people as if they don't exist.*

She had no reason to believe that such a man existed, but so long as she was dreaming him up, why not dream big?

Another flash of lightning illuminated the room, and she rose to walk to the window. She'd always loved the sound of summer storms, found the slash of the rain against the roof and windows oddly soothing. Streaks of lightning flashed and she glanced out the window. And froze. At the sight of a man exiting a nearby copse of elms to approach the house. Amid the intermittent flashes, she saw him hurrying across the lawn, head bent, carrying a shovel, his hair and clothes plastered to him. Suddenly, as if he felt her gaze upon him, he paused and looked up. She shrank back, clutching the heavy velvet curtains flanking the windows, but not before she'd gotten a good look at him. And instantly recognized him.

Heart pounding for no good reason she could think of, she waited several seconds, then peeked out the window once again. He was gone.

Had he seen her? She frowned at the question. So what if he had? *She* wasn't the one skulking about at an ungodly hour during a storm, clutching a shovel.

But what had Lord Langston been doing outside in the rain in the middle of the night, traipsing about in a furtive manner with a shovel in the first place? Why it was precisely the sort of thing that—

Her gaze jerked to the three leather bound books on the night table that comprised *The Modern Prometheus*.

—precisely the sort of thing that Victor Frankenstein had done.

Her imagination, which had always been lively, threatened to run amok. She reeled in her runaway thoughts and with a frown stepped away from the window. Surely there was a logical explanation for her host's odd behavior.

And she was determined to discover what it was.

Chapter 3

T he first mauve streaks of dawn were just seeping through her window when Sarah quietly exited her bedchamber. She'd awakened early, as she did every morning, anxious to be outside, especially so as the rain had ceased at some point during the night, and she longed to breathe in the fresh, damp scents of the air and grass after a storm.

When the carriages had approached Langston Manor late yesterday afternoon, she'd caught glimpses of what appeared to be impressive gardens and was eager to explore and make some sketches. Especially now, in this quiet predawn time, as she would have the entire outdoors all to herself.

With her worn leather satchel containing her sketch supplies tucked under her arm, she rounded the corner of the corridor. And collided with a young maid carrying an armful of snowy bed linens.

"Oh! I beg yer pardon, miss," the maid said, clutching her teetering bundle closer to her chest. "I weren't expectin' anyone to be about so early."

"My fault," Sarah said, bending to pick up both her satchel and a pillowcase that had fallen from the top of the maid's stack. "I was lost in thought and not watching where I was going." She straightened, deftly refolded the pillow case, then set it on top of the maid's bundle.

"Th-Thank you," stammered the clearly stunned young woman.

Sarah fought the urge to look toward the ceiling. Ridiculous that the maid should be surprised by a mere act of common courtesy, especially as she herself had been the one not paying attention. Good lord, she was a lowly physician's daughter, not visiting royalty. If she lived to be one hundred, she'd never grow accustomed to the formality of the world of Society that Carolyn had married into. She often wondered how her sister tolerated it.

"You're welcome . . . ?" she inclined her head, waiting for the young woman to supply her name.

"Mary, miss."

Sarah pushed up her glasses and smiled. "You're welcome, Mary."

The maid's gaze took in Sarah's plain brown day gown. "Did ye need somethin', miss? Is the bell cord in yer chamber not workin'?"

"There's nothing I require, thank you. Except perhaps directions to the gardens?" She held her satchel aloft. "I was hoping to do some sketching."

Mary's face lit up. "Oh, the gardens are beautiful, miss, especially after a rain. And so well-tended. Passionate about plants and flowers, his lordship is."

Sarah's brows shot upward. "Really?"

"Oh, yes, miss. Rolls up his sleeves and works in the garden himself. Not afraid of gittin' dirty like some gentlemen are. Even saw 'im once heading into the gardens late at night." She leaned closer and lowered her voice. "Rumor belowstairs is that his lordship is growin' some sort of night-bloomin' flowers wot requires lots of care."

"Night blooming flowers?" A sense of excitement filled her at the thought of such unusual blooms, and then she inwardly cringed, scolding her overactive imagination. Lord Langston had simply been tending his garden last night and she'd cast him in the role of a Frankenstein-like mad scientist. "Such blossoms are very rare."

"Don't know nothin' about it myself, miss, but his lordship is an expert about plants and flowers and such."

"I shall look forward to discussing it with him at the first opportunity," Sarah murmured. Perhaps she'd misjudged Lord Langston. Any man who loved plants and flowers couldn't be *all* bad. Nor could a man who was willing to spend the time to coax night blooming flowers to grow.

After Mary instructed her to exit the house through the drawing room's French windows, Sarah thanked her and headed that way. The instant she stepped outside onto the flagstone terrace, a sense of peace infused her. Deep golds and pinks stained the sky, glowing with the first hints of the rising sun's muted rays. Leaves rustled in the towering elms that speared upward as they flanked the house, providing background music for the birds' gentle morning warbles.

After drawing in a cool, deep breath scented with the lingering fragrance of fresh rain, Sarah started across the flagstones. Her breath caught at the beauty of the vast garden spread before her. Curving trails lined with well-tended borders meandered through acres of perfectly manicured lawns and hedges. Copses of trees, beneath which inviting benches were placed, would provide shade as the sun rose. Clearly her host did indeed harbor a passion for his garden, as this was one of the most beautiful she'd ever seen. She could only imagine how breathtaking it would be once it was flooded with sunshine.

Anxious to explore, she moved down the flagstone steps. The wet grass dampened her sturdy shoes and the hem of her gown, but rather than finding it uncomfortable, she reveled in the familiar and much-loved sensation. She walked slowly along, choosing curving paths at random, marveling at the gorgeous profusion of annuals and perennials. Her mind registered each one as she passed—impatiens, columbine, daisy, blue pimpernel, among dozens of others.

The soft trickle of water reached her ears, and she followed the sound. Several minutes later, after rounding a curve, to her delight she came upon a large round stone fountain from which rose a statue of a robe-draped goddess. She carried a tilted urn, pouring water in a gentle stream into a pond at her feet. A stone bench arced around a portion of the fountain, and the entire small clearing was surrounded by tall hedges. Feeling as if she'd discovered a secret hideaway, Sarah sat down and opened her sketch pad.

She'd just completed a rough outline of the fountain when she heard a soft crunch of gravel. Looking up, she saw a huge dog walk into the small clearing. The beast halted when it caught sight of her. She remained perfectly still so as not to startle the animal, hoping he was friendly. The dog lifted its massive head and sniffed the air.

"Good morning," Sarah said softly.

The beast's tail wagged at her greeting, and with his tongue lolling, he trotted toward her. Lowering his head, he sniffed at her boots, then made his way upward to her knees. She continued to remain still, giving him the opportunity to get her scent while she took in his shiny, dark, short-haired coat. Apparently satisfied that she was friend and not foe, he issued a single, deep woof then sat—right on her boot.

Satisfied that *he* was friend and not foe, Sarah smiled. "*Woof* to you as well." She set aside her sketch pad then buried her fingers in the dog's scruff and scratched. His dark, intelligent eyes dropped in doggie ecstasy and he raised a massive wet paw which he plopped on her lap.

"Oh, you like that, don't you," she crooned, then laughed when her new friend made a sound that resembled a sigh of contentment. "My dog loves that as well. How is it that you're out here all alone?"

No sooner had she voiced the question than another crunch of gravel sounded. Still scratching the dog, she looked up and watched a figure enter the small clearing. A figure she immediately recognized as being her host, Lord Langston. He caught sight of her and stopped as if he'd walked into a wall. Clearly he was as surprised to see her as she was to see him.

His gaze flicked to the huge canine pinning her in place, and with a frown, he whistled softly. The dog immediately slid his paw from her lap then stood. After shooting Sarah a look that appeared to say *I have to go now, but I'll be back,* he obediently trotted to his lordship, where he plunked his rump on the ground. Right on one of his lordship's polished boots.

Sarah rose, pushed up her glasses then offered Lord Langston an awkward curtsy, swallowing her annoyance that he'd burst upon her sanctuary and interrupted her. Especially as she had no right to be annoyed. After all, it was *his* garden, and clearly his dog. Still, why wasn't the man abed? From her observations, she'd concluded that the majority of noblemen didn't present themselves until at least noon. Of course, this was a perfect opportunity to discuss his garden and his night blooming flowers, inconvenient though the timing was.

"Good morning, my lord."

Matthew stared at the young woman, recognizing her as his houseguest with the soup-fogged spectacles from last night's dinner. Lady Wingate's sister, whose name he still could not recall. He swallowed his annoyance that she'd interrupted his quiet walk. Why in God's name wasn't she still abed? From his observations, he'd concluded that young women rarely presented themselves before noon. And when they did present themselves, they were certainly more put together than this chit with her wrinkled, wet-hemmed gown and haphazard coiffure, which listed precariously to the left, slipping from whatever moorings she'd obviously hastily shoved into the flyaway strands. And why in God's name was she looking at him in a way that made him feel as if *he* were intruding upon *her*?

Damn it all, as her host he supposed he'd have to remain here and exchange some polite, inane pleasantries with her. Which was the last thing he wanted to do. He'd needed this walk, this time alone to clear his head, to occupy his time until Daniel made his trip to the village smithy to gather information regarding Tom Willstone's appearance on the estate last night. Well, he'd do what he had to, then escape at his first opportunity.

"Good morning," he said, resigned to his fate of several minutes of forced conversation. His gaze dipped and he barely suppressed a wince at the outline of a huge, dirty wet paw print marring the front of her gown. Good God, the instant she noticed it she'd no doubt fly into the boughs. He made a mental note to mention the soiled gown to Mrs. Harbaker. The housekeeper would see to it that the garment was properly cleaned. He hoped to God he wouldn't be forced to replace it. Women's gowns cost ridiculous amounts of money.

"I see you found my dog," he said, wading into the silence.

"Actually, he found me." Her gaze flicked to the dog and she flashed a smile. "He appears to enjoy sitting on people's feet."

"Yes. Sitting—I taught him that. However, he requires a bit more instruction on where it is proper to plant his bottom." Even as he reached down to give his pet's warm, sturdy neck an affectionate pat, Matthew vowed to have a stern chat with the beast about routing out unwanted houseguests during their morning walk. "He didn't frighten you, I hope."

"Not at all. I've a dog of my own. She nearly matches yours in size. Indeed, except for their coloring, they look very much alike." Her gaze settled on his pet. "He's very sweet."

He barely managed to hide his surprise that she owned such a large animal. Most ladies he knew possessed tiny, yappy lapdogs who did nothing more than piddle on rugs, bite one's ankles, and lounge about on satin pillows.

"Sweet? Thank you, however I can assure you he much prefers to be regarded as fierce and manly."

She looked up and a tiny smile played around the corners of her mouth. "I'm certain he's both—in a very sweet way. What is his name?"

"Danforth."

"An interesting name. How did you happen to choose it?"

"It somehow . . . suited him. All alone, are you?" he asked, looking about. "No chaperone?"

Her brows rose, then her lips quirked in clear amusement. "A woman my age is more apt to serve in the capacity of chaperone rather than require one, my lord."

A woman her age? Obviously she was older than he'd surmised. Not that he'd paid particular attention. He squinted a bit in her direction. Didn't look a day over two and twenty. The muted lighting clearly hid a multitude of aging sins. And there was no denying that those spectacles and dowdy gown lent her a spinsterish air.

"Rather early to be out," he observed, proud that his voice didn't sound the least bit annoyed.

"Not for me. This is my favorite time of day. I love the soft quiet, the gently rising light, the peace and serenity of dawn. The promise of a new day filled with possibilities."

Matthew's brows rose a bit. It was his favorite time of day as well, although he wasn't certain he would have been able to express it why quite so eloquently. "I know precisely what you mean."

"Your gardens are lovely, my lord."

"Thank you—" Damn it, he wished he could recall her name. So much easier to excuse oneself when one could say, *Well, it's been lovely chatting with you, Miss Jones, but I really must be off.* Was it possible her surname was Jones? No, no that wasn't it—

"I understand you're an expert gardener and horticulturalist."

Her statement yanked him back and he squashed the urge to look skyward. Obviously his servants' mouths had been running amok. Next time he hired someone, he was going to make certain that all candidates for the job were mutes.

"It is my great passion, yes," he said, uttering the same

lie his activities had forced him to tell more times than he cared to admit.

Her face bloomed into a smile, one that showed off perfectly straight, pearly white teeth and creased deep, twin dimples into her cheeks. "It is my great passion as well." She indicated the grouping of plants surrounding the fountain. "These *hemerocallis flava* are the healthiest specimens I've ever seen."

Hemero-what? He barely suppressed a groan. Bloody hell, if he didn't have rotten luck, he wouldn't have any luck at all. What were the odds that the first woman he'd met in months who was able to discuss something other than fashion and the weather would be some bloody plant expert?

"Ah, yes, they are particular favorites of mine," he mumbled. And now it was time to escape. He slipped his foot from beneath Danforth's rump and took a backward step. And bumped into the edge of the fountain. And discovered—or rather his arse discovered—that it was the *wet* edge of the fountain. The *cold,* wet edge.

He bit back the sharp oath that rose to his lips and pushed away from the stone. Damn it, if there was anything more uncomfortable than cold, wet wool clinging to one's buttocks he had no desire to discover what it was.

Her gaze shifted to the fountain then to his hips and he saw her lips twitch. She raised her gaze back to his then said, her voice laced with amusement, "A dreadfully uncomfortable sensation I've endured myself on more occasions than I care to recall. May I offer you my handkerchief?"

Humph. As if a bit of feminine lace would speed the drying of his soaked arse. Still, some of his annoyance evaporated at her empathy for his discomfort. "Thank you, but it's barely damp," he lied, forcing his features to remain impassive as a trickle of fountain water tickled its way down the back of his thigh.

"Very well. Tell me, do you use anything special?" she asked.

"To dry my breeches?"

"To fertilize your plants."

"Um, no. Just the, er, usual."

"Surely your compost heap must contain *something* special," she said, her tone and expression earnest. "Something out of the ordinary. Your delphiniums are extraordinary and your *lanicera caprilfolium* is the most fragrant I've ever smelled."

Good God. This conversation made him feel as if he wore a bull's-eye on his wet arse while wandering about an archery field. "You'd have to consult with Paul, my head gardener, on that, as he is in charge of the post heaps."

A frown pulled down her brows and she blinked behind her lenses. "You mean the *com*post heaps?"

"Yes. Of course I do."

Her penetrating, narrow-eyed look made him feel as if he was a lad in knee pants who'd been caught doing something naughty. Definitely time for him to escape. Before he could so much as move an inch, however, she said, "Tell me about your night bloomers."

"I beg your pardon?"

"I've been trying to establish moonflowers and four o'clocks but have not been entirely successful. They must have enjoyed the rain last evening. Certainly more than you."

He stilled, suspicion immediately flooding him. "Me?"

"Yes. I saw you returning to the house late last night. Carrying your shovel."

Damn. So he *had* seen someone at the window when he looked up at the house last night. He'd thought so. Clearly she was one of those nosy women who spent all their time peeking out windows and listening at keyholes—exactly the sort he didn't want as a guest in his home. And now she was looking at him with an expression that suggested she wasn't wholly convinced he'd been merely planting flowers. Double damn.

"Yes, I'd visited the gardens," he said lightly. "Pity the rain came when it did, forcing me to abandon my work with the night bloomers. And just as I was making progress. But tell me, what were you doing up at that hour?"

His suspicions were further aroused when an unmistakably guilty look flashed across her features. Clearly she'd been up to something. But what?

"Oh, nothing," she said in a breezy tone that sounded decidedly forced. "Just restless and unable to sleep after the journey."

As a man who knew a great deal about lying, it was patently obvious she wasn't telling the truth. So what the bloody hell had she been doing? He immediately ruled out the possibility of a passionate encounter. One look at her convinced him she wasn't the type. Conspiring to steal the Langston silver? Or worse—spying on him?

His jaw tightened at the thought. Could *she* have been the eyes he'd felt boring into him at the graveyard? Given the disheveled state of her hair, she looked as if she could have been caught in the rain. Had she left her room for a midnight stroll in the gardens and accidentally happened upon him? Or had she seen him leave the house and deliberately followed him?

He didn't know, but he had every intention of finding out.

"I hope you didn't suffer any ill effects from getting caught in the rain, my lord."

"No ill effects," he said, her adroit maneuvering of the conversation away from herself not lost upon him.

"And your night bloomers were healthy?"

Damned if he knew. "Oh, yes. Those little devils are thriving."

"Thanks no doubt to your diligent checking on them late at night."

"Exactly."

"So you check on them every evening?"

Oh, yes, she was a nosy one. "It depends upon my schedule, of course."

"Of course. I'd love to see them. Which part of the garden are they in?"

Damned if he knew. "Oh, they're over that way." He waved his hand vaguely in a wide arc that encompassed three-quarters of the garden area. "Just keep following the trails and you'll happen upon them eventually."

She nodded, and a bit of the tension gripping him relaxed. As she was no longer looking at him as if his motives were sinister, she obviously believed his sojourn last night was a gardening mission. Excellent. And now it was time for him to make his escape.

"If you'll excuse me, Miss, um . . ." He cleared his throat and coughed. "Danforth and I shall continue our walk."

She tilted her head and rested her gaze on him with a disconcerting penetrating look that made him feel as if he were a pane of glass she could see right through. "You don't know my name, do you?"

It was a statement rather than a question, and to his annoyance, he felt heat flush his face—which only added to his annoyance that she was right. "Of course I know who you are. You're Lady Wingate's sister."

"Whose name you can't recall." Before he could make any attempt at politeness or even admit she was correct, she waved her hand in a dismissive gesture. "Please don't concern yourself. It happens all the time. I'm Sarah Moorehouse, my lord."

It happens all the time.

Matthew wasn't certain whether it was her words or the matter-of-fact manner in which she stated them that had him regarding her more carefully. Yes, he could see how this unremarkable woman could and would be overlooked—a state of affairs to which she'd obviously inured herself. An unexpected fissure of sympathy eased through him, followed by annoyance at himself for not recalling her name. Troublesome and nosy or not, she was his guest, and he didn't like the fact that he'd taken the same route that so many others before him clearly had.

For some inexplicable reason, he was suddenly reluctant to leave. Surely merely the result of wanting to find out more about her—such as her penchant for peering out windows and perhaps tiptoeing through the gardens in the middle of the night. Yet with no desire to resume their earlier conversation, he nodded toward her sketch pad. "What are you drawing?"

"Your fountain." Her gaze shifted to the feminine statue. "The Roman Flora, is she not?"

His brows shot upward in surprise. He might not know much about plants, but he knew his mythology very well. And clearly so did Miss Sarah Moorehouse.

"I don't believe anyone has ever identified her before, Miss Moorehouse."

"Really? The spring roses flowing from her lips are an obvious clue. And where else would the goddess of flowers be but in a garden?"

"Where else, indeed?"

"Although she was a relatively minor figure in Roman mythology, Flora is my favorite of all of the goddesses."

"Why is that?"

"She is also the goddess of spring, a season dear to my heart, as it symbolizes the renewal of the cycle of life. I celebrate her festival every year."

"Floralia?" he asked.

Her brows shot up. "You know of it?"

"Yes, however, I've never celebrated it." Intrigued, he asked, "What do you do?"

There was no missing her surprise at his interest. "It's rather silly, really. Just a bit of a private picnic in the garden."

Silly? Actually that sounded . . . peaceful. "Private? You celebrate alone?"

She shook her head, dislodging a wispy dark curl that brushed along her cheek. "No, not alone. A few select friends join me." Her dimples winked and a teasing gleam flashed behind her spectacles. "Of course, it is a very coveted and exclusive invitation. Very sought-after, you know. Not *everyone* gets to sit upon the Moorehouse heirloom blanket and partake of the feast I've prepared."

"*You've* prepared?"

She nodded. "Experimenting in the kitchen is a great passion of mine."

"I thought you said flowers were your great passion."

"'Tis possible to have more than one passion, my lord. I love finding new uses for the multitude of herbs and berries and vegetables I grow."

He was attempting to hide his surprise that an aristocratic young woman would even know the location of the kitchen, then recalled that she wasn't of the peerage. Her father was . . . a steward? Physician? Yes, something like that. Her sister's title was the result of her marriage.

"This cooking you do . . . are you good?"

"No one's cocked up their toes." Her grin flashed. "Yet."

A chuckle rumbled in his throat, feeling foreign there, surprising him. And he realized how long it had been since he'd laughed.

"Tell me about this feast you prepare for your exclusive party to celebrate Floralia."

"The menu varies every year, depending on who is attending. This year I prepared meat pies and fresh scones with blueberry jam, with strawberry tarts for dessert, for myself."

"That sounds delicious. And for your guests?"

"There were raw carrots, stale bread, a ham bone, warm milk, and a bucket of slop."

"That sounds . . . not nearly as delicious. And you claim no one has yet cocked up their toes?"

She laughed. "They are the foods of choice when your honored guests include rabbits, geese, my dog Desdemona, a litter of kittens, and a pig."

"I see. I'm assuming the pig is an actual porcine and not a human of untidy habits?"

"Correct. Even though the slop was for her, she managed to gobble up one of my strawberry tarts."

"Given the choice, I'd do the same. An interesting array of friends you have."

"They're loyal and always happy to see me. Especially when I'm toting strawberry tarts."

"No horse guests?"

She shook her head and something flickered in her eyes. "No. I'm afraid of them."

His brows shot up. "Of horses?"

"No, strawberry tarts." She flashed another grin. "Yes, horses. I like them so long as they stand at least twenty feet away."

"That must make riding difficult."

"Indeed. Riding is definitely not one of my passions."

He nodded toward her tablet. "May I see your sketch?"

"Oh . . . it's very rough. I'd only just begun."

Since looking at her rudimentary drawing was far safer than allowing the conversation to wander back to plant species he'd never heard of, he said, "I don't mind, if you don't."

She pressed her lips together, and he noted that the pressure coaxed her dimples to blossom. She was clearly reluctant, yet he could easily see that neither did she wish to offend her host. Good God, the drawing must be awful. Well, he'd take a quick peek, murmur a few encouraging words, then excuse himself. He'd certainly done his conversational duty and had learned enough for now. He had no desire to arouse her suspicions by prolonging their chat too long.

She extended the tablet with what appeared to be extreme caution, as if he were going to bite her, but instead of being offended, he was amused. Usually women were all too eager to do whatever he asked. Clearly not the case with Miss Sarah Moorehouse.

He took the pad and looked down. Then blinked. Then turned a bit so as to better capture the soft predawn light. "This is extremely good," he said, unable to keep the surprise from his voice.

"Thank you." She sounded just as surprised as he.

"If this is what you call 'very rough,' I'd be interested to see what you consider to be the finished sketch. The detail you've captured, especially here . . ." He stepped closer, until he stood next to her, then held the tablet in one hand while indicating Flora's face with the other. " . . . here, in her expression, is amazing. I can imagine her smile about to bloom. I can almost see her coming to life."

He turned his head to look at her, and his gaze traveled over her profile, noting the short, straight nose that seemed too small to support her wire-rimmed spectacles. And the gentle curve of her cheek, the smooth skin bearing a small smudge of charcoal.

As if she felt the weight of his regard, she turned to look at him, and he was struck by the fact that she was quite tall. The tops of women's heads normally barely cleared his cravat, but she was nearly on eye level with him.

She blinked behind her glasses, as if startled to find him standing there. The thickness of her lenses made her eyes appear slightly magnified, and he suddenly wished the wan light was brighter so he could discern what color they were. They didn't look especially dark, so probably blue.

"You're quite tall," she said, the words coming out in a rush. As soon as she'd uttered them, she pressed her lips together, as if the words had escaped without her permission. Even in the dull light he could see the flush that stained her cheeks.

A smile pulled at the corners of his mouth. "I was just thinking the same thing about you. 'Tis refreshing that I'm not having to stoop down to chat with you."

A huff of laughter passed her lips and she smiled. "I was just thinking the same thing about you."

His gaze dropped to her smile, to those intriguing deep dimples—which he now noticed flanked a very lush set of lips. "You've captured Flora's expression perfectly," he said. "Her air of happiness and serenity."

"Her mien is one of deep contentment and love," she said softly. "Quite understandable, as she is in her favorite place—the garden, surrounded by what she loves most." She looked down at her sketch and her voice took on a wistful note. "To spend one's existence in a beloved location, with all the things you love most, that is . . ."

"An enviable place to be?" he suggested, watching her profile.

She turned back toward him and studied him for several seconds, a favor he returned. Although she was Lady Wingate's sister, he could detect no resemblance between this woman and the stunning viscountess. No one would ever call Miss Moorehouse a beauty. Her features were too . . . mismatched. Her eyes, magnified even more by her spectacles, were too large, her nose too small. Her chin too stubborn, her lips too plump, her height completely unfashionable. Her mousy-colored hair, based on its current untidy condition, appeared to be the unmanageable sort that refused to be tamed into submission. He tried to recall something, anything he might have heard about her, but could think of nothing other than the fact that she was apparently Lady Wingate's traveling companion and a spinster. Based on that, he'd envisioned an older, dour, pinch-faced matron.

Yet while she wasn't beautiful, she was hardly old, dour, or pinch-faced. No, this woman was young. And robust. And clearly intelligent. And possessed an entrancing, dimpling smile that lit up her unusual face as if she'd swallowed a candle. A smile that offered an intriguing contrast to the wistfulness he'd detected in her voice. And large, doe-shaped eyes so devoid of guile that he found it difficult to look away from her.

Yes, but she's also nosy, and was doing something last night she doesn't wish to confess.

"An enviable place to be," she repeated softly. "Yes, that describes it perfectly. Who could ask for anything more than that?"

Me. He wanted something more than that. Something that had frustratingly remained out of his reach for almost a year. He yearned for it, yet despaired of ever finding it.

Peace.

Such a simple word.

So bloody difficult to achieve.

He realized he was staring and cleared his throat. "Are there any other sketches in your tablet?"

"Yes, but—"

Her words cut off as he opened to a random page and looked at a beautifully detailed sketch of a flower, delicately tinted with watercolors. Beneath the sketch, printed in small, precise lettering, were the words *narcissus sylvestris*—which, since he recognized the bloom, clearly was Latin for . . .

"Daffodil," he murmured. "Very nice. You're as talented with watercolors as you are at drawing."

"Thank you." Again she seemed surprised by his compliment, and he wondered why. Surely anyone who looked at these pictures could see they were excellent. "I've painted sketches of several hundred different species."

"Another passion of yours?"

She smiled. "I'm afraid so."

"And what do you do with your sketches? Frame them for display in your home?"

"Oh, no. I keep them in their sketch pads while I add to my collection. Someday I intend to organize the group and see them published into a book on horticulture."

"Indeed? A lofty goal."

"I see no point in aspiring to any other sort."

He shifted his gaze from the sketch and their eyes met. The sky had lightened enough that he could now discern that her eyes weren't blue at all, but rather a warm, golden brown. Along with intelligence, he detected a bit of a challenge in her direct gaze, as if she were daring him to dispute her ability to see her goal to fruition. He certainly had no intention of arguing the point with her. It was apparent that in addition to being nosy, Miss Moorehouse was one of those frighteningly efficient spinster types who marched on ahead, heedless of any hindrances to their progress.

"Why aim for the ground when you can shoot for the stars?" he murmured.

She blinked, then her smile bloomed again. "Exactly," she agreed.

Aware that he was once again staring, he forced his attention back to the sketch pad. He flipped through more pages, studying sketches of unfamiliar plants with unpronounceable Latin titles, along with several flowers he didn't recall the names of but that he recognized thanks to his hours spent digging holes all around the grounds. One bloom he did recognize was the rose, and he forced himself not to shudder. For some reason the damn things made him sneeze. He avoided them whenever possible.

He flipped another page. And stared. At the detailed sketch of a man. A very naked man. A man who was . . . not ungenerously formed. A man who, based on the letters printed along the bottom of the page, was named Franklin N. St—

She gasped and snatched the sketch pad from his hands and closed it. The sound of the pages snapping together seemed to echo in the air between them.

Matthew couldn't decide if he were more amused, surprised, or intrigued. Certainly he wouldn't have suspected such a drawing from this mousy woman. Clearly there was more to her than met the eye. Could *this* have been what she'd been up to last evening—drawing erotic sketches? Bloody hell, could this Franklin person who'd modeled for her sketch be someone from his own household? There *was* a young man named Frank on the groundskeeping staff. . .

Yet surely not. She'd only just arrived! He tried to recall the man's features, but as best he could remember from his brief look, his face was shadowed and indistinct—the only part of him which was.

"Friend of yours?" he drawled.

She hoisted up her chin. "And if he is?"

Well, he had to give her points for standing her ground. "I'd say you'd captured him quite well. Although I'm certain your mama would be shocked."

"On the contrary, I'm certain she'd take no notice at all." She stepped away from him then glanced in a pointed fashion at the opening in the hedges. "It was lovely chatting with you, my lord, but please don't let me keep you any longer from your morning walk."

"My walk, yes," he murmured, feeling an inexplicable urge to delay his departure. To look at more of her sketches to see if he could discover but yet another layer of this woman whose personality, in such a short period of time, had presented such contrasts.

Ridiculous. It was time to leave. "Enjoy your morning, Miss Moorehouse," he said. "I shall see you at dinner this evening." He made her a formal bow, a gesture she responded to with a brief curtsy. Then, with a soft whistle to Danforth, he departed the small clearing with the dog at his heels and headed down the path leading toward the stables. Perhaps a ride would help clear his head.

Walking at a brisk pace, he reflected on his meeting with Miss Moorehouse, and two things occurred to him: first, the woman's in depth knowledge of horticulture might be of use to him, provided he could glean the information he wanted from her without her realizing his reasons for wanting it—a challenge, given her nosy nature. He'd attempted to get such information from Paul, but while his head gardener knew a great deal about plants, he did not possess a formal education such as Miss Moorehouse clearly did. In having her as a guest, he might have stumbled upon the key to finding the missing piece to his quest.

And second, the woman had very effectively, albeit very politely, dismissed him from his own bloody garden! As if she was a princess and he a lowly footman. He'd not made an issue of it, as departing was precisely what he'd wanted to do. Bloody hell. He couldn't decide if he was more annoyed or fascinated.

Both, he decided. Miss Sarah Moorehouse was one of those annoying spinster women who peered out windows when they should be sleeping, always turned up in spots where you didn't wish them to be, and tended to see and hear things they shouldn't. Yet the dichotomy of her bookish, plain appearance and her erotic nude sketch intrigued him. As did her knowledge of plants. If she could prove to be of some use to him in his quest, well, he'd simply find a way to suffer her company.

For he'd do anything to end his quest and get his life back.

And if, by some chance, she'd followed him into the garden last night, he intended to see to it that she did not do so again.

Sarah clutched her sketch pad to her chest and stared at the opening in the hedges through which Lord Langston had just disappeared. After several long seconds, she released a lengthy breath, one she hadn't even realized she'd held.

Heavens, there was no denying his lordship was an exceedingly fine-looking specimen. Indeed, as far as appearances were concerned, he could easily qualify for the title of Perfect Man. When he'd stood next to her, her pulse had misbehaved in the most unsettling, confusing, and unprecedented way, a way she hadn't liked one bit.

Had she?

She pushed up her glasses with an impatient gesture. No, she hadn't liked it. Because as outwardly attractive as he might be, appearances in this case were deceiving, and his handsome features clearly masked the soul of a scoundrel. The man purported to be an expert on plants and flowers? Ha! Based on their conversation and the comments he'd made while looking at her sketches, she was convinced he didn't know a compost heap from a carnation. If he'd been returning from tending to night bloomers when she saw him from her window last night, why, she'd eat her bonnet. Not that she was wearing a bonnet, but by God, she'd retrieve one from her collection so she could eat it. Which once again begged the question: What *had* Lord Langston been doing with that shovel late last night?

Her imagination immediately conjured lurid images of Dr. Frankenstein, and her lips compressed. Whether or not her host's actions were sinister, they were suspicious at best, and she intended to discover what he was up to—especially as he might well be intending to court one of her friends. If he was up to no good, Julianne and Emily needed to be warned.

And Lord Langston needed to be stopped.

Chapter 4

After a vigorous ride that indeed helped clear his head, and a change of clothes, Matthew made his way to the dining room. He found himself wondering if he'd find Miss Moorehouse seated at the polished mahogany table. And then further wondering why the thought inexplicably quickened his steps. When he arrived, however, he found the dining room empty.

"Has anyone been down to breakfast?" he asked Walters, as the footman poured him a fragrant, steaming cup of coffee.

"Just one of the ladies, my lord. Can't recall her name. Thick spectacles, she has. And a hearty appetite. Was particularly fond of Cook's scones and raspberry jam."

"Ah. Clearly a woman of excellent taste," Matthew murmured, reaching for his china cup. An image rose in his mind, of Miss Moorehouse biting into a jelly-laden scone, her dimples winking as she chewed, a dab of raspberry clinging to her plump bottom lip. Of him, leaning slowly toward her, her doe eyes widening as he flicked away the bit of jelly with a leisurely swipe of his tongue.

His cup halted halfway to his lips and he blinked to dispel the unsettling—and utterly ridiculous—image. Good God, perhaps getting caught in the rain last night *had* adversely affected his brain. Infected him with some manner of fever. Either that or he'd simply been without a woman for far too long. Yes, that explained it. For there could be no other explanation as to why he'd harbor the least sensual thought about a woman who was not in the least bit sensual. And certainly not at all the sort of female to inspire such thoughts. A nosy, bluestocking spinster— just the sort of female he normally avoided as he would a bad rash.

Still, something about Miss Moorehouse had captured his interest. Something besides her knowledge of plants and penchant for staring out windows. . .

Again her image materialized in his mind's eye. It was those damn dimples, he decided. And those huge, golden brown eyes, magnified by her spectacles. Behind their intelligence they'd looked . . . vulnerable. In a way that had grabbed him by the throat. In a way he neither understood nor particularly liked.

With an effort, he shoved the woman from his thoughts, and after his solitary breakfast he entered his private study. Refusing to dwell on his impatience for Daniel's return from the village, he spent several hours going over the estate's accounts. When he finished, he set down his pen and rubbed his tired eyes. In spite of his best efforts to economize, over the course of the last few months his financial situation had deteriorated to a dangerous level. His path was clear. And inevitable.

A knock sounded at the door, and with a sense of relief at being interrupted from looking at the depressing accounts, he called, "Come in."

The door opened and an immaculately attired Tildon appeared. "Lord Surbrooke requests to see you, my lord," the butler intoned.

Finally. "Thank you, Tildon. Send him in."

Matthew closed the account books, slipped them back into the desk drawer, then locked the drawer. He'd just pocketed the key in his waistcoat when Daniel Sutton breezed through the doorway.

"So this is where you've hidden yourself," Daniel said, crossing directly to the decanters. "You've missed all the fun."

"Fun?"

His best friend nodded. "Whist and backgammon in the drawing room."

"What the devil were you doing in the drawing room? I've been awaiting your report from the village."

"I went to the drawing room in search of you, to give you my report. You weren't there, which was quite unsociable of you, by the way. One thing led to another and I ended up playing both whist and backgammon."

"You detest whist and backgammon," said Matthew, joining Daniel near the fire, where his friend had settled in an overstuffed brocade chair with a generous brandy.

"That was before you filled your house with an array of beautiful women."

"In case you've forgotten, those beautiful women are supposed to be here for *me*," Matthew said dryly.

"Well, *someone* has to keep them occupied and watch out for your interests while you're hidden away. Especially since you saw fit to invite both Berwick and Logan Jennsen, not to mention Thurston and Hartley. All notorious charmers, you know. What in God's name were you thinking?"

"That it would appear damn odd if my house party guests were all female. I'd actually only planned to invite you and Jennsen, but Berwick sent a note last week hint-ing he'd like to visit, as he'd be traveling through the area. As I thought it would be churlish to refuse an acquaintance of such long standing, I extended the invitation."

"What about Thurston and Hartley?"

"They tagged along with Berwick."

"Well, the lot of them were circling your female guests like vultures around carrion."

"At least they'll entertain the ladies, which allows me some time to do what I must." A cynical sound escaped him. "As I have the highest ranking title amongst all of them, I'm not overly concerned that I'll lack for a willing bride. The title of Marchioness of Langston is a powerful lure."

"True. Still, I managed to keep the vultures from swooping in and instantly issuing marriage offers. You can thank me later. As your oldest and dearest friend, I am, as always, pleased to assist you."

"You are, indeed, the soul of helpfulness."

Daniel shook his head and made a *tsking* sound. "I detect sarcasm in your voice, Matthew, and can only say you shall be sorry after I tell you that I've spent my game-playing time well, digging up information for you. In fact, my inquiries will greatly narrow down your search."

"Excellent. Anything that will save me time is welcome. But first, I want to hear what you learned in the village. Did you speak with Tom?"

Daniel shook his head. "No. I went to the smithy only to find it closed. I then went to the Willstone cottage where I spoke to Tom's wife. Mrs. Willstone said she didn't know where her husband was. Based on her pale face and reddened eyes, it was clear she'd been crying."

"When had she last seen him?"

"Yesterday evening, just before he left to take a walk.

Mrs. Willstone said Tom suffers from headaches and the cool night air helps. When he hadn't returned by the time the storm hit, she supposed he'd taken refuge somewhere to wait out the rain. Said it wouldn't be the first time such has happened. Even so, he's always home by morning, rain or not, to open the smithy."

"But not this morning," Matthew said.

"Correct. She'd just said that she couldn't imagine where he was when her brother entered the room. His name is Billy Smythe and I subsequently learned from further inquiries while in the village that he's a former soldier who recently moved into the Willstone cottage and started working in the smithy with Tom."

"And was Billy able to shed any light on Tom's whereabouts?"

"He certainly offered an interesting theory. According to Billy, Tom was out chasing a lightskirt. And he did not sound happy about it. Didn't like that his sister was worried and that he'd been left to do all the work at the smithy."

"He told you this in front of his sister?"

"Yes. She insisted Billy was wrong, and he insisted she was being a fool. Said he'd arrived in Upper Fladersham nary a fortnight ago and had already heard the rumors about Tom. He then went on to promise that when Tom finally drags his arse home from this last dalliance, he'll be made to understand that it was just that—his last dalliance." Daniel swirled his brandy around his snifter. "Can't say I blame him."

"Nor I. Did either of them say anything else?"

Daniel shook his head. "Under the guise of you wanting to hire Tom for some intricate ironwork, I extracted a promise from Mrs. Willstone to have him contact you here as soon as possible. I then spoke to a few other shopkeepers, none of whom had seen Tom since the previous day."

Matthew nodded slowly, staring into his brandy, then raised his gaze to Daniel's. "Thank you for doing that for me."

Not a trace of pity showed in his friend's eyes, but Matthew knew it was only because Daniel would keep his expression purposefully blank. Daniel knew why he never ventured into the village, and he was a good enough friend to never mention the reason. "You're welcome. Based on what I've told you, do you think it was Tom's presence you sensed last night?"

"I suppose so. I felt, very strongly, that someone was nearby, and he was there." Matthew supposed he should have been satisfied with what Daniel had discovered—that apparently Tom's reason for being out last night was no more sinister than a walk to relieve a headache, and perhaps an ache of a different sort.

Yet something didn't sit right. It was odd that Tom hadn't returned home, especially since he'd been heading in the direction of the village when Matthew had seen him. Perhaps he'd stopped somewhere else? Another cottage in another village? Perhaps he'd had a horse nearby and traveled a greater distance?

With no ready answers, he had no choice but to do as Mrs. Willstone was doing—wait for Tom to return home.

His thoughts were interrupted when Daniel said, "Well?"

"Well what?"

"Don't you want to know what else I discovered, with regards to your houseguests?"

"Yes, of course."

Clearly satisfied that he once again had Matthew's attention, Daniel said, "Before I tell you, I wish to hear your impressions of the lovely ladies you invited to your house party—which, by the way, would be more of a party if you actually joined in the festivities."

Matthew shrugged. "They're all . . . acceptable."

"But surely after spending the evening with them you must have formed *some* opinion. What about Lady Emily?"

Matthew considered for several seconds, then said, "She is very pretty."

"And Lady Julianne?"

"Very beautiful."

"Viscountess Wingate?"

"Stunning."

Daniel studied him over the rim of his snifter. "That's all you have to say?"

Matthew shrugged. "I discussed the weather with Lady Emily. She doesn't like the cold. Nor the rain. Nor too much sun—she freckles dreadfully, you know. Lady Julianne and I discussed Dinstory's annual musicale, which we'd both attended last Season. She enjoyed it thoroughly, while I fell asleep and nearly concussed myself when I leaned sideways in my chair and clunked my head against the wall.

"The viscountess and I began a more promising discussion on the merits of household pets, although she prefers the sort of tiny yappy dogs that cause Danforth to look at me with his most long-suffering gaze."

He stretched out his legs and crossed his ankles. "So, as I said, each of them are acceptable. None grabbed my attention more than the other. So certainly tell me if you have information that could tip the scales one way or another."

Daniel nodded. "Very well. But first let me begin by

saying that you've gone about this in entirely the wrong way. You want a wife—"

"Correction. I *need* a wife. A very specific sort of wife."

"Precisely. You need an *heiress*. Which is why, instead of inviting all these lovely young ladies here, the sort who can deplete a man's patience and strength, you should have invited some older heiresses. *Much* older. The sort who don't require new gowns every half hour. The sort who are grateful for whatever attention you give, rather than pouting when they feel neglected. In my expert opinion, if a man *must* have a wife, then the perfect wife is one who is one hundred years old and worth one hundred thousand pounds. And if she doesn't speak English, so much the better. And don't worry about her less than stellar, wizened appearance. Remember this, my friend: beauty is only a few blown-out candles away. All women look the same in the dark."

After casting that last pearl of wisdom, Daniel raised his snifter in salute, then downed the contents in a single swallow.

"Unfortunately, a one-hundred-year-old bride won't do, as I need to provide an heir," Matthew said lightly. "And I had no idea you were such an expert on the subject of choosing a wife. Especially as you don't have one."

"Just because I don't have a wife doesn't mean I don't know the characteristics of a good one. Believe me, you will not be happy with some chit who expects you to dance attendance upon her."

"I've no intention of dancing attendance upon anyone. I need money, a great deal of it, and I need it quickly. My intention is to simply choose the least troublesome heiress I can find, one who will not disrupt my life. Then, after the nuptials, I'll embark on the monumental task of settling the estate's debts and making it profitable once more."

"I've told you that I'll make you a loan—"

Matthew cut off his friend's quiet words by raising his hand. "Thank you, Daniel. I appreciate the offer, but no. The amount I owe is far too great. Even for your deep pockets."

"You mean the amount your father owed."

Matthew shrugged. "His debt became mine when he died."

"Sins of the father," Daniel murmured, the bitter twist to his mouth marring his usual easygoing good looks. "Still, there's no reason why you have to marry so bloody quickly. Take some time, at least to find an heiress you find tolerable."

Matthew shook his head. "My time has run out."

"Then perhaps you should have spent more time during the last year actually looking for this wife you're determined to have rather than burying yourself here, looking for something impossible to find. Something that most likely doesn't even exist."

"Most likely you're right. It may not exist. Or if it does, I'll never find it. But given the freedom finding it would provide me, I *had* to look. And besides—"

"It was another deathbed request from your father. I know. But for God's sake, Matthew, how much of your life are you going to give up to satisfy the selfish requests of a pain-maddened man who spent the majority of the last twenty years slinging arrows to inflict more guilt upon you?" Daniel's gaze bore into him. "His words that set you off on this impossible mission were simply a way for him to control you from the grave. What happened wasn't your fault. You've spent all these years paying for an *accident*. Trying to atone to a man for whom no apology would ever suffice."

Matthew's shoulders tensed in a vain attempt to protect against the onslaught of guilt rushing toward him. Images he fruitlessly wished he could forget flashed through his mind, bombarding him, and he closed his eyes, willing them away.

"Your father's gone, Matthew." Daniel's quiet voice broke through his painful memories. "There're no more apologies, nothing else to be done—except for you to live your life. As *you* wish."

Matthew opened his eyes and stared into the glowing embers in the grate, imagining they were the gates of Hell yawning before him. "I won't be free until I honor the promises I made. To find what I'm searching for—"

"An impossible task—if it even exists.

"—and to marry within a year."

"A ridiculous request."

"Not to my father, who was desperate that I produce an heir. I'm the last male Devenport." His stomach clenched as he said the words, nearly stumbling over them, and he forced aside the heartbreaking image of James that rushed into his mind. "It was Father's final and sole request."

"And it was just as unreasonable as the other countless requests he forced upon you over the years." Daniel fixed him with a penetrating stare. "He's *dead*, Matthew. He won't know."

A plethora of unsettling emotions swamped Matthew, and he leaned forward, set his elbows on his knees, and dragged his hands down his face. "I'm ashamed to admit how many times I've told myself that very thing—*he won't know*. But every time I do, my bloody conscience inconveniently interferes, informing me that *I'll* know. While my honor, my integrity, may be tarnished, I want them, *need* them, to still mean something. At least to me. I made promises. I intend to keep them. And it's almost a certainty that my only hope of saving the estate is through marriage."

Daniel blew out a sigh. "Very well. In that case, let me tell you what I've learned so as to narrow your search. Let's start with Lady Emily."

"What about her?"

"She won't do. Through an enlightening conversation with Logan Jennsen, who somehow knows the financial situation of every man in England, I learned that although Lady Emily's father has done a good job covering it up, he's lost nearly everything and is on the brink of ruin. Indeed, he's nearly as bad off as you."

"Damn. Of course it's better I found out now rather than after the I do's. What about Lady Julianne?"

"Now, she is a promising prospect, in spite of her not being one hundred years old. Indeed, I think she is who you should concentrate all your energies upon. She is Lord Gatesbourne's only daughter, and the earl will bestow a fortune to secure her a title. Especially one attached to a reasonably handsome, young peer as opposed to an ancient, creaking old coot with no teeth who will make his darling daughter weep to simply look upon."

"Always good to know one is more desirable than an ancient, creaking old coot," Matthew said in a dust dry tone.

"In addition," Daniel continued as if he hadn't spoken, "from what I've observed, Lady Julianne is shy and amenable. You won't have any difficulty shunting her off to some far corner of your vast holdings should you so choose."

"What about Lady Wingate?"

Something flickered in Daniel's dark blue eyes, something that was gone so quickly Matthew would have missed it had he not known his friend so well. "Lady Wingate isn't a good choice for two reasons. First, she has nowhere near enough money to rescue your estate."

Matthew frowned. "I thought Wingate left her financially well off."

"Thanks again to my conversation with Jennsen, I learned Wingate left her comfortable—some money, and a town house in Mayfair he purchased several years before his death—his only unentailed property. Rumor had it that he bought the place because, knowing what a scoundrel his brother was, he wanted to assure that Lady Wingate had a place of her own, not tied to the estate in any way, should he die." His lips tightened. "Based on the way the brother has behaved since Wingate passed, 'tis fortunate he took such precautions."

"Well, her financial situation certainly is reason enough to make her unacceptable to me," Matthew said, "but you mentioned two reasons. What is the other?"

"Lady Wingate apparently remains devoted to her dead husband's memory, in spite of the fact that three years have passed since he died. During our conversations last night and this afternoon, it was glaringly apparent that she believes the man was a paragon, one who could never be matched in her eyes. When I casually brought up the subject of the joys of marriage, she made it clear that she has no intention of ever marrying again. Apparently, she found her one true love and is content to spend the rest of her days reliving the memories she shared with him rather than making new ones."

Matthew stared at his friend, who was in turn staring

into his empty snifter with a brooding expression. "You sound as if you disapprove of her decision."

Daniel shrugged one shoulder. "Seems a bloody waste to me."

"She obviously loved him deeply."

"Yes. Enough to throw away the rest of her life, worshipping him as if he were a saint. And from all accounts, he completely adored her." He made a humorless sound. "God save me from such misery. I'll continue to enjoy my shallow love affairs in which my heart remains my own, thank you very much." He turned toward Matthew. "What about you? Can you imagine giving so much of yourself to another person? Your entire heart and soul?"

Because Daniel sounded genuinely perplexed at the prospect and he rarely asked such probing questions, Matthew seriously pondered before answering. Finally he said, "I've enjoyed the company of many beautiful women, but none of them have inspired anything near the sort of deep devotion you've just described. I can therefore only say that if one is lucky enough to find it, they'd be a fool to discard it. I, however, do not have the luxury of time to search the world for this one perfect woman who most probably doesn't exist."

"In which case, Lady Julianne is who you should set your sights upon."

An image of the beautiful, blond heiress blinked into Matthew's mind, and for reasons he couldn't explain, a wave of weariness swept through him. She was, in every way, the answer to his prayers. All he had to do was act charming, court her, and dangle the lure of his lofty title before her. Surely he could do so, and in an expeditious manner. Based upon the eagerness with which her mother had accepted the invitation to his house party, he believed his attentions wouldn't be rebuffed.

He blew out a long breath. "Only one viable candidate out of three choices."

"Yes. You didn't do a very thorough job researching your potential brides."

"I was distracted." Yes. By his damn quest. "I'll concentrate on Lady Julianne, but I'd best hedge my bets and send out invitations to several more candidates to join the party. Any suggestions?"

Daniel considered, then said, "Lady Prudence Whipple and Miss Jane Carlson both fit your requirements. Neither is particularly accomplished, but what they lack in charm and conversation, they more than make up for in wealth."

"Excellent. I'll send the invitations."

Restless, Matthew rose and walked toward the French windows. Bright sunshine streamed through the polished glass, creating wide ribbons upon which dust motes gently floated. From his vantage point he could see a wide arc of velvety, verdant lawn, part of the gardens, and a corner of the terrace. His gaze halted on the latter, on a large, round, wrought-iron table where his guests were enjoying afternoon tea, all chatting and laughing together. All except . . .

A frown pulled down his brows. Where was Miss Moorehouse? His eye was drawn to a movement on the lawn, and as if the mere thought of her had conjured her up, there she stood, frolicking in the grass with Danforth. He watched her toss a large stick that Danforth sprinted after as if it had a hunk of beef attached to it. His pet leaped upward and neatly caught the sturdy piece of wood in midair, then trotted back to Miss Moorehouse and dropped the stick at her feet. Then his dog, who was nobody's fool, flopped onto his back and presented his belly for rubbing.

Even from this distance he could see Miss Moorehouse's bright smile, indeed he could almost hear her laughter as she knelt in the grass, heedless of her gown, and gave Danforth a thorough rubdown. Then she stood, picked up the stick and tossed it again.

"What about Miss Moorehouse?" he said.

"Who?" Daniel asked from where he was seated behind him.

"Lady Wingate's sister."

He heard the chair squeak as Daniel rose. Seconds later he joined Matthew at the window and followed his gaze to the woman and dog cavorting on the lawn. "The spinster with the spectacles? The one who sits silently in the corner with her nose buried in her sketch book?"

The nosy one with the wide, doe eyes, deep dimples, and lush lips. "Yes. Do you have any information about her?"

He felt the weight of Daniel's speculative gaze but ignored it. "What do you wish to know? And more importantly, *why* would you wish to know? She's merely Lady Wingate's traveling companion and is certainly not an heiress. Her father is a physician."

"That didn't stop Wingate from marrying her older sister and making her a viscountess."

"Nooo . . ." Daniel said slowly, as if speaking to a child. "But Miss Moorehouse, while I'm certain is a nice enough woman, hardly possesses the beauty to inspire the sort of devotion her older sister did. Nor the grace, based on her present hoydenish activity. I can't imagine that there are any viscounts traipsing about who'd wish to make her their bride. Especially as she hasn't any money."

"Money being the great equalizer with regards to beauty."

"Yes. That and darkness."

"Fear not. The only interest I have in the woman is in what she may or may not know." He told Daniel about his morning conversation with Miss Moorehouse, concluding with, "She has . . . secrets. I want to know what they are."

"Understandable. But beware, my friend. We're both acquainted with her sort—a lonely, dried-up, desperate spinster who will read far too much into any attention you show her. You're probably the first man who's spared her more than five minutes. As a result, she's no doubt already halfway in love with you."

"Doubtful. She looked more suspicious than smitten."

It suddenly occurred to him that with regard to Daniel's theory about darkness being a great equalizer, he'd yet to see Miss Moorehouse up close in bright light. And for reasons he couldn't explain, he very much wanted to. No doubt because he'd have to make *some* sort of effort to befriend her if he hoped to glean any horticultural information from her.

Yes, that was the reason. Relieved to have found an explanation for his odd yearning to see her, he turned to Daniel. "I think it's about time I joined my guests."

Sarah was aware of him the instant he stepped from the house onto the terrace, followed by his friend, Lord Surbrooke. No matter how she tried to concentrate on her game with Danforth, her errant gaze continually wandered to the terrace. And it seemed every time she looked, she discovered Lord Langston looking at *her*, which rippled an uncomfortable heat through her. Botheration, even her scalp felt hot, which, as she knew, would make her already uncontrollable curls frizz even tighter. Even when she turned her back on the group to toss the stick, she found her ears straining to identify the rumble of his deep voice among the indistinct murmurs drifting across the lawn.

Determined to put some space between herself and the temptation to further exert her eyes or ears, she threw the stick toward the corner of the house, then picking up her skirts so as not to trip, ran after Danforth, who streaked forward. By the time she made three more tosses, she'd turned the corner and could no longer see the terrace.

Relieved, for reasons she didn't quite understand, she crouched down and gave the belly-up Danforth the rub-down he now expected every time he retrieved the stick.

"Oh, you are simply the complete opposite of ferocious," she crooned with a laugh to the ecstatic dog. "I wish my Desdemona were here. I think you two would hit it off famously."

"Matchmaking are you, Miss Moorehouse?"

Her heart jumped at the sound of the familiar masculine voice directly behind her. She glanced over her shoulder but couldn't make out his features, as the sun glared directly into her eyes. Turning back to the dog, she said, "I was merely suggesting to Danforth that he and my Desdemona would like each other."

He hunkered down beside her and patted Danforth's sturdy side, much to the dog's squirming delight. "And why is that?"

Her gaze riveted on the sight of his large, long-fingered hand brushing against the dog's dark fur. It was a very strong, capable-looking hand. One surprisingly sun-browned for a gentleman. One that was clearly capable of tenderness as it glided over the dog's flank. Was it also a hand capable of sinister acts? Seeing the affection he lavished on his dog, it was difficult to imagine. Still, she suspected him capable of deceit with regards to his claims of proficiency in the garden, so she needed to be wary.

"They are of similar temperament. I miss her very much."

"You should have brought her."

Sarah couldn't help but laugh. "She is hardly a lapdog, my lord—although she attempts to convince me that she is at least twice a day. There was barely room enough in the carriage for my sister and I and our luggage, let alone a dog that weighs ten stone."

"You didn't join the others for tea. Why not?"

She felt the weight of his stare and turned to look at him. And stilled at the impact of his steady gaze through compelling hazel eyes that were a fascinating mixture of brown, green, and blue, dotted with intriguing flecks of gold. They were intelligent eyes, sharp and alert, yet she detected an underlying hint of weariness in them. The result of some burden that saddened him? Or perhaps it was guilt? Guilt associated with his nocturnal shovel-toting outdoor walks?

Impossible to tell. But what *was* clear was that based on his current quizzical expression, he'd asked her a question. She had no idea what. One look into those eyes, which were no more than three feet away from hers, and she'd completely lost the thread of the conversation.

Heat eased up the back of her neck as it always did when she was embarrassed. She knew that in seconds the heat would produce blotches that would spread to her cheeks, alerting him to her embarrassment. "I'm sorry, what did you say?"

"Why didn't you join the others for tea?"

"The day was too lovely to sit and sip tea. I was actually headed into the gardens in hopes of finding your groundskeeper when I ran into Danforth. He asked me to play fetch and I complied."

The tiniest hint of a smile ghosted over his face. "He *asked* you?"

"He dashed off, returned with that stick, dropped it at my feet, then made pleading noises. Perhaps there is a person in the kingdom who could resist such an invitation, but I am not that person."

"Most ladies are quite put off by his size."

"I'm afraid I'm not like 'most ladies.'"

He frowned and nodded slowly, clearly agreeing with her, and she shoved away the ridiculous sense of hurt that piqued her.

After another pat to Danforth's sturdy flank, he rose then extended his hand to her. Sarah stared at that bare, masculine hand for several seconds, and for some insane reason her heart began to beat in slow, hard thumps. As if in a trance, she slowly lifted her hand and slipped it into his. The feel of his bare palm against hers, his long fingers closing over hers, stunned her. His skin felt so . . . warm. And his hand was so . . . large. She'd always believed her own hands oversized and ungainly, but it looked quite small nestled in his. Almost dainty.

He gave her arm a gentle tug and she rose. The instant she gained her feet, he released her, and she found herself curling her fingers inward and pressing her palm against her skirt to retain the almost magical warmth of his touch.

"Shall we walk?" he asked, nodding toward a copse of trees in the distance.

She had to swallow to locate her voice. "By all means."

They strolled in silence for nearly a minute, then Lord Langston said, "You claimed you're not like most ladies. In what way?"

She shrugged. "I don't mind getting dirty in the garden, or while frolicking with my animals. I detest embroidery, adore walking in the rain, don't mind sun freckles on my nose, can't sing worth a jot, and I'm abysmal at polite conversation."

"I'd have to disagree with you on that last one. Personally, I find it refreshing that you've yet to mention the weather."

Sarah looked at him to see if he was joking, but he looked perfectly serious. "May I then say that I'm delighted it's not just me? I cannot understand why anyone would wish to discuss the weather. Ever."

"Precisely. What is the point?"

"It's not as if you can *do* anything about it. The weather—"

"Is what it is," they said in unison.

Sarah blinked. Then smiled. "Precisely."

His gaze dipped to her mouth, and an arrow of heat shot through her. Then he looked up, met her eyes and asked softly, "So in what other ways are you unlike other ladies?"

"Well, I suppose in most ways as I'm not a 'lady.'"

"Perhaps, but I meant figuratively, as in you're a female. Do you not like to visit the shops?"

A small, feminine sigh escaped her. "Actually, I adore the shops. Especially bookstores. I just love the smell of them. The leather, the aged paper."

"Any other sort of shops?"

"The confectioner's shop has always held a special appeal. And the haberdashery. I fear I have something of a weakness for bonnets."

"Bonnets? You mean the sort you wear on your head?"

"I know of no other kind. Do you?"

"No . . .'tis just that I haven't seen you wear one."

"I was wearing one when I came outdoors but I removed it to play with Danforth." She reached up one hand and skimmed it self-consciously over her hair. "I've found that shoving my hair beneath a bonnet is the only real way to tame the wayward mess."

His gaze shifted to her hair. He studied the strands for several long seconds, then frowned, and she barely refrained from clapping her arms over her head to thwart his unimpeded view. Finally he said, "I thought your hair was brown, but here in the sunlight . . . it's more, um . . . colorful. It looks curly."

Based on his scowl, it was clear his words weren't a compliment. Even as she inwardly cringed, she had to press her lips together to keep from telling him that she already knew her hair was a disaster of spirals in an unfortunate hodge-podge of every shade of brown, thank you very much. It was therefore unnecessary for him to point out the flaw.

"Horrendously curly," she agreed with a philosophical shrug. "When unbound it resembles a mop. I fight with it on a daily basis, but sadly, it always wins."

"Does your mother have curly hair?"

"No. My mother is beautiful. Carolyn looks just like her." Anxious to change the subject, she decided it was time to put him to a small horticultural test.

"Tell me, my lord—" Her words cut off when his

shoulder bumped hers, shooting a legion of heated tingles down her arm. She inhaled sharply and caught a whiff of something very pleasant and very masculine . . . a heady combination of sandalwood and freshly starched linen. Her gaze flew to him but he continued strolling along as if nothing were amiss.

When she remained silent, he looked her way and asked, "Tell you what, Miss Moorehouse?"

Dear God, she'd done it again. Completely lost the thread of the conversation. How utterly vexing. With a frown, she forced herself to concentrate and her faulty memory kicked back to life. Ah yes, his horticultural quiz.

"Tell me, my lord, is your straff wort in the shade or in direct sunlight?"

"I beg your pardon?"

"Your straff wort. In your garden. Do you have better results when it's planted in the shade or in direct sunlight?"

He pondered for several seconds then asked, "Which tends to work better for you?"

"Shade. I find that too much sun turns the leaves brown."

"Yes, I experienced the same thing. Nothing worse than brown, shriveled leaves."

"Oh, I agree. And your tortlingers? Do they shrivel as well?"

"I'm afraid I'd need to consult with Paul. He's in charge of all the tortlingers." They rounded the corner and came within view of the group on the terrace. "Shall we join the others?"

"Actually, I'd prefer to explore the gardens some more, if you don't mind. I'd like to locate your night bloomers."

"I don't mind at all. Enjoy yourself, Miss Moorehouse. I'll see you at dinner."

They parted ways, with Lord Langston heading toward the terrace while Sarah struck out for the nearest path leading into the garden. The instant she was certain she couldn't be seen through the thick hedges, she halted and narrowed her eyes at her host through the concealing foliage.

So your straff wort requires shade, does it? Your head groundskeeper is in charge of the tortlingers? "Well, you fell into that trap, didn't you, Lord Plant Expert," she murmured to herself. "Didn't know there was no such thing as straff wort or tortlingers, did you?"

Which meant two things: Lord Langston was definitely up to something.

And she needed to discover what that something was.

Chapter 5

At dinner that evening, Sarah was once again seated at the opposite end of the table from her host, this time placed between Lord Berwick and Mr. Logan Jennsen. Lord Berwick, whom she judged to be in his early thirties, possessed the sort of dazzling blond handsomeness that guaranteed him an abundance of female attention wherever he went. He offered her a polite smile, politely inquired about her health, made a polite comment regarding the weather, then promptly turned his attention to Carolyn, who sat on his other side.

Sarah breathed a sigh of relief. Now she could concentrate on the delicious meal and not be forced to make awkward conversation. She tasted a spoonful of the creamy soup, and as was her habit, savored the flavor for several seconds before swallowing, mentally identifying the ingredients as they slid over her tongue. Fresh cream, broccoli, parsley, thyme, a hint of tarragon—

"Do you attend these often, Miss Moorehouse?"

She hastily swallowed at the sound of the deep, male voice coming from her left and turned her head. And discovered Mr. Jennsen's dark-eyed gaze resting upon her.

From her observations at several parties, Sarah knew the mysterious, fabulously wealthy American mostly remained on the fringes of the room, watching the crowd. Whether this was by his own choice or because the members of the ton held him at arm's length—or a combination of both—she wasn't sure. They invited him to their soirees—he was far too rich to ignore—yet kept him at a wary distance. As if he were an exotic beast they suspected might bite them. And of course, he was an *American*. And in *trade*. Either reason was enough for Society's elite not to get too friendly. Although they hadn't been introduced until yesterday, on the two occasions she'd seen him at London parties, she'd felt a sort of kinship with him—from one outsider to another.

Mr. Jennsen was as dark as Lord Berwick was blond; a tall, muscular, robust man. His sharp, angular features and a nose that most likely was broken at one time would prevent anyone from calling him classically handsome. But with his keen, intelligent eyes and commanding presence, he was without a doubt extremely compelling.

Clearly, since he'd said her name, he was speaking to her, a fact that surprised her, especially since Emily, who looked beautiful in her pale green muslin gown, sat directly across from him. After dabbing her lips with her napkin, she said, "I'm not certain what you mean by 'these,' Mr. Jennsen."

"These country house parties." He leaned a bit closer, affording her a whiff of fresh linen and soap. In a voice only she could hear, he said, "These deadly dull dinners."

A gurgle of surprised laughter rose in her throat at his outrageous—but heaven help her, she had to agree with him—comment. She coughed to cover the sound. "You're not enjoying the soup?"

He glanced down at his bowl. "It's *green*."

"Broccoli normally is, I'm afraid."

"Ah, well therein lies the problem. I do not like broccoli."

"Pity, as I understand tonight's menu features it prominently. Broccoli soufflé, broccoli stew, followed by sautéed broccoli, broccoli in cream sauce, and even a broccoli flambé for dessert."

He looked absolutely horrified. "You're joking."

"Yes, I am." She grinned. "But your expression was priceless."

He stared at her for several seconds then laughed. "I knew it."

"That I was joking?" She shook her head. "I think not."

"No, I mean I knew you were . . . different."

Sarah stilled then heaved an inward sigh. Apparently today was her day for having gentlemen point out her flaws.

Something must have shown on her face, for he said, "I assure you I meant 'different' in the most complimentary way, Miss Moorehouse. You have a sense of humor. And aren't afraid to speak your mind."

"It appears you suffer from the same affliction, Mr. Jennsen."

"Yes. Which is why I'm delighted to find myself sitting next to *you* this evening. Last evening I sat between Lady Julianne's matchmaking mother and Lady Emily's matchmaking aunt—a lady who is half deaf, by the way. I'm praying you'll save me from another meal spent talking for hours yet saying *absolutely nothing*. Blah blah blah, weather weather weather, marriage marriage marriage, blah blah blah." He shook his head. "I don't know how you British do it—talk in those never ending circles."

"It's an acquired skill, drummed into us from infancy.

By the time we're adolescents, we can blah blah blah about the weather and marriage all day long."

"I see. Then how is it that you escaped such drumming?"

She debated how honest she should be, but then decided she had no reason to hide behind platitudes with this self-confessed plain-speaking man. "My parents didn't care if I mastered the fine art of the weather discussion, as all their marriage hopes were pinned upon my sister. I therefore spent my time doing other things."

He nodded in an approving fashion. "Good for you. Things such as playing with dogs and walking through the gardens, I presume?" When her brows shot up, he added, "I saw you today, during tea time on the terrace. You and that monstrous dog were enjoying yourselves."

"Yes. You weren't?"

"Not nearly as much as you were. Not only was I once again seated between the chaperones, I don't particularly care for tea."

"Broccoli *and* tea?" She made a *tsking* sound. "Is there anything you *do* like, Mr. Jennsen?"

"Asparagus. Coffee." He picked up his wineglass and contemplated her over the rim. "I like the unusual. The unexpected. People who possess a sense of humor and aren't afraid to speak their mind. What do *you* like?"

"Carrots. Mulled cider. People who, like me, are . . . outsiders. People who possess a sense of humor and aren't afraid to speak their mind."

A slow smile lifted one corner of his mouth. "It seems I've discovered a kindred spirit. Thank God. I thought I was going to have to suffer through listening to Thurston and Berwick discuss fox hunting all evening."

"It is what gentlemen do during these house parties.

Ride, eat, sleep, hunt, tell embellished stories of their exploits and gambling successes." She grinned. "There's always piquet and whist with the chaperones."

He gave an exaggerated shudder. "Thank you, but no."

"Then you might enjoy those games with Lady Julianne and Lady Emily. Both are skilled card players, as is my sister. And although they may not have yet had the opportunity to prove it, I assure you, all three of them are capable of discussing more than the weather. 'Tis just that that's the first topic most ladies discuss. One must wade through the weather chatter in order to reach more scintillating topics."

"Such as?"

"Shopping. Fashion."

"God help me."

"The opera. Hunting." Her lips twitched. "Or marriage—at which time the chaperones will join you."

"You're killing me, you know." He picked up his spoon and idly circled the silver utensil through his soup. "I meant no offense to your sister and friends. It's actually Thurston and Hartley who are the dead bores. Even the chaperones aren't as bad as they are. Your sister and friends have been very charming."

"I don't doubt it for a moment. They're all very beautiful."

"Undeniably. Your sister, especially."

Sarah smiled. "Yes, she is. On the inside as well."

"Then she is indeed a rare beauty. And lucky to have a sister who thinks so highly of her."

Sarah shook her head. "*I* am the lucky one, sir. Carolyn has always been my champion. And very best friend."

The footmen cleared away the soup bowls, then followed with a course of thinly sliced ham and creamed peas.

"More green food," Mr. Jennsen whispered, cutting his gaze pointedly toward the peas.

"Don't worry," Sarah whispered back. "There are only nine more courses and then the meal is done."

A low groan escaped him, and she couldn't hide her smile.

"Remind me why I'm here and not in my London town house, eating food that isn't green?" he said.

"I've no idea. Why did you come to Langston Manor?"

"Langston invited me. I'm not certain why, as we're not well-acquainted. My guess is that he wishes at some point to discuss a business proposition. Since that is my favorite type of conversation, I'm willing to temporarily tolerate green foods." He shot her a sideways glance. "I gather you came to Langston Manor as a bride candidate?"

Sarah nearly spewed her mouthful of creamed peas across the table. After swallowing, she said, "Bride candidate? Heavens no. I'm nothing of the sort."

"Why not? Are you already spoken for?"

She stared at him, certain he was jesting, but incredibly, nothing in his eyes or his expression indicated he was teasing. "No, I'm not." She added in an undertone, "You've heard that Lord Langston is looking for a wife?"

"A rumor to that effect is floating about London. When I arrived yesterday and saw the array of beautiful, unattached houseguests, I figured the rumor must be true." Then he smiled, a very attractive smile, she decided, that was just a bit lopsided and showed even, white teeth. "So you aren't already spoken for. In spite of the green food, this meal continues to improve at a rapid rate."

Now she *knew* he was teasing. "I'm here only as a traveling companion to my sister."

"And I'm only here because . . . well, I'm not sure yet.

But for the first time since I arrived, I'm *glad* I'm here." He picked up his wineglass and held it toward her. "A toast. To finding the unexpected." He smiled. "And to new friends."

As it had done repeatedly—and very annoyingly—since he'd sat down, Matthew's gaze strayed to the opposite end of the table. What the bloody hell was going on between Miss Moorehouse and Logan Jennsen? The bloody scoundrel was looking at her as if she were a pastry and he'd just discovered a craving for sugar. Every time Matthew looked, they were laughing or smiling or had their heads close together.

"If you don't quit scowling at Jennsen, he's liable to stomp down to this end of the table and plant you a facer," said Daniel, who sat on his left, in an undertone. "You know how uncouth those Americans are."

"I'm not scowling," Matthew said. Bloody hell, were Jennsen and Miss Moorehouse making a toast with their wine?

"Of course you're not. You always have that deep crinkle between your brows and look as if you bit into a rotten egg. What I'd like to know is *why* you're *not* scowling—is it Jennsen or Miss Moorehouse who has you so disgruntled?"

Matthew forced his gaze away from the couple and turned toward Daniel. "I'm not disgruntled. I'm . . . concerned. Jennsen is monopolizing Miss Moorehouse. The poor woman must be bored to death."

Daniel's gaze flicked to the other end of the table then back. "She doesn't look bored to me. In fact, she seems to be enjoying herself immensely."

Matthew's wayward gaze shifted to the other end of the table. Yes, she was clearly enjoying herself.

"Jennsen appears happy as well."

Yes, damn it, he did. For reasons he couldn't explain, Matthew's jaw tightened.

"It seems clear you don't care for the man," Daniel said, leaning closer so they couldn't be overheard. "Why did you invite him?"

Actually, he hadn't disliked Jennsen until about fifteen minutes ago. "Same reason everyone invites him. He's rich."

"I can't see how that is of any use to you—unless you're planning to rob him?"

"Hardly."

"Hmmm. And I assume you're aware that although he's rich, the heiress you need to marry must be a *female*."

"I'm aware of that, thank you very much. I invited him because he's a brilliant financial mind. I'd planned to further our acquaintance then solicit his advice on possible investment opportunities."

Yes, that had been his plan. Now, however, he had a strong urge to send Jennsen back to London. Immediately. Before the bastard had a chance to ogle Miss Moorehouse again.

Too late. The bastard just ogled her again. Matthew felt a muscle in his jaw twitch.

"Good God, man, your face resembles a darkened thundercloud. If I didn't know better, I'd say you were jealous of the attention Jennsen's paying the mousy Miss Moorehouse . . ."

Daniel's voice trailed off and Matthew again turned toward him. And found Daniel staring at him with a stunned, dropped-jaw expression.

"I may resemble a darkened thundercloud," Matthew said lightly, "a description I disagree with, by the way, but at least I don't look like a gap-mouthed carp."

Daniel's lips snapped shut. Then he whispered, "Are you mad? She's . . . she's so . . . so . . ."

"So what?" Matthew asked, unable to squelch the chill that crept into his voice.

"So . . . not an heiress."

"I am aware of that. I've already told you I've no romantic interest in her." A tiny voice inside him coughed to life and muttered something that sounded suspiciously like *liar*.

Stupid bloody voice.

"Good God, man, I can't imagine why you would. Especially with a beauty like Lady Julianne here. Who, as you will recall, *is* the much-needed heiress. And not in the least bit . . . spinsterish." His gaze narrowed and turned speculative. "But something about this Miss Moorehouse has captured you—in much more than a simply wanting to discover her secrets sort of way. If that's all it was, your eyeballs wouldn't be shooting daggers at Jennsen. And you wouldn't be eyeing her as if she were a juicy piece of fruit you wanted to nibble upon."

"I assure you nothing could be further from the truth," Matthew said stiffly.

Liar, sneered the stupid little voice.

"If you say so."

"I do. I'm simply . . . *surprised* at Miss Moorehouse's amiability toward Jennsen."

"Surprised? That an unmarried woman, especially one so plain, would revel in the attention of an attractive, unmarried, ridiculously wealthy man?"

"While Miss Moorehouse is unmarried, she is not . . .

unattached. Her affections are engaged by a man named Franklin." His fingers involuntarily tightened around the stem of his wineglass.

"How do you know this?" Daniel asked.

"I saw a sketch of him she'd drawn."

"And her feelings are reciprocated?"

An image of the intimate sketch flashed in Matthew's mind. "I believe so, yes." He frowned. "I wonder what this Franklin's last name is?"

Daniel shook his head and chuckled. "Good God, now I've heard everything. How you get yourself into these messes, I've no idea."

"A bit of sympathy for my financial and marital plights wouldn't be unwelcome, you know."

"Oh, believe me, I'm sympathetic." Daniel lifted his wineglass and raised it toward Matthew in salute. "I wish you the best of luck, my friend. I've no doubt you're going to need it."

Sarah quietly opened her bedchamber door and cautiously peeked out. After ascertaining that the dimly lit corridor was empty, she quickly exited her room. Heart pounding, she forced herself to walk at a sedate pace and arrange her features into her most innocent expression. In case she happened upon anyone, her excuse for wandering about when she'd already retired for the night was at the ready. *I borrowed my sister's handkerchief earlier and forgot to return it.* Should she be informed that her sister's bedchamber was in the opposite direction, she'd simply pretend confusion, apologize, then turn around.

But hopefully she wouldn't come upon anyone. All the gentlemen were in the drawing room, partaking of brandy and whatever else gentlemen partook of after dinner, and all the ladies, including the chaperones, had retired. The chaperones were hopefully both asleep—because the Ladies Literary Society of London was meeting in her room at one A.M.—exactly two hours from now.

And she had a shirt to procure before they arrived.

Thanks to a conversation before dinner with the very informative maid Mary, Sarah knew which bedchamber belonged to Lord Langston. All she had to do was slip inside, grab a shirt, then slip back out. With Lord Langston in the drawing room and his valet Dewhurst enjoying his normal eleven P.M. tea break—another helpful tidbit courtesy of Mary—how difficult could this be?

A moment later, during which time she didn't meet anyone in the corridor, she finally stood outside Lord Langston's bedchamber. She drew a bracing breath then softly knocked, prepared to claim that she'd believed the room was her sister's, should anyone answer her summons. If someone did, she prayed it would be the valet and not Lord Langston himself, as he'd appeared to be in a bad temper during dinner. Every time she looked in his direction—which had annoyingly occurred far more frequently than she liked—he'd been scowling.

When no one answered her knock, she cautiously twisted the doorknob and slowly pushed open the door. After another quick glance up and down the corridor to make certain she wasn't being observed, she stepped over the threshold and closed the door quietly behind her.

She leaned her back against the oak panel, taking a few seconds to allow her accelerated heartbeat to slow. When she drew a deep breath, her senses were instantly inundated with his scent. Freshly laundered clothing and a hint of sandalwood. Just the sort of scent that would tempt her to heave a noisy, feminine sigh—if she were the sort to do such heaving—which she thankfully was not.

Her gaze slowly swept the room, noting the low-burning fire in the grate, which cast everything with a warm golden glow. The large copper bathtub set before the fireplace. The leather sofa and matching chairs near the hearth. The beautiful mahogany furniture. A dressing cabinet, washstand, and several chests of drawers. The huge bed, the navy blue counterpane neatly turned down. The night tables flanking the bed. A kidney-shaped desk and a reading stand. Her gaze lingered longingly on the trestle book stand filled with leather-bound volumes, but she shoved the longing to examine them aside and forced her gaze back to the dressing cabinet and the chests of drawers.

Which one held his lordship's shirts?

Pushing off from the door, she headed toward the closest chest of drawers. Grasping the brass handle on the top drawer, she pulled. And found herself staring at a pile of neatly folded shirts.

A breathless laugh rushed from her lips, and she quickly snatched up the top shirt. By God, this had been almost too easy!

She closed the drawer and clutched her prize to her chest. Once again Lord Langston's delightful scent filled her senses. She stilled and stared down at the snowy shirt. There was something unsettling and intimate about seeing that white material pressed against her breasts. As if in a trance, she slowly raised the garment. Then closing her eyes, she buried her face in the soft material and breathed deeply.

A vivid image of him rushed into her mind, walking

with her this afternoon in the sunshine, the warm, golden rays bouncing off his thick, dark hair. His slow smile. The way his eyes crinkled in the corners when he laughed. Those hazel eyes, which, even when he laughed, somehow looked sad to her. His deep voice—

"That will be all, Dewhurst," came Lord Langston's deep voice from the corridor. "Good night."

"Very well, my lord. Good night."

Good God.

Sarah's head jerked up so fast she knocked her glasses askew. She looked frantically about for a hiding place, but unlike her bedchamber, there was no dressing screen. With no choices and even less time, she dashed toward the heavy velvet drapes covering the windows. She'd no sooner secreted herself than she heard the door open. Then close.

She squeezed her eyes shut for several seconds and fought to contain her panic. And annoyance. Vexing man! Why wasn't he in the drawing room as he was supposed to be?

The sound of a long sigh reached her ears, followed by the gentle squeak of leather. Recalling that the leather chairs and sofa didn't face the windows, she risked peeking around the edge of the curtain.

Lord Langston, his profile clearly visible, sat in the leather chair. With his elbows set upon his knees and forehead resting in his palms, he looked incredibly weary. And inexorably sad. His dejected posture reminded her of the way she'd seen Carolyn looking whenever her sister believed herself unobserved, and sympathy arose unbidden within her. What was making him so unhappy?

Before she could consider the possibilities, he leaned down and grasped his boot. After pulling it off, he re-

moved the other. Then he stood and, to her fascination—
er, alarm—began undressing.

She felt her eyes widen and she somehow forgot to
breathe, to so much as blink, as she watched him slowly
remove his jacket. Then his cravat. Then his shirt.

Oh, my . . . The Ladies Literary Society had definitely
chosen the correct candidate from whom to take a shirt,
because the shirtless Lord Langston indeed qualified as
perfect. Her fingers curled around the edge of the curtain
and her stupefied gaze ran greedily over his broad shoulders. A fascinating sprinkling of dark hair ran across his
chest then narrowed to a thin ribbon as it bisected his flat,
muscle-rippled abdomen.

She was still drinking in the extraordinary view
when his fingers began working the buttons on his black
breeches. And before she could so much as draw a breath
into her stalled lungs, he swiftly removed the garment.

If she'd had the wherewithal to do so, Sarah would have
given thanks that her eyeballs were permanently attached
to her head, otherwise they surely would have leapt from
their sockets and bounced across the floor.

The only thing to which she could compare Lord
Langston was the scandalous statue she'd stumbled upon
in Lady Eastland's conservatory during her musicale last
month. So amazed and impressed had she been by the
sight, she'd drawn a sketch from memory—the sketch
Lord Langston had seen in the garden that morning. The
one under which she'd written *Franklin N. Stein* after the
ladies had decided to make the Perfect Man. Because up
until then, she'd believed that statue was as perfect as one
could hope to find.

Clearly she'd been harboring a gross misunderstanding.
For surely there could be no more perfect a male speci-

men than Lord Langston. While the statue had been life-like in size, nothing could have prepared her for seeing an actual naked man—literally in the flesh.

Her avid gaze tracked down his muscular form, noting the narrow hips and long legs, then settled on his groin with the sort of mesmerized fascination she normally only experienced in bookshops and gardens. On the in-triguing thatch of dark hair that surrounded his equally captivating manhood.

Dear God, was there no *air* in this room?

Before she could pull in a much-needed deep breath, he turned, treating her to an equally entrancing rear view. Merciful heavens, there wasn't a single inch of him that wasn't utterly beautiful.

The desire to move closer, to study every rippling mus-cle, to touch every bit of skin, nearly overwhelmed her. She actually had to brace her knees and grip the curtain to keep from giving in to the urge. Her lenses grew foggy and she frowned, blinking rapidly to clear the view-dis-torting annoyance. Then she realized the cause was her own rapid breaths bouncing off the velvet curtains. She leaned back slightly and forced her lax lips closed.

With a smooth grace that caused a heart-pounding, breath-stealing ripple of muscles, he approached the large copper tub. And for the first time she noticed the tendrils of steam rising above the polished rim. Her lips once again dropped open as realization enveloped her like a hot, steamy cloud.

She was about to see the very naked, very perfect Lord Langston take a bath.

Chapter 6

Heat sizzled through Sarah's body, and if she'd been able to tear her gaze from Lord Langston's naked form, she most likely would have looked down to ascertain that her skirt wasn't ablaze. Like a centuries-old elm, she stood rooted to the spot, barely breathing so as not to refog her lenses, not so much as blinking, for the sight of a naked Lord Langston lifting one muscular leg to step over the edge of the tub was not a sight to be missed.

Unfortunately, her conscience chose that moment to cough to life and make itself known.

Cease this reprehensible spying at once! Her halo-enwreathed inner voice demanded. *Avert your eyes this instant and give that poor man the privacy he deserves.*

What the poor man deserved, Sarah decided, was a standing ovation. He lifted his other leg and she tilted her head to maximize the stupefying view. Another wave of heat rolled through her. Heavens. Lord Langston was indeed blessed. Everywhere.

Her conscience once again attempted to speak, but she flicked it away as one would an annoying buzzing insect. Because really, she *had* to look. How else would she know when he finished his bath so she could determine when it was safe for her to escape? And besides, she was a scientist—of sorts. Granted, her area of expertise was horticulture and not anatomy, but she certainly possessed a scientist's love of learning. A scientist's thirst for knowledge.

Yes, and look how badly the quest for knowledge turned out for Dr. Frankenstein, her inner voice said slyly.

Stuff and nonsense. Things would have gone much better had Dr. Frankenstein's creation in any way resembled Lord Langston. Her gaze wandered down his masculine form and she barely suppressed a gusty sigh.

Much better.

She was quickly developing an unexpected expertise—and appreciation—for the male anatomy.

She watched him slowly lower himself into the steaming water, then lean his head back against the curved lip. After exhaling a long breath, he closed his eyes.

Sarah studied him, noting how, due to his height, his bent knees rose from the water. Although his features were more relaxed, she still detected signs of strain around his mouth and closed eyes. What troubled him so that even in repose peace seemed to escape him?

Her gaze rested on a lock of his dark hair that fell over his forehead, and her fingers suddenly itched with the desire to brush back the strands. Discover if they felt as silky as they looked. She allowed her imagination to wander, and in her mind's eye she envisioned herself walking toward him. Kneeling beside the tub. Sifting her fingers through his hair, then tracing them over his features. Memorizing the texture of his skin. The shape of his lips . . .

As if beckoning her, his lips parted slightly, drawing her attention to his mouth. In spite of her best efforts to ignore such things—for what was the good in admiring that which she could never have?—she always seemed particularly attracted to men's lips. And this man's were truly lovely. Perfectly shaped and enticingly full. How did they manage to look so firm yet so soft at the same time?

Again she imagined herself kneeling next to the tub, this time slowly tracing the outline of his mouth with her fingertips, then leaning forward to touch her lips to his. Her eyes slid closed and her breath caught. What would his mouth feel like against hers? And his skin . . . how would it feel beneath her palms? Rough? Smooth?

Heat pulsed through her, settling low in her belly. It was a sensation she recognized, the one that often came upon her as she lay alone in her bed, in the dark, yearning for . . . something. The sensation that left her restless and overheated and made her feel as if her skin had somehow shrunk. She shifted slightly, pressing her thighs together, but the movement did nothing to relieve her discomfort; rather, it only served to further inflame nerve endings that already throbbed.

She opened her eyes and her fingers tightened around the velvet curtain as he reached out and grabbed a thick bar of soap from a ceramic dish set on a small table next to the tub. Transfixed, she watched him drag the soap across his wet skin, washing his neck, arms, and chest. Then his hands disappeared, presumably to skim the soap over his lower body, and she cursed the copper tub that thwarted her view. Hoping to improve her line of vision, she rose up on her toes. Botheration, that didn't help.

When Lord Langston finished with the soap, he set it back on the ceramic dish, then slid low in the water to rinse, disappearing from her view. Before she could pull a much needed breath into her lungs, he reappeared and ran his hands over his wet face. Then slowly stood.

She hadn't believed anything could look more perfect than a naked Lord Langston, but obviously something could.

A naked and *wet* Lord Langston.

Water sluiced down his body, tapering into silvery trails that glittered in the glow of the low-burning fire. God help her, she didn't know where to look first. Didn't know in what order to feast her eyes upon the delicious banquet stretched before her. He raised his arms, tilted back his head, and slowly pushed his wet hair away from his face.

Sarah felt as if she'd backed into the fireplace. The sight of him was so captivating, so stimulating, so . . . *arousing,* her knees actually felt weak. Indeed, she needed to lean against the wall before she slithered to the ground in a heated, steaming lump—a most unexpected and vexing turn of events, as she did not in any way consider herself the sort of female prone to swooning. With her gaze locked upon him, she took a small step back.

And the floorboard beneath her foot squeaked.

Sarah froze as the sound seemed to echo through the room—along with the frantic pounding of her heart. Her gaze flew to Lord Langston's, but he clearly didn't suspect anything amiss, as he didn't lift his head nor hesitate in his ablutions.

Thank God. How humiliating would it be if he were to catch her in his bedchamber? Ogling his nakedness—although really, who could blame her for ogling? The mere thought of him discovering her tied her stomach into knots. Scarcely daring to breathe, she carefully moved her foot from the offending spot, relief filling her when no further sounds arose.

She watched him briskly rub a large white towel over

his body then slip his arms into a dark blue robe. Part of her breathed a silent sigh of relief that he was now covered and would hopefully go to his dressing room so she could escape. But the other part of her, the bigger part, lamented the loss of the most perfect view she'd ever beheld. Indeed, she couldn't wait to get to her sketch pad to commit the sight of him to paper—although she knew that even if she survived into the next century, she would never forget what he'd looked like. She supposed she should feel some sense of remorse over her zealous gawking, but instead her only regrets were that the show was over and that she hadn't thought to bring a telescope.

Or a fan—because by God, it was *hot* in here!

He secured the robe's sash around his waist then moved toward the darkened corner of the bedchamber farthest from her. She held her breath, hoping he would exit the room through the door there, which she assumed led to a dressing chamber. What sounded like a drawer opening met her ears, and seconds later, instead of leaving the room as she'd hoped, Lord Langston once again emerged from the shadows then started across the room, his gaze fixed upon the desk. The desk that was situated no more than five feet away from her hiding place.

Botheration, what was he doing? With the way her luck was going this evening, he'd probably taken it into his head to write a letter. Vexing man. Why couldn't he simply go get dressed as any man wearing naught but a robe would do? Had she recently thought him perfect? Obviously she was daft. He was a nincompoop who'd ruined her perfect escape and distracted her with his nakedness. His eyeball-searing, knee-weakening, brain-numbing, breath-stealing, magnificent nakedness. Which he'd had the nerve, um, decency, to cover up.

He approached the desk and she held her breath, praying that he didn't intend to sit down and compose a lengthy missive.

Her prayers were answered. Instead of sitting at the desk, he swiftly turned and yanked back the curtain.

Before she could so much as gasp, a muscular forearm rammed against her chest, pinning her to the wall. The air *whooshed* from her lungs and the impact knocked her spectacles askew. She caught a blurry glimpse of a silver blade an instant before cool metal pressed against her neck.

Too shocked to move, she stared at him through eyes that felt as if they were going to pop from their sockets, whether from shock or from the pressure of his arm or the realization that he held a knife to her throat, she wasn't certain. Unmistakable surprise flickered in his eyes, then his gaze narrowed.

"Miss Moorehouse," he said in a chilly voice that was at complete odds with the heat emanating from his body. "May I inquire as to what you are doing skulking behind my curtain?"

A spurt of anger shot through Sarah, nudging aside some of her shock and fear, and she glared right back at him. "May I inquire as to why you have a knife pressed to my throat?"

"I fear it is the way intruders are dealt with. I suggest you familiarize yourself with the feeling if you plan to continue to break into other people's rooms."

"I didn't break in. The door was unlocked. Now, if you don't mind, I'd like for you to both unhand me and remove that knife."

Instead of freeing her, his gaze raked her face. "You've been spying on me."

A guilty flush seared upward from her toes, and she knew

that within seconds her skin would resemble a blotchy mess. "I wasn't spying. I was . . . watching for my opportunity to leave your chamber." Which was true. Still, she couldn't deny his accusation wasn't without a *tiny* sliver of merit. But really, if the man didn't want women looking at him, he shouldn't remove his clothes—ever. Rather, he should take some pains to ugly himself up a bit. Perhaps allow himself to go to fat. Or wear a hideous mask.

"Are you armed?" he asked.

"Armed? Certainly not."

He stepped closer, until mere inches separated them. She drew in a sharp breath as the warmth of his body surrounded her, inundating her senses with his clean scent. A drop of water dripped from his wet hair, landing on her collarbone, where it meandered downward, tickling her skin before being absorbed by her gown.

His gaze flicked down, then again met hers. "You're holding something."

She was? She flexed her fingers and realized they were still wrapped around the soft linen of his shirt. Ah, yes, his shirt—or as she would refer to it from now on, Her Nemesis. "It's merely a shirt."

He cocked a single brow. "What sort of shirt?

Dear God, it was nearly impossible to breathe, to think, with him so close—an affliction that somehow had little to do with his arm pressing against her and the cool blade touching her neck and everything to do with the fact that no more than a thin robe stood between his nakedness and her hands.

She swallowed, moistened her lips, then said in the strongest voice she could muster, "I'll tell you what sort of shirt after you unhand me and put down the knife."

He hesitated for several more seconds, and she forced

herself to meet his penetrating gaze—no easy feat with her spectacles hanging precariously from the end of her nose. Even with only a foot separating their faces, he was still a bit blurry around the edges. Yet even so, it was clear from his expression that he was highly suspicious of her appearance in his bedchamber.

Without taking his gaze from her, he slowly lowered his arm, and she sucked in a quick breath. He then reached out to set the knife on the edge of his desk, within easy reach should he require it, she noticed. She raised her hand to her neck and pressed her fingers against the skin where the cool blade had rested. A shudder ran through her, followed by another shot of anger.

"You could have slit my throat."

"Consider yourself fortunate that I did not."

"What sort of man threatens his guests in such a manner?"

"What sort of woman hides behind curtains and spies on men while they bathe?"

Damnation, he had a point. Not that she had any intention of admitting that to him. Especially since her need to hide behind the curtain was entirely his fault. Lifting her chin, she said in her haughtiest tone, "Surely you don't believe I pose any sort of physical threat to you, my lord."

"I'm not certain what to believe, Miss Moorehouse. Nor does it escape my notice that you've avoided my question as to what sort of woman hides behind curtains and spies on men while they bathe."

"As you avoided mine as to what sort of man threatens his guests with a knife."

Satisfaction edged through her at his displeased expression. Well, fine. She was far from pleased herself. He took one step back, crossed his arms over his chest and fixed an icy glare upon her. "I await your explanation."

She pushed up her spectacles and drew a bracing breath, but his clean scent filled her head, evoking an image of him, naked and wet and pushing back his hair, and her powers of speech escaped her.

When she remained silent, he prompted, "Your explanation regarding the shirt . . . ? Did you wish to give me the garment? Or . . ." He moved—so quickly, so unexpectedly, she found herself frozen in place—and planted his hands on the wall on either side of her head, caging her in. "Or did you sneak into my room to watch me bathe?"

Annoyance shook her from her stupor. "That is a most improper suggestion, my lord. And the shirt is not a gift." She lifted the garment and waggled it beneath his nose. "It is, in fact, *your* shirt."

"Indeed? Well, then I find it very interesting that you are spouting what is proper—you who have sneaked into my room, spied upon me as I bathed, *and* attempted to steal my clothing."

"Not your *clothing.* Just your shirt."

"Ah. You seem to possess a talent for splitting hairs, Miss Moorehouse."

"Only because you seem to have a talent for making inaccurate statements—another of which is your accusation that I was *stealing* your shirt when in fact I was merely *borrowing* it."

"For what possible reason?

"A . . . scavenger hunt. An amusement the other ladies and I devised. Just a bit of harmless fun."

"I see. So you planned to return my shirt?"

"Of course."

"When? During my next bath?"

Only if I'm the luckiest woman on earth. She again

blinked away the image of him naked. Or at least she tried to. And was spectacularly unsuccessful. "Certainly not. I'd planned to return it at a time when you were not in your bedchamber. As you were not supposed to be now. I'll have you know that if you'd remained in the drawing room where you were supposed to be, this debacle never would have come to pass."

"It sounds as if you're saying the fact that you're hiding behind my curtain and spying on me is *my* fault."

"That is precisely what I'm saying."

Matthew studied her for several long seconds, completely nonplussed. Yet his bewilderment wasn't solely the result of her outrageous logic. No, it was more because he couldn't figure out why he found this exchange so exhilarating. And because he didn't know why he continued to stand so close to her, caging her in. Why the urge to move even closer was gripping him in a stranglehold. And why she hadn't demanded that he step away from her.

He wished to God she would. Wished to God he could make himself move back. Wished he wasn't consumed by this insane desire to touch her.

And insanity it was. With her prim exterior, plain clothing, thick spectacles, and outspoken nature, she was not at all the sort of woman to whom he'd ever been attracted. Yet here he stood, heart pounding simply by virtue of her nearness. And there was no point in lying to himself—while he'd sat in his bath, before he discovered her behind his curtain, he'd been thinking of her. Of those honey-colored eyes that so thoroughly fascinated him. Froze him. Heated him. Had imagined her coming to him, touching him. Kissing him. And now, here she was.

But *why* was she here? Was her story of a scavenger hunt true? Or was she, as he'd already considered, more than she seemed? Unless she was an accomplished actress, she didn't possess the least air of coyness, yet he knew she had secrets. She *looked* innocent, but she drew anatomically detailed sketches of naked men. Would she add drawings of him to her sketch pad? He found the idea utterly arousing. Irritatingly so.

He breathed in and caught a slight whiff of flowers—a teasing hint that made him want to lean closer to better catch the elusive scent, a fact that further irritated him.

His gaze took in her rumpled hair and his fingers twitched with the urge to slip out every pin and watch those untamable curls she clearly tried so hard to coax into submission cascade over her shoulders. Then he studied her face, touching upon each mismatched feature that so inexplicably grabbed him and refused to let go. Her lips . . . those full lips that were more suited to a courtesan than a spinster. Those lips that seemed to beckon him like a siren's call. And those huge eyes, magnified behind her spectacles, which gleamed with what appeared to be a hint of challenge. Indeed, Miss Moorehouse seemed exceptionally, annoyingly, calm, while he felt decidedly, annoyingly, the exact opposite of calm.

He clenched his jaw. Bloody hell, this wouldn't do at all. Common sense demanded that it was time to get this vexing woman out of his bedchamber.

Unfortunately, it seemed that common sense was not in charge because instead of sending her on her way, he leaned a bit closer. And inwardly smiled when apprehension flickered in her eyes. Ah. Excellent. She wasn't quite as composed as she'd have him believe.

"Saying that your spying on me is my fault . . . I certainly must give you points for sheer boldness, Miss Moorehouse. However, allow me to offer you a bit of advice: the next time you decide to steal something, you should make an effort to keep the floorboards from squeaking."

The annoyance that flashed in her eyes pleased him greatly. "I was *not* stealing, my lord. For you to insist I was is very nude." Her eyes widened with clear dismay. "Rude. I meant *rude*."

"Hmmm. Yes, speaking of nude—"

"I wasn't speaking of nude!"

"—you've seen quite a lot of me."

He suspected she was blushing, and wished the room were brighter so he could see if color suffused her cheeks. She pressed her lips together and he could almost see her gathering her courage. She hiked up her chin then jerked her head in a nod. "Rather unavoidable, I'm afraid."

"Most young, unmarried women would swoon at such a sight."

"I'm hardly fresh from the schoolroom, my lord, nor am I prone to the vapors."

"And it isn't as if you saw anything you hadn't already seen."

She blinked. "I beg your pardon?"

"Your friend Franklin. Based on your sketch I saw, you've seen him naked." An unpleasant sensation rushed through him as he said those words, a sensation that felt precisely like jealousy.

"Oh. Um, yes."

"Were those circumstances similar to these?"

"Cir . . . circumstances?"

"When you saw Franklin naked . . . were you attempting to steal—forgive me—*borrow* his shirt as well? Or was the occasion between you of a more . . . personal nature?"

When she remained silent, he moved closer to her, until less than two feet separated their bodies. Her chest rose and fell with her shallow breaths and she clutched his shirt against her midsection. The sight of his clothing pressed against her struck him as oddly intimate. And incredibly arousing. Bloody hell, he found *her* incredibly arousing. In a way he neither liked nor understood. But in a way he could not deny. Just as he could no longer deny the inexplicable yet gnawing need to touch her. Nor ignore the irrational, unreasonable desire to erase all thoughts of this Franklin from her mind.

Based on the sketch, she and Franklin were more than simply friends, yet she projected an innocence that strongly contradicted the intimate nature of that sketch. It was a puzzle that fascinated him. And was one he intended to solve.

"I suspect your mother wouldn't approve of your scavenger hunt," he said in a silky voice.

Her tongue peeked out to moisten her lips, a distracting flick of pink that he found himself wishing she'd repeat. "I assure you she wouldn't care one way or the other," she said softly. "My mother wouldn't notice if I ran naked through the kitchen."

An image of her, naked in a kitchen—*his* kitchen—and him feasting on her—flashed through his mind, leaving a trail of heat in its wake. He had to clear his throat to locate his voice. "I beg your pardon?"

"Forgive me, my lord. Sometimes I forget myself and am too outspoken. And say inappropriate words like 'naked.' I apologize for offending your tender sensibilities."

A frown pulled down his brows. "I assure you, my sensibilities are not tender. You, however, seem to be preoccupied with things of a 'naked' nature."

"That's not true . . ."

Her words tapered off into a soft gasp when he lifted one hand from the wall and captured a loose tendril of her hair between his fingers. She went perfectly still, and unable to resist, he moved his other hand and slowly slipped the pins from her hair, letting them fall to the floor, where they landed with soft *pings*. She made no move to stop him, just gazed at him through wide eyes that reflected a combination of wonder and shock and puzzlement—as if she couldn't believe he was touching her nor understand why he would.

He felt her tremble, heard the quickening of her breath, and grim satisfaction filled him at the realization that this . . . whatever it was that had him in its grasp, also held her.

With each pin he removed, more curls spiraled downward over her shoulders, ending at her waist. The delicate scent of flowers rose from the freed strands, and he breathed deeply. When he finished, he ran his fingers slowly down the shiny, wildly curly tresses. Touching the edge of her glasses, he murmured, "May I?" Then, without giving her time to refuse, he slipped off her spectacles. And stared.

"You look like a Botticelli painting," he whispered.

A sound of disbelief passed her lips and she shook her head, setting her curls in motion. "Hardly. He painted Venus."

"Yes. And if you were naked, you'd put Venus herself to shame."

"You require spectacles."

"I assure you, I don't."

"It is now *you* who are preoccupied with things of a 'naked' nature."

His gaze ran slowly down her length, imagining the

generous breasts and long legs her modest gown hinted at. "It seems so," he agreed softly. Reaching out, he trailed a single fingertip over her smooth cheek. Her skin felt like warm velvet. "Venus's natural state was nude, you know."

Her lips parted and a soft gasp escaped her—a sort of breathless, pleasure-filled sound that urged him to discover what other sort of erotic sounds she might make.

She nodded slowly. "Yes. I also know that she is associated with love and beauty. While I know a fair amount about love, beauty does not, in any way, apply to me."

He captured a handful of curls and slowly sifted his fingers through the satiny spirals. "I must disagree. Your hair is beautiful."

Instead of appearing complimented, she looked at him as if he belonged in Bedlam. "You truly do need spectacles."

He shook his head and gently wrapped a length of curls around his fist. Lifting his hair-wrapped hand to his face, he breathed deeply. "You smell beautiful as well. Like a garden in the sunshine. And your eyes . . ." He looked into her golden brown depths and again wished there was more light.

"Are the color of mud," she said in a flat voice.

"Are the color of honey, surrounded by rich chocolate," he corrected. "Has no one ever told you how lovely your eyes are?"

"Never," she said without hesitation.

"Not even your friend Franklin?"

She hesitated, then said, "No."

Matthew decided then and there that the man was an idiot. "Consider yourself told." His gaze dropped to her mouth. "And then there are your lips. They're . . . striking."

She said nothing for several long seconds, just stared at him with an unreadable expression. Then her bottom lip trembled slightly and a combination of weary resignation, disappointment, and something else that looked like hurt filled her eyes. Although she raised her chin, he sensed that some of the courage she'd previously displayed had seeped from her.

"Please cease these games, my lord," she said quietly. "I apologize for intruding and disturbing your privacy. It was not my intention to do so. And now, if you'll excuse me . . ." She held out his shirt.

He felt dismissed. Just as he had in the garden. Yet that flash of hurt in her eyes filled his chest with a hollow sensation he couldn't name. Clearly she believed he was making sport of her, and while part of him wished that were the case, nothing could have been further from the truth.

"You can have the shirt, Miss Moorehouse. I wouldn't want to cause you to be disqualified from your scavenger hunt."

"Thank you. I'll see that it's returned." She squinted pointedly toward his hand, which still held her spectacles. "If you'll give me back my glasses, I'll be on my way."

Which is precisely what his common sense was screaming at him to do. But everything else inside him was insisting that she stay. And that he find out if she felt as soft as she appeared. Tasted as delicious as she looked. Just one touch, one taste . . . to satisfy this gnawing curiosity.

Without taking his gaze from her, he reached out and placed her spectacles on the desk, next to his knife. Surprise flickered in her eyes. "Did you just set my glasses aside?" she asked.

"I did."

"I'm afraid I cannot be without them, my lord. Even at this short of a distance . . ." She indicated the two foot space between them with a waggle of her hand. ". . . you are blurry."

"Then I'd best move closer." He stepped forward and lifted his hands to sift them through her hair. "Is this better?"

She swallowed audibly. "Um, actually, I'm feeling a bit . . . crowded. If there's something you want—"

"There is." His gaze dropped to her mouth. And he had to swallow a groan. By God, she just looked so . . . ripe. So delectable. So kissable. "I want to kiss you."

A frown creased her brow. "You're joking."

"I'm not."

"Don't be ridiculous."

"Again, I'm not."

"This morning you couldn't recall my name."

"I recall your name now." His gaze again dipped to her lips. "Miss Sarah Moorehouse."

"Then you must be foxed."

"I'm not. Are you?"

"Certainly not. I'm—"

"As curious as I am?" He cupped her face between his hands and brushed the pad of one thumb over her plump lower lip. A tiny, breathless sound caught in her throat, heating his desire to an even higher degree.

"Curiosity, as you may recall—"

"Killed the cat. Yes, I know." He moved closer, until his body lightly touched hers from chest to knee. "How fortunate that we aren't cats."

"I . . . I cannot fathom a single reason as to why you would wish to kiss me."

Lowering his head until his lips hovered just above hers, he whispered, "Don't worry. I can fathom enough reasons for both of us."

He brushed his lips over hers once, then again, softly, searching. Her lips parted on a low sigh, and he took advantage of the invitation to deepen the kiss.

And was instantly lost. In the heady, flowery scent of her and the delicious, warm taste of her. He eased one hand slowly down her arm then around to the small of her back, and urged her closer. God, yes, she *was* soft, just as he'd known she would be. Warm and curvy, and she tasted so good . . . so damn good. And it had been so long since he'd held a woman. Kissed a woman. So damn long . . .

He sank deeper into the kiss, his tongue exploring the velvety heat of her mouth. She hesitated for several seconds, and then, with a low moan, her lips parted farther and she touched her tongue to his. And suddenly what he'd thought would be a simple kiss felt anything but. It felt hot and urgent and fired pure lust through him. And made him crave more. More . . .

Without breaking their kiss, he moved closer, pinning her to the wall with his lower body, and insinuated his knee between her legs. He might possibly have retained a small modicum of control if she'd remained passive, but instead she wrapped her arms around his neck, rose up on her toes and pressed herself more fully against him.

His body's reaction was swift and unstoppable, and with a groan he slowly rubbed himself against her, pressing his hardness against her softness.

Pleasure shuddered through him and he lost all sense of time and place. He was intoxicated by the feel of her arching against him, a sensation that made it seem as if she were melting into him. One kiss melded into another, deep, drugging exchanges that grew in urgency. Mindless, heedless, to anything save the taste and feel of her, his hands smoothed over the curve of her bottom then came forward to cup the fullness of her breasts. Her head fell limply back, and he ran his lips down the fragrant curve of her neck, his tongue tracing the frantic beat of her pulse as her fingers slipped into his damp hair. Erotic sounds vibrated in her throat and she squirmed against him, stripping away another layer of his control. His erection jerked and he pinned her more firmly between himself and the wall.

Stop . . . He had to stop this madness, because if he didn't, he was going to sweep her up in his arms, carry her to his bed, and put out this bloody fire she'd ignited. But he couldn't do that . . . for some reason . . . some reason which entirely escaped him.

You're looking for a wife, his helpful inner voice reminded him. *And this woman—who is not an heiress—is not a candidate.*

Right. And her very good friend *was* a candidate. Besides that, he wasn't entirely certain he trusted this woman, again for reasons he couldn't recall at the moment, but even in his lust-rattled brain he knew they existed. Which made this interlude a very bad idea. In every way. But bloody hell, she felt so damn good. In every way. And she made him feel better than he'd felt in a very long time. He needed to stop . . . yet he simply could not.

Reaching up, he gently grabbed one of her wrists and pulled her hand down, slipping it inside his robe and dragging her palm across his bare chest. A groan rumbled in his throat, and he urged her hand across his chest again. She'd just made a tentative, slow sweep of her own accord when a sound penetrated the fog of lust engulfing him. A low, deep sound that resembled a—

Woof.

Bloody hell. With a Herculean effort, he raised his head. And stared, captivated by the sight of her. She looked utterly aroused, and appeared lost in the same foggy haze as engulfed him. Erratic breaths puffed from between her full, moist lips, and her eyelids drooped half closed. He turned his head and shot Danforth a glare that should have sent the beast slinking from the room with his tail tucked between his legs. Instead, Danforth's gaze bounced between him and Miss Moorehouse, and Matthew could almost hear his canine musing: *Well, well, what have we here?*

Danforth gazed up at Miss Moorehouse with an adoring expression, licked his chops and issued another woof. The beast then appeared to actually *grin,* and with a firm push of his snout, nudged Matthew back a step and insinuated himself between him and Miss Moorehouse. Then sat. On Matthew's bare foot. And proceeded to pant hot doggie breath. Against Matthew's bare leg.

Bloody hell.

He turned his attention back to Miss Moorehouse. She was staring at him with a dazed expression that perfectly matched the way he felt. Her hand still rested on his chest, right above the spot where his heart pounded as if he'd just sprinted to Scotland and back.

"Good heavens," she said in a husky, breathless rasp.

If he'd felt capable of speech, he would have voiced a similar sentiment, although his most likely would have been more along the lines of *Holy bloody hell, what just happened?*

"I had no idea," she whispered. "I'd wondered . . .

but never suspected . . . not in my wildest imaginings."
A long, pleasure-filled sigh escaped her, blowing warm
against his skin. "Oh, my . . ."

He frowned. Her words made it sound as if she'd never
been kissed before. But surely a woman who'd sketched
a naked man had been kissed. Yet there was something
extraordinarily innocent about her. And her response to
him, while undeniably heated, hadn't felt the least bit
practiced. Was it possible he'd been the first?

Before he could find his voice to question her, she
blinked several times, then lifted her head from the wall
and squinted toward the floor. "I'm guessing that blurry
brown blob is Danforth?"

Upon hearing his name, Danforth issued a deep *woof*
and swiped his tail across the parquet floor.

Matthew cleared his throat. "I'm afraid so."

"How did he get in?"

"He can open doors." He glared at his pet. "I taught
him that." And right now he wished like hell he hadn't.
Damn dog was too smart for his own good. And his timing was heinous.

Or was it perfect? His better judgment told him Danforth had quite saved the day. Had put a halt to something
that never should have begun. His aroused body, however,
wholeheartedly disagreed. And one look at the moist-
lipped, loose-haired Miss Moorehouse had him longing
to snatch her right back in his arms.

Her hand slid slowly from his chest, and he immediately missed her touch. With a self-conscious sound she
pushed back her mass of disheveled hair. "I . . . I feel the
need to say something, yet I've no idea what."

She said the words without a trace of coyness or guile,
and he couldn't stop himself from tucking a stray strand

of her hair behind her ear. "You are . . . magnificent."

She nodded, her expression serious. "Yes, that seems appropriate. You are magnificent."

His lips twitched. "Thank you. But I meant *you* are magnificent."

She studied him for several long seconds, confusion flitting across her features. Then she shook her head. "I'm not. I know I'm not. And this . . . what happened between us, should not have occurred. I shouldn't be in your bedchamber and we shouldn't have . . ."

"Kissed?" he supplied helpfully when her voice trailed off.

"Kissed," she repeated in a husky whisper that had him clenching his hands to keep them off her. Then she shook her head, as if to clear it of cobwebs, and reached out to pluck her glasses from his desk. After putting on the spectacles, she looked at him. All traces of arousal and desire had vanished from her eyes, replaced by a coolness he didn't care for in the least.

"I beg your pardon, my lord. I don't know what came over me. I don't normally . . ." She frowned, then continued in a brisk tone, ". . . conduct myself in such a way. I think we should forget this ever happened."

"Do you?"

"Yes. Don't you?"

"I think you're correct that we should try. However, I think we shall fail."

"Nonsense. One can do anything one sets one's mind to. And now, I must go." She stepped away from him, then reached down to pick up his shirt, which she'd dropped. Danforth was sitting on the sleeve and she had to tug several times to slide the material from beneath his rump. And then the woman who only moments ago had trembled in his arms strode across his bedchamber and quit the room without a backward glance, closing the door quietly behind her.

He stared at the door for several seconds, then with a sigh raked his hands through his hair and slid his foot from beneath Danforth's bottom. Perhaps Miss Moorehouse would forget about that kiss, but he knew he wouldn't.

The question was, what did he intend to do about that? And about her? He had no idea. Then there was the fact that she'd seen him naked, and he'd always been taught that turnabout was fair play.

What did he intend to do about *that*?

He certainly knew what he *wanted* to do.

Hmmm. It appeared his many questions regarding Miss Moorehouse would require a great deal of thinking about. And he was hit with the very unsettling realization that thinking about her would not pose any difficulties.

Chapter 7

Ten minutes before the other ladies were due to arrive for their one A.M. meeting, Sarah stood before the cheval glass in her bedchamber and stared at her reflection. She'd changed into her plain white cotton night rail, secured the sash of her plain white cotton robe around her waist, and braided her unruly hair into a plain, single thick plait. She looked the same as she did every night—utterly plain. But she didn't feel the same.

She raised her hand and skimmed her fingertips over her lips. Her eyelids fluttered closed and a sigh of pure pleasure escaped her. Never, not even in her wildest dreams, not once during the countless hours she'd lain awake at night imagining being kissed, touched by a man, had she ever suspected that the actual act could be so incredibly wondrous.

The delicious sensation of his body pressing against hers, his lips on hers, his tongue touching hers, his hands sifting through her hair, skimming down her back, urging her closer. The knee-stealing feel of her palms skimming across his chest, the sound of his rapid breathing, the heart-stopping sensation of his hardness nestled against the juncture of her thighs. Heat rippled through her and she clamped her legs together in an effort to lessen the aching throb where he'd pressed so intimately against her, but her effort proved futile.

He'd felt so *warm*. So strong and broad. Being wrapped in his arms was like being cuddled in a heated blanket fresh from drying in the sunshine. His wet hair had slipped through her fingers like dampened silk. He'd held her, kissed her, touched her, with a fiery passion she'd never dared dream she would experience outside her imagination. And as active as her imagination was, she had never conceived of a scenario like the one she'd shared with Lord Langston.

Why? *Why* had he kissed her like that? She opened her eyes to study herself and shook her head, utterly confused. Nothing reflected in the mirror would inspire a man's passion. Perhaps he really had been foxed, although she hadn't detected the smell, or taste, of spirits about him. As humiliating as it was to consider, most likely he'd been thinking about some other woman. Pretending she was someone else. Someone beautiful. There was no other logical explanation. Unless . . .. . .

Perhaps he'd kissed her in order to distract her from the fact that he kept a knife in his bedchamber—a knife he'd pressed to her throat when he believed her an intruder bent on doing him harm. Did all gentlemen keep weapons at the ready as Lord Langston did? Perhaps. Or perhaps it was only those gentlemen who had something to hide. And she'd been considering just that about him . . . until he completely changed the direction of her thoughts with his kiss.

Another sigh escaped her. Regardless of whether he'd been thinking of someone else or attempting to divert her, now she knew of this magic she'd overheard other ladies discussing. This enchantment Carolyn had often alluded to. It was intoxicating. Addicting. And, she very much feared, unforgettable. Would her sister, her friends, be able to tell? Did the heated, pulsing glow she felt within show on the outside?

She leaned closer to the mirror. No. She still looked like plain, bespectacled Sarah on the outside.

A soft knock sounded on the door, and she pulled her gaze from the mirror to quickly cross the room. She opened the door to find Carolyn, Julianne, and Emily in the corridor, clutching bundles against their robes.

"It looks as if you all were successful in your scavenger hunt," Sarah said after the trio had entered and she'd closed and locked the door.

"Yes," said Emily, her eyes glowing with excitement. "Did you get Lord Langston's shirt?"

Among other things. Heat crept into her face. "Yes." She cleared her throat. "Everything went smoothly for all of you, I trust?"

"I was in and out of Lord Thurston's bedchamber—cravat in hand—in less than one minute," Emily reported with a smug grin while setting her treasure on the bed. "It was almost too easy."

"Same for me," said Julianne, adding the pair of Lord Berwick's boots she'd procured. "I didn't encounter anyone, but my heart was pounding so hard I thought I might swoon."

"Plucking Lord Surbrooke's breeches from his wardrobe was as simple as picking daisies in the garden," Carolyn said with a smile, holding her offering aloft before setting it on top of the other things on the bed.

"Sarah asserted that men are nincompoops," Emily

said with a devilish grin, "and it would appear, at least in regards to this situation, she is correct." She turned to Sarah. "How did you fare?"

Sarah's face burned hotter and she knew the blotches were on their way. "Fine. No problems." At least none she was willing to share. She added Lord Langston's shirt to the pile and forcibly banished from her mind the image of him, wet and naked, and instead concentrated on Carolyn's smile.

"We'll be able to fashion a very fine facsimile of our Perfect Man with these articles," Sarah said. "All we need are some rags or batting with which to stuff Mr. Franklin N. Stein."

"We could go to the village and buy batting," Julianne said. "The gentlemen have an archery tournament scheduled for tomorrow so the timing is perfect. I'd love an excursion to the shops."

"That's a sentence we should teach our Perfect Man to say," Sarah said with a grin. "'I'd love an excursion to the shops.'"

The ladies laughed, and Emily suggested, "Let's make a list of things our Perfect Man would say and do."

They all agreed to the idea. Sarah sat at the escritoire while the others seated themselves upon the bed's ivory counterpane. Pen in hand, Sarah asked, "Besides loving an excursion to the shops, what else would he say?"

Julianne cleared her throat and adopted a deep voice. "'Spending the day at my club isn't important, darling. I'd much rather be with you.'"

"'I'd *love* to dance again, my dear,'" added Emily in a manly tone.

"'You're the most beautiful woman I've ever seen,'" came Carolyn's suggestion.

"'The most intelligent woman with the most interesting opinions,'" added Emily.

"'I could talk to you for *hours*,'" said Julianne, her words ending on a wistful sigh.

"'Are you tired, my dear? Why don't you sit on the settee and let me rub your feet.'"

They all broke into giggles at Carolyn's last suggestion, and Sarah's hand flew across the vellum to jot down each idea.

"'I love the sound of your name,'" said Emily.

An image of Lord Langston, dressed in his robe, his hair wet, his eyes roaming her face, flashed through Sarah's mind. *I recall your name . . . Miss Sarah Moorehouse.*

"'Your hair is beautiful,'" said Julianne.

Sarah's hand hesitated and she closed her eyes, hearing his voice say those exact words.

"'Your eyes as well,'" added Emily.

Has no one ever told you how lovely your eyes are?

"'You smell beautiful,'" added Carolyn.

"Like a garden in the sunshine." The words Lord Langston had murmured escaped Sarah before she could stop them and her head jerked up. And found her sister and friends nodding in approval.

Knowing her face was flaming, Sarah applied her attention to her list with renewed zeal.

"I think he should say 'I want to kiss you' with unwavering frequency," Julianne decreed.

I want to kiss you. The words reverberated through Sarah's mind, pulsing heat to her every nerve ending. She'd heard those very words only a short time ago. And they had indeed been perfect.

"And 'I love you' as well," said Carolyn softly. "Those are the loveliest words I've ever heard."

The wistful note in her sister's voice tugged at Sarah, and she said softly, "I love you, Carolyn."

Just as she'd hoped, her sister smiled. "I love you too, poppet."

Sarah pushed up her glasses then asked, "What are some of the things our Perfect Man will do?"

"You mean besides accompany us to the shops, dance and talk with us, and tell us how magnificent we are?" asked Emily.

Again Lord Langston's huskily spoken words drifted through Sarah's mind. *You are . . . magnificent.* She cleared her throat. "Yes. Besides that."

"Flowers," Julianne said. "He should bring flowers."

"And plan romantic outings," added Emily.

"Take the time to find out our favorite things then give them to us," said Carolyn. "They don't have to be expensive or elaborate. Just . . . thoughtful." Her gaze took on a faraway expression. "My favorite gift from Edward was a single pansy. He'd pressed the flower—which is my favorite—into his own book of Shakespeare's poems, between the pages of my favorite sonnet. The flower came from the patch of garden where we'd shared our first kiss." A small smile touched her lips. "It cost nothing, yet to me that gift was priceless."

Sarah made a notation on her list, then looked up and asked, "Anything else?"

"I think our man now is quite perfect," Julianne said. "All we need to do is assemble him."

"Let's meet here tomorrow afternoon after your shopping excursion," Sarah suggested.

"Aren't you coming?" asked Carolyn.

"I'd prefer to stay here and explore the garden, do some sketching, if you don't mind. The grounds are spectacular." Her lips twitched. "Perhaps you lovely ladies can entice some of the gentlemen to accompany you to the shops."

Emily looked toward the ceiling. "Highly unlikely. They'd no doubt prefer to run a few foxes to ground. I sat next to Lord Thurston at dinner, and the man, while exceedingly handsome, is a bore. He was unable to discuss anything other than horses."

"But he isn't unpleasant," Julianne said. "Indeed, all the gentleman are agreeable. And Mr. Jennsen seemed quite taken with our Sarah."

"I noticed that as well," Carolyn said. "The man couldn't take his eyes off you."

It was Sarah's turn to look toward the ceiling. "He was merely being polite. And grateful not to have to discuss the finer points of fox hunting with Lords Thurston and Berwick as he'd done at dinner the night before."

"Lords Langston and Surbrooke are both amiable," Emily admitted. "Of course that may change if Mama and Julianne's aunt Agatha don't cease their nonsubtle matchmaking efforts."

"Which are directed toward Lords Berwick, Thurston, and Hartley as well," Julianne added. A frown puckered her smooth brow. "Do you suppose one of the gentlemen present could be a Perfect Man?"

Emily shook her head. "No. Such a man doesn't exist, which is the entire reason we've had to make him up." She blew out a dramatic sigh. "But wouldn't it be wonderful if he did?"

After all agreeing it would indeed be wonderful, albeit unrealistic, Sarah gathered up the articles of clothing and hid them in her portmanteau, which she secreted in the bottom of her wardrobe. The ladies bid each other good-night, promising to meet the following afternoon to bring Franklin N. Stein to "life."

Sarah closed the door after their departure, but seconds later there came a quiet knock. She opened the door and found Carolyn standing in the corridor. After her sister entered the room, she said, "I know you must be tired Sarah, but . . ." She reached out and clasped Sarah's hand. "I wanted to tell you how happy I am that you're here with me."

Relief filled Sarah that nothing amiss had prompted Carolyn's return to her bedchamber. "There's no where else I'd rather be."

"I know, and I'm grateful. This time with you, Julianne, and Emily, and our adventures with the Literary Society, are exactly what I need." A small smile touched Carolyn's lips. "Of course, I'm sure you suspected as much."

"I can't deny I'd hoped you'd enjoy yourself."

"As I'd hoped the same for you, Sarah." Carolyn's eyes searched her face. "And I can see that this trip has been good for you. I'd hoped that being away from your usual routine, being away from Mother, would enable you to spread your wings a bit." Her smile flashed. "And I knew you would enjoy the marquess's renowned gardens."

Sarah blinked. "Do you mean to tell me that all this time I thought we'd come here for *your* benefit, you'd planned to come here for *mine*?"

Carolyn grinned. "There's a saying about great minds thinking alike."

Surprised and touched, Sarah said, "True. But you've no need to be concerned for me, Carolyn. I'm perfectly content."

"Yes, I can see that. There's a . . . glow about you, and I'm delighted about it."

Heat rushed into Sarah's cheeks. Before she could say anything, Carolyn gave her a peck on the cheek then said, "Good night, poppet. Sleep well." And then she was gone, closing the door quietly behind her.

Sarah heaved out a long, slow breath. Clearly her inward glow *did* show, at least to Carolyn, who knew her better than anyone. Thank goodness her sister was ignorant of the source. Which called to mind Julianne's question: *Do you think one of the gentlemen present could be a Perfect Man?*

She made an impatient sound, annoyed with herself for being so fanciful and impractical. No, the Perfect Man did not exist. He was merely a figment of their imagination. Although . . . Lord Langston had certainly been perfect as far as kissing was concerned. And he'd said several of the things on their Perfect Man list. And based on their previous list of traits the Perfect Man should have, in addition to being a good kisser, Lord Langston was handsome, witty, and intelligent. And she could attest firsthand that he was stunningly passionate and made her insides flutter. She wasn't yet sure if he was kind, patient, generous, honorable, and honest. Certainly those last two traits were suspect, given the secrets he obviously had. Certainly he knew far less about horticulture than he'd led people to believe. And besides, he didn't wear glasses—so how perfect could he be?

Still, even if he were the Perfect Man, of what use would that be to her? He would never be *her* Perfect Man for she'd never be the sort of woman such a man would want. Indeed, it was a very good thing he wasn't the Perfect Man or else she might fall madly in love with him. And that would be a disaster of gargantuan proportions that would only bring her heartbreak.

But, if after finding out more about him it turned out he was *close* to perfect, he would be a good match for Julianne or Emily. In which case she needed to stop thinking about him. Immediately. She needed to forget his kiss. The feel of him touching her. The texture of his skin beneath her fingers. The taste of him.

Unfortunately, she suspected that would prove easier said than done.

"Excellent shot, Berwick," Matthew said as his guest's arrow landed in the nine point golden ring on the archery target set up across the lawn.

Lord Berwick lowered his bow. "Thank you. I believe that puts me in the lead."

"True, but Jennsen still has one arrow left to shoot," Matthew reminded him.

After observing the quiet, steady determination Jennsen had displayed for the past two hours on the archery field, Matthew didn't question why the man was such a financial success. Although far less experienced in the sport than any of the other archers, one by one Jennsen had unraveled his opponents, never appearing as if he so much as broke a sweat. Even on those occasions when his shot proved less than brilliant, his quietly confident demeanor often shook the other shooters, forcing them to make costly errors. Over the course of play, the atmosphere had deteriorated from amiable rivalry to chilly tension, especially during the last two rounds. Hartley and Thurston had given in to frustration several times, Thurston going so far as to break an arrow across his knee.

All the rounds had proven very competitive with close scores. Daniel won the first round, and Matthew the second. Hartley and Thurston tied in the third, the victory going to Hartley with the tie-breaking shot. Jennsen had taken the fourth round and Berwick the fifth. They'd all agreed this was the last round, and it now came down to the final arrow.

"Jennsen needs a ten point shot to win," Thurston said, eyeing the American. A cold gleam entered his eyes. "Anyone care to make it interesting?"

Logan Jennsen flicked a cool glance Thurston's way, then settled his gaze on Berwick. "I've a fiver that says I make my shot."

One of Berwick's blond brows cocked upward and a coolly amused smile touched his lips. "I've a tenner that says you won't."

"I'm in," Hartley said, looking at the American with the same lack of friendliness Thurston had. "My money's on Berwick to win."

"Mine as well," Thurston agreed. He turned toward Daniel. "What about you, Surbrooke?"

Daniel smiled. "I'll go with Jennsen to win."

Matthew noticed the annoyance that flickered in Berwick's eyes. "You'll miss your blunt when it's gone," Berwick said, a hint of chill in his tone.

Daniel shrugged. "It's mine to miss."

"And you, Langston?" Berwick asked, fixing his blue gaze on Matthew. "What's your bet?"

Matthew raised his hands in mock surrender, hoping to diffuse the frosty tension permeating the warm air. "As host, it would be impolite for me to show any partiality. I'll therefore remain neutral and wish you both the best of luck."

Still, Matthew made a mental bet, placing his money on Jennsen. Everything in the man's demeanor made it clear he was accustomed to getting what he wanted, and what he wanted right now was to best Berwick and cut Hartley and Thurston down a notch or two.

Matthew had heard rumors that Jennsen's decision to abruptly leave his native America was prompted by more than a simple wish to expand his business, that his past was less than sparkling clean. He had ignored the gossip as coming from Jennsen's competitors, but now, seeing the cold-eyed determination and unwavering control with which the man conducted himself on the archery field led him to wonder if those rumors might in fact be true.

With the same unruffled calm he'd displayed through all the matches, Jennsen lifted his bow and took aim. Seconds later the arrow tip found its home in the ten point gold ring. He turned toward Berwick, and Matthew noted that no triumph gleamed in Jennsen's dark eyes. Rather, he regarded Berwick with a cold, indecipherable expression that Berwick returned with his own icy glare before finally giving a tight jerk of his head to acknowledge his loss.

"I'll settle my debt when we return to the house," Berwick said in a curt voice.

Thurston and Hartley mumbled their concurrence, although their displeasure was obvious. Jennsen merely inclined his head in response.

"Well, that was fun," Daniel said in a patently over-bright tone. "I for one could use a brandy. Anyone else?"

"A brandy," Thurston agreed, sounding as if he were speaking through clenched teeth. He turned toward Matthew as the group walked across the lawn toward the targets to retrieve their arrows. "And a game of whist with your lovely female guests, Langston."

"Excellent suggestion," Hartley said. "Lovely women,

all three. Too bad you didn't invite more, Langston."

Matthew refrained from mentioning the two additional invitations he'd dispatched, or the fact that Hartley and Thurston unexpectedly tagging along with Berwick had thrown off his male to female ratio. "Yes, they're all lovely," he murmured.

"Lady Julianne, especially," Berwick said, his composure back in place. "She's one of the most beautiful women I've ever seen."

Matthew barely refrained from looking skyward. Bloody hell. The last thing he needed was a determined rival for Lady Julianne's attentions, especially with time so short.

Jennsen turned toward Hartley and said, "You said all *three* women are lovely. There are actually four—and yes, all of them are lovely."

Hartley's brow puckered in confusion. "Four? Surely you don't mean to include Lady Gatesbourne or Lady Agatha?"

Matthew's shoulders stiffened. Damn it, he knew all too well to whom Jennsen was referring.

"I meant Miss Moorehouse," Jennsen said mildly. His gaze shifted, and Matthew was treated to the same inscrutable stare Jennsen had fixed upon Berwick only a moment ago.

"Miss Moorehouse?" Hartley repeated in an incredulous tone. "Surely you jest. She is naught but Lady Wingate's traveling companion."

"And most assuredly *not* lovely," Thurston said, his lip curling with distaste.

"Unless one was without benefit of any lighting at all," Berwick added.

"I completely disagree," Jennsen said. "But I've always believed that beauty is in the eye of the beholder." His dark gaze challenged Matthew. "Wouldn't you agree, Langston?"

Matthew's jaw tightened. Clearly Jennsen was staking a claim of some sort upon Miss Moorehouse—something that certainly shouldn't have mattered to him or bothered him in the least, especially given his situation and his need to court Lady Julianne. But damn it, it *did* bother him. A tide of unwanted yet undeniable hot jealousy washed through him, and it was only with the greatest effort that he managed to tamp it down.

Returning Jennsen's stare, he forced a calmness into his voice he was far from feeling and said, "Yes, I agree that beauty is in the eye of the beholder."

And so long as he kept his eye trained where it needed to be—on Lady Julianne—all would be well.

After partaking of a brandy in the drawing room with his male guests, Matthew begged off a move to the billiards room and instead made his way to his private study. Once there, he tried to concentrate on the estate's account ledgers, but the task proved frustratingly impossible. And for no good reason. With the men engaged with billiards and the ladies not yet back from the village, the house was quiet. Even Danforth wasn't snoring on the hearth rug as he usually would be at this time of day. There was no excuse for him not to be making good use of this uninterrupted time to go over his finances, to see what else could be sold, to find another way to cut expenses.

Unfortunately he knew that no matter how hard he pored over the ledgers, he was out of options save two.

The very practical "marry an heiress" option, or the "succeed at his quest" option, which sadly, over the past year, had miserably failed. Yet even if he succeeded at his quest, honor dictated that he still needed to decide upon a wife. And soon. And given his failure thus far at his quest, an heiress his wife would have to be.

Although the house was quiet, his thoughts were anything but. No, his thoughts were filled with images of *her*. And the passionate kiss they'd shared. A kiss that had somehow tested his restraint as no other kiss ever had. Perhaps because she was unlike any other woman he'd ever kissed. Regardless of her questionable level of experience—and he judged that in spite of her penchant for sketching naked men, she wasn't very experienced at all—she was . . . natural. Unpracticed. Completely lacking in guile and vanity. And he found that irresistibly alluring. That and those huge eyes. Those luscious curves. And those soft, plump lips . . .

He dragged his hands down his face. Bloody hell, he'd wanted to know how she felt, how she tasted, and now he knew, and he'd been unable to think of anything else since she'd left his bedchamber. Certainly his erratic performance on the archery field reflected his distraction. This preoccupation with a woman who was in every way the complete opposite of what he was normally attracted to utterly baffled him. He'd always preferred demure, soft-spoken, classically beautiful, petite, blue-eyed blondes. Someone like Lady Julianne. Yet for some reason, Lady Julianne—who was also conveniently the much-needed heiress—had failed to capture his attention.

Instead he'd been grabbed in a stranglehold by an outspoken, brown-eyed, dark-haired, tall, bespectacled spinster who would never be described as a classic beauty. But there was something about her that somehow ensnared him. In a way he couldn't name because he'd never experienced the feeling before. And based on Logan Jennsen's behavior and words, Matthew wasn't the only one affected by her. Bloody damn hell.

But unlike him, Jennsen was free to pursue whomever he wished. Not that Matthew wished to pursue Miss Moorehouse. Even removing the heiress factor from the equation, she wasn't his type at all. Which only made this situation of her occupying his thoughts more confusing and irritating.

He blew out a frustrated sigh and was about to force his attention back to the hated ledgers when he heard a familiar *woof*. His gaze drifted to the open French windows through which a shaft of bright afternoon sunlight streamed. Apparently, Danforth had roused himself from whatever spot he'd found to nap in. Probably a patch of warm sun on the terrace. Lucky beast.

Another *woof* sounded, followed by a soft feminine laugh. A laugh he instantly recognized. A laugh that had him sitting up in his chair as if a plank had been shoved down the back of his breeches.

"Silly dog, sit *still*." Miss Moorehouse's laughter-filled voice floated in through the open glass-paneled doors that led out to the far corner of the terrace.

As if in a trance, he rose. He'd made it halfway across the Axminster rug toward the French windows when Danforth came bounding through the opening. Tongue lolling, tail wagging, the dog made a beeline for him. He greeted Matthew with a trio of deafening barks, then sat. Right on his boot.

Seconds later Miss Moorehouse burst into the room

from the terrace. "Come back here, you mischievous beast. I'm not finished—"

Her gaze fell upon Matthew and her words chopped off as if sliced with an ax. She halted as if she'd slammed into a wall.

Matthew's heart ridiculously seemed to trip over itself. He stared at her, noting her plain gray day gown and disheveled chignon from which dozens of shiny tendrils had escaped. A bonnet hung halfway down her back by its satin strings, which were tied loosely around her neck. A rosy glow suffused her cheeks, and her chest heaved as if she'd run some distance.

She moistened her lips, a gesture that had him pressing his own lips together to keep from mimicking her. She shoved up her glasses, which had slid halfway down her nose, then offered him an awkward curtsy.

"Lord Langston. I beg your pardon. I thought the gentlemen were engaged in archery."

"We finished our tournament. I thought the ladies had gone to the village."

"I remained behind to further explore your extensive gardens. I hope you don't mind."

Not so long as you don't start spouting Latin flower names at me. Or asking him how his straff worts and tortlingers were faring. "Not at all."

Her gaze moved around the room and she frowned. "This is not the drawing room."

"No. This is my private study."

Her cheeks turned crimson. "Oh. Again, I must beg your pardon. I didn't mean to intrude."

She *was* intruding. On his privacy and his very boring, er, productive work with the ledgers. He should send her on her way. Absolutely. Instead he found himself saying,

"You're not intruding. In fact, I was just about to ring for some tea. Would you care to join me?"

Good God, where on earth had *that* invitation sprung from? He hadn't been about to ring for tea at all. In fact, it was hours before his usual tea time. It was as if he'd lost all control over his lips.

At the mere thought of lips, his gaze dipped to her lush mouth. He tried not to look, tried to tear his gaze away from those plump lips that he knew tasted warm and delicious, but it seemed as if he'd lost all control over his eyeballs as well.

She studied him for several seconds, as if he were a puzzle she was trying to decipher, then said, "Tea sounds lovely. Thank you."

Danforth chimed in with what sounded like an approving *woof*. Most likely because the beast knew that with tea came his favorite snack—biscuits.

Well, perhaps this was for the best. After all, hadn't he decided to spend some time with her to decide if she might, with her extensive knowledge of plants, help him in his quest? Yes, he had. It was *necessary* that he spend time with her. So long as he kept the conversation away from straff wort and tortlingers, he'd fare well. Which reminded him, he needed to ask Paul about the straff wort and tortlingers so Miss Moorehouse wouldn't again catch him unawares.

"Please make yourself comfortable," Matthew said, indicating the grouping of chairs near the fireplace. He wriggled his boot from beneath Danforth's rump and crossed to the bell cord near his desk. By the time he put away the ledgers, Tildon had answered his summons. After ordering tea to be served on the terrace, Matthew joined Miss Moorehouse at the fireplace.

Rather than sitting, she stood before the hearth, staring up at the portrait hanging above the marble mantel. He followed her gaze and looked at the painting that never failed to tighten his gut.

"Your family?" she asked.

He felt a muscle tick in his jaw. "Yes."

"I didn't know you had a brother and sister."

"I don't. Not anymore. They both died." The words came out more clipped than he'd intended, but while he thought about James and Annabelle every day, he rarely spoke about them. He felt the weight of her stare and turned toward her. And found her regarding him through very serious eyes.

"I'm so sorry for your loss," she said softly.

"Thank you," he said by rote, years of practice allowing him to shove back the grief that had once paralyzed him. He'd learned how to live with the grief. The guilt, however, never went away. "It happened a long time ago."

"Yet the loss of a loved one is a pain that never heals."

He raised his brows, surprised, as her words so closely mirrored his thoughts. "You sound as if you know this from experience."

"I do. When I was fourteen my dearest friend Delia, a girl I'd known since childhood, passed away. I still miss her and shall continue to do so for the rest of my life. And I loved my sister's husband Edward as if he were my own brother."

He nodded. She understood the grief. "Your friend, how did she die?"

Deep pain flashed in her eyes, and it took her several seconds to answer. "We . . . we were riding. I suggested a race." Her voice dropped to a whisper and she looked at the floor. "Delia's horse went lame just before the finish and she was thrown. Her neck broke in the fall."

He instantly recognized the guilt in her voice. How could he not? It was a sound as familiar to him as his own voice, and a deep sense of empathy rolled through him. "I'm sorry for your loss as well."

She looked up then turned to face him. Their gazes met and the area around his heart went hollow at the bleak expression in her eyes. It was a look he knew all too well. "Thank you," she whispered.

"I believe I now understand why you fear horses."

"I haven't ridden since. It's not exactly fear that stops me, it's more . . ."

"Not wanting to revisit painful memories." It wasn't a question—because he knew the answer. Knew precisely how she felt.

"Yes." She studied him through her huge, magnified eyes. "Now *you* sound as if you speak from experience."

He quickly debated what, how much, to say. It was something he never talked about. But that bleak look cried out to him, grabbed him by the gut. Brought out all his protective instincts. Made him want to comfort her.

After clearing his throat, he said, "I do. It's the reason I never go to the village."

Although she said nothing, he saw understanding dawn in her expression, and she nodded once. She might not know what happened, but she knew his aversion to the village had to do with his siblings' deaths. And she understood. And didn't question him. Simply stood with him in quiet, shared understanding.

Something inside him seemed to expand. He very much liked that about her. She didn't find it necessary to fill silences with nervous chatter or to ask him endless questions as so many other women did. Although she was outspoken, there was a quiet patience and self-possession about her that appealed to him greatly.

And before he could even think to stop himself, he found himself saying, "I was eleven. I was supposed to be studying mathematics but instead I went to the village to see my friend Martin. He was the butcher's son. My father had specifically told me not to go to the village, that people were falling ill to a fever and he didn't want anyone at Langston Manor exposed to it."

He drew a deep breath, and the words came faster, pouring out of him like poison from a lanced wound. "But I heard that Martin was sick and I wanted to see him. Bring him some medicine the doctor had left the last time I was ill. So I went. By the next morning, I was feverish. Two days later both James and Annabelle fell ill. I survived. They didn't. Neither did Martin."

He stopped speaking. He felt out of breath. Emptied. And his knees weren't quite steady. His brother and sister had died because of him. He had survived for reasons he could not, would not, ever understand, but somehow just saying the words out loud—the words he'd kept trapped inside for so long—afforded him a small sense of relief he hadn't felt in years. Perhaps there was some merit to the theory that confession was good for the soul.

His thoughts were interrupted when she reached out and clasped his hand. He looked down. Her slim fingers lightly held his. She gently squeezed, and he reflexively returned the gesture.

"You blame yourself," she said softly.

He raised his gaze to hers. Her eyes were soft with an understanding and compassion that seemed to compress his chest. "If I'd done what I'd been told . . ." His voice trailed off, unable to say the words that echoed through his mind. *They'd still be alive.*

"I understand. Exactly. I wasn't supposed to race my horse. If I hadn't suggested we do . . ." She pulled in a deep breath. "It's a pain I live with—"

"Every day," they said in unison.

She nodded. "I'm very sorry for what you've suffered."

"And I'm sorry for what you've suffered." He hesitated, then asked, "Do you ever . . . have conversations with your friend?" He'd never asked anyone that question, fearing they'd think him a candidate for Bedlam.

"Frequently," she said, nodding. The movement sent her glasses sliding down her nose, and she pushed them back up with her free hand—the hand that wasn't holding his. He flexed his fingers, fitting her palm a bit more snugly against his, finding undeniable comfort in the warmth of her skin pressing against his.

"I visit Delia's grave regularly," she said. "I bring her flowers and tell her all the latest happenings. Sometimes I bring a book and read to her. Do you talk to your brother and sister?"

"Nearly every day," he said, feeling as if an enormous weight was lifted from his shoulders by simply admitting that out loud.

A fleeting smile flitted across her face, then, as if she could read his thoughts, she said, "I thought I was the only one. It feels good to know it's not just me."

"Yes, it feels good." Just as standing next to her and holding her hand felt good. Inordinately so. In a way that confused him yet made him feel . . . not so alone.

"Now I understand the sadness in your eyes," she mur-

mured. His surprise must have shown because she added,
"I find myself observing people, a habit born of my love
of sketching and spending too much time sitting in corners at too many parties."

"Sitting in corners? Do you not dance?"

A whisper of wistfulness passed over her features,
gone so quickly he wondered if he'd imagined it. "No.
I attend the parties merely as my sister's companion.
Besides, gentlemen prefer to dance with dainty, elegant
young women."

She said this last in a matter-of-fact tone, and it suddenly dawned on him why she didn't dance.

No one asked her.

An image embedded itself in his mind, of her at a
soiree, sitting alone in the corner, watching while all the
dainty, elegant young women danced. And he knew without a doubt that he would have been one of the gentlemen
dancing with a dainty, elegant young woman, bypassing
the bespectacled, plain Miss Moorehouse. A fissure of
shame seeped through him at the realization, along with
something that felt like a sense of loss. Because, as he'd
discovered upon closer inspection, while she wasn't a
classic beauty, she wasn't plain at all.

Clearing his throat, he asked, "You've observed sadness in my eyes?"

She nodded. "That and . . ."

Her voice trailed off and a hint of red shaded her
cheeks. "And what?"

After a brief hesitation she added, "Secrets." Then she
shrugged. "But everyone has secrets, don't you agree?"

"Including you?"

"Especially me, my lord." A teasing gleam entered
her eyes, and her smile flashed, affording him a quick

glimpse of her dimples. "I am, of course, a woman of great mystery."

He found himself returning her smile. "And I am, of course, a man of great mystery."

"Yes, I suspected as much," she said in a light tone, and he couldn't tell if she was serious or not.

She slid her hand from his, and he immediately missed her touch. Turning once again to face the painting, she said, "Your brother was considerably younger than you."

"On the contrary, he was nearly a decade older than I."

She frowned, then looked back and forth between the portrait and him twice, finally staring at him with a half-confused, half-amazed expression. "You mean *you* are . . ." Her words evaporated and a fresh rush of color suffused her cheeks.

"The short, pudgy, pasty-faced lad with the glasses. Yes, that's me. In all my six-year-old glory. The tall handsome young man is my brother James."

"There is a remarkable resemblance between him and you. And none whatsoever between you and the six-year-old boy."

"Around age sixteen I somehow sprouted up and outgrew the pudginess." He might no longer resemble that shy, awkward, lonely boy on the outside, but on the inside . . . he still knew that boy very well. The boy who hadn't been able to beg, borrow, or steal his father's attention—until James died. And even then he'd only gained it to be reminded everyday that James's death was his fault. As if he didn't already know that. As if that didn't eat at him every minute.

"The transformation is . . . remarkable," she said. She turned back toward him. "What happened to the glasses?"

"By the time I was twenty I no longer needed them. The

doctor explained that he'd seen such cases, that as children grow, their eyesight can change. Sometimes for the better, sometimes for the worse. Mine changed for the better."

"You are very fortunate, my lord. Mine changed for the worse."

He tilted his head and studied her for several seconds, as one would a work of art. "Yet your spectacles suit you. I occasionally still wear glasses, when I'm reading small print."

She stared at him then blinked. "Oh, my."

Those were the same two words and the same husky rasp she'd murmured last night after he'd kissed her. His gaze involuntarily dropped to her mouth. And he immediately realized his error as desire hit him low and hard. Her lips looked moist and plump and were slightly parted, and the urge to kiss her again grabbed him in a vise grip.

Kissing her again was an extremely bad idea. But bloody hell, he wanted to. So very much. Here, in the sunlight, where he could see her, read her every reaction.

Before he could reach for her, however, a knock sounded on the door. Mentally cursing the interruption, he called out, "Come in."

Tildon entered and announced, "Tea is served on the terrace, my lord."

After thanking the butler, who closed the door quietly after him, Matthew drew in a slow breath before returning his attention to Miss Moorehouse. His common sense told him it was fortunate Tildon had knocked at just that second, or else he most likely would have kissed her again. Oh, bloody hell, who was he attempting to fool? He *definitely* would have kissed her again.

Which was not how he should be spending his time with her. No, he should be engaging her in conversation, finding out more about her in order to determine what secrets she might have, and to decide if she could help him with his quest. He didn't need to know if she was a good kisser.

He already knew.

She was.

Phenomenally good.

He inwardly frowned and shifted to relieve the growing discomfort occurring in his breeches. Damn it, this unwanted desire for her was simply unacceptable. What he needed to do was pull his attention away from her lips and concentrate on the task before him: to find out more about her. And to that end he extended his elbow and inclined his head toward the terrace. "Shall we?"

Chapter 8

Sarah needed to find out more about him.

Which meant she couldn't dwell upon the way he made her feel.

Seated at the square, linen-topped, wrought-iron table on the terrace, she eyed the intricately carved silver tea service Tildon had set out. In addition to tea, a polished platter held an assortment of delicate cucumber and watercress sandwiches on thin slices of crustless bread, scones with strawberry jam, and freshly baked, still warm biscuits.

The scents wafted toward her on the gentle summer breeze, but they weren't what made her mouth water. No, Lord Langston was doing that, effectively distracting her from her goal:

She *had* to find out more about him.

Hopefully, something to make him less attractive. Something that didn't stir her blood, as when she'd discovered he was a marvelous kisser. Or something that didn't grab her heart like the story of what had happened to his brother and sister. Because grab her heart he had. And dear God, she didn't want him to. Couldn't allow him to.

Yet how could she possibly ignore the empathy and

sympathy she now felt toward him? She knew the pain he carried with him every day because she carried that same ache that no passage of time completely numbed. He *knew*. He *understood*. And that drew her to him more strongly than any manner of handsome looks ever could.

Although . . . there was no denying his extreme good looks, and as much as she didn't wish to notice them, she was merely nearsighted—not blind. In those few seconds before Tildon had knocked on the door, she'd thought Lord Langston had meant to kiss her again. And rather than being appalled or outraged or disinterested or any of the other things she *should* have felt, instead her heart had pounded in anticipation and it required all her where-withal not to throw her arms around his neck and press her body against his. To experience again the wonder she'd felt in his arms last night. To feel his hands on her, urgent, demanding, coaxing her closer while his tongue mated with hers.

Her gaze roamed down his masculine form as he dismissed Tildon then moved toward the table and sat down in the seat next to hers. A sigh escaped her, and warmth that had nothing to do with the afternoon sun rushed through her.

"Are you all right, Miss Moorehouse?"

His voice yanked her from her wayward thoughts and she discovered him watching her. With an expression that suggested he knew she'd been staring at him.

Botheration. She could practically feel the blotches creeping up her neck.

"I'm fine, thank you," she said in her most prim voice.

"You look . . . flushed."

"'Tis merely the result of the sun," she lied, inwardly wincing at the falsehood.

"Would you prefer to have our tea inside?"

Yes, preferably in your bedchamber while I watch you bathe.

A horrified *ack!* rose to her lips, and Sarah clamped her mouth closed to contain it. Good God, this was not good. She needed to forget about their kiss. Absolutely needed to forget about kissing him again. And positively needed to forget about seeing him naked.

What she needed to do was . . . something. Something that she couldn't recall. She frowned and forced herself to concentrate. Oh, yes. She needed to focus on finding out his secrets. Excellent. Because even though she'd felt a deep kinship with him and he'd appealed to her sympathies by his story and the fact that he'd talked about something she sensed he didn't easily discuss, he still had secrets—namely the nature of his late night "gardening" missions. Certainly there was no point in asking him outright what he was up to. No, she'd need to finesse the conversation. Encourage him to talk about other things, and hope he'd inadvertently reveal something.

But how best to proceed? Most likely by adopting a conspiratorial air and appealing to his vanity. From her observations, she'd concluded that men enjoyed feeling as if they were being told secrets, and they were not immune to flattery.

Picking up her china tea cup from which a fragrant curl of steam rose, she said, "Your transformation from the child depicted in the portrait to the man you've become is extraordinary, my lord."

He shrugged. "I believe many children go through what could be called an awkward phase."

"Not all children. Take my sister, for instance. She was beautiful as an infant and remains so still today."

"Your sister is older than you."

"Yes. By six years."

"Then how do you know she was a beautiful infant?"

"My mother told me so. With alarming frequency. I believe she hoped the reminders would encourage me to outgrow the 'awkward' phase, as you called it, that I've exhibited since birth."

After a quick sip of tea, she said, "Mother thinks I've remained plain merely to vex her. She insists I've no need for my spectacles and if I'd simply sit still for several hours and allow her to use an iron to flatten out my unruly curls, I wouldn't be *quite* so unattractive. Although she did warn me that of course no matter what I did I'd never be half as lovely as Carolyn, but I should at least *try*."

He paused in the act of raising his teacup to his lips and frowned. "Surely she didn't say that to you."

"Oh, she did. Quite often." In fact, she still did, but the words no longer had the power to sting her. "As a young child I found it quite devastating, mostly because I didn't want Carolyn, whom I adored, to dislike me as our mother did for something I couldn't help."

She took another sip of tea then continued, "But Carolyn has always been my champion. Indeed, our mother's overt favoritism toward her has always been a source of embarrassment for her—her even more so than for me. Carolyn is a warm, loving person and has never failed to give me her unconditional love. Which has made me love her even more in return."

He studied her over the rim of his cup. "You seem very matter of fact about your mother's view."

"While I think she could have perhaps been more diplomatic, she didn't say anything that wasn't true. Anyone with eyes can see that Carolyn is stunning and I'm not. It's simply the truth, no more, no less." Her lips twitched. "Of course, I occasionally go out of my way to prove to Mother that regardless of looks I don't deserve the status of favorite."

His eyes immediately lit up with interest. "Oh? What do you do?"

"You'll think me awful."

"Doubtful. Based on what you've told me, I wouldn't think it awful if you said you'd dumped a hip bath filled with water over your mother's head."

Her face must have flamed red, because he asked, his voice filled with laughter, "*Have* you dumped a tubful of water over her head?"

"No. But I can't deny I've considered it."

"On more than one occasion, I'd wager."

"Almost daily," came her dry reply.

"Yet you've resisted. Clearly you are of a strong constitution."

"Not particularly. 'Tis more a case of the tub being too heavy for me to lift."

He laughed, a deep, rich sound. His teeth flashed white and his smile reached all the way up to his eyes. The effect was . . . dazzling. "Have you not heard of a pail?"

"I have. But I try only to vex Mother, not infuriate her."

"And how do you go about vexing her?"

"It certainly isn't difficult. I love the warmth of the sun on my face, so I'll remove my bonnet in the garden—a *crime*, as far as Mother is concerned, as my skin freckles, which only serves to make me more unattractive. I sometimes pretend to misunderstand her. For instance, if

Mother says, 'I feel faint,' I might reply, 'Why, yes, I have
some paint. Shall I fetch it for you?'" Sarah struggled to
keep from smiling. "She is convinced I am going deaf.
And then I play what I privately call the Senses Game
with her. I'll say things such as, 'I can't hear you, I don't
have my glasses on.'"

He grinned. "How about, 'I can smell it, I'm not deaf,
you know.'"

"'I'm not deaf, I can see it.'"

"'I'm not blind, I can smell it."

Sarah laughed. "Exactly. Mother heaves a beleaguered
sigh, looks skyward and mutters under her breath—
an oath or a prayer for patience, I'm not sure which. I
shouldn't find it humorous, but I do. And now you know
my greatest secret—I'm not very nice."

"My dear Miss Moorehouse, if giving a verbal tweak
constitutes your grounds for saying you're not very nice,
then I suggest you reassess your criteria, because that
simply doesn't qualify you for a Heart of Evil."

"Perhaps not, but really, in many ways my lack of
beauty has worked in my favor. Since all Mother's attention was always focused on Carolyn, I was afforded free-
doms many young girls were not."

"Such as?"

"While Carolyn was trapped with Mother, receiving
endless lessons in deportment and dancing and proper
posture, I ran about outside in the sunshine, sketching
flowers, cultivating the garden, exploring the countryside,
enjoying long walks, swimming in the lake." She reached
for a biscuit and shot him a smile. "I'll have you know
I'm excellent at fishing *and* catching frogs."

Amusement gleamed in his eyes. "Somehow I am not

surprised. When I was a boy I used to catch frogs. Caught the occasional fish as well. I haven't done either in years." He sipped his tea, then leaned back in his chair. "What about your father?"

"Papa is a physician who's often gone for days at a time treating patients in other villages. His time at home is spent mostly in his study, reading medical journals. To this day whenever I see him he gives me an absentminded look, pats me on my head, then sends me on my way—in precisely the same fashion as he did when I was three."

He nodded slowly, his gaze turning thoughtful. "I rarely saw my mother when I was a child, and my memories of her are a bit of a blur. I remember her always looking beautiful, always on her way to some soiree or another. I suppose she cared for me, although I don't recall her ever saying so. After James and Annabelle died, I saw her even less, as I was away at school most of the time and took to spending most holidays with my friend Daniel, Lord Surbrooke." He paused, then added quietly, "My mother died when I was fourteen."

"And your father passed away last year," Sarah said softly.

"Yes." A muscle ticked in his jaw. "He was shot. By a highwayman attempting to rob him. The man who killed him was never caught. He literally got away with murder."

"I'm sorry. Sorry for your loss and that you're . . . alone."

He regarded her with such an unsettling expression, Sarah inwardly cursed her runaway tongue. "Forgive me, my lord. I meant no offense. Sometimes my thoughts become words before I can stop them."

"No offense taken. I have a few close friends and many

acquaintances, so in that respect I'm not alone. But my lack of family, yes, in that way I am."

"I'm surprised you aren't married."

"Really? Why?"

Sarah realized this was a perfect opportunity to flatter him—although anything complimentary would be merely the truth. "You're handsome, titled, personable, a great—" *kisser*—"gardener. All the prerequisite qualities to ensure an abundance of female attention."

"I could say the very same about you, Miss Moorehouse."

She grinned. "That I'm handsome, titled, and personable?"

He returned her smile. "Well, you're not titled."

"Nor am I handsome." She leaned a bit closer to him and lowered her voice, as if imparting a great secret. "Only gentlemen and very old, very severe women are referred to as such."

"True. A more appropriate way to describe you would be 'uniquely attractive.' And you certainly are personable."

It suddenly occurred to Sarah *he* was the one doling out the flattery. And she wasn't certain whether to allow herself to be flattered, or to be highly suspicious of his motives. Certainly suspicion was much smarter.

Before she could decide his intent, he continued, "However, what I meant is that I'm surprised *you* aren't married."

She stilled, and full-blown distrust assailed her at his ridiculous statement, which could only be an attempt to curry her favor. Clearly this man was up to something. Or he was an absolute nincompoop. Either way, an almost giddy sensation of relief filled her because she would never, could never, find a man who was either up to something or a nincompoop attractive.

Feeling much better, she raised her brows. "And why would that surprise you, my lord?"

"Are you fishing for compliments, Miss Moorehouse?"

"Certainly not." Good lord, she knew better than to engage in such a useless exercise. "I'm merely curious as to why you're surprised."

"I suppose because you seem very . . . nurturing. And loyal."

"Rather like a spaniel."

He laughed. "Yes. Except you're taller. And smell much better."

She hid her smile behind her teacup. "Thank you. I think."

"And you're very intelligent."

A snort escaped her. "While I'm grateful for your assessment, based on my observations, most gentlemen do not necessarily find intelligence an attractive trait in a woman."

"Well, disloyal as this may seem to my gender, I'll share a little secret with you." He scooted his chair closer and their knees bumped beneath the table, shooting a heated spark up her leg. Leaning toward her, he said in a very serious voice, "I regret to inform you that many gentlemen are, unfortunately, nincompoops."

Sarah blinked, not certain if she were more stunned or gratified or fascinated that his assessment of many members of his gender so closely mirrored her own. Certainly his opinion, and his willingness to express it, surprised her, and their shared thinking on the subject filled her with a warmth she couldn't quite describe, a warmth completely separate from, though no less compelling than, the one resulting from his nearness.

His knee remained lightly touching hers, so lightly that she supposed it could be accidental. But the warmth, mixed with a hint of challenge, glittering in his eyes, indicated he knew very well what he was about.

Move your leg away, her inner voice commanded. Yes, she certainly should move her leg away. Push back her chair. Put some distance between them. End this unwise, forbidden contact that had heat coiling through her entire body.

Instead, her entire body betrayed her and did exactly what it wanted to do—lean closer to him. Until less than two feet separated their faces.

"Tell me, my lord, do you fall within the ranks of the nincompoops?"

"What if I told you I most certainly do not?"

"I'd say you were lying."

Instead of taking offense, he appeared amused. "Because you think I'm a nincompoop?"

"Because I think *everyone* is, occasionally."

"Even you?"

"Oh, most especially me. I'm always saying or doing something I shouldn't."

"Really? Such as?"

"I'd say my most recent foray into nincompoopdom occurred seconds ago when I suggested not only that my host was lying, but a nincompoop as well." That and the fact that her knee remained, most improperly, pressed against his. Indeed, the contrast between their innocent conversation and the very *un*-innocent press of his leg against hers curled a heated exhilaration through her that she'd never before known.

He shifted, increasing the contact between his leg and

hers, and her heart jumped. "I find your candor refreshing," he said softly.

"Do you? Most people find it appalling."

His gaze turned serious and searched hers. "I've always preferred the brutal truth to insincere platitudes. And I'm afraid, given my title and position, more often than not I'm offered insincere platitudes. Most particularly by women."

"If these women are complimenting your appearance or your home, surely you cannot accuse them of being insincere."

He shrugged. "But what is their motive for doing so?"

"I'd venture to guess it's because they find both you and your home attractive."

"But again I must ask *why*. For instance, both Lady Gatesbourne and Lady Agatha have been *extremely* complimentary since the moment they arrived. They've complimented my person, my home, my garden, my dishes, my furniture, my cravat, my dog—"

"Surely you agree that Danforth is worth complimenting," she broke in with a smile.

"Naturally. However, when Lady Gatesbourne informed me he was a 'darling doggie,' Danforth was sitting on her shoe and her face bore an expression of absolute horror. I may occasionally be a nincompoop, but I know insincere flattery when I hear it."

"Both ladies are merely striving to make a good impression, my lord."

"Yes. Because Lady Gatesbourne has a marriageable daughter, and Lady Agatha has a marriageable niece. They are not interested in *me*, they are interested in my title. Do you have any idea how it feels to be pursued for such a reason?"

"No. I don't." Actually, she had no idea how it felt to be pursued at all.

"It is . . . disappointing. Believe me, those fine ladies do not compliment me because they are so taken with my family's china or the way my cravat is tied."

"Is it not possible they are? After all, your family china *is* lovely."

One dark brow quirked upward and he shot her a mock severe look. "Are you saying my person, my home, my garden and my furniture are not?"

Sarah couldn't help but laugh. "Now it would appear you are shamefully *looking* for compliments."

"Only because you seem so stingy with them," he said, his injured sniff belied by the mischief twinkling in his eyes.

She forced herself not to smile and instead made a *tsking* sound and waggled her finger at him. "You've no need for compliments from me. 'Tis clear your head is already swelled as a result of the flattery everyone else piles upon you."

"I may not *need* a compliment from you, but I'd like one just the same."

She hoisted her chin and pursed her lips into a prim pucker. "I feel it my honor bound duty not to add to your vanity."

"Then may I be permitted to add to yours?"

She laughed. "I assure you I have no vanity—"

Her words and laughter sliced off when he captured her hand and lightly entwined their fingers. "No vanity?" he said softly, the pad of his thumb circling lightly against her palm. "Surely your friend Franklin showers you with compliments."

She had to swallow twice to locate her voice. "He's not very talkative."

"Ah. The strong, silent sort."

"Exactly."

"Then please, allow me . . ." He studied her hand, tracing a single fingertip slowly around each of her fingers. Her embarrassment over the faint charcoal stains from her sketching evaporated under the tingles of delight shooting up her arm. "You're a very talented artist."

Pleasure suffused her, but she felt compelled to correct him. "I'm hardly an artist—"

This time he cut off her words by touching his fingers to her lips. He shook his head. "The correct response to a compliment, Miss Moorehouse, is 'Thank you.'" He slid his fingers slowly away from her mouth.

"But—"

"No 'but.'" He leaned closer. "Just 'Thank you.'"

Less than a foot now separated their faces, and it was increasingly impossible to think about anything other than erasing that small amount of space.

"Th-thank you."

A faint smile touched his lips. "You're welcome. I myself cannot draw worth a jot. Would you consent to doing a sketch of Danforth for me?"

"I'd be delighted. Actually, I was working on one when he dashed into your study."

"And you followed him."

"I did."

"And now here you are. Having tea. With me." He said the words so softly a tremor ran through her.

"Yes. Here I am." *With my knee pressed to yours and your hand holding mine. And my heart pounding so hard I fear you can hear it.*

A slight frown pulled down his brows. "But where is your sketch pad?"

It took her several seconds to recall. "I set it down in your study. On the chair near the fireplace."

"Ah. That explains why I didn't notice it earlier."

"Really? How?"

"I was too busy looking at you."

Her first thought was that he was jesting, but no hint of teasing lit his intense, serious gaze.

Part of her, the dreamer part she'd ruthlessly kept buried for more than two decades, the part of her that secretly, uselessly, longed to hear words such as he'd just spoken, struggled to break free of its confines. To bask in his flattering words, the heated way he was looking at her, the breathless way he was making her feel.

But then the other part of her, the practical, pragmatic, unsentimental part that knew better stepped forward and issued her a stern warning. *Do not foolishly allow yourself to be swayed by such nonsense or to read too much into his words.*

Right. Don't be foolish. She cleared her throat. "Looking at me? Did I have charcoal on my face?"

He shook his head. "No. Indeed, your skin is . . ." He released her hand and brushed his fingers over her cheek. "Remarkable."

"On the contrary, it is freckled from the sun."

"Ah, yes, your penchant for removing your bonnet while outdoors. I can see your freckles quite clearly here in the sunlight. Yet contrary to your opinion, those tiny imperfections do not detract. Rather, they make me want to touch each golden dot." His fingertip skimmed slowly across her cheek then down the bridge of her nose.

He must want something, her inner voice cautioned. *And he is using his very considerable charm in an attempt to get it.* Based on her observations, gentlemen often used flattery for their own purposes. Indeed, she'd planned to use such a ruse in the hopes of gaining information from him.

But what on earth could he possibly want from her? Surely not information. What could she possibly know that he'd be interested in? Nor could his motive have anything to do with desiring female companionship, for if so, he'd certainly turn his charm toward either Emily, Julianne, or Carolyn. No, there must be some other reason. But what?

She didn't know, but she needed to remain wary. Keep up her guard. But dear God, it was difficult to do when he was looking at her like this. As if she was something precious and rare. And very, very lovely.

His gaze dipped to her lips. "When we were in my study . . . could you tell how much I wanted to kiss you?"

Could you tell how much I wanted you to? The words rushed into her throat, begging to be spoken, and she clenched her teeth to contain them. Heart pounding, she shook her head and her glasses slid down her nose. Before she could push them up, he reached out and performed the task. Then he gently cradled her cheek against his warm palm.

"Can you tell how much I want to kiss you right now?" he whispered.

Words failed her. Indeed, her lungs seemed to fail her. It felt as if fire licked beneath her skin, melting her insides, arrowing heat to every nerve ending. An insistent, impatient throb pulsed between her thighs. And he hadn't even kissed her. Had barely touched her.

She moistened her lips and noted how his eyes seemed to darken at the gesture. "I cannot imagine why you would wish to do so, my lord."

"No?" He frowned and brushed the pad of his thumb

over her bottom lip. "Perhaps that is part of the reason. Because you can't imagine why. Because you don't expect it. I find you remarkably refreshing."

"I assure you I am completely unremarkable."

"I disagree. But even if you are, I assure *you* it's in a most refreshing way."

Utterly confused, embarrassingly flattered, she forced herself to say, "I think perhaps the bright sun has addled your wits, my lord. I'm certain you've only to raise a finger and women flock to you."

His gaze searched hers with an intensity that curled her toes inside her sensible, sturdy walking shoes. "And if I raised a finger, Miss Moorehouse, would *you* flock to me?"

In a heartbeat. The words echoed through her mind, and seemed to shove a lifetime of common sense and propriety aside with a single push. Dear God, this man's effect on her was unsettling in the extreme, to the point of being frightening. She was normally so sensible, but right now she felt the complete opposite of sensible. She wanted him to kiss her again—so badly she ached. Wanted to feel his touch. His hands on her. Her hands on him.

She shouldn't want those things. Those things were not meant for her. Most especially not with a man like him. A man who could have any woman he wanted. A man she wasn't even certain was trustworthy.

Yet in spite of all that, she *did* want those things. With an intensity that shook her. It was as if the dam behind which she'd trapped all her secret longings had sprung a leak, flooding her with desires she'd tried so desperately to contain and ignore. She wanted to again feel the wonder, the awakening, she'd experienced when he'd kissed her. And when would she ever have another opportunity?

Never, that deeply buried part of her whispered. *You'll never have another chance. Never with a man like this.*

"Lord Langston, I—"

The sound of approaching voices cut off her words. Looking beyond his broad shoulders, she noted the group walking across the lawns. Leaning back, she said, "The ladies have returned from the village."

He didn't glance over his shoulder. "That isn't what you were going to say."

She hesitated, then shook her head. "No."

"Tell me."

"I—"

"There you are, my lord," came Lady Gatesbourne's high-pitched voice. Sarah noticed her ladyship quicken her pace, the feathers in her turban bouncing in an eye-hazardous manner. Seconds later the entire group descended en masse on the terrace.

Lord Langston stood and offered the ladies a formal bow. "Did you enjoy your visit to the village?" he asked.

"Oh, it was most exciting," exclaimed Lady Agatha. "Indeed, the entire village is buzzing with the news."

"What news is that?" asked Sarah.

"It concerns a Mr. Tom Willstone, the blacksmith."

Sarah noticed the quick flash of interest in Lord Langston's gaze. "What about Mr. Willstone?"

Lady Gatesbourne dotted her glistening face with her lace handkerchief. "He'd been missing since the night before last but was found early this morning, just outside the village."

Lord Langston's brows puckered in a frown. "Did he explain where he'd been?"

"I'm afraid not," broke in Lady Agatha, who was all but twittering. "He was dead. Apparently murdered."

Lord Langston's features turned to stone. He glanced at Carolyn, Emily, and Julianne, who all nodded, their expressions grave.

"'Tis true, my lord," Carolyn said quietly.

"Murdered?" he repeated. "How?"

"It appears he was bludgeoned to death," reported Lady Gatesbourne with ill-concealed relish.

"Then buried in a shallow grave near a copse of trees," added Lady Agatha.

Sarah went perfectly still as an image flashed through her mind. Of Lord Langston. Returning home in the rain. The night before last. Carrying a shovel.

Chapter 9

Matthew entered his private study followed by Daniel. The instant he closed the door behind them, he headed toward the decanters and poured two generous drinks. He handed one to Daniel then downed a hefty swallow of the potent liquor. After drawing a bracing breath, he told Daniel what he'd learned moments ago about Tom Willstone.

Shaking his head, he concluded, "We might not know what Tom was doing when I saw him the night before last, but now we know why he never returned home. When I saw him, I was more suspicious of his motives for being on my property than concerned for his safety." His fingers tightened on his snifter. "Someone murdered him, most likely quite soon after I saw him."

Daniel studied him over the rim of his brandy snifter. "Please tell me you're not blaming yourself."

He shook his head. "While I'm sorry he's dead, I don't blame myself for his fate."

"Good. What do you suppose happened to him?"

"There are a number of possible explanations. Maybe he fell victim to a robber."

"That is indeed a possibility. Village gossip has it that Tom always carried a gold pocket watch. From what you've said, it apparently wasn't recovered with his body. People have killed for lesser trinkets."

"Yes," Matthew agreed. "But not usually in Upper Fladersham. Perhaps the murder had something to do with his brother-in-law Billy Smythe's assertion that Tom had a lover. If this other woman had a husband or brother or another lover besides Tom, any of them might not feel too kindly toward him."

Daniel nodded. "True. You'll recall from my recounting of my visit to the Willstone cottage, Billy wasn't too happy with him."

"No, he wasn't. If the allegations of a lover are true, Tom's wife wouldn't have been happy with him either."

"And lovers have been known to seek revenge, especially if they are no longer wanted."

Matthew nodded slowly. "Yes, but Tom was a big man. Although I suppose even a big man can be felled if he's coshed hard enough."

"Right. Like on the back of the head with a large rock. Or a shovel that could then be used to dig a grave."

"I cannot imagine a woman burying him."

"It was a shallow grave," Daniel pointed out. "Not impossible for a woman to carry out."

"Not impossible, but not likely either."

"Perhaps she wasn't alone. Maybe the wife *and* the brother-in-law did Tom in."

"Perhaps. But . . ." Matthew looked into his brandy, then raised his gaze to meet Daniel's. "While it's possible that Tom was spying on me, another possibility is that he wasn't—that during an innocent stroll home he stumbled upon someone. Someone who *was* watching me."

"Someone who wouldn't have wanted to be seen spying on you," Daniel said.

"Exactly. Which means the poor bastard could be dead simply because he was in the wrong place at the wrong time."

"Which means Tom's murderer might know you're looking for something."

"Yes. And might be just waiting for me to find it."

"So he can kill you too. Then take it for himself."

Matthew winced. "Not a pleasant thought, but one we must consider."

"Well, it's a damn good thing no one saw you wandering around that night carrying a shovel from your digging expeditions or *you* might be a suspect in Tom's murder."

Matthew's hand paused halfway to his mouth and he went perfectly still. *I saw you returning to the house late last night. Carrying your shovel.*

"Bloody hell," he muttered.

"What's wrong?" Daniel asked.

"Someone did see me returning to the house that night."

"Who?"

"Miss Moorehouse."

Daniel pondered the information for several seconds then said, "Those bloody spinsterish types seem to spend an inordinate amount of time peeking out windows. Why do you suppose she was awake at that hour?"

"Said she couldn't sleep."

"Well, let us hope that Miss Moorehouse doesn't add one plus one and come up with the wrong sum and assume that just because you were traipsing about in the rain at an ungodly hour toting a shovel that you're a demented murderer."

"The picture of me you paint warms my heart. And I wasn't traipsing about, I was *walking*. Surely she wouldn't believe me capable of murder." *Would she?* Come to think of it, it seemed as if she had given him an odd look just before he'd left the terrace to find Daniel.

"Who knows what sort of insane notions women get into their heads?" Daniel said with a dark frown. "Their minds are like vipers' nests, writhing with all sorts of unpleasantness and poison."

"You, my friend, are far too cynical."

"And you, my friend, are—for reasons I cannot fathom—suddenly not nearly cynical enough. Tell me, was the night before last the first time you sensed being watched?"

"Over the course of the past eleven months I've dug countless holes and never sensed it before then."

"Is it possible that the presence you felt was that of Miss Peeking-out-the-Windows Moorehouse?"

Matthew shook his head. "I was not near the house."

"Perhaps she'd ventured out into the rain."

"She didn't tell me she had."

Daniel's brows rose. "Perhaps she didn't want you to know."

"Why would she spy on me?"

"Who the bloody hell knows why women do half the things they do? But since you hadn't sensed being watched before that night—the first night after Miss Moorehouse's arrival, by the way—then I'd venture to say chances are this situation with Tom has nothing to do with you. But you'd best keep up your guard. Certainly if someone is waiting for you to find what you're looking for, you're safe until you find it."

"A very comforting thought," Matthew said dryly.

"Do you intend to search tonight?"

"I intend to search *every* night, at least until my year-long time limit runs out."

"Which is in approximately three weeks."

"Twenty-eight days to be exact."

"At which time you'll be getting married."

Matthew's fingers tightened on his snifter. "Yes."

"Which means, in that short time span you'll need to"—he ticked off items on his fingers—"decide on a bride, ask her to marry you, gain her and her family's permission and approval, and, since time is so short, arrange for a special license."

"Yes."

"And how is that all progressing?" Daniel asked in an innocent voice.

"Very well, thank you for asking."

"Indeed? Have you accomplished even *one* of those things?"

"As a matter of fact I have. I've already procured the special license. Did so last month."

"Excellent," Daniel said with an approving nod. "Now all you need is someone to stand beside you and speak vows that shall join you together until one of you cocks up your toes."

"What a quaint way to put it."

"Until the cold, clammy hand of death separates you."

"I understand, thank you. Have you always been such a pain in the arse, or is this merely a recent phenomenon?"

Daniel ignored his sarcasm and asked, "Have you spent any time with the most likely bride-to-be candidate, Lady Julianne?" Before Matthew could answer, Daniel rushed on, "Why no, you haven't. Although from what you've said, you *were* engaged in a very cozy tête-à-tête on the

terrace with Miss Peek-out-the-Windows Moorehouse."
He raised his brows. "Care to explain?"

"There is nothing to explain," Matthew said, forcing
his suddenly tense shoulders to relax. "We were having
tea. Not a tête-à-tête. As I told you, I think she has secrets.
I want to know what they are."

"A good idea, given she saw you sneaking back into
the house carrying an incriminating shovel the same night
a man was murdered."

"I wasn't sneaking. I was *walking*."

Daniel regarded him for several long seconds then said
quietly, "I've no idea what you see in her, but regardless,
you'd do well to recall that she has no money."

"I am well aware of that."

"Good. As I have your best interests at heart, I spent
some time chatting with Lady Julianne and her mother at
breakfast this morning. Would you like my opinion?"

"I suppose I might as well say yes, as I'm certain you'll
give it to me anyway."

Daniel smiled. "How well you know me. Lady Julianne is a lovely young woman with a horribly overbearing mother who all but smothers her. She is agreeable
and amenable, and based on the cordial way she treats
her mother, she has the patience of a haloed saint. If you
could get her away from that termagant, she'd make an
acceptable wife. Certainly one who wouldn't argue with
you or complain about being shipped off to a country estate. However, if that dreadful woman is to become your
mother-in-law, I'd strongly advise you give her as wide a
berth as possible."

"Thank you for that information. Although I'm
curious—if Lady Julianne is so lovely and amenable, why
don't you want her for yourself?" He shot his friend a

narrow-eyed look. "Are you interested in someone else?"

Was that a flicker in Daniel's eyes? Before he could decide, his friend said lightly, "It's clearly missed your notice that *I'm* not shopping for a bride. My only interest is in helping you secure the wife you're so determined to have. And even if I were to suffer a severe blow to the head and decide I wanted to leg shackle myself to some woman, I'd certainly not choose someone like Lady Julianne. Virginal innocents are not to my tastes. She'd bore me to tears within a week. Still, she'll suit nicely for you."

"Because I don't mind being bored to tears?"

"Because you're desperate for a wife and she has to be an heiress. And young enough to bear children. I really don't think you're in a position to be all that choosy. A bit of boredom is not a terrible price to pay for all you'd stand to gain. But you'll be better able to form an opinion of Lady Julianne after you've spent some more time with her. I'd suggest you begin with dinner this evening."

"Dinner?" Matthew frowned. He'd intended to seat Miss Moorehouse next to him.

"Yes, dinner. You know, that meal we eat after the sun goes down. Sit Lady Julianne next to you. Relegate me to the far end of the table, where, on your behalf, I'll do my utmost to discover Miss Moorehouse's secrets and determine whether she believes you're a shovel-toting murderer, thus leaving you time to charm the lovely heiress you need so badly. Unless you'd prefer to sit Miss Moorehouse next to Logan Jennsen once again? Based on how famously they got on last evening, neither would complain at the arrangement."

Matthew's entire body was seized by an unpleasant feeling that resembled a cramp. "I'll seat Jennsen next to the lovely Lady Wingate. That should keep him occupied."

For a fleeting second Daniel looked as if he'd just bitten into a lemon. "Better yet, seat Jennsen between Lady Gatesbourne and Lady Agatha. That will keep both ladies well occupied."

Yes. And it was no more than Jennsen deserved.

At dinner that evening, Matthew sat at the head of the table with Lady Julianne on his right and Berwick on his left. He glanced down the table, noting Logan Jennsen engaged in conversation with the loquacious Lady Agatha, who was no doubt regaling him with the grisly details of Tom Willstone's murder. Lady Gatesbourne, who sat on Jennsen's other side, watched the man with avid interest, her eyes glittering with undisguised avarice. No doubt calculating how many hundreds of thousands of pounds Jennsen was worth. A smiling Lady Emily was holding court with Hartley and Thurston, both of whom had regained their good humor after their losses on the archery field.

Daniel was seated next to Miss Moorehouse, and Matthew trusted his friend to draw her out as best he could. So all was well. He should have been relaxed and enjoying himself and focusing on the beautiful Lady Julianne. But he wasn't.

No matter how hard he tried, he could barely keep his mind on their conversation. Thank God Berwick seemed happy to chat with her across the table, as Matthew had once again dropped the conversational ball.

His gaze refused to cooperate and remain on Lady Julianne and instead kept straying to the opposite end of the table, where it seemed Daniel and Miss Moorehouse were getting along very well. At that moment she smiled at Daniel, a lovely dimpling smile that reached all the way to her eyes, making them glow behind her spectacles with amusement. He heard the deep rumble of Daniel's laughter and his shoulders tensed.

Bloody hell, there was no mistaking the unpleasant sensation gripping him. It was jealousy. He wanted that lovely smile directed toward him. Not his best friend. *He* wanted to be the one laughing with her. Not his best friend.

And what was this? Logan Jennsen said something across the table to Miss Moorehouse that caused her to turn her radiant smile in his direction. Damn it, she was glowing as if she were lit from within. And Jennsen—who was supposed to be occupied with Lady Gatesbourne and Lady Agatha—was once again looking at Miss Moorehouse as if he were an explorer who'd just happened upon a cave filled with sparkling jewels.

Bloody bastard. Jennsen had more money than the damn royal family—*he* didn't have to marry an heiress. And from the looks of it, he didn't have any interest in the heiresses sitting in his midst. No, he seemed to have eyes only for Miss Moorehouse—whom he'd described as lovely.

Bloody bastard.

"Don't you agree, Langston?"

Berwick's voice yanked him from his reverie and he jerked his attention back to his dinner companion. "Agree?"

"That Lady Julianne looks exceptionally lovely this evening."

Matthew turned toward Lady Julianne and offered her a smile he prayed didn't look as tight as it felt. "Extremely lovely." And it was the truth. Dressed in a pale

peach gown that highlighted her delicate features, golden
hair and flawless ivory complexion, she was simply stunning. Her father was no doubt being showered with offers for her. Indeed, it looked as if Berwick was already
half in love with her. A quick scan of the table confirmed
that Hartley and Thurston also kept casting their gazes
in Lady Julianne's direction. He shouldn't even have to
think twice about courting her then offering for her. What
the hell was wrong with him?

And once again his gaze strayed to the opposite end
of the table. To spectacles and a pair of huge doe eyes.
To a dimpling smile and loose strands of unruly hair. To
fingers that bore faint traces of charcoal. To full lips and a
plain gray gown that somehow in no way detracted from
her appearance.

Just then Miss Moorehouse looked beyond Daniel
and her gaze met his. And he felt as if he'd been punched
in the chest. The murmured conversations and delicate
clinking of silverware against china faded away. For several surreal seconds it seemed to him as if they were the
only two people in the room and that something private
and intimate passed between them.

Heat rushed through him, as if she'd touched him, and
although he tried to keep his features composed, he wondered if she could see her effect on him. Then a quizzical
look entered her eyes, one that made him feel as if he
were a puzzle she was attempting to solve.

"She has *such* a way with the needle and thread," Lady
Gatesbourne said, her voice rising above everyone else's.
Miss Moorehouse blinked several times, as if coming out
of a trance. Indeed he felt as if he were pulled out of a
trance himself.

Without moving her head, Miss Moorehouse flicked

her gaze toward Lady Gatesbourne then looked toward the ceiling. A laugh rose in Matthew's throat, which he managed to smother, but he couldn't stop from smiling. From the sound of it, Lady Gatesbourne was extolling, rather loudly, the virtues of her modiste in between enthusiastic sips of wine.

If nothing else, the woman would sleep well tonight. With any luck, she might fall asleep before dessert was served. Good God, the thought of that woman being his mother-in-law was enough to put him off the entire idea of marriage. And certainly wasn't doing anything to help his appetite.

Miss Moorehouse smiled in return then reverted her attention to Daniel. Matthew picked up his wineglass and contemplated the claret contents, trying to figure out a topic of conversation with which to engage Lady Julianne. Finally he turned to her and said, "Tell me, Lady Julianne, have you read any books of interest lately?"

Why that question should cause her eyes to widen with what looked like panic and her cheeks to flame, he couldn't imagine. "Oh, um, not especially, my lord." She cast her gaze downward and appeared to be fidgeting with her napkin.

Good God, he'd thought it a simple, innocent enough conversation starter, but she appeared about to succumb to the vapors. He was about to change the subject to the surely safe topic of the weather when she looked up and said in a rush, "But we've recently formed the Ladies Literary Society of London."

"We?"

"Lady Wingate, Lady Emily, Miss Moorehouse, and myself."

"A literary society," he said, nodding in approval.

"Reading and discussing Shakespeare's works, are you?"

More color rushed into her face. "We've only just formed. Things of that sort are in our future, I'm sure."

Bloody hell, she blushed at the drop of a bonnet. Not that he didn't appreciate a beguiling blush, but good God, all he'd mentioned were *books*. Certainly she didn't appear to be made of sturdy stuff. Regardless, he forced himself to press on, but decided he'd best change the subject since anything literary appeared about to send her into a swoon.

"Tell me, Lady Julianne, what are some of your favorite things to do?"

She considered for several seconds, then said, "I enjoy playing the pianoforte and singing."

"Are you good?"

"I am passable and endeavoring to improve." The tiniest hint of mischief glinted in her eyes. "However, if you ask my mother, she will tell you that I sing like an angel and my talent at the pianoforte is unrivaled."

Hmmm. Lady Julianne was not only lovely, but modest. And appeared to have a sense of humor. Both very promising.

Yet again his gaze strayed to the end of the table. And he saw both Jennsen and Daniel listening intently to something Miss Moorehouse was saying. His fingers tightened around his crystal wine goblet and he forced his attention back to Lady Julianne. "What else do you enjoy?"

"Reading. Embroidery. Riding. Dancing. The usual sorts of things ladies enjoy."

Yes, the usual things. The problem was, it seemed he'd developed a freakish—and completely inconvenient—preference for the *un*usual.

"I'm also very fond of animals," Lady Julianne continued. "I love riding my mare when we're rusticating at the country estate, and walking my dog in Hyde Park when we're in London."

He forced himself to keep his wandering gaze on her and concentrate on this positive bit of information. That she enjoyed riding and liked animals was certainly good. "What sort of dog have you?"

Her face lit up and she named a breed of the sort of small, yipping, ankle-biting, carpet-piddling beasts that slept on satin pillows and that one constantly tripped over and Danforth utterly disdained.

"When I return to London, I'm planning to purchase several more in the same breed so Princess Buttercup has some companions," Lady Julianne enthused.

Matthew stared at her over the rim of his wineglass. "Your dog's name is Princess Buttercup?"

Lady Julianne smiled, a dazzling smile that no doubt lured most men like a siren's call. "Yes. And the name suits her perfectly. I commissioned my modiste to make her several tiny doggie outfits, complete with bonnets."

Good God. Danforth would never forgive him. He could just see his dog's reaction if he were to bring such a creature into their midst. "Do you like large dogs?"

"I like all dogs, but personally prefer small breeds. Large dogs cannot sit on your lap, and they can all but pull one off one's feet when attempting to walk them on a lead. Of course, they don't frighten Princess Buttercup. She's quite fierce and doesn't hesitate to snap at beasts far larger than herself."

He instantly pictured a snapping Princess Buttercup dressed in tulle and a minuscule bonnet, her tiny teeth attached to Danforth's tail while a very unhappy Danforth glared at him.

The picture of domestic bliss he'd been attempting to

paint in his mind vanished like a puff of steam in a brisk wind. Which was utterly ridiculous. Except for the Princess Buttercup situation, Lady Julianne was perfect in every way. Perfect for him in every way. What more could he possibly ask for in a wife than a woman who was a beautiful, witty, modest, amenable, demure, animal lover who also happened to be the much-needed heiress? Nothing. He couldn't ask for anything more.

Yet once again his gaze strayed to the end of the table. And he froze. Daniel had clearly abandoned his conversation with Miss Moorehouse, as he was now talking to her sister, Lady Wingate, who sat on his other side. Miss Moorehouse, however, didn't look in the least bit abandoned. No, she was speaking to that bastard Jennsen, who was hanging on her every word as if pearls of wisdom dripped from her lips. Her lovely, full, lips. That she'd just moistened with the tip of her tongue. A quick glance at Jennsen confirmed that he'd seen the gesture. And had liked what he'd seen.

Bloody hell.

How much longer until this endless dinner concluded?

"Well?" Matthew said to Daniel the instant the last guest departed the drawing room and they were finally alone.

"Well what?" Daniel asked, settling himself in Matthew's favorite chair before the hearth and stretching out his legs.

Matthew tried to curb the impatience in his voice and failed. "You know what. How did your conversation with Miss Moorehouse go?"

"Very nicely. How did yours with Lady Julianne go?"

"Marvelously. What did you learn about Miss Moorehouse?"

"Lots of interesting things. Did you know that she has a talent for—"

"Sketching. Yes, I know. Tell me something I don't already know."

"Actually, I was going to say a talent for conversation. *Real* conversation. Not just because she is able to intelligently discuss an impressive array of subjects, but because she also *listens*. Intently. As if what you're saying is of the utmost importance and interest to her."

Matthew stood before the fireplace and leaned his shoulder against the marble mantel. An image of Miss Moorehouse as she'd appeared on the terrace earlier today flashed through his mind, her huge eyes fixed upon him, her head tilted as she carefully listened to his words. As if nothing mattered more than what he had to say. "Yes, I've noticed that about her. What else?"

"She is keenly observant. Notices small details about people and things. She asked me a number of questions about you."

"What sort of questions?"

"Mostly about your absorption with gardening. She's apparently quite the expert on the subject."

"How did you respond?"

"I was vague, saying you enjoyed all things concerning the outdoors. She's either romantically interested in you—which I warned you might happen—or she's suspicious of you, having seen you carrying that shovel."

The thought of Miss Moorehouse harboring romantic feelings for him absolutely should *not* have pulsed heat through him.

"Did you learn anything else?" Matthew asked.

"She enjoys cooking and baking, using ingredients from her own garden, which is, I gather, quite extensive. Did she tell you about the Dutton sisters?"

Matthew shook his head. "Who are they?"

"A pair of elderly sisters who live about an hour's journey from Miss Moorehouse's home. One sister is nearly blind and the other requires a cane to walk. Miss Moorehouse walks to the Duttons' cottage every day, regardless of the weather, and brings them a basket of food she's cooked herself."

Matthew's brows rose. "She told you this?"

"No. Her sister told me. She further told me Miss Moorehouse refuses to accept money from the Duttons. And that she often brings baked goods to several other families in the area, one in particular, a young woman named Martha Browne who was widowed six months ago. She already has three small children and is due to give birth to a fourth child in two months. According to Lady Wingate, Miss Moorehouse is a tremendous help to Mrs. Browne and beloved by her children."

Matthew stared into the fire. While he hadn't known these things, they certainly didn't surprise him. He could easily picture Miss Moorehouse in the role of loving caregiver. Nor did it surprise him that the recipients of her generosity were people who were in some way broken.

"There is an air of . . . something about Miss Moorehouse," Daniel said softly. "I don't know quite what to call it. I'm certain comparisons between her and her beautiful sister have been common her entire life, a situation that would leave many women bitter. But instead, it seems to have bestowed in Miss Moorehouse a particular compassion toward people, especially those less fortunate."

"Yes, I've noticed that about her as well."

"I must say, it is a particularly attractive quality, and quite unusual amongst women of our social set. Perhaps it's because she wasn't born into our social set that she is so unique."

Unique. Yes. That described her perfectly.

"She's very matter-of-fact," Daniel continued. "Outspoken, but not in an off-putting way, as Lady Gatesbourne is. I'm not ashamed to admit when I'm wrong, and I believe I was wrong about Miss Moorehouse. Not only did I not discover any deep dark secrets, I tend to doubt she has any. Indeed, she's quite the breath of fresh air. I see why you find her so interesting. Indeed, I find her so myself."

Matthew wished that he could call the feeling jolting through him anything other than jealousy, but there simply was no other name for it. He actually had to clench his teeth to keep from saying the two words that rushed into his throat.

She's mine.

He shook his head and frowned. Ridiculous. Damn it, what was wrong with him? She wasn't his. He didn't want her.

Yet the instant that last thought entered his mind, he rejected it. Because as much as he didn't *want* to want her, by God there was no denying that he *did* want her. With an intensity that stunned him. Which was inconvenient in the extreme, as he couldn't have her. She was not the woman he needed to focus on. He needed, badly, to focus on Lady Julianne—Miss Moorehouse's good friend.

Bloody hell.

Daniel folded his hands over his stomach and looked up at him from his slouched position. "Jennsen clearly thinks she's a breath of fresh air as well."

Matthew's hands clenched. "Yes, I noticed."

Daniel nodded. "I assumed you did, since you kept looking down toward my end of the table."

"To see how you were doing with Miss Moorehouse. I noticed you spent a good deal of time speaking with Lady Wingate."

"She was an excellent source of information regarding her sister. Besides, I'm not one to ignore a beautiful woman, especially one who's sitting right next to me." His gaze probed Matthew's. "About Miss Moorehouse— based on the way she was looking at you when she thought I wasn't looking at her, she is . . . infatuated. Paying further attention to her will only serve to falsely raise her hopes."

Matthew frowned. Part of him knew Daniel was correct—that paying further attention to Miss Moorehouse was an exercise in futility. Yet the thought of not doing so made him feel as if a weight rested upon his chest.

"You could break her heart, Matthew," Daniel said quietly. "Surely you don't wish to do that."

"No." Daniel was right. This . . . attraction or whatever it was he felt for her had to be forgotten.

"Good. Now tell me, how went your conversation with Lady Julianne?"

He ruthlessly shoved the image of Miss Moorehouse from his mind. "Fine. She is lovely, demure, sweet-natured, and loves animals."

"*And* is an heiress," Daniel reminded him. "She sounds perfect."

"Indeed she does."

"You won't want to fanny around in pursuing her in earnest. Did you see the way Berwick was looking at her? The man is smitten."

Yes, he'd noticed. And hadn't cared a jot. Wasn't touched by even the slightest twinge of jealousy.

"Even though Thurston and Hartley lavished their attentions on Lady Emily tonight, I'd wager to say that they are smitten with Lady Julianne as well," Daniel continued.

Matthew stared into the fire and tried, truly tried, to dredge up even a tiny flicker of jealousy at the thought of another man courting Lady Julianne.

And found nothing.

Then the image of Miss Moorehouse he'd only a moment ago managed to push from his mind returned. But this time he imagined her smiling across the table at Logan Jennsen . . . then that bastard Jennsen pulling her into his arms and kissing her. And it felt as if a red haze dulled his vision.

With an exclamation of disgust, he pushed away from the mantel and dragged his hands down his face. Then he strode toward the door. "I'll see you in the morning."

"Where are you going?" Daniel asked.

"To change my clothes then go dig some holes. Pray that I find what I'm looking for."

"I wish you luck. Would you like some company?"

Matthew halted, turned, then cocked a brow at his always perfectly turned out friend. "*You'd* be willing to dig holes?"

"I'd prefer not to. But I'd gladly stand watch while you do. There's a killer wandering about, you know."

"I know. And I thank you for the offer, but I'd prefer that you get some sleep. That way you can act as host tomorrow afternoon, thus allowing me several hours to continue my search during the day. Besides, we agreed that Tom's murder might not have anything to do with me. And even if it does, we also agreed that I'm most likely safe until, or unless, I find what I'm looking for."

"'Most likely safe' doesn't sound all that promising, Matthew. And what if you actually find it?"

"I'll hardly jump about like a jackanapes and announce it at the top of my lungs. I'll be armed. And accompanied by Danforth, who has better eyesight and hearing and a superior sense of smell than you—no offense intended."

"No offense taken. And I'll be happy to take over your hosting duties. I'm not the least opposed to spending my time with a bevy of beautiful young women."

"Excellent." He resumed his walk to the door.

"Matthew . . . you realize this search is almost for a certainty a waste of time?"

He paused, then nodded. "I know. But I have to try."

"Well then, be careful, my friend."

Matthew quit the room, closing the door behind him, then headed for the stairs, feeling completely out of sorts, and it was all *her* fault. This digging of the holes would be good for him tonight. Yes, he'd dig lots and lots of holes that would, like their countless predecessors, yield nothing. He'd dig until he was exhausted and couldn't think anymore. Until he was too tired to want that which he couldn't have.

Miss Sarah Moorehouse.

Damn it, he suspected he was going to need to dig a *lot* of holes to accomplish that particular feat.

When he reached the top of the stairs, he noted the procession of servants carrying steaming buckets of water. One of his guests had clearly ordered a bath. A fissure of envy snaked through him. A hot soak certainly sounded much better than hole digging. Perhaps he'd order one for himself when he returned.

He was about to turn in the direction of his bedchamber

when the servants halted and the one in the lead knocked. On the door to the bedchamber belonging to—

"Miss Moorehouse? Yer bath-water's arrived."

Matthew quickly ducked into the small alcove and remained out of sight until the last of the servants had disappeared into the bedchamber. When the corridor was again empty, he quickly headed toward his own chamber, a smile tugging at his lips.

His digging would have to be postponed for a while.

Right now he was much more interested in a bath.

Chapter 10

Wearing only her loosely knotted robe, Sarah added several drops of lavender oil to the steaming water in the copper tub set up before the fireplace in her bed-chamber. She dipped her fingers beneath the surface and slowly stirred, noting that the hot water would need to cool a bit before she entered. But that was fine. She had plenty to keep her occupied.

Turning, she stared at the man sitting across from her on the settee. The dim light from the low burning fire cast him in intriguing shadows, and her pulse quickened just gazing upon him. Her avid gaze moved over him, taking in broad shoulders covered in a snowy linen shirt, loosely tied cravat, black breeches and boots. He remained utterly still, utterly silent, as if waiting to obey her every command. A smile curved her lips.

Franklin N. Stein was indeed the Perfect Man.

Well, except for the fact that his right leg was some-what fatter than his left. But that was only because they'd run out of stuffing. Of course, they wouldn't have run out of stuffing if they hadn't, amidst much giggling, overly gifted Franklin in other areas of his breeches in a manner that surely wasn't anatomically possible.

And there was the slight problem of him not having

any hands. And the slightly larger problem of him not having a head.

Sarah frowned at the headless yet extremely well endowed Franklin. No, that simply wouldn't do. Carolyn, Emily, and Julianne had departed her bedchamber after helping her stuff and assemble Franklin, and she'd hidden him in the wardrobe while the tub was being filled. But she'd dragged him out again after the servants departed. She simply couldn't enjoy her bath then go to bed and leave their creation in such a deplorable condition.

Crossing to the wardrobe, she pulled out her oldest night rail. Then she moved to the bed and stripped the white pillowcase from one of the pillows. After stuffing her night rail into the linen case, she formed the bundle into a round shape. She then set the makeshift head between Franklin's broad shoulders. Stepping back, she examined her handiwork.

A bit lumpy, but definitely an improvement. Except now he had no neck. Of course, that had to be better than not having a head. But now that he had a head, he really needed a face.

And instantly a face—the perfect face—materialized in her mind. Intelligent hazel eyes. Chiseled features. Firm, full lips that didn't smile nearly enough, but when they did smile. . .

Oh, my.

Her heart stuttered as she recalled how Lord Langston had smiled at her across the dinner table. In spite of the fact that she'd sat next to the very charming Lord Surbrooke and across from the very entertaining Mr. Jennsen, part of her had remained preoccupied with Lord Langston. Who'd spent the long meal conversing with Julianne. Julianne, who had looked absolutely stunning.

Sarah closed her eyes and tried to fight back the unwanted feeling that had pressed on her all evening, but she could no longer do so. Jealousy flooded her, and with a groan she buried her face in her hands.

Since there was no stopping it, she decided she might as well just let the feeling come, allow herself to wallow in it for several minutes, then lock the useless emotion back in the furthest corner of her soul.

Damnation, she didn't want to feel jealous, and most especially not of one of her dearest friends. Jealousy was a foolish, empty emotion that served no purpose, that only came upon her when she stupidly wished for things she could not have. Such as beauty.

She'd long ago accepted the limitations of her appearance. Instead of uselessly railing against the fates that had chosen not to bless her with the sort of stunning looks they'd bestowed upon Carolyn, she'd concentrated her time and energy on her interests in horticulture and drawing. She'd forced herself to set aside the sort of feminine dreams that occupied the minds of most girls, impractical dreams of love and romance and grand passion, and in doing so had found great satisfaction within the confines of her garden and sketch pad. Her great passions were of the nonromantic sort. She was fulfilled by her interests, her friendships, her pets, her love of cooking, and was quite content with her life.

Yet every once in a while, most often when she lay in bed at night, alone, surrounded by quiet darkness, a sense of emptiness would sneak up and ambush her. Make her ache for the things she didn't have, would never have. Love, a magical romance, and a grand passion. A husband and children to love.

Allowing herself to entertain such thoughts always angered and frustrated her. She led a very satisfactory life, one for which she should be thankful, grateful. She had a sturdy roof over her head, and unlike her widowed friend Martha Browne, never lacked for food, and unlike her friends the Dutton sisters, was in excellent health. And most of the time she was content.

But sometimes, like now, she wanted *more.* Wanted the things that Carolyn had had with Edward—love, magic, and passion. Wanted Emily's vivacious beauty, which caused not one, but two men to dance attendance on her all evening. Wanted the sort of quiet beauty that Julianne possessed. The sort that turned heads. That made a man seat her next to him at dinner. And gaze upon her as if she were the loveliest woman he'd ever seen.

Sarah sank onto the settee and pressed the heels of her palms harder against her eyes to hold back the moisture that threatened to spill over. Stupid! Stupid, useless thoughts. Ridiculous, futile dreams that served no purpose but to make her ache with a loneliness and emptiness that could never be filled. She needed to bury these thoughts, once again lock them away in the deepest recess of her soul where they couldn't haunt her. Taunt her. Or hurt her. Until the next time she foolishly allowed them to see the light of day.

She drew a shuddering breath and impatiently dashed away the wetness beneath her eyes. Feeling something pressing against her shoulder, she lifted her head. Franklin, as if sensing her mood, had tilted toward her and his stuffed shoulder now touched hers. Commiseration—a lovely trait in the Perfect Man. Unfortunately, his lumpy head had rolled off his shoulders and now rested on the floor near his booted feet. The tendency to literally lose one's head—not quite so lovely. Obviously a needle and thread were called for.

With a sigh, she pushed Franklin upright, plucked his head from the floor and plopped it back on his shoulders. Then she straightened her spine. Enough. She'd wasted enough time wishing for things she couldn't have. Wanting a man she could never have and whom she shouldn't even want in the first place. A man whose interest in her was both suspect and most certainly fleeting. A man who, for all she knew, was a dastardly murderer.

Yet the instant that last thought formed in her mind, her heart vehemently rejected it. There had to be another reason Lord Langston had been returning to the house carrying a shovel the night Mr. Willstone was killed. But what? She knew his claims regarding night blooming flowers were false. Was he capable of the sort of sinister experiments Dr. Frankenstein had conducted? Dear God, surely not. But that simply brought her back to the same question: What had he been doing that night?

With an impatient sound, she rose. Time to put aside these thoughts and get into the tub. But first she needed to take care of Franklin—best not to leave him sitting about unprotected while she was indisposed. After tucking his unwieldy body under one arm and his head under her other arm, she walked to the wardrobe and hid him in the farthest corner. He didn't look particularly comfortable, and his head wasn't on quite straight, but given the tight quarters, there was nothing she could do. Good thing he didn't have a neck, because if he did, he'd definitely have a crick in it by morning.

She closed the wardrobe's double oak doors, then crossed the room, her bare toes sinking into the thick carpet. After setting her spectacles on the table next to the tub, she untied her robe's sash and shrugged out of the garment, allowing it to puddle at her feet. Then she carefully stepped over the copper edge and slowly sank into the hot water.

A satisfied *ahhhh* rushed past her lips. Bending her knees to compensate for the fact that she was longer than the tub, she scooted lower, until the fragrant heat reached her chin. Then she rested her head on the curved copper lip, closed her eyes and let the warmth seep into her, the only sound in the room the steady ticking of the mantel clock.

The heat and steam loosened her tense muscles, and she let out a long, deep, contented sigh. And was suddenly reminded of another bath. . .

An image of Lord Langston took shape behind her closed eyes. Rising from the tub. Water sluicing down his wet, naked form. Lifting his muscled arms to push back his wet hair. *Oh, my.* There was nothing quite so perfect as a bath—unless it was watching a perfect male specimen take a bath.

"There's nothing quite so perfect as a bath—unless it's watching a perfectly lovely woman take a bath."

With a gasp, Sarah's eyes popped open at the soft, deep, familiar voice whose words so closely reflected her own thoughts. She sat abruptly upright, sloshing water over the side of the tub, and squinted toward the fireplace. Although he was blurry about the edges, there was no mistaking the figure leaning his shoulder nonchalantly against the mantel as anyone other than Lord Langston. He held a long swath of white material in one hand, and when she squinted harder, she realized it was her robe.

She snatched her glasses from the table, slid them on, then crossed her arms protectively over her chest. Glaring up at him, she noted that he'd removed his jacket, waistcoat, and cravat, leaving him dressed in a white shirt, black breeches, and black boots. His shirt was open at the throat and he'd rolled back the sleeves to his elbows.

Her heart seemed to perform a somersault. He looked deliciously undone, wonderfully masculine, and wickedly handsome. When she raised her gaze to his, she found him looking at her, a lazy smile curving his lips.

"What are you doing here?" she asked in a whispered hiss.

He raised his brows and adopted an innocent expression. "Is it not obvious? I'm watching you bathe. As you watched me." He lifted the hand that held her robe. "And borrowing an article of your clothing. As you borrowed one of mine. It's a little something I like to call an eye for an eye." His gaze flicked to her chest. "Or tit for tat, if you prefer."

Surely it was anger that made her pulse race and her heart pound so hard. Hugging her knees closer to her chest, she said, "You mean revenge."

He made a *tsking* sound. "Revenge is such an unattractive word." His gaze slid slowly over her and his eyes seemed to darken. "And allow me to assure you, there is nothing in the least bit unattractive about the picture you make in that tub. You look delightful. Very . . . Botticelli-esque."

A blush seemed to suffuse her entire body, right up to the roots of her untidily upswept hair, which she was certain resembled a pigeon's nest on top of her head. "You're making sport of me, my lord." Dear God, was that breathless sound her voice?

"I'm doing nothing of the kind. Instead of skulking behind a curtain to watch you bathe as you did me, I'm merely being up-front and honest."

Without taking his gaze from hers, he pushed off from the mantel and dragged an armchair to the edge of the tub. After laying her robe over the back of the chair, he sat. Making a rolling gesture with his hand, he said, "Please, continue. Don't mind me."

"Continue?"

"With your bath." He leaned forward and rested his forearms on the edge of the tub. His fingertips dipped below the surface and lazily circled in the water. Mischief gleamed in his eyes. "Do you need help finding the soap?"

The thought of his hand delving farther beneath the surface stole every bit of air from her lungs. Unable to speak, she shook her head, an action that sent her glasses sliding down her nose. Before she could push them up, he plucked them from her face and set them on the table.

"They'll only get foggy from the steam," he said. "And you won't need them. I've every intention of remaining close by."

She had to swallow to find her voice. "This is extremely improper." Finally—her common sense roused itself.

"You didn't seem to think so when you entered *my* bedchamber and watched me bathe. This is clearly a case of someone who shall remain nameless"—he leaned a bit closer and lowered his voice—"but we both know I'm referring to you—finding fault with someone else for faults that are conspicuously their own. I believe that it is referred to as the pot calling the kettle black."

Botheration. Vexing as it was, she couldn't deny he had a point. "But this can hardly be considered fair. You didn't know I was watching you bathe."

"No." A devilish smile curved his lips. "If I'd known I had an audience, I would have put on a much more entertaining show." He stroked a single fingertip up her calf, eliciting a gasp and a frenzy of tingles. "You've seen mine, Sarah. It's only fair that I see yours."

The sound of her name spoken in that husky, deep whisper sent a heated tremor through her. She had indeed seen his, and it was a sight she'd never forget. Sadly, however, she greatly feared that she would not prove so unforgettable. But the way he was looking at her . . . behind the teasing glimmer, his eyes were dark, steady, and intense. And there was no missing the glitter of challenge as well. She could almost hear him asking, *Do you dare?*

Did she?

As recently as a few short days ago, she would have answered with an emphatic no. She wasn't the sort of woman to bathe in front of a man. Yet a few short days ago she also would have sworn she wasn't the sort of woman to hide behind a curtain and watch a man bathe. Or share a mind-numbing intimate kiss with a nearly naked man.

She drew in a shaky breath. Where was her outrage at this invasion of her privacy? Why wasn't she demanding he leave at once? Why did she, at this moment, inexplicably feel more *alive* than she could ever recall feeling—except for those magical moments she'd spent in his arms? Instead of saying or feeling what she should, she remained silent, rendered mute by an exhilaration and anticipation that bordered on pain.

No man had *ever* looked at her like this. Ever made her feel like this. So breathless. So reckless and bold. So filled with wants she couldn't even name.

So *alive.*

No man except him.

"Would you like me to wash your back?"

His voice was a seductive whisper that curled around her, persuading her to comply, to accept his challenge.

Her better judgment tried to warn her to refuse, but her heart—so filled with wants and curiosity and desire—drowned out the sound.

Without a word, without taking her gaze from his, she slowly unwrapped one hand from around her knees then moved it unsteadily along the bottom of the tub until she found the soap. Lifting her hand from the water, she held out the rectangular bar.

Eyes glittering, he took the bar from her, then moved to the head of the tub. She heard his boots creak as he crouched down behind her. "Lean forward," he instructed softly.

With anticipation snaking through her, she did as he bid, wrapping her arms tighter around her bent legs and resting her chin on her upraised knees. His hands scooped warm water over her shoulders then began to touch her in a way that she could only describe as magical. His soapy palms and fingers glided slowly up and down her back, over her shoulders, massaging her in a way that produced the most delightful, pleasurable sensations she'd ever experienced. She no more could have squelched the moan of pure pleasure vibrating in her throat than she could have stopped tomorrow from coming.

"Feel good?" he asked, his breath blowing warm against the back of her neck.

"Yes." Good lord, yes. So much better than merely good.

"Your skin is beautiful. So incredibly soft. Did you know that this . . ." He traced his fingers down the center of her spine, under the water, then circled them lightly over the small of her back. " . . . is one of the most sensitive spots on a woman's body?"

She had to swallow twice to locate her voice. "I . . . I believe it." His fingers continued their slow caress, and she could no longer speak. Could only feel. Tingles vibrated through her entire body, and every breath melted into a sigh of pleasure. His hands moved slowly back up, then he smoothed water over her back and shoulders, rinsing them of soap.

"More?" he asked softly.

God yes. Please yes. Don't ever stop. Indeed, it seemed her entire existence had boiled down to the word *more.*

A small part of her tried to interject, tried to tell her that she had to stop this madness. That this had gone far enough. Was completely improper. Could lead to scandal. Ruin. But her body refused to be denied the flood of wondrous sensations coursing through it.

"More," she agreed.

Lightly clasping her shoulders, he urged her to lean back. She obeyed, but modesty forced her to cross her legs and fold her arms over her chest.

Seconds later his soapy hands began their magic all over again, this time massaging their way down one arm, gently lifting it from her chest, and stroking her skin all the way to her wrist. Her eyelids drooped closed when he caressed each finger until she was limp with pleasure.

Her other arm fell away from her chest of its own accord, and he lavished the same treatment on that limb. Next he wrought his magic on her neck, then worked his way slowly downward, over her collarbone, then to the rise of her breasts.

She forced her heavy eyelids open and watched his hands slip beneath the surface to curve beneath her breasts. Her breath caught and she involuntarily arched her back. His thumbs brushed over her nipples and they hardened into tight peaks, begging him to repeat the sensual caress.

With rapt attention she watched his long fingers play

over her wet breasts, circling and lightly tugging on her nipples, each teasing pull drawing a groan from her. The sight of his hands on her, his skin so dark against hers, left her breathing hard and aroused in a way that made her feel as if he'd set her on fire. The folds between her legs felt heavy and swollen and they ached with the need to be touched. She squirmed, rubbing her thighs together, but rather than soothe, the movement only served to enflame her further.

He rolled her nipples between his fingers and gently tugged. "You feel so good, Sarah. So soft and warm." His words brushed passed her ear. She turned her head, seeking, searching, and then his lips were on hers. Gentle, persuasive. Too gentle. She wanted, needed, more.

With a sigh she parted her lips and he slowly deepened the kiss. She felt as if he was sinking into her and she was melting into him. The sensation of his tongue touching hers, his hands caressing her breasts, filled her with an ever growing heated urgency that demanded something . . . something she couldn't name but that she desperately wanted. Needed. With an aching intensity that couldn't be denied.

In the next instant his hands and lips were gone, leaving her bereft and dragging a moan of protest from her. Before she could question him, he was standing beside the tub, looking down at her. Although she couldn't see his face clearly, she could hear his ragged breaths.

"More?" he asked in a gravelly whisper.

Sarah stared at him, this man who in mere days had stirred her emotions more, and in unprecedented ways, than anyone she'd ever known. Her mind, heart, and body all ached, begged to know more.

But did she dare?

If she said yes, would she regret her decision tomorrow? Perhaps. But in her heart she knew she'd regret it more if she missed this opportunity she never thought she'd have.

"More," she whispered.

He held out his hands, and with her decision made, she put her hands in his. He gently pulled her to her feet. Standing in front of him, water trailing down her skin, she remained still while his gaze slowly traveled down her wet form. A trail of heat followed his perusal, as if tiny flames were lit everywhere his gaze touched, evaporating her modesty.

When their eyes once again met, he whispered, "Perfect."

It was not a word she ever would have used to describe herself. Not a word she ever thought any man would ever say to her. Her heart thudded in response, then nearly stalled when he reached up and gently pulled the pins from her hair, dropping them on the carpet. Her unruly curls fell from its haphazard upsweep, the ends brushing her hips. Then he slowly sifted his fingers through the strands.

"Perfect," he repeated. "If Botticelli could see you, he'd declare you his muse. I pity him that he'll never have the pleasure."

"I cannot fathom a single reason as to why you would say that."

"Really? You said something similar in my bedchamber with regards to my desire to kiss you. Therefore, I shall answer as I did then: 'Don't worry. I can fathom enough reasons for both of us.'"

He touched a single fingertip to the base of her throat and dragged his hand slowly downward. Sarah's eyes drifted closed. Locking her knees, she focused her attention on his hand, absorbing the myriad heated tingles coursing over her skin. With slow, feathery caresses he awakened every pore, layering sensation on top of sensation. When he palmed her breasts, teasing her nipples into tight arousal, a long sigh escaped her.

"Open your eyes, Sarah."

She dragged her eyelids open and stared into his beautiful hazel eyes, darkened with an unmistakable passion she'd never thought to see. Never dreamed to inspire.

He stepped closer then lowered his head. His tongue circled her distended nipple, then his lips closed over the sensitive bud, sucking gently. Sarah gasped at the intimacy, at the knot of pleasure that tightened low in her belly. Lifting her hands, she sifted them through his thick hair, reveling in every wondrous draw of his lips.

As he lavished the same attention on her other breast, his hands coasted down her back to cup her buttocks. A guttural groan rose in her throat, a sound she didn't recall ever before making. He kissed his way up her chest and neck, along her jaw.

"Sarah . . . Sarah," he whispered, his lips and breath tantalizing her skin. And then his mouth slanted over hers and her arms wrapped around his neck and her mind emptied except for one word. *More . . . more. . .*

As if he heard her silent plea, he deepened the kiss, his tongue dancing with hers. One large hand slipped lower, down the back of her thigh, then lifted her leg until her foot rested against the edge of the tub. Any embarrassment she might have felt at being so openly exposed dissolved at the first touch of his fingers against the aching folds between her legs.

She gasped into his mouth and would have simply slithered back into the tub if not for his strong arm wrapped so securely around her waist. He tormented her with a slow circular motion that maddened and enflamed her until she undulated in shameless need against his hand. He groaned and lifted his head, pressing kisses along her jaw.

"So soft," he whispered against her neck. "So hot and wet. So . . . perfect."

Yes, perfect. The way he was touching her, teasing her feminine flesh, was perfect. And pushing her closer to a precipice that remained just out of reach.

And suddenly she was there, hovering, until his next magical touch propelled her over the edge into a hot, dark abyss of pulsing pleasure that dragged a ragged cry from her throat. She buried her face against his shoulder and for an endless, mindless moment her entire being narrowed down to the place between her thighs where he continued to stroke with such perfection. Then the spasms subsided, leaving her limp and languid in the most wickedly delicious way.

She drew a deep breath and her senses flooded with the scent of his skin. Sandalwood and clean linen and *him*. She slowly raised her head and found him regarding her through serious hazel eyes.

"Sarah," he whispered.

"Lord Langston," she whispered back.

One corner of his mouth twitched. "Matthew."

"Matthew." The mere act of saying his name elicited a tingle. She slowly lowered one hand from around his neck, dragging her palm down to slip it inside the open neck of his shirt to rest against his chest. She splayed her fingers against his warm skin, absorbing the feel of his heartbeat, the slight tickle of his dark chest chair against her palm. "Matthew . . . what have you done to me?"

He reached up, cupped her cheek in his palm and brushed the pad of his thumb over her cheekbone, looking at her as if she were an enigma he couldn't solve. "What have *you* done to *me*?"

"Not nearly the same wondrous thing you just did to me. I . . . I've never felt like that before."

Something she couldn't decipher flickered in his gaze. "I'm delighted to have been the first." He pressed a kiss against her forehead, then in one smooth motion lifted her from the tub. When he slowly lowered her, her body dragged along his. With her feet on the carpet, his hard arousal pressed against her belly and she wished he was as naked as she. Wished there was nothing to thwart her from satisfying her burning curiosity to discover and explore the texture of every bit of his skin.

After setting her on her feet, he stepped away and retrieved her robe from the back of the chair. Standing behind her, he held the garment so she could slip her arms into the sleeves. He then moved to stand in front of her and deftly tied the ribbon around her waist.

"I believe we're even now," he said.

She raised her brows. "Not exactly."

"Oh? You saw me bathe, I saw you bathe."

"I only *saw* you bathe. You *helped* me bathe. And, um, then some."

Instead of looking amused as she'd expected, his expression remained serious. Reaching out, he captured her hands and entwined their fingers. "Is that what you want, Sarah?" he asked softly, his gaze searching hers. "To help me bathe?"

An immediate yes rushed onto her tongue, but she forced herself to suppress it. Because based on his tone, his expression, he was not asking her in a playful, teasing way. In as light a tone as she could muster, she said, "I'll think on the matter." And she would. Indeed, she doubted she'd be able to think of anything else.

"As for helping you bathe," he said, "I'm afraid I couldn't stop myself." His gaze skimmed down her form and a muscle ticked in his jaw. Meeting her eyes once more, he said, "And now I must leave. Before I find myself in that exact same situation once again—unable to stop myself." Lifting her hands, he pressed a warm kiss to the backs of her fingers. Then he released her and walked swiftly to the door. He quit the room without a backward glance, closing the door with a quiet click behind him.

Sarah turned toward the tub and for several moments remained perfectly still, staring at the water, reliving their incredible, magical interlude. Surely she should be feeling regret. Shame. Embarrassment at the liberties she'd allowed him. Instead she felt exuberant and exhilarated. And understood what it was ladies whispered about behind their fans at soirees.

She turned and her gaze fell upon the bed. She supposed she should climb beneath the covers, but how could she possibly sleep when her mind was so full of what she'd just experienced?

Knowing sleep was many hours away, she walked toward the window, where she pushed aside the heavy green velvet curtain. The full moon hung in a star-studded sky, an iridescent pearl against black satin sprinkled with glittering diamonds. Silvery moonlight illuminated the garden below. Her gaze swept over perfectly manicured grass. Immaculately trimmed hedges. A copse of soaring elms.

A shovel-toting figure moving toward the copse of soaring elms.

She gasped and pressed her nose closer to the glass. Even if she hadn't recognized Matthew, there was no mistaking Danforth trotting at his heels. Whatever his lordship had been up to the other night, he was clearly up to it again—and not even a quarter hour after departing her bedchamber. All her questions and concerns about him that he'd dissolved with his drugging kisses and intoxicating caresses came roaring back, smacking her from the stupor into which he'd lulled her.

Her sated languor was squashed by disgust at herself for being so effortlessly and completely seduced into forgetting all her questions and concerns. She dashed to the wardrobe and dressed as quickly as possible in a dark brown gown. Recalling Tom Willstone's death, she grabbed the brass poker from the stand next to the hearth, as she had no intention of placing herself in danger. Thus armed, she quit the room and hurried toward the stairs, determined to find out once and for all what the infuriatingly distracting Lord Langston was up to.

Chapter 11

Matthew walked down the darkened garden path, all his senses on alert. In addition to the knife he normally kept tucked in his right boot, he'd slipped another blade into his left boot and brought Danforth along for further protection. If indeed someone was watching him, waiting for him to find that which he sought, that person would have one hell of a fight on their hands getting it away from him—if he ever managed to find it. And just in case Tom Willstone's murderer was still lurking about, he had no intention of being caught unawares.

He headed toward the far northwest corner of the garden, an area he dreaded visiting. If he'd known the first thing about gardening a year ago when he began this quest, he would have planned to dig in the northwest corner during the winter months, when the roses weren't in bloom. But he hadn't known at the time, and now the northwest corner was the last unexcavated section of the garden left for him to dig. So he would go where the roses were.

And not just a few roses. No, there were *hundreds* of roses. All lovely and fragrant. All just waiting to make him sneeze.

As if powered by the mere thought of his nemesis flowers, his nose twitched. The sneeze came upon him so suddenly, so violently, he had no time to stifle it. Two more followed in quick succession before he was able to muffle the sound by shoving his handkerchief beneath his nose.

Bloody hell. Clearly he was nearing his destination. So much for a stealthy arrival. Of course, he would have realized he was nearing his destination if his brain weren't so jumbled—which was completely *her* fault.

Muttering an oath, he firmly shoved all thoughts of that distracting woman aside and fashioned a makeshift mask for his lower face by tying the ends of his handkerchief behind his head and pulling the square of linen over his nose. As it had in the past, this helped his nose, but did little for his eyes, which felt grittier and itchier with each step that drew him closer to the rose garden.

Heaving a sigh of resignation, he made his way down the rose-lined pathway. When he reached the far border, he stopped, looking around, listening. Although nothing seemed amiss, he once again felt as if he were being watched. He glanced down at Danforth, noting the dog's alert stance. Did he sense an intruder?

Matthew waited nearly a minute, but when Danforth didn't issue so much as a warning growl, he decided it was time to get to work. He trusted Danforth's canine senses to pick up on any intruders. If he'd brought the beast with him the night he'd seen Tom Willstone, perhaps the man would still be alive.

With the same patience he'd used for the past year, Matthew began digging a trench along the base of the shrubs, hoping this one would yield the results he sought. As he rammed the shovel into the dirt, his mind wandered—to the precise thing he was trying not to think about.

Her.

And not to just any thoughts about her. No, his mind instantly drifted into sensual waters that did nothing for his concentration. Halting his digging, he leaned on the shovel's wooden handle and closed his eyes. And instantly imagined her in the bath. All wet, satiny skin, lounging in a tub of steaming water. Pictured her looking up at him with those beautiful eyes, then slowly rising from the water, like the Botticelli painting she so closely resembled.

The feel of her skin, her hair, her wet, swollen sex, the flowery scent of her, the erotic sounds she'd made, were all branded in his mind. He'd gone to her bedchamber intending only to stay a moment, just to see the look on her face when she realized he intended to pay her back in kind. And then leave.

Isn't that what he'd intended?

He opened his eyes and shook his head. God help him, he didn't know. All he knew was that he'd taken one look at her and been completely captivated. Thoroughly seduced. And utterly unable to walk away.

It was those damn eyes. So huge and liquid and soft. Like golden pools of honey a man could simply drown in. And every time she looked at him, that's exactly what he felt like—a drowning man. Yet it was so much more than just her eyes. It was . . . everything. It was just . . . *her.*

Never had a woman affected him so strongly so quickly. He tried to recall any woman who'd fascinated him as this one did, who filled every corner of his mind, whom he ached to touch as he did this one, who eroded his control so completely, and he failed utterly. Which, given his circumstances, was very bad indeed.

An agonized groan vibrated in his throat. How had this happened? How was it possible that this woman, who was nothing like the sort of woman he'd always imagined himself with, nothing at all like the sort of woman he'd always pursued in the past, was the only woman who had ever affected him this way? This profoundly?

Bloody ridiculous, that's what it was. And bloody annoying as well. Yet also bloody undeniable.

Still, this inexplicable attraction to her must simply be because she *was* so completely opposite of every woman he'd ever been attracted to. Which meant that this . . . attraction or whatever one wanted to call it, was merely some odd aberration that would hopefully go away.

He cheered a bit at the thought. Yes, surely it would go away. It was merely the result of too many sleepless nights. Too much worrying. Too much pacing in front of the hearth rug. Too much hole digging.

And surely another factor was that he'd been too long without a woman. No doubt *any* woman who'd arisen from a steaming tub of water and stood before him wet and naked would have aroused his ardor. His inner voice guffawed and called him a bloody idiot. *You've walked away from other women,* it reminded him. *But you couldn't have walked away from Sarah in that tub if a gun were held to your head.* He shot his annoying inner voice a frown and told it to shut the hell up.

Damn it, such thoughts were not serving his purpose well. Heaving a frustrated sigh, Matthew set his boot on the flat end of the shovel to begin another trench. He'd just lifted the first mound of dirt when Danforth, who'd been sitting quietly, suddenly stood. The dog lifted his nose, his nostrils twitched, and his entire body tensed as if ready to spring into action. A low rumble sounded from his throat, and in the next instant he raced down the path.

In a flash, Matthew retrieved the knife from his right

boot, and with the weapon in one hand and the shovel in the other, he ran after Danforth.

As he neared the end of the rose garden, he heard a crashing in the underbrush followed by several deep *woofs*. Seconds later Matthew rounded a corner in the path and skidded to a halt. And stared. At Danforth, who, instead of cornering and holding at bay a potential threat, was a tail-wagging, tongue-lolling bundle of canine happiness as he gazed up adoringly at Sarah, upon whose shoe he happily sat. Sarah stood with her back pressed against the thick trunk of an elm. She patted Danforth's head with one hand, clutched a fire poker with the other, and was making frantic shushing sounds.

Danforth, clearly sensing his presence, turned his head. He appeared to be grinning. Matthew could almost hear the beast saying, *Look who I found! What jolly fun!*

Hmmm. This new trick of Danforth's of finding Sarah in places where she wasn't expected—clearly he'd taught him that. And was damn glad he had.

She looked up and stared at him over Danforth's head with a nonplussed expression Matthew wagered matched his own. Surely he should have been annoyed at finding her here. Spying on him. Yes, the frantic pounding of his heart was the result of just that—pure annoyance. It might *seem* like anticipation, but it most certainly was not. And this sudden heat coursing through him? That might *feel* like a rush of desire, but it was certainly nothing more than irritation. And certainly he wasn't imagining her naked. And wet. And melting in his arms.

Reaching up, she pushed her glasses higher on her nose then frowned. "Lord Langston? Is that you?"

Good God, the woman was daft. "Of course it's me. What are you doing here?"

Rather than answering his question, she asked one of her own. "What is wrong with your face?"

His face? He reached up and encountered his forgotten handkerchief. With an impatient gesture he yanked the linen down and glared at her. "There is nothing wrong with my face. What are you doing here?" he asked again.

She lifted her chin. "What are *you* doing here?"

Without taking his gaze from her, he stalked forward. When he stood directly in front of her, he issued a quiet whistle that Danforth instantly obeyed by rising and then moving to stand next to him.

"*I* am working in my garden," he said in a perfectly calm voice.

Her brows shot upward and she nodded her chin toward the blade he clutched in his hand. "Indeed? What sort of gardening are you doing with that knife? Stabbing your night bloomers to death?"

"What are *you* doing with my fire poker? Searching the underbrush for blazing logs?"

"I brought it with me for protection. You'll recall that a man was killed not far from here."

A shiver of dread, accompanied by a good dose of anger that she'd come out here alone, rippled through him. "I do indeed recall, which therefore again begs the question you've yet to answer: What are you doing here?"

"Walking. Enjoying the night air."

He moved a step closer to her. Her eyes widened but she didn't attempt to move away. "After your bath?"

"Yes. Believe it or not, bathwater does not render one incapable of walking."

"If it was night air you sought, you could have achieved your goal without leaving the comfort of your bedchamber," he said silkily. "You could have opened your windows and paced about your room and not have risked running into a murderer. You are either very brave or very foolish."

"I assure you I'm not foolish. I brought the fire poker, which I was fully prepared to use"—she shot him a pointed glare—"and still am, if necessary. I also knew that with you and Danforth so close by, I wasn't in any real danger."

"And how did you know Danforth and I were close by?"

"I saw you from my window. Now it is your turn to answer my question, which you've ignored. What are you doing with that knife?"

"I carry it for protection against intruders."

"I was harboring the impression that I was a *guest*, not an intruder."

"My guests are all asleep at this hour."

"As opposed to wandering about in the garden."

"Precisely."

"Then perhaps you should write up an instruction manual for your guests, as I was not aware I was required to retire at a certain time."

"An instruction manual is an excellent idea. I'll be certain to include a chapter on how guests should not spy on their hosts."

"In that case, I'd suggest also adding a chapter on how hosts should not deliberately lie to their guests."

"So you admit you were spying on me?"

She hesitated, then jerked her head in a nod that sent her glasses sliding downward. "Yes."

"Why?"

"In order to find out why you'd lied to me."

"And what exactly do you think I lied about?"

"The reason for your nocturnal visits to the garden." She hiked her chin up a notch. "Whatever you're doing out here has nothing to do with night bloomers or any other sort of gardening."

"Upon what are you basing such an accusation?"

"Tell me, my lord, are your tortlingers planted in this area of the garden?"

Matthew hesitated for a beat, cursing himself for neglecting to ask Paul. "No."

"How about your straff wort?"

"No. As I'm sure you can tell, this area of the garden is reserved primarily for roses." *Ha. So there.* Even he knew enough about roses to fool a self-proclaimed gardening expert.

"So then your tortlingers and straff wort are elsewhere in the garden."

"Obviously."

"You'd be willing to show them to me?"

"Of course. But not now."

"Why not?"

"Because right now I'm going to escort you back to the house then continue with my business, which is none of *your* business."

"You'll do nothing of the kind. Because I'm not leaving. What you'll do instead is explain to me what you are doing out here. Without uttering any further falsehoods."

"I don't like being called a liar, Sarah."

"Then I strongly suggest you stop lying." She paused for several seconds then said, "There are no such things as tortlingers and straff wort."

"I beg your pardon?"

She repeated her statement, very slowly, as if he were a half-wit.

Matthew went perfectly still, then inexplicably had to fight the urge to laugh. Not at her, but at himself. Bloody hell. She'd given him ample rope and he'd very neatly hanged himself. He wasn't certain if he was more annoyed or amused or impressed.

"I see," he said, unable to squelch his grudging admiration.

"Then I'm sure you can also see that I am due a satisfactory explanation for your nocturnal garden visits."

"Actually I don't see that at all. What I do on my own property is none of your concern. Just because we've seen each other naked doesn't mean I'm obligated to offer you explanations."

"It *is* my concern if you don't wish for me to believe that during your visit to the garden several nights ago you were digging a shallow grave for Mr. Willstone."

"Is that what you believe, Sarah? That I killed Tom Willstone?" Before she could answer, he moved one step closer to her. "Because if I did kill him, surely you realize that there'd be no reason for me not to kill *you*." Another step closer. Now less than two feet separated them. "Here. Now."

Her gaze never left his, and for the space of one heartbeat it felt as if she'd looked into his soul. "I don't believe you killed him," she said softly.

"Really? As you said, you saw me that night with a shovel, and there's no point in not admitting I've lied about my gardening expeditions. So why don't you believe I killed him?"

She again studied him for several long seconds before replying. And he gritted his teeth to keep from falling into the damn vortex of her gaze.

Finally she said, "Because I listen to my heart. And

my heart tells me you are a man of honor. That you would not, could not, kill anyone. That a man who still so strongly carries the guilt of his siblings' deaths, who still mourns their loss after all these years, is incapable of ending someone's life."

Her words seemed to burn a hole through him. There was no question that she meant what she'd said, and damn it, her unquestioning belief in him left him . . . humbled. Vulnerable. Unsettled and confused. He would have expected such belief from Daniel, his closest friend, but not from a woman who barely knew him. Even his own father hadn't believed him to be a man of honor.

Yet she did.

He had to swallow to find his voice, and then only managed to say, "Thank you."

"You're welcome." Reaching out, she laid her hand on his arm. "Tell me what you're doing out here. Please."

The debate of whether to take her into his confidence was swift, decided by a combination of the concern in her eyes, the warmth from her hand, and his sudden weariness at keeping his doings secret. If he told her, given her expertise with plants, then he could simply ask for her help, which is exactly what he'd wanted to do.

After tucking his knife back in his boot and jabbing his shovel's tip into the soft dirt, he drew a deep breath and began, "During the years prior to my father's death, we only saw each other upon occasion, and each of those meetings were tense and awkward. He always made certain I was fully aware of his disapproval—that I wasn't worthy of the title. And that it was my fault that James, who had been worthy and more of a man than I'd ever be, was dead."

Just saying those words stung him, hurt him, as they

had every time his father had flung them at him. "Three years ago, after one such tense meeting, our normal round of arguments turned uglier than usual and all communication between us broke off. I didn't hear from him again until he summoned me as he lay on his deathbed."

Matthew closed his eyes, the image of his pale, dying, pain-ridden father forever emblazoned in his mind. The shot from the highwayman's pistol had fatally wounded him, but not in a merciful, quick way. It had taken him a long, painful day to die.

Opening his eyes, he stared at the ground and continued, "When I arrived at Langston Manor from London, I learned from Father's steward that the estate was heavily in debt. Father was always a gambler, but apparently he'd suffered a long run of extremely bad luck. He'd lost everything that wasn't entailed and owed huge sums to the servants and dozens of merchants and shopkeepers. Even to the steward himself."

He drew a deep breath, then still looking at the ground, said quietly, "When I saw Father, he was close to death. Extremely weak, and laboring for every breath. He haltingly told me he had something of the utmost importance and secrecy to tell me, but before he would impart this information, he demanded a promise that I would do something for him. I'm not certain if it was guilt or pride or the need to show him I was honorable or a combination of all three, but I said I would do whatever he asked."

Looking up, he said, "He extracted a promise that I would marry within the year and set about producing an heir. It is a promise my honor demands I keep."

She nodded slowly. "Of course it is." Realization dawned in her eyes. "The year is nearly over."

"Yes. In twenty-eight days."

"So the rumors that you're looking for a bride are true."

"They are."

He could almost see the thoughts aligning in her head. "Which is why you invited my sister, Lady Emily, and Lady Julianne to your home. To choose one of them to be your wife."

"Yes."

She frowned. "But why have you not cast your net wider? You've not been in London—there have been dozens of soirees over the past several months, all attended by dozens of eligible young ladies."

"I haven't wanted to leave the estate. Haven't wanted to take time away from my search."

"Search?"

"It pertains to my father's great secret." Matthew could almost feel his father's hand weakly clutching his, see his eyes desperately trying to convey all he wanted to say while each torturous breath rattled in his filling lungs, his terror at knowing he was nearly out of time.

"With his last breaths he told me that the night before he was shot he'd won a huge sum gambling—more than enough money to pay off his debts and put the estate back to rights again. He hid the money, here on the estate."

Comprehension widened her eyes. "In the garden."

"Yes. But his words were so faint, so halting, he was nearly impossible to understand. He died, still trying to speak. Afterward I wrote down what he said as best as I could recall, and I've been searching ever since, trying to find this cache of money so as to pay off the debts I inherited upon his death."

She nodded slowly then pushed off from the tree and paced in front of him. He stepped back to give her room, watching as she clearly absorbed all he'd told her.

"I believe I understand now," she said, continuing to pace. "Because you have so little time left before your year expires, you didn't want to leave your estate and thus your search for the money. Yet, in order to honor your promise to your father, you need to find a bride. And since you are so deeply in debt and may indeed never find this windfall he spoke of, it is now necessary that your bride be an heiress. Therefore, you invited three women you believed to be wealthy marriage prospects to your home, intending to choose one of them while still searching for the money." She halted and met his gaze. "Is that accurate?"

"I don't believe I could have explained it better myself."

She pushed up her sliding glasses then asked in a soft voice tinged with obvious disapproval, "You'd marry purely for money?"

He dragged a hand through his hair. "Unfortunately I don't have the luxury not to. I cannot allow the estate to fall into ruin. A great many people are counting on me. They depend on this estate for their livelihoods. Nor can I ignore the Langston history and the fact that this home has been in my family for generations. The burden of those responsibilities weighs heavily upon me, and I take those obligations very seriously."

His gaze shifted to Danforth, who stood quietly beside him, then returned to hers. "And I'm certain you're aware that many marriages amongst members of the peerage are based on the advantageous combining of fortunes and titles rather than sentimental affairs of the heart."

"Yes." Indeed, Julianne had said on many occasions

that she was well aware she'd be married for her money. "The fact that you've told me all this, I gather it's not merely to explain yourself because you think I would otherwise report your shovel-toting late night excursions to the authorities. It is because you believe my expertise with regard to plants and flowers may help you find some clue in your father's last words. Correct?"

He nodded. "You've again explained it perfectly. Would you be willing to help me?"

Instead of answering, she asked, "Have you not asked your groundskeeper Paul to assist you?"

"Not directly. I've asked him some general questions and professed an interest in gardening, but other than that I haven't asked anyone to help me. I haven't wanted to risk that word might spread. If I'd confided in Paul, he could have inadvertently said something to one of the villagers or servants, and the next thing you know, every person within a ten mile radius would be digging holes in my garden."

"How do you know I won't do the same? Tell someone your secret or attempt to find the money and keep it for myself?"

The urge to touch her became too strong to ignore. Reaching out, he gently brushed his fingertips across her smooth cheek. "My heart tells me you won't."

She stared at him for several seconds, then something that looked like hurt—or perhaps disappointment— flashed in her eyes. She stepped back and his hand fell to his side. Then she once again commenced pacing.

"Of course," she murmured. "Now I understand. That is why you've been so . . . attentive. So charming. The reason you kissed me. Invited me to tea. Came to my bed-chamber this evening. You want my help."

Matthew snagged her arm as she passed him and pulled her around until she faced him. "No." The word came out more harshly than he'd intended.

"You don't want my help?"

"I do. But that is not the reason for my attentions toward you."

Again that flash of disappointed hurt shimmered in her huge eyes, cutting him off at the knees. "It's quite all right, my lord. I understand—"

"Matthew. And *no.* No, you don't understand," he insisted, his voice taking on a rough edge. She *didn't* understand, and he wanted, needed, for her to do so. Grabbing her other arm, he pulled her closer.

"That was supposed to be the reason," he admitted, hating himself for the hurt those words brought into her eyes. "Spend time with you, talk to you, because I wanted information, wanted to tap into your expertise without revealing why. But it didn't work out that way. Every time I spoke to you, I forgot what I was supposed to be doing. Forgot everything. Except you." He brushed his thumbs over the velvety smooth skin of her upper arms. "I've been attentive to you because I can't get my mind off you. I kissed you the first time because I couldn't stop myself from doing so. I invited you to tea because I desired your company. I came to your bedchamber tonight because I couldn't stay away. I touched you then for the same reason I'm touching you now—because I can't keep my hands off you."

Her gaze searched his, then she shook her head. "Please stop. It isn't necessary for you to say such things. I'll help you, or at least try to."

"Damn it, you *still* don't understand." He barely resisted the urge to shake her, and cursed every person in her life who'd ever made her feel inferior. "It *is* necessary that I say such things, because they're true. Every time I'm near you, something happens to me. You just . . . *do* something to me. Just by looking at me. Just by being in the same room as me. I can't explain it, as it's something I've never experienced before. And to be perfectly honest, I'm not certain I like it."

They stared at each other, and he swore the air between them crackled. Then her brows rose, and damn it, she actually looked amused.

"Well, at least you've ceased your flattery. Although you might want to be careful not to be too insulting. After all, you are dealing with a woman who's holding a fire poker."

"Oh? Do you intend to cosh me?"

"If necessary."

"And what would make it necessary? If I did something . . . untoward?"

"Yes."

Giving into the desire that had gripped him the instant he'd seen her standing beneath the tree, he erased the distance between them in one smooth step. Her breasts brushed against his chest and that whisper of a touch scorched him. He leaned down until only a hairbreadth separated their mouths.

"Then you'd best prepare to cosh me," he whispered against her lips, "because I'm about to do something *very* untoward."

Chapter 12

The fire poker dropped from Sarah's nerveless fingers. Even if she'd had the opportunity to brace herself, nothing could have prepared her for this fierce, hungry kiss. He slanted his mouth over hers, demanding a response. And everything, every thought, fell away except him.

Closer. She wanted him to hold her closer. Wanted to feel more of the heat that seemed to pump from his skin, warming her in the most delicious way. Wanted his arms tighter around her. His body pressed closer to hers.

As if he'd read her mind, he gathered her closer, lifting her off her feet. She wrapped her arms around his neck and held on for all she was worth. She felt him move, then realized that he'd turned them so his back now rested against the tree.

He spread his legs and yanked her into the V of his thighs, a spot where the fit was . . . perfect.

Yet whereas in her bedchamber he'd slowly, gently seduced her, now he swept her away in a fury of passion that tasted of both frustration and dark need. His tongue invaded her mouth while his hands urged her ever closer. The heat and scent of his body surrounded her like a flaming blanket, while the exquisite feel of his hard arousal pressed against the juncture of her thighs, instantly reigniting the fire he'd just recently put out. He rubbed himself against her, shooting sparks through her that loosened her knees.

One deep kiss led to another, then his lips left hers to skim across her jaw. She arched her neck to afford him better access, and he immediately took advantage of the invitation, kissing his way down to touch his tongue to the hollow at the base of her throat. She tunneled her fingers through his hair, threw back her head, completely and utterly saturated in decadent sensation.

With a deep groan, he lifted his head, but instead of kissing her again, he gently brushed back strands of hair from her face. With an effort, she dragged her eyes open. And found him regarding her through very serious eyes.

Her confusion at his ending their kiss must have shown, because he said softly, "Please don't think I stopped because I don't want you. The problem is that I want you far too much. My ability to resist you is only so strong, and I'm afraid I've reached my limit."

Everything inside her, all the dormant feelings he'd awakened with his kisses, his touches, shoved aside her propriety, which begged her, commanded her, to remain silent. Summoning all her courage, she said, "What if I don't want you to resist?"

His eyes seemed to darken. "Believe me when I say that it is nearly impossible for me to do so. If I hadn't stopped when I did . . ."

"If you hadn't stopped, then what?"

His gaze searched hers. "Do you not know? Even after what we shared in your bedchamber are you unaware of what happens between men and women?"

Heat flooded her face. "I know what happens."

"Because you've experienced it with Franklin?"

"No! I've never . . . no. No one has ever touched me, kissed me, the way you have." She dipped her chin and stared at his chest. "No one has ever wanted to."

He lifted her chin with his fingers until their gazes met. "*I* want to." A humorless sound escaped him. "So badly I can barely think."

"I know that should frighten me. I wish that it did. I'm ashamed to say that it doesn't."

"You should be frightened. I could hurt you, Sarah. Without meaning to."

Her gaze searched his. She knew he didn't mean physically, which could only mean that he feared she would come to care for him. Which she greatly feared was already happening. And that her heart would break because, as she'd just learned, he'd soon have to marry someone else—

She froze as the implications hit her like a bucket of icy water.

Marry someone else. . .

How could she have forgotten that, for even an instant? The realization of what she'd done, what she would have done if he hadn't stopped, suffused her with a sense of horrified shame. He was bound to marry someone else. Within the next few weeks. And worse, that someone else would most likely be one of her dearest friends.

Dear God, if he married Julianne, how could she ever look either of them in the eye again? How could she ever look at herself again?

She stepped back, out of his embrace, not sure if she was more relieved or humiliated at the ease with which he let her go. Acute mortification washed through her and she wished she could simply vanish.

"What have I done?" she whispered.

He reached for her, but she stumbled back two steps, shaking her head. What had she been thinking? She hadn't been thinking at all, that was the problem. He'd touched her, kissed her, and she'd forgotten everything except for him. The way he made her feel. Which would have been bad enough had he been someone else, but the fact that he might, in a very short time, marry her friend, made this interlude even more unacceptable. In every way.

She pressed a hand to her churning stomach. "I must go."

He stepped toward her but made no move to touch her. "Sarah, you did nothing wrong."

"Didn't I?" Her voice hitched, mortifying her further. "You are a man looking for a wife. And casting your eye in the direction of one of my dearest friends, someone I love."

He dragged his hands down his face, looking as tortured as she felt. "I accept full responsibility for what happened between us."

"A generous offer, but one I cannot accept. You took no liberties I didn't freely offer. Indeed, you were the one who had the strength, the sense, to stop. If you hadn't, I would have agreed to whatever you wanted."

That humbling, humiliating truth lodged a lump in her throat. "You've clearly set your sights on Julianne," she said, hating the knifelike stab those words caused, hating even more the fact that he didn't deny it. "What are your feelings toward her?"

"Other than believing her to be a nice young woman, I have no feelings toward her." Again he dragged his hands down his face. "I haven't been able to think of anyone but you."

"I'm not an heiress." And for the very first time in her life, she wished she was.

"I am, unfortunately, aware of that."

"Which means that this . . . whatever this momentary madness between us might be called . . . is finished. And if you do pursue Julianne, you'll have to tell her the truth of your financial situation."

"I assure you, the young lady—be it Lady Julianne or someone else—as well as her father, will be in full possession of the facts," he said in a stiff voice. "Believe it or not, most heiresses do not expect to make love matches."

The air between them felt thick with tension. A breeze blew a lock of her disheveled hair across her face and she impatiently pushed it aside. "I've never had to fight temptation of this sort before," she said, "and I can only say that's a good thing because clearly I have no talent for it. But I shall simply have to develop that talent. Immediately."

She drew a deep breath then continued, "I offered you my help in deciphering your father's last words and I'll not renege on that. But there can be no further intimacies between us."

Their gazes held for several long, tense seconds, then he slowly nodded. "There can be no further intimacies between us," he agreed in a flat voice. "I beg your sincerest pardon for my behavior."

"As I beg yours. And now, if you'll excuse me, I'll return to the house."

"With my escort," he said, his tone making it clear he'd brook no arguments.

Since she didn't wish to prolong her escape any longer than necessary, she merely nodded, and after picking up the fallen fire poker, walked toward the house as quickly as she could.

When they reached the French windows through which she'd left the house, he rested his hand on the brass knob. "If you'll come to my study tomorrow morning after breakfast, I'll show you the list of my father's last words."

She nodded. "I'll be there."

He opened the door and she slipped inside.

His hand brushed her arm, shooting a tingle through her, but even when he whispered, "Sarah," she didn't turn around, afraid that if she did she wouldn't find the strength to keep moving. She hurried toward the stairs, desperate to be alone. When she arrived in her bedchamber, she closed the door behind her then leaned against the oak panel, her chest heaving from her haste and the effort of holding back the misery that threatened to choke her.

For a tiny, magical moment in time she'd allowed herself to forget who she was, the proper sort of woman she'd always been. She'd felt like a wilted plant someone finally remembered to water, drinking in every drop of the wondrous feelings coursing through her. But then reality had returned, with a particularly hard thump.

She needed to forget his kiss. His touch. His smile. His laugh.

She needed to forget *him*.

Unfortunately, that was the last thing she wanted to do. And the only thing she could do.

Would she come?

The next morning Matthew paced in front of the desk in his private study, asking himself the same question that had haunted him ever since she'd walked away from him last night. Would Sarah come to his study as she'd promised? Or would she change her mind?

Perhaps she'd spent a sleepless night, as he had. Perhaps she'd spent the night packing her belongings, preparing to leave and never return.

The thought of her going filled him with an ache he couldn't name. He paused and glared at the ormolu mantel clock, only to discover, much to his frustration, that no matter how intense a glower he shot at the timepiece, the minutes did not pass more quickly.

With a tired sigh, he moved to the chair by the fire and sank down onto the cushion with a weary plop. Setting his elbows on his spread knees, he rested his head in his hands and closed his eyes.

An image of her instantly materialized in his mind. As she'd looked last night in her bedchamber, naked, wet, aroused, her hair disheveled from his impatient hands. Her eyelids droopy with arousal, her lush lips moist and parted and kiss-swollen. Her hands splayed against his chest. Her soft curves melted against him. Then, as she'd looked in the garden, so vulnerable that all the desire he'd somehow managed to control earlier exploded. It had required every ounce of his strength to halt the madness that overtook him the instant he touched her.

If you hadn't stopped, I would have agreed to whatever you wanted.

Her words had haunted him through the long night, conjuring dozens of sensual images. Of things he wanted to do with her. To her. How the night would have turned out far differently if his bloody conscience hadn't intruded.

But why? Why this woman? What was it about her that had him so undone?

And suddenly an answer came to him. He frowned and mulled it over for several seconds, trying it on as he would a new cutaway jacket—to see how it fit. And the more he mulled, the more he realized that he couldn't deny the realization. In addition to being painfully attracted to her—

He genuinely liked Sarah Moorehouse. Very much. Actually, he suspected, far too much.

He liked her outspokenness. Her intelligence and wit. Her compassion. Her love for her sister. The way she rose above the petty unkindnesses shown to her by her own mother. Her talent. The hint of vulnerability she worked so hard to hide. The look of her. The scent of her. Her laugh and her smile. The fact that, unlike the young women he normally associated with, her interests didn't run to soirees and husband hunting—or, in the case of the more mature women in his social set, to soirees and choosing the next man with whom to indulge in an affair.

Everything about her simply pleased him.

Which, he realized, was a first for him.

He had a number of female acquaintances whom he liked but wasn't attracted to in *that* way. There'd also been a number of women in his past he'd physically desired but ultimately hadn't liked very much outside the bedchamber. Was he so attracted to Sarah because he liked her? Or did he like her because he found her so attractive?

Bloody hell, he had no idea. All he knew was that seeing her in the bath, touching her, watching and feeling her climax, was an unforgettable experience that he needed to find a way to forget. Damn it, if she were only an heiress—

He froze. He only needed to marry an heiress if he didn't find the money. If he found it, he could marry whomever he wished.

He could marry Sarah.

Elation coursed through him, eliciting a quick burst of

laughter. Bloody hell, why hadn't he thought of that before now?

Then reality returned with a sharp slap. After months of fruitlessly searching, there was virtually no chance of finding the money, assuming it even existed.

But still, there remained that tiny flicker of hope that he'd succeed. A flicker that had now taken on an even greater meaning because finding the money would not only solve his financial problems, it would free him to marry a woman he genuinely liked, admired, and deeply desired.

Do not get your hopes up too high, his inner voice warned, an admonishment he forced himself to heed. He'd be a fool to pin his hopes, his future, on something so nebulous. He therefore tucked away the minuscule flame of hope deep in his heart, before it could burn out of control, and concentrated on the sober, unromantic actuality of his situation: failure was almost guaranteed.

When Sarah arrived, he'd show her the piece of vellum upon which he'd written his father's last halting words, see if she could shed any light upon them from a horticultural viewpoint. Then he'd set upon his task with renewed vigor and pray for success. And if he failed, he'd simply have to forget about her.

Well, perhaps not so simply, but he *would* forget about her. He'd have to. There was no other choice. She was simply a *woman.* What had Daniel said about them? Oh yes, that they were all the same in the dark.

Except . . . he'd been with her in the dark on several occasions and would have known her even if his eyes were closed. Her scent was embedded in his brain as if branded there. His fingers would know the silky texture of her hair, her satiny skin, even without benefit of light. He would instantly recognize the taste of her kiss. That soft sound of surprise and arousal that vibrated in her throat every time he touched her.

He pressed the heels of his palms against his eyes and shook his head. *Don't think of touching her. Don't think of the way she tastes, the way she feels. Just don't think of her at all.*

Yes. He needed to think of Lady Julianne, whose beautiful face . . .

He couldn't even recall. Especially now that the hope of marrying Sarah was rooted in his brain.

"Argh!" he muttered into his hands.

A knock sounded at the door, and he jumped to his feet as if a giant spring were attached to his buttocks. "Come in," he said.

The door swung open and Tildon appeared. "Miss Moorehouse to see you, my lord."

He shot himself a fierce mental frown when his heart seemed to skip a beat at the mere mention of her name. Good God, he was behaving like a green schoolboy.

"Thank you, Tildon. Send her in."

He tugged his jacket into place and straightened his shoulders, fully prepared to embrace an air of utter nonchalance. What difference did it make that he'd seen her naked? Caressed her naked body? He'd seen other women naked. Caressed their naked bodies. Just because he couldn't at the moment recall either the name or face of any of those other naked women didn't mean a thing.

She is merely a woman. Precisely. Just like any other woman. A woman who was so wrong for him as to be laughable. A woman who would disappear from his life in a matter of days, never to be seen or thought of again.

Excellent. With everything now in its proper perspective, she could walk through that doorway and he'd be fine. He'd be—

She walked through the doorway and he felt as if he'd been smacked on the back of the skull with a skillet. His heart turned over at the sight of her eyes, so huge behind her spectacles, vulnerable honey brown pools that bore the unmistakable traces of having shed tears. And her lips . . . which still bore the unmistakable signs of having been kissed.

She'd clearly attempted to ruthlessly pull back her unruly hair into a neat chignon, but several tendrils had escaped, and his fingers itched to plunge into the silky strands and disarray the rest. Garbed in an unadorned, mud brown gown, she should not have ignited his desires in the slightest. Yet one look at her and it was as if all his fine resolutions sprouted wings and flew out the window.

There was no nonchalance. No indifference. Where disinterest should have ruled, intense heat held court. Yet something more than merely desire squeezed him in its grip. He knew what desire, pure lust, felt like. They were simple, basic emotions that were easily satisfied. But there was nothing simple about the way this woman made him feel. Yes, it was desire, lust, but something more.

Because he didn't simply want to make love to her then go about his day. No, he wanted to talk to her. Take a walk with her. Laugh with her. Share a meal with her. Find out all about her. And while the fact that he wanted all those things utterly confounded him, they were undeniable.

There can be no further intimacies between us.

She'd said it, and rightfully so. And he'd agreed— rightfully so. Good God, she wasn't some experienced woman with whom he could contemplate an affair. She was a virgin. A guest in his home. And he needed an heiress to marry. He wouldn't make more a muck of things than he already had. If he found the money, he'd ask her to marry him. But since he couldn't count on succeeding, he needed to proceed as he had been—on the premise that an heiress was necessary. There was nothing left to do other than get on with the reason she'd come to his study.

Clearing his throat, he said, "Please come in. Would you care for some tea?"

She shook her head. "No, thank you." Her glasses slid downward with the movement and he watched her push them back into place, clenching his fingers to squelch the urge to go to her and do the deed himself.

He dismissed Tildon with a nod and the butler left, closing the door quietly behind him. The soft click of the lock falling into place seemed to Matthew to reverberate in the quiet room, along with the rapid beat of his heart.

For the sake of propriety, and to save himself from temptation, he knew he probably should have instructed Tildon to leave the door ajar, but he couldn't risk anyone overhearing them. He cast about in his mind for something innocuous to say, but his mind was blank. Except for the image of her in his arms. Should he ask if she'd slept well? No—if he did, she might feel compelled to ask him the same question, and what could he say? Certainly not the truth. Because the truth was that he hadn't slept at all. That he'd spent the entire night convincing himself she meant nothing to him. That he could forget her.

One look at her had proved him utterly wrong. Indeed it had taken exactly one instant in her company to show the folly of all those hours spent telling himself whatever he felt for her was an aberration. Clearly it wasn't.

But until such time as he might locate the money, he

needed to keep his feelings to himself. It would be unfair and cruel to dangle an offer of marriage before her that would most likely never come to fruition.

"Do you have the written words you'd like me to look at?" she asked in a voice completely devoid of emotion.

The question yanked him from his stupor and he nodded. "Yes. The list is on my desk." He crossed the room, then held out the chair for her.

She hesitated for several seconds before walking briskly toward him. When she stopped in front of the chair, he stood directly behind her. And had to grip the chair's cherrywood spindles so as to not to reach out and embrace her. The back of her neck, that bit of ivory skin he knew felt like warm velvet and tasted faintly of flowers, was less than two feet away from his lips.

The knowledge that he had only to take one step forward to brush his mouth against her skin had him drawing in a sharp breath—which only resulted in further torture. Her scent, that subtle floral fragrance that made him feel as if he stood in the midst of a sunshine-filled garden, invaded his senses and he had to grit his teeth to contain the groan that rose in his throat.

Unlike him, she appeared perfectly composed, a fact that irritated him no end. Excellent. He couldn't very well desire her if he were irritated. In fact, the more irritable, the better. She sat, and he pushed in the seat, then moved to stand beside her.

"This is what I wrote after those final minutes with my father," he said, pointing to the piece of ivory vellum on the desk. "He was nearly impossible to understand, the words halting and most of them not much more than mere whispers and stutters."

She ran her finger slowly down the list of words, saying each one as her finger passed over it. "Fortune. Save estate. Hidden here. Garden. In garden. Golden flower. Fern. Fleur-de-lis."

Continuing to look at the words, she said, "Tell me about your search thus far. Based on this, I'm guessing you've looked near all the golden or yellow flowering plants."

"Yes. Claiming a long suppressed interest in all things horticultural, especially yellow flowers—my favorite color—I consulted with Paul, who was only too happy to point out the multitudes of golden-hued blooms in the garden and everywhere else on the estate."

She turned and looked up at him. "*Is* yellow your favorite color?"

"No." His gaze shifted to her gown, then returned to her eyes. "I prefer brown. And you, Sarah? What colors do you prefer?"

Her gaze held his for several seconds, a delicate wash of color suffusing her cheeks. Then she turned back to the vellum. "I like all colors, my lord," she said, not so subtly emphasizing the formality of the last two words. "After digging near the golden flowers, did you then dig near the ferns?"

"Yes. Near the acres and acres of ferns. Like the golden flowers, there are ferns all over the estate. Just when I think I've found the last bunch, another crop sprouts up. It's kept me very busy this spring."

He leaned forward and pointed to the final words. "I'm not certain 'fleur-de-lis' is accurate. As I said, he was very difficult to understand."

"The literal translation is 'flower of the lily,'" she murmured. "There are an abundance of lilies in your garden, of many different varieties."

"And I have dug in, under, and around all of them. After my initial search of the golden flower and fern areas proved unsuccessful, I drew a grid map of the estate grounds and have systematically searched each area. The rose garden, where you found me last night, is the last section left to search. Based on him saying 'hidden here,' I'm certain my father meant the gardens here at Langston Manor. Even so, I've searched the small garden area behind the London town house, as well as the conservatories both here and in London, but found nothing."

"That means you've already searched the areas where the irises are planted?"

"Unless they're roses, I've searched. Why do you ask?"

She turned and looked up at him once again. Because he was leaning down, her face was less than a foot from his. He grimly noted the slight catch in her breath, the darkening of her eyes. Apparently she wasn't as indifferent as she seemed. Well, good. Because damn it, he disliked suffering alone.

She cleared her throat then said, "I ask because although the literal translation of 'fleur-de-lis' is lily flower, the character itself is considered to be a symbol of the iris."

Matthew stilled. "I didn't know that. Are you certain?"

"Yes." Her gaze searched his. "Is that of some significance? I thought you'd already searched near the irises."

"I did. And found nothing." A fissure of hope seeped through him. "But 'iris' could be an important clue because it's not only the name of a flower."

"What else is it the name of?" she asked with a mystified expression.

"Iris was my mother's name." That fissure of hope grew stronger. "And my mother's most beloved part of the estate was an area my father had built especially for her, in honor of her favorite flower. And it's the one place I haven't finished searching."

Comprehension dawned in her eyes. "The rose garden."

Chapter 13

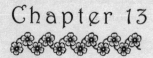

$\mathcal{S}$arah looked into his beautiful hazel eyes and saw the hopeful excitement glowing there. Indeed she could almost feel it emanating off him in waves.

He reached out and laid his hand over hers. "Thank you."

One touch. God help her, that's all it took and her stern resolve to remain indifferent melted like sugar in hot tea. And that simply wouldn't do.

Slipping her hand from beneath his, she eased back the chair, then stood. "There's nothing to thank me for," she said, her fingers involuntarily curling into a fist to retain the heat from his touch. "We don't know if those words mean the rose garden is the right place, and even if they do, that's where you're digging now anyway."

"You don't understand. I've been searching for nearly a year. With no results. I began this quest with high hopes, but as more and more time passed, it's been increasingly difficult to remain hopeful. Lately, I've come to regard every day as bringing me one day closer to failure. This is the first time in months that I've experienced any hope. So I thank you." One corner of his mouth quirked upward. "If it weren't for the roses, this news would be perfect."

"What do you mean?"

"I don't care for roses. Or more accurately, they don't care for me. Every time I'm near them I sneeze."

"Ah. That explains the achoos I heard last night."

"Yes."

"I must say, they made it easy to find you."

"Just as your scent made it easy for Danforth to find you."

"It is difficult to be stealthy with Danforth's keen nose about."

"Even more difficult when you're surrounded by flowers that make you sneeze."

The camaraderie she'd felt from their first meeting relaxed some of her tension and she couldn't help but smile. "You'd make a terrible thief."

"If I were stealing roses, yes. Luckily that is the only flower that affects me that way."

"No sneezing around the tortlingers?"

"None. Nor the straff wort. Nor around the . . . what flower is the scent you wear?"

"Lavender." She shot him a mock stern look. "Which, if you knew the first thing about flowers, you would know."

"I believe we've already established that my knowledge is severely limited." Before she could reply, he said softly, "The scent of lavender doesn't make me sneeze."

"I should hope not, lest you'd be sneezing all the time. It is extremely prevalent in your garden." Refusing to contemplate the cause for the husky note in his voice, she said briskly, "I've an idea to propose to you, one which may appeal to you, especially given your sensitivity to roses."

"I'm listening."

"If you'd like, I'd be willing to assist you in your rose

garden digging. Neither my sister nor my friends would think it in the least bit odd if I joined you, as they are well aware of my love of gardening. Indeed, they'd think it more odd if I sat about with an embroidery hoop. You've numerous acres to cover, and if I assisted you, the work would get done twice as fast, which would mean half the time for you amongst the sneeze-inducing roses."

"You would be willing to do that?"

"Yes."

There was no missing his surprise. "Why?"

"A number of reasons. I love being in the garden under any circumstances, and it is where I'd hoped to spend this afternoon anyway, while the group takes the horseback ride they were discussing at breakfast."

She linked her fingers together, drew a bracing breath, then continued with the speech she'd been rehearsing in her head for past several hours. "And I'd like to help you. I could claim that the reason is because I find the thought of this treasure hunt of sorts exciting and I'd therefore like to be a part of it—which is true. But in the interests of complete honesty, I also know how important it is for you to honor your father's wishes and to put your family's estate back to rights. I . . . I think there was a kernel of friendship forming between us before our very . . . ill-advised, um . . . kiss, and I'd like for that friendship to continue—platonically, of course. Especially as there is a chance you may marry one of my dearest friends."

She waited for his answer, all the while hoping that he wouldn't discern that she hadn't been completely honest with him. That her offer was also self-serving and born of a fact she couldn't ignore—if he found the money, he'd be free from the need to marry an heiress. And even though her common sense and better judgment firmly reminded her that this man could have any beautiful society diamond he wanted, her heart couldn't let go of the hope that if he were free to choose, he might choose *her*. A ridiculous, crazy, insane hope she'd tried mightily to kill, but one that remained stubbornly alive. And one that compelled her to help him. To speed up the digging process. And that gave her even more incentive to pray for his success.

He studied her with an expression she couldn't decipher then asked softly, "You're not afraid to spend the afternoon alone with me in the garden?"

Of course I am. "Of course I'm not." Actually, it wasn't him she was afraid of, but herself. Still, as she'd had more than two decades of practice at hiding her desires, surely she could do so for a single afternoon. "You agreed there would be no further intimacies between us, and you are a man of your word."

He said nothing for several seconds, just continued to look at her with that same unreadable expression. Finally, he quietly replied, "In that case I accept your offer. What time is the group going for their ride?"

"Someone suggested leaving around noon, and they planned to discuss with you making a picnic of the excursion."

"Excellent. I'll see that those arrangements are made and beg off from the outing. Shall we then meet in the rose garden at quarter past noon? I'll bring a shovel and gloves for you."

She smiled. "I'll be there."

When Sarah arrived at the rose garden at precisely quarter past twelve, she was enthusiastically greeted by a *woof* from Danforth, who promptly sat on her shoe, and a mighty sneeze from Lord Langston, who'd pulled down the piece of white linen that completely hid the lower half of his face in order to say hello.

"Are you all right?" she asked, watching him settle the cloth back in place.

"Yes. As long as I keep this handkerchief in place."

She tilted her head and pursed her lips. "You may not have the noiseless stealth of a thief, but you certainly have the look of one."

"Thank you. Your kind words warm my heart." He held out a shovel. "As you can see, I've started on the row containing the yellow roses first. I dig a trench along the base of the bushes, about two feet deep. After about a six foot distance, I go back and fill in the hole. That way, if I have to abandon the project quickly, I don't have too much of a distance to refill." He glanced at the familiar worn sack she carried. "You brought your sketch pad?"

"Yes. I thought in case we took a rest, I'd work on that sketch of Danforth I promised you." Her gaze fell on the large knapsack near his feet. "Have you taken up sketching as well?"

"It's a picnic lunch, prepared for us by Cook while she packed the hampers for the horseback riding party. This way we won't have to return to the house should we get hungry—unless you'd prefer to do so."

"Not at all. I enjoy eating outside, and often bring simple meals with me when I'm working in the garden."

"Excellent. Shall we start?"

"By all means."

Sarah set down her leather satchel then reached for the shovel and leather gloves he held out to her. When she grabbed the handle, her fingers brushed against his. A heated tingle raced up her arm and she inwardly frowned at her body's reaction. A quick look at Lord Langston showed him staring off into the distance.

Clearly he hadn't even noticed the contact. Which of course should have pleased her. And did—for the most part. She simply had to squash the tiny part of her that felt both confused and peeved that he was so unaffected when the barest touch of his fingers rendered her unable to catch her breath. Clearly she was entirely forgettable. Which, of course, she'd always known. But she'd never known how it felt to be forgotten by a man.

Good that you're getting a taste of it now, because if you find the money, he'll forget you in a heartbeat, her inner voice warned ominously. *He'll still marry a beautiful young Society gem.*

Taking the shovel, she forced the voice aside and concentrated on the task at hand. They worked with a minimum of conversation, the sounds of their shovels digging into the dirt accompanied by the chirping of birds and the rustling of leaves in the warm breeze. Sarah quickly established a steady rhythm, aided by softly humming to herself, as was her habit when she worked in her own garden. Danforth found himself a shady spot nearby, much as her beloved Desdemona always did. The thought of her pet brought a wave of nostalgia for home, although between the beautiful gardens and Danforth, this place felt nearly as comfortable as her own home.

She'd just finished filling in another six foot trench that had yielded no results when Lord Langston asked, "Would you like to stop for something to eat and drink?"

Sarah dug her shovel tip into the ground, and wiping her damp forehead with the back of her glove, turned toward him. And stilled. While she had no doubt that she looked like something that had been dragged behind a carriage for several hundred miles, he looked utterly perfect. And completely, unfairly so. After two hours of hoisting dirt in the hot sun, he should look like she felt—overheated, grimy, sweaty, and disheveled. And while he was clearly grimy, sweaty, and disheveled, on him it somehow looked masculine and delicious. And utterly perfect.

Because she'd at first so fastidiously kept her errant eyeballs on her work rather than on him and had eventually lost herself in her task, she hadn't noticed that he'd removed his waistcoat and cravat. But there was no missing it now.

He'd pulled his handkerchief from his face and held it wadded in one hand. He'd rolled back his sleeves to his elbows, baring muscular forearms browned by the sun. His snowy shirt—which wasn't quite so snowy any longer—was open at the throat, and she spied the shadow of his dark chest hair in the V-shape opening before the linen thwarted her view. The material was limp and wrinkled from his exertions and clung to his form in a way that brought a feminine sigh of appreciation to her lips.

Raising one hand, he combed his fingers through his dark hair, which, like his skin, glistened from his exertions. He then settled his hands on his hips, drawing Sarah's avid gaze downward. His spread fingers rested on dirt-streaked fawn breeches, as if pointing to his fascinating groin.

Heat that had nothing to do with the sun scorched her as she vividly recalled what he looked like without his breeches. And the wickedly delicious sensation of his hard flesh pressing against the apex of her thighs.

He sneezed, then asked, "Does that meet with your approval, Sarah?"

Approval? Her gaze snapped up to his. His blank expression made it impossible to tell if she'd been caught staring, but she strongly suspected she had been. Good lord, she could feel the hot blotches of embarrassment creeping up her neck. She had no idea what he was asking that met with her approval, but since everything she could see looked fine, she said, "Yes, that's . . . perfect."

With a nod, he set down his shovel then snatched up the knapsack. "There's a lake on the property—lots of trees and shade." He sneezed again. "And no roses. It's only about a ten minute walk. Would you like to eat there?"

Food. Of course. "That sounds lovely."

"Excellent." He let loose with another pair of sneezes, then indicated with his hand a path heading away from the rose garden.

With Danforth leading the way, he fell into step beside her, and in less than a minute he exhaled an audible sigh of relief. "Much better." She felt the weight of his stare but resolutely kept her gaze fixed on Danforth and the path ahead. If she were to look at him, she feared she'd lose her concentration. No doubt walk into a tree and render herself unconscious.

"Are you all right?" he asked.

Botheration, she must look even worse than she thought. "Yes, I'm fine. And you?"

"Fine, although a bit warm. The shade here along the path is most welcome."

It was indeed. She'd felt as if she were melting when she looked at him, although that had nothing to do with the bright sunshine. "I'm sorry our search wasn't successful," she said.

"As am I." He was silent for several seconds then said, "Thank you for your help. I enjoyed your company."

"I wasn't much company. We barely spoke."

"Conversation wasn't necessary. It was just nice not to be out there alone."

An image of him as she'd seen him that first night, returning in the rain with his shovel, flashed through her brain. With her mind filled with the story of Frankenstein at the time, she thought he looked guilty. But now, upon reflection, she realized he'd looked . . . dejected. Lonely. She knew all too well what lonely felt like.

Several minutes later the path ended at a clearing, in the center of which a large oval lake glistened, its dark blue surface glass smooth except for a pair of regal white swans floating near the shore. Danforth took one look at the swans and bounded toward the water as if he were shot from a catapult. Sarah couldn't help but laugh at the dog's enthusiastic splashing and barking as he dashed into the lake. With disdainful squawks of protest, the swans flapped their white wings, skimming the surface to resettle on the far end of water. Clearly satisfied that he'd rousted the intruders, Danforth left the water and trotted back toward them.

"I should warn you," Lord Langston said, "that Danforth will—"

His words were cut off when Danforth gave his large body a vigorous, all-over doggie shake. When he finished, Sarah turned toward Lord Langston and struggled not to laugh at the drips of water dotting his face.

"Danforth will shower us with lake water?" she provided in her most helpful fashion.

He wiped his wet face with his wet arm and glared at his wet dog. "Yes."

"Thank you for the warning."

He turned back toward her. "Does your dog do that?"

Sarah couldn't help but laugh. "Every chance she gets.

Get Sarah Wet is Desdemona's favorite game." She leaned down and ruffled Danforth's scruff, much to the dog's delight. "Oh, you think you're very funny, don't you?" she asked him.

For an answer, Danforth barked twice, then streaked back toward the lake.

Lord Langston shook his head. "You realize he took that as encouragement and we're going to be on the receiving end of another dousing."

Sarah grinned. "I don't mind. Indeed, the cool water feels good after the hot sun."

"You wore your bonnet today," he said. "I thought you preferred to garden without it."

She lifted one hand to touch the wide brim she'd chosen specifically to help shield him from her view. "Normally I do, but for once I thought I'd heed my mother's admonishments. Bad enough that I'm dirty and smelly and now doused with doggie lake water. If I also had a sunburned face, Danforth would try to bury me in the woods."

"Doubtful." He lowered his voice to a conspiratorial whisper. "He'd merely attempt to drown you with . . . what did you call it? Doggie lake water. Brace yourself. Here he comes."

Seconds later Danforth skidded to a halt in front of them and once again gave himself a mighty shake.

"Can dogs chortle?" Lord Langston asked in a dark voice, once again mopping his face while glaring at Danforth's retreating rear end as the dog dashed back toward the water. "Because I believe I heard that beast *chortle*. With evil glee."

"Actually, I think it was more of a snicker than a chortle."

He heaved an exaggerated sigh, and Sarah had to press

her lips together to keep from laughing. "I used to swim in this lake as a boy, you know."

"And now look at you. You don't even need to jump in. Danforth brings the lake to you."

"Ah, yes. I am a lucky man."

After Danforth treated them to a third dousing then raced back toward the lake, Sarah asked, "Does he ever get tired?"

"Oh, yes. Around midnight usually." He held out a wet, non-too-clean, rumpled square of linen. "May I offer you my handkerchief?"

She extracted a wet, non-too-clean, rumpled bit of lace-trimmed cotton from the pocket of her gown and held it out to him and grinned. "May I offer you mine?"

He arranged his features into an exaggerated stern frown. "Why Miss Moorehouse, are you insinuating that I'm not looking my best?"

She raised her chin and gave an injured sniff. "Why Lord Langston, are *you* insinuating I don't look—"

Her words were cut off by another spray of lake water courtesy of Danforth. After he stopped shaking, he turned in a circle, barked twice, then dashed off toward a nearby copse of trees.

"He just told us he's off to chase some wildlife," Lord Langston said. "He won't expect us to wait lunch for him, but he'll be highly insulted if we don't save him some." He inclined his head toward the lake. "Would you care to join me for a bit of hand washing?"

"Absolutely, although I'm afraid more than my hands require washing after this outing."

"Not at all. You look fresh as a daisy."

She burst out laughing. "Yes, a daisy that's been trod upon, doused with water, and speckled with dirt."

Crouching at the edge of the water, she dipped her handkerchief and used it to refresh herself as best she could, noting from the corner of her eyes that Lord Langston simply cupped his hands and splashed water onto his arms, face, and neck. When he stood, she arose, then stilled as he reached up and pushed back his damp hair with his hands, in just the same way he had when he'd risen from his bath.

An image of him gloriously naked and wet slammed into her mind, heating her to the point where she felt certain steam must be rising from her moist clothes. Her handkerchief fell from her fingers, landing in a wet plot on the toe of her boot.

They both bent at the same time and bumped heads.

"Ouch," they said in unison, both rising, both holding a hand to their foreheads.

"I'm sorry," he said. "Are you all right?"

No. And it's entirely your fault. "Yes, thank you. Are you?"

"I'm fine." He held out her handkerchief. "Your handkerchief, however, has seen better days."

Taking extra care not to touch him, she reached for the wet cotton square and murmured, "Thank you."

"You're welcome." One corner of his mouth lifted. "You've been a remarkably good sport about all this. You haven't uttered even one complaint."

"That is only because you've promised to feed me, and I don't want to jeopardize my chances of a meal. After I've eaten, I'll complain all you like."

"And I'll nod sympathetically and pretend to listen, as a perfect host should. Shall we?" He extended his arm with a flourish, his eyes dancing with mischief. She hadn't planned on touching him, but given the obvious playfulness of the gesture, she felt churlish to refuse.

Resting her hand lightly on his forearm, she pretended she was touching a piece of wood. There. See? She could do this. Spend time with him in a strictly platonic way. Enjoy his company, his conversation, the way ordinary friends did. Even touch his arm. Everything was going perfectly.

They picked up her satchel and his knapsack and set up their casual picnic underneath a huge willow, on top of a blanket he pulled from the top of the knapsack.

"Let's see," he said, pulling the wrappings off each bundle as he removed them. "We have hard-boiled eggs, ham, cheese, chicken legs, meat pies, asparagus, bread, cider, and strawberry tarts."

"That's good for me," Sarah said with an approving nod that sent her glasses sliding downward. "What did your cook pack for *you*?"

"A woman with a hearty appetite, I see."

"Most assuredly. Especially after two hours of digging and a doggie lake bath."

He shot her a mock reproachful look. "I thought you weren't going to complain until *after* you ate."

"Sorry. I forgot myself. As for the food, a bit of everything sounds perfect. Would you like me to serve?"

"Will I end up with anything on my plate?"

"Probably. Maybe."

He waggled his brows. "Hmmm. Methinks you merely want to get your hands on my chicken legs."

She smothered a laugh and gave an injured sniff. "Certainly not. It's your strawberry tarts I'm after."

While he poured the cider, Sarah prepared two heaping plates. After handing him his serving, she sat next to him so they both faced the lake, making certain to keep a respectable distance between them. There. See? She could do this. Sit next to him and watch the water and enjoy a meal.

They ate in silence for several minutes, both looking at the lake, and she simply enjoyed the beautiful day and the lovely setting. Birds trilled and ribbons of sunlight winked through the rustling leaves, glittering on the calm water.

"Do you come to this lake often?" she asked, keeping her gaze steadfastly on the glasslike surface.

"Nearly every day. I either walk here or ride. It's my favorite spot on the estate. I find the water very peaceful."

"I can see why. It's . . . perfect. What do you do out here every day?"

"Sometimes I swim, sometimes I skip rocks, sometimes just sit under this tree. The trunk of this willow has a flat part that is quite comfortable. Some days I bring a book, other days I only bring my thoughts." From the corner of her eye she saw him turn toward her. "Do you have a lake at your home?"

"No. If I did, I'd be torn as to where to spend my time—at the lake or in the garden."

"You could always plant a garden near the lake."

She allowed herself to turn toward him. Alternating ribbons of golden sunlight and dusky shadows trickled between the willow's slender leaves, painting him with an intriguing palate her artistic eye immediately longed to capture. His hazel eyes rested on her, looking more green than blue, most likely due to the verdant foliage surrounding him. Dear God, she wasn't certain if the word beautiful should be used to describe a man, but it certainly summed up *this* man.

Although her breath hitched under the impact of his

regard, she was quite proud that she didn't drop the piece of cheese she held. There. See? She could do this. Look into his eyes and remain coherent and not drop her cheese.

"A garden by the lake," she murmured. "That would solve the problem." After taking a sip of cider, she asked, "What sort of books do you like to read?"

"All sorts. I recently reread *Paradise Lost* and am mulling over what to start on next. Perhaps you have a recommendation? I understand you're a member of the Ladies Literary Society of London."

Sarah nearly spewed a mouthful of cider. After swallowing and coughing several times, she asked, "How do you know about that?"

"Lady Julianne mentioned it at dinner last night. So tell me, what does a ladies' literary society do?"

Good heavens. She could feel blotches creeping up her chest. "We, um, choose books to read and then discuss them."

"What sort of books?"

The blotches reached her neck. Thank goodness she hadn't removed her bonnet. At least the brim offered her some protection should the blotches creep higher. Returning her attention toward the lake, she said, "Literary works. Would you care for another egg?"

"No, thank you."

She felt the weight of his stare and kept her own gaze focused straight ahead on the water. "Where do you suppose Danforth is?" she asked.

"Why are you changing the subject?"

"What subject?"

"The Ladies Literary Society of London."

"Perhaps you missed the word 'ladies.'"

"Which would obviously prevent me from being a member, but surely doesn't prevent you from discussing it with me."

"Are you a lady?"

"No."

"Are we in London?"

"No."

"Do you see any literary tomes upon this blanket?"

"No."

"I believe that's enough said."

"Hmmm. The lady doth protest too much, methinks."

She hoisted her chin. "As a member of the Ladies Literary Society of London, I am well acquainted with *Hamlet,* my lord. Your quote from act two, scene three, however, is in error in this case."

"Is it? I wonder . . ."

She applied her attention to her hard-boiled egg, but found it difficult to concentrate knowing he was staring at her.

Then he chuckled. "Ah. I believe I understand. You ladies aren't reading literary works at all, are you?"

Botheration. The man was too clever by half. Before she could even think of an answer, he continued, "So what are you reading? Something salacious and scandalous, I'll wager. Something that would send your mamas racing for the hartshorn."

Adopting her most prim tone, she said, "I'm certain I don't know what you're talking about."

"Come now, Sarah. You've piqued my curiosity."

"Didn't we at some point determine that curiosity killed the cat?"

"Yes. And immediately thereafter determined that we weren't cats."

Memories flooded her and her heart skipped. Of course. And then he'd kissed her. And she hadn't been the same since that moment.

"Tell me," he urged softly.

"I've nothing to tell."

"If you do, I'll tell you something about me that no one else knows."

Unable to stop herself, she turned toward him, noting the teasing challenge in his eyes. Warning bells rang in her brain, reminding her that it was that same teasing challenge that had convinced her to allow him to watch her bathe. And look at the havoc *that* had wreaked.

Yes. It was the most unforgettable experience of your life.

True. Which was not good, as she had to forget about it. And thinking about it now, while she was alone with him, was a particularly poor idea.

And while she was sure she could accomplish the task of forgetting about her bath—most likely—now the dratted man had found another way to tempt her. A way she knew she'd never be able to resist. She moistened her lips. "A secret for a secret?"

His gaze flicked down to her mouth. "Yes. Sounds like a fair trade to me. Would I have your word that what I tell you will not leave this shady spot?"

"Of course." The words popped out before she could stop them. "Would I have your word?"

He laid his hand over his heart. "On my honor, your secret would be safe with me."

After a quick mental debate, she decided no harm could come from telling him, especially as he'd given his word. And the prospect of hearing his secret was simply too tantalizing to pass up. There. See? She could do this.

Swap silly secrets just as she would with any of her other friends.

"Very well. I admit that the Ladies Literary Society focuses on . . . less traditional works."

"Such as?"

"Well, we've only recently formed and therefore have thus far only read one book."

"Which I take it wasn't authored by Shakespeare."

"Correct. We read *Frankenstein*."

Keen interest flared in his eyes. *"The Modern Prometheus,"* he murmured.

"Have you read it?"

"I have. It's an interesting choice for your ladies' group, one which would understandably raise eyebrows, given the grisly nature of the story and the scandalous behavior of the author."

"Which is precisely why we named ourselves as we did—to avoid those raised eyebrows."

He nodded thoughtfully. "I'd wager that you had a strong reaction to the book."

"Why do you say that?"

"Because you are one of the most compassionate people I've ever met. I've no doubt you'd describe Dr. Frankenstein as a nincompoop. And I easily imagine that the plight of the monster tugged on your soft heart."

An odd sensation ran through her at his eerily accurate assessment, which, while correct, still sounded somewhat insulting. She raised her chin. "Dr. Frankenstein created a being that he utterly rejected solely because of its appearance. To call him a nincompoop is to actually insult all the other nincompoops. And if feeling sympathy for a poor, abused, unloved creature makes me softhearted, then so be it."

"It does indeed make you softhearted—and I mean that in the most complimentary way. I've no doubt that if *you'd* come across the monster, his entire life would have been different. You'd have accepted him, unconditionally. Helped him. Taken him under your wing and shown him the kindness he so desperately wanted and needed."

His words stilled her. "How do you know that? Perhaps I would have been horrified by his frightening size and visage."

"No. You would have taken his ugly, gigantic hand in yours, led him to your garden, where you would have taught him the finer points of tortlingers and straff wort, and conversed with him as if he weren't different in any way. You would have befriended him and helped him, just as you've befriended and helped the Dutton sisters and Martha Browne."

She blinked and stared. "How do you know about the Duttons and Martha?"

"Your sister spoke of them to Lord Surbrooke, who in turn mentioned them to me. It is very kind of you to help them as you do."

"They're my friends. It has nothing to do with kindness."

"It has everything to do with kindness. With decency and generosity. Loyalty and compassion. You possess all those traits, Sarah."

"Anyone would do those things—"

"No, they wouldn't. And they don't. Some people do, people like you, and we should all be grateful for that. But there is a lot of selfishness in the world. Don't fool yourself into thinking that your soft heart isn't a very special and very rare gift."

Pleased warmth suffused her at his words, and a heated

blush rushed into her cheeks. "I . . . I don't know what to say."

He shot her a reproachful look. "I believe we already had a lesson on what to say when one is given a compliment."

Yes. She remembered. Vividly. It was when they'd had tea on the terrace, and he told her she was a talented artist. She recalled her pleasure at his words. Words spoken before she knew he had to marry within the next few weeks. Marry an heiress. Who would most likely turn out to be Julianne.

She swallowed then nodded. "In that case, thank you."

"You're welcome."

She found herself staring at him, trapped by his gaze, unable to look away. Heat suffused her with smothering awareness and an almost painful yearning to touch him. A suffocating desire for him to touch her. And a flood of useless wishes that all revolved around her suddenly turning into an heiress.

Dear God, perhaps she *couldn't* do this. Couldn't be alone with him and pretend she didn't want and need. Didn't feel all the desires and emotions storming through her.

But since her only alternative was to jump up and run down the path, she forced herself to look at the water. And to say something to dispel the sudden tension she felt.

Bending her knees, she wrapped her arms tightly around her calves. "I've shared my secret. Now it is your turn."

"Yes, I suppose it is. Promise you won't laugh?"

"I promise." *I won't laugh. I won't touch. I won't indulge in useless fantasies of things that can never be.*

"Very well. When I was a lad of ten, I dreamed, as I suppose many lads do, of being a pirate. Sailing the mighty seas, captaining my own ship, partaking of swash-buckling sword fights, looting exotic ports of call."

Surprised and amused, she turned toward him. She wasn't certain what she'd expected him to say, but certainly she hadn't anticipated anything so fanciful. *"Looting?"*

He looked skyward with an expression of pure mascu-line exasperation. "Of course *looting*. How else do you think pirates get their booty? I wanted to be a pirate, not a philanthropist."

A smile tugged at her lips. "Naturally. Continue."

"I realized that it unfortunately would be a number of years before I was old enough to be a pirate, but being not only determined but also impatient, I decided to be the pirate of Langston Manor, and that this lake," he extended his arm to encompass the water, "would be my mighty sea.

"I named myself Blackguard and spent that entire sum-mer secretly building a pirate ship. I kept it hidden in that thicket." He nodded his chin toward an overgrown area near a copse of elms.

"How large was this fine ship?" Sarah asked.

"Not much bigger than I was. I suppose *some* would have called it a rowboat, but only someone completely lacking in imagination."

She bit the insides of her cheeks to keep from smiling. "I see. Did you finish the boat?"

"Ship," he corrected in a very serious voice. "Yes, I did. I even carved a mermaid figure for the prow. She didn't look much like a mermaid—I wasn't much of a carver and I accidentally hacked off her tail. And her head. But

what was left of her proudly rode on the bow."

He turned to gaze upon the water. After stretching out his legs, he leaned back on his forearms and continued, "On the day of the maiden voyage, I dressed in my finest pirate wear and launched *Blackguard's Booty*. Seeing her bob on the surface was my finest hour. The culmination of months of planning and secret work. I'd rowed nearly to the center of the mighty sea when my fine ship suddenly sprung a leak. Being a good captain, I'd come prepared for just such an emergency in the form of a bucket. I began bailing, but seconds later *Blackguard's Booty* sprung another leak. Then another. And another."

He turned back to her. "I can tell by your expression that you have an idea where this story is headed."

She had to fight to maintain a straight face. "To the bottom of the lake?"

He blew out a long sigh. "I'm afraid you're correct. In spite of my valiant bailing efforts, it quickly became apparent that the battle was lost. Therefore I stood, saluted, and like generations of pirate captains before me, went down with my ship."

"Very brave and noble of you," she said in her most grave tone.

He shrugged. "It was the least I could do."

"So *Blackguard's Booty* . . . ?"

"Remains at the bottom of the lake. Along with my spectacles, which I lost somewhere between leaks ten and eleven. My father was none too pleased when I arrived home with my finest breeches and jacket ruined and my glasses gone."

"What did you tell him?"

"That I'd suffered a mishap at the lake. Which was perfectly true."

"You didn't tell him of this boyhood desire to loot and swashbuckle?"

"I've never told anyone." He shot her a frown. "You'll recall your promise not to laugh."

"I'm not laughing," she said, trying her best not to. "Although I must admit it's difficult when I can so vividly picture you standing in your leaky rowboat, saluting, with ever-rising water lapping around your waist."

"Ship," he corrected with an injured sniff.

"Clearly you changed your mind about becoming a pirate."

"Which is good. Turns out I wasn't much of a pirate. Or a boatbuilder."

"'Tis fortunate you knew how to swim."

"Yes. But other than that, the entire episode was a total failure."

"Oh, but it wasn't. Just because your boat didn't prove seaworthy doesn't take away from your success."

"Success?" He chuckled. "Madame, you clearly missed the part of the story where I went down with my ship."

"I did nothing of the sort. Your success was in your determination to build a boat. Your perseverance in completing it. Most people wouldn't have even attempted such a project, let alone seen it to fruition. And the crowning achievement of your success was your final noble gesture of seeing it through to the end."

He nodded slowly, then said, "As captain of the ill-fated *Blackguard's Booty*, I thank you for your kind words. If only you'd been around twenty years ago, my pride might have recovered more quickly."

"I doubt it. Twenty years ago I would have laughed myself into a seizure at the sight of Blackguard going down with his rowboat." She grinned, then in her best underwater imitation, added, *"Glub glub glub."*

His lips twitched, but then he quickly narrowed his eyes. "You're laughing."

"I'm not. I'm smiling."

He smiled back, a slow smile that reached all the way to his eyes and stole her breath. Filled her once again with the overwhelming awareness of him that she'd managed to push aside during his tale. "We're now even," he said.

"Yes." Damnation, she sounded as breathless as she felt. Desperate for something to say, she blurted out, "Where do you suppose Danforth is? I'd hoped to work on his sketch before we return to the rose garden."

"You intend to return to the garden with me? I thought perhaps two hours of digging would be exertion enough for you for one day."

Her inner voice urged her to claim fatigue. But as she'd been doing frequently of late, she ignored the voice. "I'm not the delicate hothouse bloom you clearly mistake me for, my lord. I assure you I'm up for the task. Unless you'd prefer to dig alone."

He shook his head, his gaze steady on hers. "No, Sarah. I'd prefer to be with you."

His softly spoken words seemed to hang in the air between them. and she realized with a profound sense of sadness that that would be her preference as well—and not merely in regards to digging in the garden.

And she was once again forcefully reminded of the heartbreaking uselessness of wanting things she could not have.

Chapter 14

One week after Sarah's first digging expedition, the Ladies Literary Society of London gathered at midnight in her bedchamber. The storm that had started several hours earlier continued unabated, rain and wind rattling the windowpanes. While Sarah was delighted to spend this time with her sister and friends, part of her yearned for what the storm had prevented—another late night digging expedition in the rose garden with Lord Langston. The same sort they'd engaged in every night for the past week.

Because Lord Langston needed to spend the daytime and evening hours entertaining his guests, by mutual agreement they, along with Danforth, had spent several hours each night digging trenches in the acres of rose garden after everyone had retired. And tonight, because of the storm, there'd be no digging. Which meant there'd be no Lord Langston. Which, her common sense insisted, was good. And if her heart disagreed, well, that was simply too bad. With each unsuccessful outing bringing their search closer to failure, she had committed herself to listening to her common sense, and for the past week she'd been successful—in all her deeds, if not always in all her thoughts.

Now, dressed in their night rails and robes, the Ladies Literary Society sat on Sarah's bed, legs tucked beneath them. Franklin, his lumpy head finally sewed on, albeit in a slightly crooked manner, sat propped against the headboard. Several days ago, during a Literary Society meeting held in the afternoon while the gentlemen went hunting, Sarah had drawn Franklin a face, his features decided upon by secret ballot. Each Literary Lady cast her votes for which gentleman possessed the best eyes, nose, mouth, and jaw. Based on the results, Franklin possessed Lord Langston's eyes, Lord Berwick's nose, Mr. Jennsen's mouth, and Lord Surbrooke's jaw.

"It's positively eerie how much Franklin looks like a combination of all the gentlemen," Emily said.

"Except for the lumpy head," said Julianne. "And I don't believe any of the gentlemen possess one leg that is fatter than the other."

"I also doubt any of them—or any man, for that matter —is quite as . . . *endowed* as our Franklin," Carolyn said.

Muted laughter met her comment, and an image of Lord Langston rising from the bath materialized in Sarah's mind. He came close.

"You did a wonderful job on the face, Sarah," Carolyn said with a smile.

She firmly blinked away the unsettling image. "Thank you. And now I hereby call our meeting officially to order. Does anyone have any comments?"

"I'd just like to point out," Julianne said, "that this is the exact sort of stormy night during which Dr. Frankenstein created his monster." She hugged her arms around herself and shot an apprehensive glance toward the dark, rain-streaked windows.

"So the atmosphere is perfect," Sarah said in a soothing tone, knowing Julianne was frightened by storms. "And that's all it is—atmosphere."

"It's also the sort of night when that poor Mr. Willstone was murdered," Julianne added. "Mother keeps harping about a crazed killer on the loose."

"There's been no sign of any strangers lurking about," Carolyn said, patting Julianne's hand. "Mr. Willstone was wandering about alone in the middle of the night. We're surrounded by an entire household to protect us."

"Yes, so let us speak of less distressing things," said Emily. "I know that we agreed we'd bestowed our Perfect Man with every attribute, but given that Franklin sits here among us, I think there's one more thing we should add to our list of things the Perfect Man should do."

"What is it?" Sarah asked.

"The Perfect Man must not only be willing to sit in a room filled with gossiping women and listen politely, but he must also be the soul of discretion." Emily waggled her brows. "Because Franklin is about to hear an earful."

"Impossible—he has no ears," Carolyn quipped.

Their laughter dispelled the gloomy mood. Julianne scooted closer to Emily and asked, "What's the gossip? Tell, tell."

"Don't ask me," Emily said, treating them all to her most innocent expression. "Ask Sarah."

Sarah suddenly felt the weight of three pairs of curious eyes gazing upon her, and her stomach dropped. Good lord, had Emily somehow found out about her late night digging excursions?

"Me?" she asked, horrified that the word sounded like a guilty squeak.

"Yes, you," Emily said, giving her arm a playful push. She leaned closer toward the center of the square they formed and whispered loudly, "Sarah has made a conquest."

Good God. She *did* know. "It's not what you think—"

"Of course it is," Emily said. "'Tis obvious Mr. Jennsen likes you."

For several seconds she sat with her mouth open, midword. Then she shook off her surprise and frowned. "Mr. Jennsen?"

Emily looked toward the ceiling. "Don't tell me you haven't noticed."

Before she could reply, Carolyn said, "I've noticed his partiality toward you as well, Sarah."

"As have I," added Julianne.

A heated flush suffused Sarah, and she knew the blotches of embarrassment were on their way. "He has been kind and charming to all of us."

"Yes," Carolyn agreed, "but especially to you." A frown puckered her brow. "Which rather worries me. He *seems* a decent man, but there is something about him that is, well, rather . . . dark. And secretive."

"No doubt his American upbringing," Julianne said. "Which is why he hasn't been fully accepted into Society."

"That and he's in *trade*," Emily said with a sniff. "Personally, I think he's a nincompoop. Lording his wealth over everyone, casting his jaded eye toward our Sarah. Why, he's nothing more than a common colonial. He presents himself as a diamond, but he is nothing more than a paste gem."

Surprised by Emily's comments, Sarah felt driven to defend the man. "I've not found anything offensive about Mr. Jennsen," she said. "In fact, he's been very kind to me."

"Perhaps not *offensive*," said Emily, "but I do think that beneath his perfectly tailored clothing lurks a man who is a bit vulgar and more than a bit uncivilized. Which makes him not good enough for our Sarah. But what about the other gentlemen? Personally, I find both Lord Langston and Lord Berwick handsome."

"True," said Julianne, "but Lord Berwick is more personable. Lord Langston is rather . . . somber. And he doesn't seem to be at all the passionate sort." She heaved a wistful sigh. "I've always dreamed of a darkly passionate suitor."

"Perhaps he'd surprise you." The words popped out of Sarah's mouth before she could stop them, and she barely refrained from clapping her hand over her runaway mouth. Good lord, next she'd be telling them all precisely how passionate Lord Langston could be. But Julianne would have to find that out for herself—and that was something Sarah simply couldn't think about.

Emily nodded. "Sarah's right—perhaps he'd surprise you. And Lord Langston is the one rumored to be looking for a wife," she added with an arch look in Julianne's direction. "You're the one he particularly asked to partner with him in whist."

Even in the dim light Sarah could see Julianne's blush, and a rush of guilt and discomfort at the topic suffused her. Anxious to move the conversation away from Lord Langston, she said, "What about Lord Surbrooke?"

"He's another one with secrets, I think," said Emily.

"And perhaps some sadness," Sarah said. "Even when he laughs, happiness never quite shows in his eyes. And Lord Berwick?"

"Handsome," said Julianne.

"Charming," added Emily.

"Polished, but rather shallow, I think," said Carolyn. "I sat next to him at dinner this evening and overheard his conversation with Lord Thurston, who sat across from us, about how incompetent servants can be. Lord Berwick mentioned that he was missing a pair of boots—a pair his valet swears he packed, but obviously didn't. His lordship didn't notice the boots' absence until the gentlemen went hunting, as they were the pair he likes to wear for such outings."

"Oh, dear, I hope our little prank hasn't caused difficulties for Lord Berwick's valet," said Sarah, her gaze shifting to Franklin. "I suppose we should think about dismantling our Perfect Man and returning the articles of clothing."

"I can't bear to think of pulling him apart tonight," Julianne protested. "This is his first meeting with us since gaining his face and having his head sewn on."

"True," Sarah agreed. "Very well, we'll wait a day or so to dismantle him. Now, let's continue our assessments. What of Lords Thurston and Hartley?"

"Witty and nice, and nice but boring," said Carolyn, ticking off her vote for each gentleman on her fingers.

"Agreed," said Emily and Sarah together.

"Yes," said Julianne, "although they both strike me as rather . . . lecherous." She gave an exaggerated shudder. "Plus, Lord Thurston has horrid breath."

"Ewwwww!" they all said in unison, then collapsed into giggles. Emily laughed so hard she flopped onto her back. Franklin, thrown off balance, promptly tilted over on top of her.

"Speaking of lecherous," Carolyn said with a laugh, reaching out to reseat Franklin. "The Perfect Man would *never* behave in such an ungentlemanly way. Perhaps Franklin isn't so perfect after all."

Sarah chuckled with the others, but an image rose in

her mind, of Lord Langston, holding out his hands to her as she sat in the bathtub. Of him kissing her while he caressed her wet, naked body. Most assuredly not the sort of behavior that would be considered gentlemanly.

Yet in spite of that, to her, he was still perfect.

Unfortunately.

Matthew stood at his bedchamber window and stared out into the darkness. Rain lashed against the glass panes, accompanied by howling gusts of wind, and he cursed the fates that had brought the inclement weather. If not for this bloody storm, he'd right now be in the rose garden digging trenches in the moonlight—certainly not his favorite place to be or his favorite thing to do. But they'd taken on new meaning and enjoyment over the past week because of his companion.

Sarah.

He closed his eyes and blew out a long sigh. This past week following that first afternoon digging expedition with Sarah had simultaneously proven both the most enjoyable and the most frustrating he'd ever known. But tonight, because of the storm, there'd be no digging. Which meant there'd be no Sarah.

Which meant there'd be no companionship. No moonlit walk to the lake, as they'd done after each unsuccessful digging expedition. No sharing stories of childhood adventures and mishaps. No skipping stones along the water's glasslike surface. No tossing sticks for Danforth to fetch. No frog catching, as they'd indulged in last evening. No smiles. No laughter. No easing of the knot of loneliness that had gripped him so tightly for so long.

No profound sense of happiness.

Of course, it also meant he was spared the torture of being close to her yet not able to touch her. The torment of inhaling the seductive scent of lavender that clung to her soft skin and gloriously unruly hair. The agony of clenching his teeth every time their shoulders or fingers accidentally brushed. The frustration of wanting her so damn badly yet having to pretend that he felt nothing warmer for her than tepid friendship.

It had indeed been a week of torturous contentment.

Last night, after watching her enter her bedchamber, he'd gone to his room and paced until dawn, unable to sleep, unable to erase her from his mind. With failure to find the money looming ever larger, he'd told himself that surely after spending more time with her, he'd discover aspects of her nature he didn't like. Quirks that annoyed him. Personality traits that he didn't admire.

But now, a week later, he could only laugh at the folly of that belief. The more time he spent with her, the more he wanted to spend with her. For all his hope of finding something about her he didn't like, their excursions only served to reinforce all the things he already liked and admired about her. Not only that, but he also discovered new aspects of her, all of which greatly appealed to him.

She was fiercely determined and optimistic, refusing to allow him to give up hope that the money would be found. And she was patient and tireless, never once complaining about the strenuous work or the blisters that formed on her hands. She hummed while she worked, a habit that made him smile because she was clearly tone deaf—a flaw he should have found irritating but instead found utterly endearing.

Highly concerned for their safety, he'd brought his knives each night, and a pistol as well, but not once had he sensed any threats or anyone watching them, nor had the ever alert Danforth. If someone had previously been watching him, it seemed clear they'd abandoned the endeavor. And just this evening he'd heard through the servant gossip grapevine that Elizabeth Willstone's brother Billy Smythe had abruptly left Upper Fladersham, fueling speculation that he was responsible for Tom's death. A very sad outcome for the Willstone family, but a huge relief, as far as his own circumstances were concerned.

He'd left Sarah at her bedchamber door each night around three A.M., his heart heavy with a sense of loss at departing her company. He'd then spent each day filled with impatient anticipation for their nightly sojourn into the garden.

Yet each digging expedition that brought them closer to completing their search of the rose garden also brought them closer to failure. As much as he didn't want to acknowledge that fact, in his heart he knew it was only a matter of time. He estimated that they would finish within the next five nights—time that he could have shortened, but doing so would then shorten the time he spent with Sarah, and he craved those hours alone with her too fiercely to give them up any sooner than necessary.

So, five nights remained. At which point there'd be nothing left to search. And no further hope that he'd find the windfall his father claimed to have left behind. No further hope he'd be free to marry whom he wanted.

That depressing thought had him opening his eyes and dragging his hands down his face. Turning away from the rain-splattered window, he paced across the room and sat heavily in the armchair set before the fire. Danforth, sprawled out on the hearth rug, rolled to his feet, padded over to him, then promptly sat on his boot. After Danforth shot him a questioning look that clearly indicated the beast knew all was not well, the dog plopped his massive head on Matthew's thigh and heaved a doggie sigh of commiseration.

"You said a mouthful," Matthew said, lightly scratching behind Danforth's ears. "You have no idea how lucky you are to be a dog."

Danforth licked his chops then glanced longingly at the door.

Matthew shook his head. "Not tonight, my friend. There will be no Sarah tonight."

Danforth's entire body seemed to droop at the news, a sentiment Matthew keenly understood.

No Sarah tonight. . .

The words echoed through his mind, filling him with an ache he couldn't name. An ache that only grew when he considered that in a mere five days from now, there'd be no Sarah *any* night. Ever. The house party would be over and she'd be gone from Langston Manor. He'd soon after be married—thus fulfilling his promise. To an heiress—to satisfy his responsibilities to his title.

An heiress . . . He leaned his head back to stare at the ceiling, and an image of the lovely Lady Julianne materialized in his mind. Over the past week, he'd made a concentrated effort to spend time with her, sitting next to her at several meals, partnering her in whist, inviting her for a turn around the garden, all under the watchful eye of her very unsubtle mother—not to mention the baleful glares of Hartley, Thurston, and Berwick, all of whom clearly much admired Lady Julianne.

With a groan, he lifted his head and stared at the dancing fire. From every aspect, a match between him and Lady Julianne would be perfect. She had the money he needed, he had the lofty title her family desired, and she possessed a most pleasant disposition. She was, in every way, perfect.

Yet the mere thought of marrying her brought on an unpleasant sensation akin to a cramp. No matter how he tried to picture himself sharing his life with her, the image simply wouldn't form in his mind.

And that's when the realization suddenly hit him. Smacked him so hard, he abruptly sat bolt upright.

Perfect though Lady Julianne may be, he simply *could not* marry her. *Would not* marry her. Not with this unquenchable desire for Sarah burning in his veins. Marrying one of Sarah's dearest friends would mean constant reminders of the woman he truly wanted, frequent visits, and he knew in his heart, in his soul, that he wouldn't be able to stand it. It was an untenable situation that would dishonor both him and Lady Julianne, a very decent young woman who deserved more than a man who lusted after her closest friend.

For his own sanity, when Sarah left his home he needed her to leave his life as well. He needed an heiress, but he'd simply have to look elsewhere. By virtue of her friendship with Sarah, Lady Julianne was no longer a viable candidate—indeed, she never truly had been—something he should have realized sooner. And surely would have if he hadn't been so distracted by his attraction to Sarah.

He exhaled a long sigh of relief. Now that he'd made the decision to cross Lady Julianne off his list of marriage candidates, it felt as if at least a portion of the crushing weight pressing on him was lifted. He'd received letters today from Lady Prudence Whipple's and Miss Jane Carlson's households stating that neither would be able to join the house party, as they were both traveling on the continent. But London was littered with wealthy young women anxious to marry a title. In spite of time being tight, the fact that he was young and not hideous would ensure him success.

However, that meant that a trip to London was now necessary, and time was indeed short. His year was up in only three weeks. Which meant that he had to accelerate the digging pace to complete the search. After a quick mental calculation, he decided they could finish in the next three nights, rather than five. Which meant only three more nights with Sarah, a realization that felt like a knife twisting in his gut. And, barring an unlikely but still hoped for success, he'd then leave immediately for London.

To find a bride.

Who wasn't Sarah.

Bloody hell, if only she were an heiress, all his problems would be solved. If only he hadn't made bloody deathbed promises that his honor demanded he keep. If only he hadn't inherited the bloody title and all the responsibilities—and crushing debts—that went along with it.

He dragged his hands through his hair. No point dwelling on if onlys. He knew what he had to do, and that was that.

Gently nudging Danforth's chin aside, he arose and made his way toward the decanters, where he poured himself a generous brandy. He tossed back a swallow, savoring the warmth against his tight, dry throat. His gaze fell upon his desk, and he instantly thought of the contents of the top drawer. They seemed to beckon him like a siren's call.

As if in a trance, he set down his snifter and walked

across the room. Slid open the top drawer. And withdrew the two drawings. Holding them in his hands, he studied the first one, which depicted Danforth sitting on the grass, his rump settled on what was obviously a man's black boot. His pet was so realistically drawn, Matthew could almost imagine him breathing. Could nearly feel the beast's weight upon his foot.

He carefully set the drawing on top of the desk then studied the second sketch. It portrayed him as a bespectacled boy dressed in pirate garb, saluting with a stoic expression while standing in a half-sunken rowboat set in the middle of a lake. A headless, tailless mermaid adorned the bow of the ship, along with the name of the ill-fated vessel: *Blackguard's Booty*. She'd captured the moment so vividly, so accurately, it was as if she'd been there.

Last night, after their digging expedition, she'd given him the rolled sketches tied with a ribbon. When he teasingly said it wasn't his birthday, she blushed and replied that it wasn't much of a present.

Oh, but how wrong she'd been. He'd stared at the drawings, much like he was doing now, speechless from the lump of emotion swelling his throat. They were . . . perfect. And unique. Just like the woman who'd made them for him.

He now stared at the sketch for several more seconds, then turned it over to read the brief inscription: *For Lord Langston, in memory of a perfect day.*

She'd signed her name, and he gently brushed his finger over her neat, precise signature, his imagination instantly recalling how it had felt to touch her soft skin. Something nudged his leg, and he blinked away the mental pictures of her that haunted him day and night and looked down. Danforth had joined him and was looking up at him with an expectant expression which he then shifted toward the door.

Matthew shook his head. "Sorry, old boy. As I said, it's just you and me tonight."

Danforth gave him what appeared to be a reproachful look. Then, in a flash, the dog nipped between his teeth the ends of the sketch Matthew had laid on the desk. Before Matthew could recover his surprise, the beast dashed for the door, the sketch flapping from his jaws.

It took Matthew several seconds to recover his surprise. Then he demanded in a sharp tone, "Stop."

Danforth did indeed stop. Directly in front of the door. But only long enough to lift one massive paw and employ the door opening trick Matthew had taught him. In a heartbeat the beast disappeared into the corridor.

"Bloody hell." Determined to rescue his sketch, Matthew took off at a dead run after his suddenly insane dog.

He entered the corridor and looked both ways. Danforth stood at the end of the long hallway, sketch dangling from his jaws, tail wagging as if this were some grand game and he was waiting for his master to join him and play.

"Come here," Matthew commanded in a quiet whisper, not wanting to rouse the household.

The normally obedient Danforth instead turned the corner and disappeared from view. Thoroughly aggravated, Matthew jogged down the corridor. When he turned the corner, he halted as if he'd walked into a wall. Danforth stood halfway down the hallway.

Directly in front of Sarah's bedchamber.

"Come here," he said in a whispered hiss. When Danforth didn't move, Matthew strode toward him. "If you've ruined my sketch, you'll never see another beef bone," he vowed. "Or another of Cook's biscuits. It'll be nothing but mush for you from now on."

Danforth didn't appear the least bit concerned about those threats to his dietary happiness. Indeed, he appeared not to be paying the slightest attention to Matthew. No, instead he lifted his paw, set it on the brass doorknob, and once again employed his favorite trick. Matthew broke into a run. The door swung open, and before Matthew could get close enough to stop him, Danforth—and his sketch—disappeared into the room.

Matthew skidded to a halt just outside the door. Bloody hell, what to do now? Her bedchamber . . . the one place on the entire planet he most wanted to be, but the one place he knew damn well he shouldn't venture anywhere near. She might be in the bath. Or in the process of undressing. Heat scorched him at the mere thought.

But . . . perhaps she was asleep. Why, she most likely already was! And he *had* to enter the room—he needed to rescue his sketch before Danforth's drool ruined it. In fact, it was his *duty* to retrieve the gift she'd given him. If she happened to be in the bath or undressing when she should be sound asleep, well, that was hardly his fault.

He drew a bracing breath, cracked his knuckles, then walked into the den of temptation, er, the bedchamber.

The instant he stepped over the threshold, his gaze flew to the hearth. No steaming tub was set before the fireplace filled with a wet and naked Sarah. Damn. Er, good. He then looked toward the bed. Empty. He scanned the room, his gaze halting on the sight of her, standing in front of the wardrobe. His heart executed the tumbling maneuver it seemed to perform whenever he laid eyes on her.

She wore a plain white night rail that covered her from her chin to her toes, a completely modest ensemble that should not have set his blood on fire. She held his sketch in her hands and gazed at him, her eyes huge with obvious surprise. Danforth, who appeared to be grinning, sat at her feet—actually, most likely *on* her feet, Matthew didn't doubt, rendering her unable to move. And it occurred to him that Danforth was one damn smart dog.

She flicked what looked like a nervous glance over her shoulder, then moistened her lips, a quick flick of pink that made Matthew clench his jaw. "Lord Langston . . . what are you doing here?"

He hated that she insisted upon the formality of his title. He wanted to hear her say his name, watch her lips press together then pucker softly as she said each syllable. And although he'd invited her to do so, she adamantly kept to his title.

"Danforth," he said, shaking his head. "That devil. He snatched the sketch you'd drawn of him from my desk, and before I could stop him, entered your room. As you know, he's quite adept at opening doors."

"Yes, I know." Her gaze again flicked over her shoulder toward the wardrobe behind her.

She looked and sounded nervous. Agitated. Clearly his presence had her rattled. Well, good. Why should he be the only one suffering?

"I apologize for Danforth's behavior."

"There's no need." She held out her hand. "Here's your sketch."

He didn't reach for it. "Thank you, but I believe he had a reason for bringing it to you. I think he wants you to write a brief message on the back, as you did for the other sketch." Lowering his voice to a conspiratorial whisper, he confided, "He was a trifle insulted that you hadn't. He told me so."

Her lips twitched and she looked down at the dog. "Is that true, Danforth?"

Danforth gazed up at her adoringly and made a pitiful whine. By God, that dog truly was smart. And a talented actor. If only he were human, he could walk the boards at the Lyceum Theater.

"I apologize for the oversight and will correct it immediately," she said in a properly contrite tone.

Matthew watched her ease her foot from beneath Danforth's rump then walk to the escritoire in the corner. In an effort not to stare at her while she busied herself with her task, he looked around the room, noting the stack of books on the bedside table. The robe laid neatly across the bottom of the bed. The hairbrush and comb on the dresser.

The pair of men's black boots visible beneath the partially closed wardrobe doors.

Matthew's gaze halted. Then narrowed. Then widened. He stared at the masculine footwear for several seconds in stunned disbelief. He then blinked several times, certain he was seeing things. But no, there were the boots, clearly visible from the ankles down. Which could only mean—

There was a man hiding in the wardrobe.

A man who, based on Sarah's agitation and looks over her shoulder, she was perfectly aware of being there. And as she'd shown no signs of fright, she clearly welcomed his presence.

He actually felt the blood drain from his head. Bloody hell, she was entertaining a man! A man who wasn't him. A cowardly bastard who'd obviously ducked into the wardrobe the instant the door opened, interrupting their tryst. A tryst that wasn't with him.

Anger, shock, outrage, jealousy, and—damn it— hurt all collided in him, crashing through him, leaving him dazed and battered. And darkly furious.

His first reaction was to march to the wardrobe, yank open the doors, and call out the bastard cowering behind the oak panels. But that could wait. Instead he walked to the escritoire with slow, measured steps. When he stood opposite Sarah, the desk between them, he planted his hands on the polished wood and leaned closer.

"Sarah?"

She looked up from her writing on the back of the sketch. "Yes, my lord?"

"What were you doing when Danforth came into the room?"

Something glinted in her eyes, and her gaze flicked to the wardrobe. Color bloomed on her cheeks. She might as well have had the word *guilty* branded across her forehead. "Nothing."

"Nothing? Come, come. You must have been doing *something*."

"No. Just . . . sitting by the fire."

He regarded her steadily, biting back the fury and hurt churning in his stomach. "You're a terrible liar," he said, proud of how calm he sounded.

She lifted her chin. There was no missing the annoyance that now sparkled in her eyes. "I've never aspired to be a good one. And I'm not lying. I was sitting by the fire."

By God, if he weren't so angry, he'd be tempted to applaud her show of bravado. Instead, he straightened and without a word stalked toward the wardrobe. He knew the exact instant his destination became clear to her because he heard her gasp and the sound of her hurrying after him.

"Lord Langston, what are you doing?"

He couldn't speak—pure rage had rendered him mute.

Never in his entire life had he felt such violence toward another person as he felt toward the whey-faced milk-sop skulking in the wardrobe. The bloody bastard she'd clearly invited into her bedchamber. A man who'd no doubt dared to touch her. Kiss her.

No doubt, his inner voice taunted in agreement. *Just as* you've *dared. So how are you any different from the bastard skulking in the wardrobe?*

His jaw clenched so hard he marveled that it didn't snap. A feral growl vibrated in his throat and he reached for brass wardrobe handles.

"Stop," she said from behind him. "Please don't—"

Her words were cut off when he yanked open the wardrobe doors, so hard one of the top hinges broke, leaving the panel yawning at a lopsided angle. Prepared to knock the bastard clear to France with his first punch, Matthew reached in and grabbed the man by the cravat and yanked him forward.

And found himself staring into his own eyes.

Or rather, a charcoal rendering of his own eyes, along with a nose, mouth, and jaw that weren't his yet seemed somehow familiar. All drawn upon a lumpy head. Which had no hair. Or ears.

Fist still drawn, he froze, except for his eyeballs, which skimmed down over this . . . whatever the bloody hell it was he held. It appeared to be a life-sized replica of a man. A man wearing . . . his shirt? A man who possessed no hands, one leg that was considerable fatter than the other, and sported what appeared to be an impossibly enormous erection.

He lowered his fist, then turned toward Sarah, who stood several feet away, her hands clapped to her cheeks, her face frozen with a wide-eyed expression of mortified horror.

"What the bloody hell is this?" he asked, giving the thing a hard shake. Apparently too hard a shake because there came a tearing sound. The lumpy head rolled off its shoulders and flopped onto the floor.

Sarah instantly bent to retrieve it, then straightened, holding the bundle protectively beneath her arm. Matthew's own eyes stared back at him, looking so lifelike he found himself touching his head to make certain it was still attached to his shoulders. When he raised his gaze back to hers, there seemed to be fire spewing from her eyeballs.

"Now look what you've done," she fumed. "Do you have any idea how long it took me to sew on his head so it wasn't crooked?"

He stared at her, nonplussed. A deafening silence swelled between them, until he broke it by saying, "I've no idea how long it took you—obviously not long enough. And now I have a question. What the bloody hell is going on? And what the bloody hell *is* this thing?" He again shook the headless, grotesque figure. "Where did it come from, why is it wearing my shirt, and why does its lumpy head bear a replica of my eyes?"

She raised her brows. "You said *a* question. That was five."

"All of which I want answered. Immediately."

She pressed her lips together and regarded him steadily for several heartbeats, then jerked her head in a tight nod, which sent her glasses sliding. After pushing them back up, she said, "Very well. There is nothing going on save that you saw fit to barge into my bedchamber unannounced and uninvited. This *thing*—as you so rudely called it—is a life-sized facsimile of a man. It came from the imaginations of the Ladies Literary Society. In addition to your shirt, he is also wearing Lord Thurston's cravat, Lord Surbrooke's breeches, and Lord Berwick's boots. He is doing so because if he weren't, not only would he have been impossible to stuff, he would have been naked."

She raised her chin, then continued, "His lumpy head bears, in addition to your eyes, Lord Berwick's nose, Mr. Jennsen's mouth, and Lord Surbrooke's jaw, as our intent was to fashion the Perfect Man." She made a sound that resembled an injured sniff. "Other than the eyes, there is no resemblance to you."

"I should hope not. I do have ears, you know. And hair. Not to mention a neck and—"

"I *meant*," she cut him off in a quelling tone while narrowing her eyes, "that he is the epitome of gentlemanly behavior. He wouldn't be so brash as to barge into a lady's bedchamber nor cast aspersions on the unfortunate shape of someone else's head."

"If his dog had run off with something of great importance to him and he was too lily-livered to do what was necessary in order to retrieve it, then he is the epitome of a nincompoop." He scrubbed his free hand over his face. "Good God, you've got me talking about this *thing* as if he's real. As if he has a name."

"As a matter of fact, he does have a name."

"Really? And what is his name? Lord Lumpy?" His gaze flicked down to the tremendous bulge in the front of the thing's breeches. "Earl Enormous? Sir Anatomically Impossible?"

"No." Reaching out, she snatched the thing's body away from him and clutched it against her bosom. After a brief hesitation during which he could almost hear her debating with herself, she said, "Allow me to introduce you to my very good friend Mr. Franklin N. Stein."

Chapter 15

Sarah stood perfectly still and watched myriad expressions flash across Lord Langston's face—disbelief, confusion, then finally, unmistakable annoyance. Well, good. Why should she be the only one who was annoyed?

"You made a facsimile of your friend Franklin?" A humorless sound passed his lips. "Why? Did you miss him that much?"

She tightened her hold on Franklin's headless body, gripping so hard that a puff of stuffing squeezed up from the gaping hole in his neck. She'd debated whether to tell Lord Langston the doll's name, whether to admit that Franklin didn't really exist, but in the end she simply couldn't lie to him. Besides, he'd find out eventually. Surely, after he and Julianne were married his new wife would share with him the story of how Franklin came into being. So there was no point in not admitting the truth now.

She cleared her throat. "I haven't missed Franklin at all."

He narrowed his eyes. "The fact that you're clutching a replica of him to your bosom indicates otherwise."

"I'm not *clutching,* I'm holding," she informed him, clutching Franklin even closer, "and only because he cannot stand on his own."

He shot an askance look at the front of Franklin's overstuffed breeches. "I can see why."

"And it would be impossible for me to miss him, as he doesn't exist."

"Doesn't exist?" His brows furrowed into a frown. "What nonsense is this? I saw your sketch of him. Perhaps you've forgotten? It was the very detailed drawing of the very naked man. You even wrote his name beneath the picture."

Drawing a deep breath, she explained about seeing the statue of the naked man in Lady Eastland's conservatory, making the sketch, then the decision of the Ladies Literary Society, after their reading of Frankenstein, to fashion for themselves a man—the Perfect Man. She told him everything, concluding with, "So you see, Franklin doesn't really exist, except in our imaginations. And here." She moved her arms to lift Franklin's body and unattached head.

He regarded her with an expression she couldn't decipher. "So there was no naked man."

"No *real* naked man," she corrected. "Except . . . you."

"Yes, except me," he agreed in a soft, silky voice. His eyes glittered and he took a step toward her. Startled and more than a little alarmed at how her heart lurched at his nearness, she took two quick steps back. Her shoulders hit something hard. The wall.

He took another step forward. "Tell me, Sarah," he said, his quiet, deep voice touching her like a soft, dark caress, "did you sketch *me*?"

Her breath caught. The way he was looking at her, with that knee-weakening smoldering heat she hadn't seen during the past week, turned her insides to porridge. His eyes darkened, flaring with the exact fire that had flamed just before he'd kissed her. Touched her intimately.

Desire gushed through her, bringing with it a rush of dismay at the humbling realization that clearly the only reason she'd been able to control her hunger for him this past week during their digging excursions was because he hadn't looked at her like this. Like he craved her. Wanted to devour her in one huge gulp.

A hefty dose of anger suffused her. At him, for making her want him. For being everything she'd always wanted yet didn't dare dream to hope for. And at herself, for longing to forget all the reasons wanting him was wrong. For yearning to take what she wanted and to hell with the consequences.

For allowing herself to fall utterly, hopelessly, in love with him.

The truth she'd tried so hard to deny walloped her without mercy. She loved him. She wanted him. So badly she ached with it.

But she could not have him. Like so many other facets of her life, she needed to accept that and get on with things. And the first thing she needed to do was finish this conversation and get him out of her room. Before she said or did something that she'd regret. That they'd both regret.

Straightening her spine, she said, "You know I sketched you. I gave you the picture, in all your adolescent pirate glory."

He moved another step closer, until less than two feet separated them. And she knew that if she hadn't been holding a headless stuffed man. she would have given in to her deepest urges and pressed herself against him.

He planted his hands on the wall, on either side of her head, caging her in. "I meant naked, Sarah. Did you sketch me in all my *naked* glory?"

Numerous times. "Not even once."

He made a soft *tsking* sound. "You really are a dreadful liar. Shall I look through your sketch pad to discover the truth?"

Annoyance—and dismay—rippled through her. "You wouldn't dare."

"Words that only serve to challenge. And I think you'd be surprised at what I would dare."

Refusing to let him think she was intimidated, she asked in her haughtiest voice, "And if I did sketch you?"

"I'd be . . . flattered. And wonder how often you might look at those sketches." His gaze dipped to her lips and a tingle ran through her. When his eyes once again were raised to hers, he whispered, "I'd wonder how often you might think of me. Wonder if it was anywhere near as often as I think of you."

Her heart stumbled and suddenly she felt trapped. By his words and his nearness. His velvety, seductive voice. And her own resolve, which was evaporating with alarming speed. Giving up all pretense of bravado, she pressed herself closer against the wall and shook her head. "Stop. Please."

"Because, Sarah . . . I think of you all the time."

Her womb clenched with a stark, raw hunger that frightened her. She squeezed her eyes shut and prayed for the strength to resist him. To withstand her fierce desire for him. "This is wrong. I cannot . . . I want you to go."

"I'm not going to marry Lady Julianne."

His words hung in the tension-filled air. Opening her eyes, she gave him a searching look. He appeared in dead earnest. "I beg your pardon?"

"I'm not going to marry Lady Julianne."

It took her several seconds to absorb his statement.

Then comprehension dawned and her breath caught. "You found the money?"

"No."

The flare of hope that had ignited in her heart vanished in a blink. "Then I don't understand. You said you needed to marry an heiress."

"Unfortunately I do—unless a miracle occurs and we find the money in the next few days. But that heiress will not be Lady Julianne."

An overwhelming sense of relief that was purely selfish warred with loyalty for her friend. "But why? You seem to have a liking for each other." True, although based on what Julianne had said earlier, Sarah didn't believe for a moment her friend would be heartbroken. "And I assure you, you'll not find a lovelier, more sweet-natured woman."

"The problem is neither her beauty nor her sweet nature. The problem is that she is your friend."

His expression indicated that she should understand what he was talking about. His expression was dead wrong. She didn't have a clue. That being the case, she leaned forward and discreetly sniffed.

He blinked. "Do I smell?"

"Yes. Like sandalwood and fresh linen."

"What were you expecting?"

"Brandy. Or perhaps whiskey. Certainly spirits of some nature."

"I assure you I am completely sober. Sarah, I cannot marry your friend when I desire *you* so very much." He brushed his fingertips over her cheek, and her insides quivered from the feathery contact. "Such an arrangement would be an awkward, untenable situation for us all. Therefore, barring success in locating the money, I plan to leave for London four days from now to embark on the unwanted but necessary task of finding a different heiress."

His gaze searched hers. "Do you count as friends any other heiresses? Tell me now so I can cross them off my list of potential candidates."

It was difficult to speak, especially when his words, *I desire you so very much,* continued to echo through her brain. Caught between a swirl of surprise, confusion, relief, and desire, she shook her head and managed to say, "No."

"Excellent."

Matthew's gaze dipped to her lips and he swallowed the groan that rose in his throat. Bloody hell, had he just said that he desired her *so very much*? If he'd ever in his life uttered a more monstrous understatement, he couldn't recall the details. And he could tell by the way her chest rose and fell with her quick breaths, the way her honey brown eyes gazed at him so intently, that he wasn't alone in his desire.

Damn it, he should leave her bedchamber. Immediately. He knew it, his inner voice was screaming at him to do so, but his feet refused to move. Instead he cupped her face in his palm and stroked the pad of his thumb lightly over her lush bottom lip.

"My speaking of desiring you," he whispered. "Did I shock you?"

She shook her head, sending her glasses downward in that familiar way that both amused him and tugged on his heart. "No. But . . ." Her words trailed off and she looked at the floor.

He touched two fingers beneath her chin until their gazes once again met. "But what?"

She swallowed, then said, "But you should refrain from making such knee-weakening statements until I'm already seated, lest I might crumple into a heap at your feet."

Her admission clearly meant that she'd suffered the same torment as he this past week. *Thank God.* Surely the selfishly motivated sense of relief and elation that suffused him didn't speak well of him, but he couldn't stop the feelings.

"Sarah . . ." Hell, just saying her name pleased him. He breathed in and the subtle scent of lavender teased his senses. And it seemed as if that one single breath completely unraveled him, loosened the confining ties on the hunger for her he'd suppressed all week. Desire hit him so fiercely he wouldn't have been able to step away from her if his very life had depended upon him doing so.

There was no longer a question of loyalty to her friend. Surely, then, just one kiss would be all right. Just one, to satisfy this desperate yearning. Just one, to relieve this edgy pressure that demanded relief. Just one, and then he'd stop.

He lowered his head and touched his lips to hers. A soft reacquaintance after a week-long absence that felt more like a decade. Her lips parted on a sigh, and in a heartbeat he was lost, sinking deeper into the soft velvet of her mouth. He felt her toss aside the bundles she held, and then her arms were around his neck and she was pressing herself against him. And all semblance of control vanished like a puff of steam in a gale force wind.

With a growl, his arms went around her, crushing her to him but unable to get her close enough. One hand plunged into her soft hair, holding her head still, while his other hand settled on the small of her back, pressing her nearer still. His tongue danced with hers, explored the satin of her mouth. Wild, reckless need pulsed through him and he stepped forward, pinning her to the wall with his lower body.

The feel of her soft curves cradling his erection dragged a guttural groan from his throat. He rubbed himself against her, slowly, each drag across her body jolting him with waves of shocking pleasure.

Touch her. Had to touch her. Just once more. Just one touch . . .

He lowered one hand and curled his fingers into the cotton of her night rail, dragging the material upward until he touched her drawers.

Skin. Had to touch her skin. Just one touch.

He skimmed his hand upward, and her soft, warm breast filled his palm. She gasped against his mouth, that erotic, delicious sound that had haunted him since the first time he heard it. Her nipple pebbled beneath his touch and he teased the tip between his fingers, gently tugging, absorbing her shudders of pleasure.

And he realized that just one kiss, just one touch, wasn't going to be enough. He wanted more. He wanted everything. So badly he was all but shaking. Which meant he had to stop this madness. Right now.

With an effort that required every ounce of his shredded strength, he slipped his hand from beneath her gown, eased his body away from hers, and lifted his head.

The sight of her, breathing hard, parted lips moist from his kiss, hair disarranged from his impatient hands, glasses fogged over, grabbed him by the throat. Never in his life had he wanted a woman more.

He gently slipped off her glasses, and she regarded him through droopy lids. "You stopped," she said, her voice a husky whisper. "Why?"

"As I told you the last time we found ourselves in each others' arms, my ability to resist you is only so strong, and I'm afraid I've reached my limit."

For several heartbeats the only sound in the room was the mingling of their ragged breaths. Then, with her gaze steady on his, she whispered, "And as I asked you the last time we found ourselves in each others' arms, what if I don't want you to resist?"

Reaching out, he brushed back a wayward curl from her forehead with fingers that shook. "The selfish part of me that wants you so badly wouldn't give you a chance to think or change your mind. But the part of me that cares for you, that doesn't want to hurt you in any way, would find it necessary to ask if you've considered all the ramifications. All the consequences. Because they are numerous. Much more so for you than for me."

"I have. Indeed, as much as I've tried not to, over the past week I've thought of little else."

"Sarah . . . as my situation stands right now, I have nothing to offer you. And as much as I might wish it otherwise, the chances of my situation changing by finding the money is very poor."

"I know that it is your duty to marry an heiress. I understand that you're leaving here in four days' time and we'll most likely never see each other again after that. I'm aware that pregnancy could be a risk, but I also know from whispers I've heard that there are ways to prevent it. And I'm hopeful you know of those ways . . . ?"

At his nod, she continued, "I realize that by giving myself to you I'll render myself unmarriageable." Reaching up, she framed his face between her palms. "But you wouldn't be taking anything away from me, as I'd never planned to marry. Indeed, I'm already considered an unmarriageable spinster and have been for years. I accepted long ago that marriage and children were not in my future. I'd planned to live out my life doing what I've always done—sketching, taking care of my garden and my pets, enjoying my friendships, my relationship with Carolyn. You are the first, nay, the *only* man who has ever wanted me."

Her bottom lip trembled and his heart rolled over at the sight. This woman, with her imperfect features that were somehow so perfect, and her utter lack of vanity, inspired something in him, a tenderness that no one else ever had. Looking at her now, so vulnerable, so soft-eyed, yet so earnest, he couldn't imagine any man who wouldn't want her.

"Matthew . . . you've awakened feelings and desires and passions I'd never thought to experience. Never knew existed. Even if it is just for tonight, I want to experience again the magic you made me feel before. I want to make you feel that same intense pleasure. I want to experience everything I can. Just this once. With you."

Matthew laid his hand over hers, which rested on his cheek, then turned his head to press his lips against her palm. He wanted to tell her that more than anything he wanted those very same things. Just this once. With her. But such a lengthy speech was beyond him. So he said the only word he could manage.

"Sarah . . ."

Heart pounding so hard it felt as if it would bruise his ribs, he took her hands and led her to the bed.

"Stay right there," he said softly.

One corner of her lips quirked upward. "I've no intention of running away."

He placed her spectacles on the night table, then set about lighting every candle and lamp in the room. After he'd lit the first two, she asked, "Wh-What are you doing?"

"Giving us more light."

She gave a nervous laugh. "Darkness is a great beauty equalizer, you know."

He didn't comment until he'd finished, until the entire room was illuminated with a golden warm glow that resembled a summer morning. Then he returned to her and clasped her hands, entwining their fingers.

"You're beautiful, Sarah. Inside. Outside. Everywhere. I want to see all you of you. Every expression. Every pleasure. Every inch of soft skin." He raised their joined hands and kissed her fingers. "Unless you'd prefer not to see me?"

She shook her head. "Oh, no. I want to see everything." She cleared her throat. "Of course, without benefit of my spectacles, I'll need to get close. *Very* close."

A chuckle rumbled in his chest. He couldn't imagine anyone other than her amusing him at this moment. "You may get as close as you like. Consider me at your disposal."

Interest flared in her eyes. "A most intriguing invitation, especially for a person who possesses a great thirst for knowledge."

"Delighted to help in any way I can." He turned her hand and touched his tongue to the center of her palm, loving the way her pupils dilated at the gesture. "Any possibility you'd make me a similar offer?"

"I thought I already had."

He smiled. "Ah. So you did. In that case . . ." He released her hands and turned his attention to her delightfully mussed hair. After slipping off the white satin bow that held together the ends of her haphazard braid, he slowly separated the thick strands until they surrounded her in a mass of riotous curls whose ends brushed her hips.

"If only I were an artist," he murmured, sifting his fingers through her magnificent hair. The gilded light picked up every subtle shade of amber and brown in the glossy strands. "I'd paint you just like this. And put Botticelli's Venus to shame."

When she appeared about to protest, he shot her a mock warning glare. She pressed her lips together then said, "Thank you."

"Excellent. You are a most apt pupil."

"Again I thank you. And point out that I'm eager to learn more."

"How extremely fortunate for me." He applied his fingers to the row of small buttons that ran halfway down the front of her night rail. He slowly flicked them open, savoring each inch of skin as it was revealed. After opening the last button, he slipped the material off her shoulders. White cotton glided down her body to pool at her feet, leaving her dressed in only her drawers, a garment he quickly saw join her night rail. Taking her hand, he helped her step from the mound of her clothing, then allowed his gaze to skim down her naked form.

Bloody hell, she was all blushing ivory skin and soft feminine curves, and she stole his breath. He knew he needed to go slow, to gently seduce her, and he certainly wanted that—for both of them. But it was going to prove a challenge to remain in control with his body so strongly opposed to the wait.

Touching a single fingertip to the hollow of her throat, he slowly dragged his hand downward, lightly tracing the fascinating patterns of pale gold dots on her skin. There were hundreds of them, each one a delight to be explored.

"I didn't notice these freckles before," he said, circling a particularly fascinating one just above her nipple. "By mere firelight they aren't visible, but now . . ." He leaned down to touch his lips to the gilt-kissed spot. " . . . they are a sight not to be missed."

"Oh, my . . ." she murmured as his tongue swirled around her taut nipple. "Might you have any pale freckles I could explore?"

He lifted his head to brush his lips across hers. "There is only one way to find out."

Straightening, he started to unfasten his shirt, but she laid her hands on top of his. "May I?" she asked.

Her request both aroused and intrigued him. Although inexperienced, his Sarah clearly didn't lack courage, nor did she plan on remaining passive.

His Sarah. The words reverberated through his mind, and his inner voice coughed to life to inform him that she wasn't his. Would never, could never, be his.

In the realm of forever, that was indeed true. However, for this night she was his. And he was hers. And that would have to be enough.

He lowered his hands to his sides. "As I said, I am at your disposal."

"That is indeed lovely. Except . . . I'm not quite certain what to do with you."

He laughed. "You're off to an inspired start. Don't lose your nerve now. Take off my shirt."

She nodded, and although she fumbled at bit, she managed to open his shirt and pull the tails from his breeches. Placing her hands on his chest, she slowly separated the material, then pushed it over his shoulders and down his arms, where it joined the heap of her garments.

She stepped closer and her breasts brushed against him. Before he could recover from that shocking pleasure, she leaned forward and pressed her lips to the center of his chest.

"I don't see any freckles here," she said, her breath warm against his skin.

She kissed her way across his chest in gentle nibbles while her hands skimmed up and down his back. A low rumble of approval vibrated in his throat. Her hands on him just felt so . . . incredibly . . . good.

Not wanting to interrupt her exploration but unable to keep from touching her, he rested his hands on her hips and lightly kneaded her supple flesh.

He watched her kiss her way across his chest, then, with her lips hovering above his nipple, she asked, "Is it safe to say that if I find something highly pleasurable, you would as well?"

"Absolutely—" His answer ended with a quick intake of breath when her tongue swirled around his nipple. Bloody hell, she *was* an apt pupil. He closed his eyes, instantly imagining all the things he planned to do to her—and her responding in kind. The mere thought shaved several more layers off his rapidly diminishing control. Not a good sign, as he hadn't even removed his breeches yet.

After kissing her way back again, she lifted her head and reported, "I discovered only three freckles and one small scar. Right here." She ran her finger over the faded mark. "How did that happen?"

"As a pudgy, clumsy youth, I found out the hard way that I wasn't good at climbing trees. There's another scar on the back of my thigh, courtesy of that same tumble." He heaved an exaggerated put-upon sigh. "I suppose you'll want to see *that* scar as well."

"If it's not too much trouble," she answered in a prim tone.

"I'll attempt not to complain overly much."

He sat on the bed and pulled off his boots, then stood.

Holding his hands out to his sides, he flicked his gaze down to his obviously tented breeches, then murmured, "Have at it."

In that extremely apt way of hers that he was coming to appreciate more and more with each passing second, she quickly figured out the way of things and unfastened the front placard of his breeches. With his straining erection finally free of the confines of the snug material, he helped her remove the garment. After tossing it on their pile of discarded clothing, he stood before her and allowed her to look her fill, as she'd allowed him.

"Oh, my," she whispered, her gaze riveted on his jutting arousal, which seemed to swell further under her avid scrutiny. She slowly extended her hand, and his entire body tightened in anticipation of her touch. "May I?" she asked.

"I may actually expire if you don't," he said through gritted teeth.

Her fingers brushed over him, and his eyes slammed shut at the intense rush of pleasure. Bloody hell. She'd barely touched him and already he'd forgotten how to breathe.

"You're so hard," she said, her voice filled with wonder as her fingers danced over him.

"You have no idea."

"Yet so silky smooth."

Opening his eyes, he watched her fingers lightly encircle him, a sight that all but smote him where he stood. When she gently squeezed, a low growl escaped him. Looking into his eyes, she gave him another gentle squeeze, which elicited another groan.

"You seem to like that," said his very apt pupil.

"You have no idea."

Sheer delight glittered in her eyes, and she continued her explorations, each caress sweet torture. He skimmed his hands upward to tease her taut nipples. "It occurs to me that you're doing more exploring than I am," he said, his voice sounding as if he'd swallowed gravel.

"'Tis only fair. If you'll recall our last encounter in my bedchamber, you've already touched more of me."

One hand trailed down to brush over the dark curls at the apex of her thighs. Her breathing hitched at the caress, and he said, "I'm not likely to ever forget without benefit of a severe coshing."

She flashed a teasing grin and arched her body back, away from his fingers. "There will be none of that—not while I'm exploring. It's far too distracting. While you are clearly experienced in these matters, I am not. I'm merely attempting to catch up a bit so as not to bore you."

"I assure you, there is no . . . *ahhh* . . ." Damn. Inexperienced though her touch might be, it was driving him to the brink of insanity. "No chance of me being bored. Although I seriously don't know how much more of that I can take."

A slow smile curved her lips, and her eyes danced with mischief. "Then I must be doing it correctly. Because that is precisely how you made *me* feel."

"I believe I detect a bit of the revenge seeker in you, Sarah. It is an aspect of your nature I wasn't previously aware of."

"If I recall correctly, revenge is exactly what *you* were seeking the last time you entered my bedchamber. Hmmm . . . to quote a very wise man who, oddly enough, greatly resembles you, 'Finding fault with someone else for faults that are conspicuously their own . . . I believe that it is referred to as the pot calling the kettle black.'"

The entire time she spoke, her fingers never ceased their maddening strokes, and he now stood in jeopardy of spilling into her hands. "This talent you have of recalling my words verbatim—I'm not sure I like it."

Her smile widened, deepening her dimples. "When the words are used against you, I'm certain you don't. But, as I've discovered, you *do* like this . . ."

She stroked her fingers along his aching length, and with a groan, he reached down and stilled her hand. "That's all I can take."

"Very well. I'll see if I can find that other scar you mentioned."

He wanted to simply snatch her against him, pin her beneath him, and put out this fire raging through his veins. But one look at the budding passion and discovery gleaming in her eyes, and he couldn't deny her. Fisting his hands at his sides and praying for strength, he again said, "Have at it."

Her fingers slid from his erection and he breathed a sigh of relief as she slowly walked around to stand behind him. His relief was short-lived, however, when she lightly circled her fingertips over the small of his back.

"You told me that this is one of the most sensitive spots on a woman's body." Her warm breath blew across his shoulders, tensing them. "Is it one of the most sensitive for a man as well?"

Bloody hell. It was one thing for him to stand still and allow her to explore, but quite another to attempt answering questions. Her fingers skimmed over his lower spine again. It felt as if every muscle in his body jumped in response. Gritting his teeth against the tingling pleasure, he ground out, "Seems so."

"Interesting. Now where is that scar?" Her fingers

cruised lower, tickling over his buttocks and the backs of his thighs. A shudder ran through him, and he knew his control was about to snap.

Her arms came around his waist and she stepped close behind him, pressing her front again his back. The feel of her skin touching his from shoulder to knee, while her hands skimmed over his abdomen . . . one more touch and—

Her fingers grazed the tip of his erection, and he was done. He turned and in one fluid motion scooped her up in his arms and deposited her on the counterpane, where she landed with a gentle bounce. He climbed onto the bed, gently parted her thighs then knelt between them. He drew a careful breath at the sight of her glistening sex, and reaching out, lightly caressed the swollen, wet folds.

A long sigh escaped her and she squirmed against his hand. She was ready. Thank God, because he couldn't wait any longer.

He settled himself between her splayed thighs then lowered his mouth to hers for a long, deep kiss, his tongue matching the slow, teasing glide of the head of his penis along her wet cleft. Slowly lifting his head to end the kiss, he looked down into her beautiful, wide eyes and felt his heart shift. "As you are so fond of asking—may I?"

"As you are so fond of answering—I may expire if you don't."

He propped his weight on his forearms and watched her face as he slowly entered her, absorbing every nuance of her expression. When he reached the barrier of her maidenhead, he paused for an instant, then thrust. Her eyes widened and she gasped.

"Did I hurt you?"

She shook her head. "No. Just . . . surprised me."

Buried to the hilt in her exquisitely tight, wet heat,

Matthew struggled to remain still. When he could no longer do so, he rocked his hips slightly. Again her eyes widened.

"Oh, my . . . Do that again."

"My pleasure."

Bloody hell, there he was, uttering another huge understatement. With his gaze on hers, he withdrew nearly all the way from her body then slowly sank deep into her slick heat. Again, again, long delicious slides into her body that clamped around him like a velvet fist.

Her breathing deepened, quickened, her eyes slid shut and her lips parted. She wrapped her arms around his neck and moved beneath him, awkwardly at first, but it didn't take her long to match his rhythm. He watched her arousal build and fought to keep his own in check. His thrusts lengthened, quickened, deepened, until she cried out and arched beneath him.

The instant her rippling tremors subsided, he withdrew, an effort that nearly killed him. With his body pressed tightly against hers, his release thundered through him, racking jolts of pleasure that dragged a long groan from his very soul. Utterly spent, he collapsed on top of her, buried his face in the fragrant warmth of her neck and closed his eyes.

When his breathing had slowed to something that resembled normal, he lifted his head. And found her looking up at him through glowing eyes.

"Oh, my," she whispered. "That was . . ."

He brushed a damp curl from her cheek. "Yes, it was."

She cleared her throat. "Um, Matthew?"

"Yes?"

"Do you recall how I said I want to experience everything I can, just this once, with you?"

One corner of his mouth quirked. "I'm not apt to forget such an arousing statement."

"Well, I've changed my mind."

"I'm afraid it's a bit too late."

She shook her head. "No, I mean the 'just this once' part. I'm afraid that I found that so incredibly delightful that 'once' is simply not going to be enough."

"I see. So you wish to have your wicked way with my body again tonight?"

"If you don't mind terribly much."

"I'll try to grin and bear it."

Her smile bloomed and she pulled his head down for a kiss. And as his lips met hers, he knew that just once wouldn't be enough for him either.

When his inner voice informed him that one million times wouldn't be enough, he managed, with a great deal of effort, to ignore it.

Chapter 16

ꙮꙮꙮꙮꙮꙮꙮꙮꙮ

$\mathcal{D}$ull gray streaks of a rain-soaked dawn were just touching the sky when Matthew slipped from Sarah's bed. Before reaching for his clothes, he gazed down at her, momentarily unable to look away from the picture she made, her hair fanned out across the pillows, one bare shoulder peeking from beneath the counterpane. After they'd made love a second time, she'd fallen asleep, her head pillowed on his chest, one arm slung across his abdomen, one thigh nestled between his.

He'd remained awake, staring at the ceiling, listening to her breathe, brushing gentle kisses against her hair. Absorbing the feel of her cuddled against him.

But now their night was over and he needed to return to his own bedchamber before the household arose. With his gaze still resting on her sleeping form, he scooped up his breeches from the floor and donned them. Leaving her bed and walking out of this room were proving far more difficult than he'd anticipated. He'd expected to enjoy their night together, seducing her, introducing her to lovemaking, teaching her to enjoy pleasure.

But he hadn't expected to feel as if *he* were the one being seduced. The one being introduced to the beauty of lovemaking. The one being taught all the nuances of true pleasure. In spite of his previous experiences, it was at her unpracticed hands that he'd learned the difference between merely slaking one's lust and sharing the physical act of lovemaking with someone you cared for.

Nor had he anticipated the profound sense of peace that filled every crevice of his being. It seemed as if he'd exhausted himself for years searching for that elusive calm to fill his soul. Never would he have expected to find it in the arms of a virgin spinster. In fact, if anyone had suggested he would, he'd have laughed.

Which just showed he had a lot to learn. And Sarah—sheltered, innocent Sarah, who hadn't seen or done even a fraction of things he had—knew more about life and love, generosity and kindness, than anyone he'd ever met. And in only a few short days she'd be gone from his life. Unless he found the money.

If he did, he could—and would—marry Sarah. At the mere thought, all the lonely darkness he'd envisioned looming on his horizon turned bright gold with sunshine. Which meant he *had* to find the money. It *had* to be there. He had three days and the remaining acres of the rose garden in which to find it. And by God, he was determined to do so.

He grabbed up his wrinkled shirt and quickly finished dressing. Then, after brushing a tender kiss against Sarah's temple, he quit the room, closing the door quietly behind him.

Striding quickly down the corridor toward his bedchamber, he'd just rounded the corner when he halted. Walking toward him, less than a dozen feet away, was Daniel. Daniel who was frowning and looking down and clearly hadn't noticed him yet. Daniel who'd obviously been outside because he was soaking wet and more than a little bedraggled.

At that moment Daniel looked up and his footsteps faltered. Their gazes met, and for just an instant something flashed in Daniel's eyes, something Matthew couldn't decipher; a look he couldn't recall ever seeing from his friend before.

Matthew's brows rose and his gaze ran down Daniel's sopping, mud-splattered clothes. "Where have you been?"

In the exact same manner, Daniel's brows rose and his gaze ran over Matthew, noting, Matthew knew, the rumpled, disheveled state of his clothing. "I think it's obvious where I've been," Daniel said in a low voice, walking closer to him. "Outside."

"Any particular reason? The weather is foul, in case you hadn't noticed."

"I noticed. As a matter of fact, I was looking for you. When I discovered you weren't in your bedchamber, I concluded you'd insanely decided to go digging in spite of the storm."

"And you thought to help me?"

"I thought, at best, to stop you. At worst, to make certain no harm came to you. But clearly my conclusion as to your whereabouts was dead wrong." His gaze shifted up and down the corridor. "I'd like to change into dry clothes. Shall we continue this discussion in my bedchamber?"

Matthew nodded his agreement. Anyone could come upon them in the corridor, and he didn't want to risk being overheard.

Once in Daniel's chamber, Matthew leaned against the mantel and stared into the glowing embers while his friend changed clothes. When Daniel joined him, his hair was still damp but he wore clean fawn breeches and was shrugging into a fresh white shirt.

"Why did you go to my bedchamber?" Matthew asked.

"I couldn't sleep. I thought perhaps you might be suffering the same fate and would care to join me in a brandy." He gave Matthew's disheveled clothing a speculative look. "Since you weren't in your own bedchamber—or outside—the question is, in whose bedchamber were you? The beautiful heiress you're hoping to marry, whose fortune you need so desperately? Or the plain spinster, whom you can't take your eyes off of, who lacks the much-needed fortune?"

Matthew pushed off from the mantel and narrowed his eyes. Before he could speak, however, Daniel held up his hand. "No need to respond. The answer is obvious. Which presents you with quite a conundrum."

"It does nothing of the kind."

He gave Matthew a searching look. "You're planning to take Miss Moorehouse as a mistress? Rather awkward, seeing as how she and Lady Julianne are such close friends. Quite frankly, I'm surprised you'd suggest such an arrangement and even more surprised that Miss Moorehouse would agree to it."

"There is no arrangement. Nor is there a conundrum because I've no intention of marrying Lady Julianne."

Daniel halted in the act of fastening his shirt. "You found the money?" he asked sharply.

"No. I've decided to find a different heiress—if necessary." He related his plan to finish searching the rose garden over the next three days, then depart for London if the money wasn't found.

When he finished, Daniel said, "So I'm assuming your departure for London will mark the end of your spectacularly unsuccessful house party."

"Yes." He frowned. "Although I wouldn't call it spectacularly unsuccessful. Haven't you enjoyed yourself?"

"Certainly. But ensuring my good time was not the reason for this gathering. It was to procure yourself an heiress. I suppose it's useless to point out that if you'd concentrated your energies on Lady Julianne, you could right now be preparing to marry a woman that most men would sacrifice a limb—or two—to wed."

"Pointing that out would not be helpful, no."

"Still, all isn't lost as far as Lady Julianne. You could still—"

"No," Matthew cut in, his tone terser than he'd intended. "Lady Julianne is out of the question."

"Because of her friendship with Miss Moorehouse."

"Yes."

"I see," Daniel said, nodding his head slowly. "Have you told Miss Moorehouse you're in love with her?"

Matthew blinked. "In love with whom?"

Daniel looked toward the ceiling. "Miss Moorehouse, you dolt."

For several seconds it felt as if the floor beneath Matthew's feet shifted. "When did I say I was in love with her?"

Daniel gave a quick, brittle-sounding laugh. "You didn't have to say it. My friend, you are as transparent as glass, at least to someone who knows you well. Every time you look at her, speak to her, you light up as if you swallowed a candelabra. Your feelings for her are plain in everything you've said and done." Daniel cocked his head and gave him a questioning look. "Don't tell me you didn't know."

"Know what? That I look as if I swallowed a candelabra?"

"No, you dolt. That you're in love."

Matthew shot his friend an icy glare. "That's the second time you've called me a dolt."

"You can thank me later for my forthright honesty."

"I'll do nothing of the sort." He frowned and turned to stare into the fire. Daniel's words seeped through him, the truth stunning him, yet somehow not surprising him. Finally he turned back to his friend and after clearing his throat said in a somewhat sheepish voice, "It would appear I've fallen in love."

"At least now that you've admitted it, I can stop calling you a dolt. What do you intend to do about it?"

"Do?" Matthew shoved his fingers into his hair. "There's nothing I can do other than what I've *been* doing—search for the money, which unfortunately isn't looking hopeful—and, barring a last minute success, plan to marry an heiress."

"And your feelings for Miss Moorehouse?"

Matthew briefly squeezed his eyes shut and let out a long sigh. Suddenly weary, he said quietly, "If the money isn't found, I'll simply have to ignore them. There is more at stake here than my personal feelings. I made promises. I gave my word. I have responsibilities to many people other than myself."

Daniel nodded in an approving manner. "Wise decision. As I once told you, one woman is much the same as another, especially in the dark. Even more so after several brandies. 'Tis therefore foolish to base one's marriage on anything other than purely practical reasons—money, heir-begetting, titles, property. To base it on something as nebulous as the capricious yearnings of the heart is tantamount to idiocy."

"Right."

"And it's not as if you have a choice, assuming the money isn't found. You *must* marry an heiress."

"Right." By God, this talk with Daniel was making him feel much better.

"And it's not as if Miss Moorehouse will be left without companionship."

"Right." He frowned. "What?"

"No need to worry that Miss Moorehouse will suffer from loneliness after you embark on your lifelong journey of wedded bliss. Jennsen's already making plans for her to visit his London home."

A sensation akin to steam spewing from his ears shot through Matthew. "Jennsen? How do you know?"

"He told me this evening over the backgammon table."

"And Sarah agreed to this?" The mere thought tightened his stomach into an aching knot.

"He hasn't asked her yet. But he intends to." A muscle ticked in Daniel's jaw. "Intends to ask Lady Wingate as well, so the entire thing is all proper."

"Bastard," Matthew uttered.

"Damn bloody bastard," Daniel agreed. "But as you'll be wed to someone else, you certainly can't begrudge Miss Moorehouse consolation in the company of another man."

No, he couldn't. But damn it, he did. With every cell in his body. His hands tightened into fists. The thought of Jennsen touching her, kissing her, making love to her, made him feel sick inside. Made him want to break something. Like Jennsen's damn jaw.

Daniel cleared his throat. "I feel it necessary to point out that you've fallen in love with the wrong woman. Your life certainly would have been much easier had you lost your heart to Lady Julianne."

"I agree. But since I didn't, there's only one thing I can do."

"What's that?"

"Hope and pray that I find the money."

Later that afternoon, Matthew strode across the lawn toward the groundskeeper's cottage. The rain had finally stopped and the grass resembled wet dark green velvet glittering beneath the intermittent bursts of sunshine as puffy clouds blew across the cerulean sky. Tildon was arranging for tea, and Matthew wanted to speak to Paul then return to join his guests.

One guest in particular.

Bloody hell, it was now going to be even more of an exercise in torture to keep his expression and words neutral. To hide his desire.

His love.

As he neared the groundskeeper's cottage, he saw Paul exit the modest bungalow-style dwelling and make his way along the flagstone walkway. When Paul caught sight of him, the groundskeeper halted as if he'd walked into a tree. He cast a quick look back toward the cottage, then raised his hand to shade his face from the sun.

"Afternoon, m'lord," he called so loudly Matthew wondered if the man's hearing had become afflicted—or if he believed Matthew's had.

"Good afternoon, Paul. Are you all right?"

"Fine, m'lord," Paul continued to holler. "Just surprised to see ye here. Is there somethin' ye be needin'?"

Matthew noted the ruddy color staining the grounds-keeper's cheeks and the glance he shot over his shoulder toward the cottage. "I want you to cut flowers for several special arrangements I'd like in place as soon as possible, definitely by dinner this evening. You'll need to cut enough for larger displays for the dining room table and foyer and a smaller one I've yet to decide where to place."

"Very well, m'lord. Any special sort of flowers ye'll be wantin'?"

"Yes. Lavender."

"And what else?"

"Nothing else."

Paul blinked. "That's the only sort of flower ye want cut for all them arrangements?"

"Yes. Just lavender."

"Very good, m'lord. I'll get to that right away. The blooms will be especially bright after the soakin' they got last night." He chuckled. "Guess you got yerself a soakin' as well."

Matthew frowned. "What do you mean?"

"Saw ye last night, digging away in the rose garden. Guess they don't make ye sneeze in the rain, eh?"

Everything in Matthew stilled. "You saw me last night, digging in the rose garden?" he repeated, just to make certain he'd understood correctly.

"Yes, m'lord."

"At what time?"

Paul pursed his lips and scratched his head. "'Bout three A.M. or thereabouts. Rain had tapered off some by then."

"What were *you* doing in the rose garden at three A.M.?" Matthew asked casually.

Something flickered in Paul's eyes. Before Matthew could decide what, the groundskeeper chuckled. "Oh, ye know how it is when ye can't sleep. Sometimes a walk helps to tire the body out. Since the rain had nearly stopped, I just wandered about some. If there's nothin' else, m'lord, I'll get me tools and start on cuttin' that lavender ye be wantin'."

"There's nothing else, Paul. Thank you."

With a nod, the groundskeeper turned and walked back toward the cottage. Just before he entered, Matthew noticed a shadow move behind one of the curtains. After Paul closed the door, Matthew started slowly down the path toward the house, his mind buzzing with two things. First, Paul clearly hadn't been alone. His yelling had obviously been a warning to whoever was in the cottage that Matthew was there. Second was the disturbing knowledge that someone had been digging in his rose garden last night. A man he knew damn well wasn't him.

So who was it? And why was he digging? Had he found out about the money? Or had whomever it was seen him digging and deduced he was looking for something of value—something the poacher wanted to find first?

The only two people he'd told about the money were Daniel and Sarah. Sarah was with him all last night. And Daniel. . .

Daniel had been in the rose garden. Matthew blew out a long breath and dragged his hand down his face. Daniel had been looking for him. An activity that certainly didn't require any digging. His friend would never betray him. Which meant that someone else must have found out about the money. Or at least suspected. And was looking for it.

By his own admission, Paul had also been in the rose garden. And the groundskeeper was clearly hiding something.

Could Paul have found out about the money? Had Paul been the person watching him on those nights he'd felt the weight of someone's stare? But why would Paul have mentioned seeing someone if he himself had been the person digging? Still, something didn't ring true about Paul's story. Who the hell walked in the *rain* to help themselves sleep? Perhaps Paul suspected he'd been seen and had told him his tale in order to explain his presence in the rose garden.

Or perhaps someone besides Daniel and Paul had been in his suddenly very busy rose garden last night.

But who?

He didn't know, but he was determined to find out.

Until he did, however, if someone were lurking in the dark, someone who knew or suspected the money existed, then digging at night with Sarah was out of the question. While he didn't relish placing himself in jeopardy, he sure as hell wasn't going to risk placing her in danger. He'd have to finish the rose garden digging alone. Preferably during daylight hours. He'd ask Sarah for some plausible excuse should anyone question him—aerating the roots or some such nonsense. In fact, with time so short, he'd need to get in some digging right after tea. He'd prevail upon Daniel to keep the guests occupied while he did so. He'd also tell Daniel about this latest development and enlist his friend's aid in discovering the identity of the mystery digger, as well as Paul's guest.

During dinner that evening he planned to announce his looming departure for London, thus marking the end of the house party. His jaw tightened. And if there was a traitor in his midst, he intended to know about it before he left.

After a delicious dinner then the usual cards and backgammon in the drawing room, the party broke up for the evening and Sarah made her way to her bedchamber. Since Emily was suffering from a headache, the Literary Ladies had quietly agreed to meet in Sarah's room before lunch the next day in order to dismantle Franklin so they could return his clothing to their rightful owners.

When she reached the top of the stairs, she bid the other houseguests a cheery good night, her gaze seeking out Matthew but not finding him. He'd led the way up the stairs while she remained near the back of the group. Clearly he'd already turned the corner at the end of the corridor on his way to his bedchamber.

She continued down the hallway toward her bedchamber, forcing her steps to remain slow and measured—an overwhelming challenge given the unread note all but burning a hole in the deep pocket of her gown.

Matthew had surreptitiously pressed the small folded missive into her palm an hour ago in the drawing room. Flustered not only at the gesture but at the fleeting touch, she'd quickly slipped her hand into her pocket and moved close to the fireplace in order to be able to blame the flame's heat for the rush of color she felt flood her cheeks. For the past hour it had proven nearly impossible to sit still, to converse with the other guests, when every fiber of her being was consumed by the desire to escape and read her note.

The walk down the corridor seemed endless, but she

finally reached her room. The instant she closed the door behind her, she pulled the small piece of ivory vellum from her pocket. With trembling fingers she unfolded it and read the missive, which consisted of three words: *Enjoy your bath.*

Bath? A frown pulled down her brows and she looked up. And saw the copper tub set in front of the fireplace. Entranced, she crossed the room. Curls of fragrant steam rose from the water, beckoning her to slide into the soothing warmth.

He'd apparently ordered this treat for her, to be indulged in before their digging expedition. Although completely unfamiliar with receiving romantic gestures, she decided she like them very much—although her inner voice warned her not to grow accustomed to them.

She quickly shed her clothing and approached the tub. Bending at the waist, she leaned over and swirled her fingers through the water, testing the temperature.

"Now *that* is the most captivating sight I've ever seen," came a familiar deep voice from directly behind her.

With a startled gasp Sarah straightened and spun around. Matthew stood less than two feet away. He wore a wicked grin, a loosely knotted silk robe, and, as far as she could tell, nothing else.

She pressed a hand over the spot where her heart rapped in her chest, no longer from surprise but simply from his presence. And the smoldering fire burning in his eyes. The sight of him made her want to repeat his *most captivating sight I've ever seen*, but before she could find her voice, he erased the space between them in a single step, yanked her into his arms, and kissed her as if he were starving and she were a banquet feast.

With a moan, she parted her lips, wrapped her arms

around his neck and pressed herself against him. Beneath the cool silk of his robe she felt the delicious heat of his skin. His hard arousal nestled against her belly and desire gushed through her at the potent reminder of how he'd felt thrusting deep inside her.

After a searing, deep kiss, he lifted his head to run his mouth down her neck.

"You have no idea how much I've wanted to do that . . ." he whispered, his breath warming her skin, eliciting a delightful shiver. "All. Day. Long." Each word was punctuated by a nipping kiss along her collarbone.

"I think I may have some small inkling," she replied, tilting her neck to give his marauding lips better access. "Oh, my. Is that why you're here? Because you wanted to kiss me?"

"Among other things. First, I need to tell you that our nighttime digging expeditions must cease." He went on to reveal his disturbing conversation that afternoon with Paul, concluding with, "I cannot expose you to any danger. Therefore I'll finish the digging during the day."

"And I'll help." When he looked about to argue, she said, "You're armed, Danforth will be with us, and it will take half the time if we work together. Perhaps Lord Surbrooke can join us as well for even further protection."

He frowned. "I'll think on it. But it also occurred to me there are three more nights before I depart for London— assuming I have to leave at all. It further occurred to me that it would be a terrible pity to let them go to waste."

"I see. And when did that occur to you?"

"About ten seconds after I left your bed this morning."

She clung to him and sighed as one of his hands cupped her bottom and the other palmed her breast. "Then clearly you're slow-witted because those same things occurred to me about three seconds after you'd made love to me. The first time."

"Ah." The simultaneous tugging on her nipple and tickling of the fingers of his other hand over the highly sensitive small of her back dragged a long moan from her throat. "I knew you were an apt pupil."

"Yes. Who is very eager for her next lesson. Although, I've already learned something since you've arrived—I now know what melted wax feels like."

"What does it feel like?"

"Hot. And liquidy." Pressing her hands against his chest, she leaned back and looked at him through her askew glasses. With a tender smile, he slid them from her nose and reached out to set them on the mantel. "How did you manage to get your robe, enter my room, and undress in such a short amount of time?"

"I slipped away for several minutes after dinner and brought my robe here. I hid it in the wardrobe, where Franklin promised to watch it for me. When everyone was preparing to retire, I came here instead of continuing down the corridor to my own chamber." He hooked his hand beneath the back of her thigh and lifted her leg, settling it high on his hip, opening her for his touch. She gasped as his fingers lightly stroked her feminine folds, which already felt heavy and swollen.

"As for my speed in undressing," he continued, his devilishly skillful fingers destroying her concentration, "you'd be surprised at how fast a man can remove his clothing when faced with the delightful prospect of making love to a beautiful woman."

"Beautiful . . . ?" The word came out on a sigh of pleasure. "I cannot fathom a single reason why you would call me that."

"I know. Which only serves to make you more beautiful. But don't worry. I can think of enough reasons for both of us."

He touched a particularly sensitive spot and she squirmed against his hand, eager to feel that delicious jolt again. Slipping her hands inside the V opening in his robe, she leaned forward and pressed her lips to his chest. "I'm enjoying my bath very much."

His deep laugh vibrated against her lips. "And we haven't even entered the water yet."

She lifted her head and eyed him with interest. "We?"

"I thought my very apt pupil's next lesson should involve the joys of bathing together." His hands slipped from her body and he took a single step back. A groan of protest rose in her throat, but before she could voice it, he'd shrugged his robe from his shoulders, turning her groan into a sigh of appreciation.

He nodded toward the tub. "Join me?"

"I cannot fathom one reason why I'd say no."

One corner of his mouth tilted up. "Neither can I."

He stepped over the edge and settled himself in the water. Sarah planted her hands on her hips and stared down at him with a mock glare. "How can I possibly join you? There's no room left."

His eyes glittered up at her and he patted his thighs. "There's plenty of room." He held up his hand, and Sarah placed her hand in his. Their palms met and he wrapped long, strong fingers around hers. "Step in so you're facing me, with your legs outside mine," he instructed. She gingerly stepped over the edge and did as he bid, her legs forming a bridge around his.

He looked up at her with a wicked grin. "What a delightful view."

"I was just thinking the same thing, although you are rather blurry."

"Easily remedied, especially if you kneel."

Intrigued and aroused by the prospect, she gripped the sides of the tub and slowly lowered herself onto her knees. His fascinating arousal rose between them, and she reached out with one hand to stroke her fingers over the velvety tip. He sucked in a quick breath and retaliated by cupping her breasts in his warm, wet hands.

"Now what?" she asked.

His gaze skimmed over her with a heated thoroughness that elicited an all over body blush. "It would appear you're in charge," he said, one hand slipping between her legs. "What would you *like* to do?"

"Kiss you," she whispered. "Make love to you."

The way his eyes darkened at her answer sizzled awareness to her every nerve ending. "I'm all yours," he said, his voice a husky growl. "Have at it."

Oh, my. Leaning forward, she touched her mouth to his, once, twice. Softly, experimentally. He allowed her to take the lead, whispering words of encouragement that stripped away any hesitancy. She ran her hands over his chest, stroked his arousal, teased his lips with her tongue, delighting in his reactions. His moans, the avid way he watched her, his increasingly ragged breaths, all filled her with a sense of feminine satisfaction she'd never suspected existed.

He trickled cupped handfuls of warm water over her shoulders then smoothed his hands down her wet body. While she continued to lightly stroke him, he sat up and, grasping her hips, laved her nipple with his tongue then drew the aching point deep into the heated silk of his mouth. Desperate to have him inside her, Sarah spread her legs as far as the tub allowed and circled her hips over his arousal, brushing the head over her feminine folds where an insistent beat pulsed.

With his gaze steady on hers, he helped her position herself. Settling her hands on his shoulders, she slowly lowered herself, a long moan escaping each of them as he filled her. When he was buried to the hilt, she experimentally rocked her hips, a movement that sent a shudder of delight through her entire body. Closing her eyes, she threw back her head and repeated the motion.

Again he let her take the lead, set the pace, murmuring encouraging words, his hands ceaselessly caressing her breasts, her abdomen, her buttocks. Tension coiled deep within her and she rocked faster while he thrust harder, pushing her closer to the precipice of ultimate pleasure. With a gasp she soared over the edge, her body tightening, throbbing, pulsing around his for an endless moment. No sooner had the tremors subsided than she felt him withdraw. Holding her tightly against him, he buried his face between her breasts and groaned as his release overtook him.

Resting her cheek on his damp hair, Sarah sifted her fingers through the thick silky strands. And knew she would have been content to stay like this forever. Wrapped in his arms. His skin touching hers. In her mind she sketched a mental image of them together, just like this, which she told herself she'd commit to her sketch pad. A charcoal picture she could look at over the years when heated memories of him were all she'd have.

Because unless the miracle she'd been praying for was realized, three days from now that's all she would have of him.

Chapter 17

Three days later, with the bright afternoon sun gilding the landscape in a manner Matthew prayed was a harbinger of good fortune, he and Sarah stood in the rose garden, shovels in hand, prepared to dig in the two last remaining rows of roses. The bad news was, they'd yet to find anything. The good news was, no one had disturbed them during the afternoon hours, nor had Matthew, or Danforth, or Daniel—who'd joined them when he wasn't playing stand-in host—sensed any intruders.

Matthew's gaze met Sarah's over the hedges and he had to firmly plant his feet and grip the wooden handle of his shovel to keep from going to her. Yanking her into his arms. Burying his face in the warm, fragrant spot where her neck and shoulder met.

The last few days spent in her company were filled with moments he'd never forget. Of hard work and disappointment at their failure to locate the money. Of laughter and smiles and sharing dreams and reminisces. And then the nights . . . hours spent exploring each other, sharing passion, whispering in the dark, holding her while she slept. Then rising to look out her bedchamber window, his gaze searching the gardens for any sign of intruders—and seeing none.

Neither mentioned the imminent end to their time together or the unlikely odds of finding the money with the
ever shrinking area left to search. Yet the knowledge hung
heavy between them and weighed on Matthew's heart.
How he was going to find the strength to walk away from
her, he didn't know. For now, he could only offer up one
last prayer that they'd be successful.

"Ready?" he asked, his throat tight for reasons that had
nothing to do with his reaction to roses.

She nodded, which sent her glasses sliding, which
made him grip his shovel handle all the tighter to keep
from reaching out to push the spectacles back into place.
She smiled, but her expressive eyes reflected the grave-
ness of the moment. "Ready."

He pulled his handkerchief into place over his nose
and mouth. They dug in silence, the only sounds those
of the rustling leaves, the warbling birds, and their shovels slicing into the dirt. With each shovelful that yielded
no results, Matthew's spirits sank lower. After he finally
shoveled up the last scoop of dirt in his final ditch, the
culmination of a nearly a year's worth of his time and
energy, he stared into the empty space with unseeing
eyes.

Bloody hell, he felt . . . gutted. He crouched down,
leaned his sweaty forehead against the shovel handle and
closed his eyes, overcome by a sense of weariness and
defeat he'd never before known. He'd sensed in his gut
that it would come to this, yet still, he'd hoped. But now
it was done. His fate decided. No more hope. No more
Sarah. Tomorrow morning he would leave for London. To
embark on the next phase of his life. Without her.

He knew that for the rest of his life he'd be haunted by
his memories of her. His love for her. And the question of

the money—had it really existed and he'd just failed in his quest to find it, in spite of his best efforts to do so? Was it still buried somewhere, beneath some golden flower he'd failed to see, mocking him? Or had the bastard who'd been digging during the storm found the treasure he'd worked so hard to locate? Unfortunately, he'd never know.

He breathed out a long, weary sigh and was just about to push himself to his feet when Sarah's excited voice reached him from the other side of the hedge.

"Matthew, I think I've found something."

It took him several seconds to emerge from the fog of defeat surrounding him. When he did, he jumped up and raced around the hedge.

Sarah, her face damp and red from her exertions, was on her knees, frantically pushing aside dirt with her hands. He noted she was nearly at the end of her row, with only a few feet left to dig.

"My shovel hit something hard," she said, glancing up at him, her eyes filled with excitement and hope.

He knelt next to her and together they pushed aside the dirt. Less than a minute later their hands stilled. And they stared at what they'd uncovered.

"Oh, my," she whispered.

He swallowed, barely able to do so around the lump in his throat, a lump lodged there at the sight of the brick they'd uncovered. Not the money, just a . . . brick. The letdown after that spike of last minute hope was nothing short of crushing.

The tears shimmering in Sarah's eyes told him she felt exactly the same way. Her bottom lip trembled and a single tear trickled down her cheek. And his heart simply broke in two.

"Sarah . . ." He pulled her into his arms and absorbed

her quiet sobs, each one a barbed lash against his heart.

"I th-thought I'd found it," she whispered against his neck.

"I know, sweetheart. So did I."

"I can't believe it wasn't there. I was so hopeful . . . so sure . . ." Another sob racked her, and he pressed his lips against her disarrayed hair. Bloody hell, seeing and hearing her cry was killing him.

She looked up at him and brushed at the wetness on her cheeks with shaking fingers, her tear-soaked eyes filled with determination. "I still have several more feet in which to dig. I want to finish. It could be there."

He cupped her face in his hands, softly brushing at the remnants of her tears. There were a thousand things he wanted to tell her. Share with her. Tens of thousands of tomorrows he wanted to spend with her. And the pain of knowing it wasn't going to happen made it nearly impossible to breathe.

"I'll finish," he said.

Ten minutes later he had to once again admit defeat.

"Nothing," he said in a flat voice.

He turned and held out his dirty hand to her. She slipped her equally dirty hand into his, and he led them away. Once they were a safe distance from the rose garden, he pulled the handkerchief from his face and stopped. She turned to him and their gazes met. He felt the need to say something, but God help him, he had no idea what. As it was, he had to clear his throat to find his voice.

"Thank you for your help."

Her bottom lip quivered and he prayed she wasn't going to cry again. He felt like a frayed thread about to snap, and seeing her tears again would cut him off at the knees.

"You're welcome," she whispered. "I'm only
failed."

"As am I." More than he could ever hope to convey.

"Saying good-bye to you . . . it's going to be difficult."

"Sarah . . ." No more words came, and with a groan,
he pulled her into his arms and buried his face against her
hair. Difficult? It was going to prove damn near impossible.

Drawing a shaky breath, he lifted his head and looked
into her eyes. The most beautiful eyes he'd ever seen. "We
still have tonight," he said. "One more night."

And then he'd leave and do what had to be done, keep
the promises he'd made, see to his responsibilities, save
the estate his father had run into financial ruin. He'd retain his honor, his family's honor. But by doing so, he
would lose Sarah, the one thing that meant more to him
than anything else.

Yet as awful as he felt right now, tomorrow he knew
he'd find out what heartbreak really felt like.

That night's dinner turned into an impromptu celebration
to commemorate the end of the house party. Food and
wine flowed freely, and Sarah tried her best to hide her
misery and partake of the festivities. Luckily everyone
else, with the exception of Matthew, whom she tried her
best not to look at lest she lose her composure, appeared
in high spirits, so it wasn't necessary for her to do more
than nod, smile, and toss in an occasional comment.

As was her habit, she spent most of the meal observing those around her. Lady Gatesbourne and Lady Agatha
were deep in conversation with Lord Berwick, both ladies

clearly sizing him up as potential husband material, much the way an undertaker sized up one for a coffin.

Emily and Julianne were engaged in lively conversation with Lord Hartley, while Carolyn was laughing at something Matthew said. Lords Surbrooke and Thurston were chatting about horses, a conversation to which Mr. Jennsen, who sat next to her, appeared to be listening.

She was proven wrong, however, when Mr. Jennsen said to her in an undertone from the corner of his mouth, "You'll have my undying gratitude if you rescue me from this deadly boring horse talk."

Sarah couldn't help but chuckle. "And here I thought you were fascinated."

"Hardly. I was merely attempting to appear so in my quest for bettering my manners."

"Is there something wrong with your manners?"

"You haven't noticed?"

"Noticed what?"

He regarded her through very serious eyes. "It's a good thing you're sitting down because what I'm about to tell you may come as a shock." He leaned closer. "I'm an *American*. From *America*."

Sarah feigned surprise. "Never say so. You? An upstart colonist?"

He held his hand over his heart. "I swear it's true. Which means I must brush up on my manners—of which I apparently have none. Especially if I hope to entice a certain young lady to visit me when next she is in London."

Given the steady way he was looking at her, there was no mistaking whom he meant, and a blush heated her cheeks. "I . . . I don't know when that might be."

"Whenever your time might allow," he said lightly. "It is an open invitation, for both you and your sister, or whoever else you might be traveling with." His gaze rested on hers. "I've very much enjoyed your company and would like to see you again."

"I . . . I'm flattered."

"Don't be." He flashed her a wicked grin. "After all, I'm just one of those uncouth Americans."

"I've enjoyed your company as well," she said. And she had. But she had no wish to give him false hope, and she knew that once she arrived home, it would be a long time before she and her broken heart would be ready to leave again. "But—"

"No buts," he said softly. "There's no need for excuses or explanations. Like you, I am observant. Just know that I wish you every happiness, and should you return to London, I'd be delighted to escort you around the city. You've only to ask."

Sarah's blush fired hotter. She wasn't certain what his observations had told him, but she suspected he'd fathomed that she held more than a passing interest in Matthew. "I thank you for your offer of friendship."

"You're welcome."

He didn't add that the offer could be for more than friendship, but he didn't need to—it was there in his eyes for her to see. Sarah reached for her wine and took a sip to hide her dismay. Until she came to Langston Manor, no man had ever looked at her twice. Now two men had made it clear they cared for her.

If only her heart wanted Logan Jennsen instead of Matthew. But that was as useless as saying if only they'd found the money.

She had one last night with Matthew, a few stolen hours that would have to last her a lifetime. She intended to treasure every moment.

* * *

It was after midnight by the time the party broke up and everyone made their way toward their bedchambers. The instant Sarah entered her room, she quickly removed her clothes and dressed in the one thing she wanted most to wear—Matthew's shirt that she'd borrowed for Franklin, who was dismantled, his clothing returned to the rightful owners. She would return the shirt to Matthew tonight— after he removed it from her body.

Several minutes later a soft knock sounded on the door. Heart pounding, she watched the door swing open. Matthew entered, holding a small bouquet of lavender. After he'd closed and locked the door, she emerged from the shadows.

He stilled when he saw her, his gaze moving slowly down her form, his eyes filled with a combination of heat and tenderness that stole her breath. With his gaze steady on hers, he walked toward her, halting when less than two feet separated them.

"You're wearing my shirt," he said.

She nodded. "You'll recall that I said I'd return it."

"Yes." He reached out and rubbed a bit of the material between his fingers. "But I think you should keep it. On me it looks quite average, but on you, it looks . . . extraordinary." He held out the bouquet. "For you."

Sarah took the flowers and lifted them to her nose to breathe in the lovely fragrance. "Thank you. They're my favorite."

"I know. And they're now mine as well."

Looking at him over the top of the purple blooms, she said, "The bouquets in the dining room and foyer were magnificent."

"I wanted you to know I was thinking of you."

While taking another deep breath of the flowers, she noticed something shiny nestled between the blooms. She reached in and stilled at the sight of the object she withdrew.

A brooch. In the shape of a single, perfect iris, the deep purple enamel flower and emerald green leaves edged with gleaming gold.

"It's beautiful," she whispered, her fingers tracing over the vivid colors.

"It was my mother's," Matthew said softly. "I hope you'll wear it. And remember me fondly."

Fondly? Dear God, if only such a lukewarm word could describe her feelings for him. Blinking back the hot moisture pooling behind her eyes, she said, "Thank you, Matthew. I'll treasure it always. I have a present for you as well." She walked to the escritoire, laid down her flowers and brooch on the polished surface, then picked up a rolled vellum scroll tied with a ribbon. When she returned to him, she handed him the gift.

He wordlessly removed the ribbon then slowly unrolled the pages. He looked at the first sketch, which depicted two plants whose heart-shaped flowers dripped from curved stems, and smiled. "Straff wort and tortlingers," he said, reading the words she'd written beneath the imaginary plants. "I somehow knew they would look exactly like this."

He turned to the second sketch and stared at it for a long moment, a muscle ticking in his jaw. When he finally looked up, the emotion in his gaze made her heart skip a beat. "You . . . as Venus. It's absolutely perfect. Right down to Venus wearing spectacles. Thank you."

"You're welcome."

He carefully re-rolled and tied the sketches then crossed the room to set them on the escritoire next to her flowers. Then he walked back toward her, but when he reached her, he didn't stop, just picked her up and with her toes dangling above the floor brought her to the bed, setting her on the edge of the mattress.

Without a word he knelt before her then reached out to unfasten his shirt, which she wore. After sliding the linen off her shoulders and down her arms, he trailed a single fingertip from the hollow of her throat to her navel.

"Lie back," he whispered, his voice hoarse.

After she'd done as he bid, he parted her legs with his hands then lifted her thighs and set them on his shoulders. Her modesty dissolved at the first stroke of his tongue along her sensitive folds. Never in her life had she imagined such intimacy. He made love to her with his mouth, his lips and tongue caressing while his fingers danced over her flesh with wicked perfection. When her climax overtook her, it dragged a cry from her that seemed to come from the very depths of her soul.

Limp and languorous, she watched him remove his clothes. Then he covered her body with his and the magic started all over again. She tried to memorize every touch. Every look. Every sensation. For she knew they would be her last.

And when she awoke in the morning, he was gone.

Matthew was two hours down the road heading toward London when he reined Apollo to a halt and leaned forward to pat the gelding's brown neck. The mauve of dawn that had stained the sky when he left Langston Manor had given way to a pale blue dotted with fluffy clouds. His guests wouldn't be departing his home until early this afternoon, but he'd been unable to stay. Couldn't bear to say good-bye to Sarah in front of everyone. He wanted his last image of her to be of her sleeping after they'd made love, her hair spread around her like a curly brown halo.

Just ahead the road split, the left fork continuing southwest toward London, and right fork heading . . . not toward London.

He stared at the roads for several long moments while myriad images flashed through his mind. Images that he knew would haunt him until he breathed his last breath.

He knew what he had to do. He couldn't turn back.

But before he went to London, he realized there was somewhere else he needed to go first.

Pressing his heels to Apollo's flanks, he turned and headed up the right fork.

Chapter 18

Sarah stood in her bedchamber and stared at the bed, every crevice of her heart and mind crowded with memories. Pale streaks of late morning sunshine, weak courtesy of the thick cloud cover, cast ribbons of lackluster color across the counterpane that perfectly matched her mood. A footman had just removed the last of her belongings. All that was left to do now was wait for the carriages to be loaded. And then she'd be on her way home. Back to the life she'd always known. The life that had always been enough.

Until she'd come here.

Until she'd fallen hopelessly, recklessly, profoundly in love. With a man she couldn't have. She'd known from the onset the extreme likelihood that things would end this way, but a tiny flame of hope had burned in her chest, unable to be extinguished, that the money would be found. That Matthew would therefore not have to marry an heiress. That he could marry whomever he wanted. And that someone would be her.

Foolish, ridiculous dreams that she should have known better than to pin her hopes upon. She'd known, of course, that she risked her heart. But somehow she hadn't anticipated that when it broke it would hurt this much. Hadn't realized it would leave such a gaping, raw, hollow space in her chest. Hadn't known her very soul would be lost along with her heart.

She walked to the window and looked down at the gardens below. Did the money Matthew's father claim to have hidden there truly exist? Or were his words simply the ramblings of a pain-ridden delirious man drawing his last breaths?

Reaching into the pocket of her gown, she withdrew the slip of paper on which she'd written Matthew's father's last words. She held the list toward the meager sunlight and studied it for what felt like the thousandth time. *Fortune. Save estate. Hidden here. Garden. In garden. Golden flower. Fern. Fleur-de-lis.*

Surely there was a clue she was missing. She again mentally ran through the Latin names of every golden flower and species of fern she could think of, but nothing offered a new suggestion. After staring at the words for another minute, she blew out a sigh, refolded the paper and tucked it into her pocket.

With a final glance around, she quit the room, closing the door behind her, the soft click reverberating through her soul like a death knell.

In the foyer, she was greeted by Danforth, who, after a tail wagging greeting, resumed what appeared to be a vigil by the window nearest the front door. Tildon, who also greeted her when she entered, explained, "Danforth takes up residence in that spot whenever his lordship is away."

And when he returned, he'd have a new bride with him. *Stop. Stop thinking about it.* Yes, she needed to stop thinking about it. Because when she did, it hurt so much she could barely breathe.

Sarah moved to the window and scratched behind Danforth's ears. The dog looked up at her with dark, adoring eyes that seemed to say, *Oh, yes, that's the spot.*

"Good-bye, my friend," she whispered. "I'll miss you."

Danforth tilted his head and issued a rumble in his throat, as if to ask, *What's this? You're leaving, too?*

"I'm sorry you weren't able to meet my Desdemona. I think you two would have gotten along like bacon and eggs."

Danforth licked his chops at the mention of his two favorite foods, though as far as she could tell, *all* foods were his favorites. She gave his head a final pat, then, after bidding farewell to Tildon, she left the house.

There was a beehive of activity in the curved drive. Footmen carrying trunks and smaller luggage items to the various waiting carriages, others securing them to the vehicles, the travelers standing about in small groups, saying their good-byes, waiting to depart. Sarah spotted Carolyn, who was speaking with Lords Thurston and Hartley. When she approached, she heard her sister say, "Will you gentlemen please excuse me? I need to speak with my sister."

Although both gentlemen seemed reluctant to relinquish her company, they moved off, joining Lord Berwick and Mr. Jennsen, who stood nearby.

"You quite saved me," Carolyn said in an undertone after she and Sarah had walked several yards away. "Heavens, I believe Lord Hartley was about to propose!"

"Propose what exactly?"

A short huff of laughter came from Carolyn. "I'm not quite sure, but I didn't wish to hear it, no matter what it was." They halted near Carolyn's carriage, which bore the

Wingate crest on its black lacquered door, and her sister gave her a searching look. "Are you all right, Sarah?"

Before Sarah could answer, Carolyn hurried on, "I would have thought you'd be anxious to return home, but you're pale and your eyes . . . you look so sad."

To Sarah's mortification, tears pooled in her eyes. "I'm tired," she said. Her conscience slapped her, because while the statement was certainly true, it was hardly truthful.

Carolyn reached out, clasped her hand and offered her a smile surely meant to be encouraging. "Tonight you'll be sleeping in your bed. You'll rest better in your familiar surroundings."

Sarah swallowed the lump of misery that rose in her throat at the prospect of her own bed—in which she'd lie alone. And not sleep.

Carolyn gently squeezed her hand. "I'm grateful to you for these last several months, Sarah. I couldn't have faced reentering society without your help and support."

Sarah returned the gentle squeeze. "Yes, you could have. You're much stronger than you think."

Carolyn shook her head. "Finding the desire to go on without Edward has been . . . difficult. But after three years, I felt that he would have wanted me to embrace life again."

"Of course he would have. He loved your smile, as do I. It is a gift to see it again."

"Attending all those soirees with me when I know you would have preferred being home, pursuing your own interests . . . I don't know how to thank you."

"There is no need as *you* are my dearest interest. I would attend one hundred soirees if it would make you smile."

"One hundred?" Carolyn said in an amused voice.

"Yes. So please don't ask me to." Sarah gave an exaggerated shudder. "I believe I'd go mad."

"I promise not to take advantage of your good nature. Especially after you so kindly formed the Ladies Literary Society of London for my benefit."

"Not for your benefit," Sarah protested, but Carolyn shook her head.

"*My* benefit. And I love you for it." An impish grin curved her lips. "I'd say our first venture into scandalous literature was a huge success. I can't wait to begin our next selection."

"Nor can I. Based on my research of the subject, our next foray promises to be a thrilling adventure tale with enough scandal attached to it to make any matron reach for the hartshorn."

"Which is precisely why we chose it," they said in unison, then laughed.

"I imagine you'll relish getting back to your own garden," Carolyn said, "although the gardens here are spectacular."

Sarah nearly drowned in the wave of sadness that washed over her. "Yes, they are."

"Did you have a favorite spot?"

"It would be difficult to choose, but perhaps the area where the statue is." *Where I had my first conversation with Matthew.* "It was like a hidden garden within a garden."

"Yes, that was a lovely section. Which goddess was the statue?"

"Flora." Sarah frowned. "Flora . . ." she repeated slowly, her words to Carolyn tickling something in the back of her mind. *Hidden. Garden within a garden.* And Matthew's father's last words . . . *Garden. In garden.*

Her heart seemed to skip two beats. Could Matthew's

father have literally meant garden *in* garden? Could he have meant the area where the statue of Flora was located?

She closed her eyes and pictured the area. Were there any golden flowers surrounding Flora? *Golden flower, golden flower* . . .

Golden flower.

An idea hit her so hard she gasped. Good lord, was it possible? Her eyes popped open to find Carolyn staring at her.

"Are you all right, Sarah?"

She was so excited she could barely stand still. "Yes, I'm fine. But I must go—I, um, left something in the garden." A statement she prayed would turn out to be true.

"One of the footmen can retrieve it for you—"

"No! I mean, that's not necessary. We'll be cooped up in the carriage for so long, I'd enjoy a quick walk. I'll be back as quickly as I can. Don't leave without me."

"Of course not—"

But Sarah didn't wait for her sister to finish. She had already turned and was striding back toward the house, her mind racing. Behind her, she heard amidst the buzz of conversations a male voice ask, "Where is your sister off to in such a hurry, Lady Wingate?" And her sister's reply, "She left something in the garden . . ."

She heard no more as she entered the house and hastily told Tildon she'd left something in the garden. The butler favored her with an odd look, but she continued on, practically running across the foyer then toward the drawing room, where she exited the house.

The instant she hit the flagstone terrace, she hiked up her skirts and ran, Matthew's father's final words reverberating through her mind. *Golden flower, golden flower* . . . Dear God, if she were right . . .

By the time she reached the hidden alcove where Flora gently spilled water from her urn, Sarah's lungs felt ready to explode. Breathing hard, she dropped to her knees and, heedless of the bits of gravel digging into her skin through her gown, began to examine the base of the statue, running her fingers over every inch of the stone. Hope burned through her veins, growing stronger with every rapid heart beat. She *had* to be right. *Had to be.*

She'd completed nearly a quarter of the way around the circumference when she noticed a crack in the stone. A crack that appeared too perfectly straight to have occurred naturally. Scarcely able to breathe, she applied her fingers to the thin opening and discovered a small, rectangular-shaped section that appeared to be loose.

She tried to pry it farther apart, but quickly realized she'd require some sort of tool. Jumping to her feet, she cast her gaze about for something, anything, a stick that might aid her, but a hasty search yielded nothing. Damnation, she'd have to return to the house. Or—the grounds-keeper's cottage was closer. She'd caught a glimpse of Paul working at the other end of the garden during her mad dash across the terrace, which meant he wasn't at the cottage. Which suited her, as she didn't wish to answer any questions. She'd just borrow a tool or a knife and he'd never be the wiser.

She'd just turned in that direction when she heard foot-falls crunching in the gravel. Based on the sound, clearly a man. A man in a hurry. Seconds later that man appeared, skidding to a halt at the sight of her.

Sarah stared. In stunned amazement. At Matthew.

Chest heaving, he asked, "What are you doing here?"

She blinked twice to make certain it was truly him and not some figment of her broken-hearted imagination.

When he didn't disappear, she moistened her dust dry lips. "What are *you* doing here?"

Matthew drew several deep, calming breaths, then slowly approached her. She appeared to be frozen in place. When an arm's length separated them, he stopped. And forced himself to keep his hands at his sides. If he didn't, he'd give into the craving to pull her into his arms, and if he did, he'd lose all hope of saying all the things he needed to.

"I'm here because there's something I need to tell you, Sarah."

She appeared to shake off whatever manner of trance she'd fallen into at the sight of him. "Matthew, I'm so glad you're here. I think I've—"

He touched gentle fingertips to her lips. "I can't let another second go by without telling you that I love you."

When he'd stopped her from continuing, she appeared about to argue with him, but now her eyes widened. "You love me?"

"I love you. So much I can barely think straight. I was halfway to London when I realized I couldn't do it."

"Do what?"

Unable to keep from touching her, he clasped her hands, entwining their fingers. "Continue to London."

"So you came back. And I'm so glad you did because I've—"

"No. I didn't come back."

She raised her brows and gave him a pointed up and down stare. "Yet all evidence indicates the contrary."

"I mean I *did* come back. Obviously. But not right away. I paid a visit to your family before returning home."

"That's wonderful. I must tell you—" Her words cut off as his clearly sank in. "My *family*?"

"Yes. Instead of continuing to London, I visited your parents."

"But why? I cannot fathom a single reason why you would do that."

His lips twitched at her familiar saying. "Don't worry. I can fathom enough reasons for the both of us."

"I'd be fascinated to know even one of these reasons."

"Actually, there is only one reason." He lifted one of her hands and pressed a kiss against her fingers. "I told them I wished to marry their daughter."

He searched her eyes for her reaction, hoping to see joy. Instead, he saw complete and utter shock. In fact, her skin went totally pale. Not precisely the reaction he'd hoped for. When she remained silent, he said, "The only other time I've ever seen a more flabbergasted expression was in your parents' parlor several hours ago."

"I . . . I cannot imagine that they were more shocked than I am."

"Well, at first I admit there was a bit of confusion."

"I imagine so."

"They assumed the daughter I wished to marry was your sister."

She blinked. Then nodded. "Yes, I'm certain they *would* assume that."

"When I told them I meant their daughter Sarah—"

"I'm certain my mother didn't believe you."

"As a matter of fact, she didn't." Matthew's jaw tightened as he recalled his conversation with Sarah's mother. Her lips had puckered like a drawstring and she'd basically told him he was a fool to even look at Sarah when Carolyn was so very lovely.

He'd taken a great deal of satisfaction in giving the woman who'd shown so little kindness toward Sarah the set-down she so richly deserved. He made certain she understood that he'd tolerate no such disparaging comments in the future or further insults against Sarah, who, she'd be wise to recall, would soon be Marchioness Langston. Sarah's father had remained silent during the entire exchange. When it was over, however, he'd shot Matthew an approving look. Indeed, he looked as if he wanted to applaud.

"Although your mother didn't believe me at first, I managed to convince her I meant you. And only you. Always you." His gaze searched hers, and the stunned confusion in her eyes prompted him to say, "And now, it seems, I need to convince *you*."

Lifting their joined hands, he pressed them to his chest. "Sarah, I fell in love with you in this very spot, the first time we spoke. Since that moment, you haven't been out of my thoughts for so much as a second. Your eyes, your smile, they grabbed me by the heart, and I've been yours since that day.

"I kept fooling myself into thinking I could walk away, make a life without you, marry someone else to save the estate my father gambled into the ground. And I did a good job of convincing myself I could do it—until I actually had to walk away. In fact, I made it two hours down the road before I realized what a complete nincompoop I was."

He looked into her beautiful eyes, which still appeared stunned. "I love you, Sarah. I know I'm asking you to take on the life of an impoverished peer, but I swear I will do everything in my power to make certain you're always comfortable. I'll do my utmost to see that the tenants are compensated and that the estate doesn't fall down around our ears—but you need to know that there will definitely be difficult financial times ahead. There's a good chance there will *always* be financial difficulties. If I'm unsuccessful in paying off what my father owed, I may even face debtors' prison."

Her eyes flashed at that. "If anyone tries to take you to prison, they'd have to get through me first."

One corner of his mouth lifted. "I didn't realize you were such a fighter."

"I've never had anything to fight for. Until now." She slid one hand from his and rested her palm against his cheek. "I love you too. So much I can hardly stand it."

"Excellent. I'm very relieved it's not just me."

He lowered himself to one knee before her. "Deathbed promise or no, I cannot, will not, marry anyone other than you. Sarah, would you do me the honor of becoming my wife?"

Her eyes glittered and her bottom lip trembled. Bloody hell, he knew what that meant—tears were on the way. He hastily stood, and the instant he did, she threw her arms around his neck. Then she buried her face against his chest and cried as if her heart were breaking.

A feeling akin to panic invaded him. Damn it, this sobbing was worse than mere tears. He patted her back and pressed desperate kisses against her hair. "Dare I hope this is your very unusual way of saying yes?"

She lifted her head, and tenderness stabbed him through the heart. Her golden brown eyes looked like wet topaz jewels glittering behind her askew spectacles.

"Yes," she whispered, then laughed, a quick spurt of joyous sound that brought with it a flash of dimples. "Yes!"

Elation swept through him and he slanted his mouth over hers for a deep, lush kiss filled with love and passion and hope for the future. Just as he was losing himself in the taste of her, however, she pushed against his chest.

After he reluctantly lifted his head, she said, "Matthew, I must tell you—there's still hope."

He bent his head to trail his lips along her fragrant neck. "I know. Now that you've said yes—"

She shook her head and her chin bumped his temple. "No—I mean hope that we might find the money."

He straightened and looked at her with a frown. "What do you mean?"

"After pondering your father's last words and a conversation I had with my sister just a little while ago, an idea occurred to me. While talking to Carolyn, I referred to this area as a 'hidden garden within a garden.' It struck me that is very close to your father's words: 'garden, in garden.' Did you search here?"

"No." He extended his hand to encompass the area. "It's surrounded by hedges. There aren't any ferns. Nothing that resembles a fleur-de-lis or an iris. Nor are there any golden flowers."

"Exactly. But perhaps the problem all along was looking for some sort of golden flower. You said it was very difficult to understand what your father was saying. What if he wasn't saying 'golden flower' at all." Her eyes took on an excited glow. "He said there was a fortune, and clearly you assumed, as I did, that meant notes. Paper money. But what if the fortune wasn't in notes but in *gold*. As in gold coins. What if he was really saying 'gold in Flora'—meaning the gold was hidden in the fountain?"

Matthew frowned, casting his mind back to those last moments of his father's life. Then he nodded slowly, a kindling of hope flaring to life inside him. "It's possible."

"As soon as it occurred to me, I rushed here. I was examining the base of the fountain and I found a crack and a loose section of stone just before you arrived. I think the money may be hidden behind it."

He stared at her, dumbstruck. "And you're just telling me this now?"

She looked skyward. "I *tried* to tell you—several times—but you were too busy proposing. Not that I'm complaining, you understand."

A bark of amazed laughter escaped him, and he caught her up in his arms and spun her around. After setting her back on her feet, he said, "Have I told you lately that you're brilliant?"

"Actually, I don't believe you've *ever* told me that."

"A heinous oversight on my part. You are absolutely brilliant. Thank God you've agreed to marry me so I can spend the rest of my life telling you so every day."

"No point in saying I'm brilliant until we know if I'm right."

"Even if you're not, it was still a brilliant bit of deduction. Now where's that loose stone?"

Taking him by the hand, she led him toward the front of the fountain then knelt and pointed. "See the crack and loose stone?"

"I do indeed." Excitement rippled through him. Slipping his knife from his boot, he applied the blade to the thin line. For several minutes the only sounds were the trickling fountain and the scraping of the knife against the stone.

"It's coming loose," he said, unable to keep the anticipation from his voice. He set down the knife and managed to wedge a fingertip on either side of the stone. By rocking it back and forth, little by little he eased it out.

"Almost there," he said, getting a better grip on the

coarse rock. A moment later the brick-sized stone slid out to reveal a dark opening. Matthew looked at Sarah, whose gaze was fixated on the cavity.

"I think you should have the honors," he said, nodding toward the hole.

She shook her head. "No. You look. It's your fortune."

"We'll look together since it's *our* fortune."

"All right."

They were about to each reach a hand into the dark opening when a voice behind them said, "A lovely sentiment, but actually, it's *my* fortune."

Matthew pivoted around and found himself staring into familiar eyes. But instead of the friendship he was accustomed to seeing there, undisguised hatred now glittered—a sentiment rendered even more obvious by the pistol aimed at the center of his chest.

Chapter 19

Keeping his gaze steady on those cold blue eyes, Matthew said calmly, "Well, this is a surprise."

"A pleasant one—for me. I'd given up hope of recovering the money your father stole from me. Now, I want you both to stand—very slowly and very quietly. And Matthew, if I see you reach for that knife, I'll blow a big hole right through Miss Moorehouse." Lord Berwick shook his head and made a *tsking* sound. "And I know you wouldn't like that."

Moving with excruciating care, Matthew rose, his mind searching for an escape. He fought against his first and strongest instinct, which was to step in front of Sarah. If Berwick fired the pistol at this close range, he could possibly kill both of them with his one shot. Better that the pistol remained aimed at him.

As soon as they'd both gained their feet, Berwick said to him, "Kick the knife toward me. Get it close enough so I can reach it."

Matthew obeyed, then watched Berwick pick up the blade.

"Thank you. Now hands on top of your heads, if you please."

"So polite," Matthew said dryly, raising his arms.

"There's no reason not to behave in a gentlemanly manner."

"Excellent. Then let the lady go."

Berwick shook his head sadly. "I'm afraid I can't do that. She'd raise the alarm, and that would turn this very simple transaction into a debacle." He looked briefly at Sarah. "If you move or make a sound, I'll shoot him. Do you understand?"

From the corner of his eye Matthew saw Sarah nod. He wanted to look at her, somehow reassure her, but he didn't dare take his eyes off Berwick.

"You cannot possibly think you're going to get away with this," he said.

"But of course I will. I'm going to take back my money, which your father stole from me, then depart."

"My father possessed many bad habits but he wasn't a thief. He won the money gambling."

"But he won it from me. It was *my* money." Anger flashed across his features. "I wasn't supposed to lose. I *couldn't* lose. I'd sold everything I could to get that money—it was everything I had. I needed to triple it to get out of debt. And I would have—if your stupid father, who hardly ever won, hadn't been struck by the most incredible streak of luck I've ever witnessed. It was as if he couldn't lose. And I couldn't win. And that wasn't at all the way the game was supposed to go."

Matthew nodded. "I see. So you invited him for a game, planning to fleece him. Rather pointless, as he didn't have any money to lose."

"Oh, but he did. He bragged about recently having won a huge sum. The game was to be just the two of us. Very high stakes. And I was supposed to win." Berwick narrowed his eyes at Matthew. "And I should have gotten it back. I would have, except he didn't have it with him in the carriage as he should have. So I made him pay. With his life."

Everything inside Matthew stilled as realization hit him like a brick to the head. "You . . . *You* were the highwayman who shot him."

The fury burning in Berwick's eyes transformed his features from handsome to demonic, but it didn't begin to match the fury gripping Matthew. "He deserved nothing less. He should have had the money with him, but he didn't. I don't know how he disposed of it, but somehow he did. I kept waiting to hear after his death that you'd paid off his debts, but after several months passed and you hadn't, I realized you either didn't know about the money or, if you did, you didn't know where it was located.

"Then I began hearing interesting rumors. About you becoming reclusive, not venturing off the estate, eschewing Society—and all due to a sudden passionate interest in horticulture." Berwick smiled, a cold upturning of his lips that didn't reach his eyes. "Very interesting, as I know that flowers made you sneeze."

"Not all flowers, only roses," Matthew corrected.

Berwick merely shrugged. "I realized that you must be looking for the money in the garden. Over the past several weeks I've observed your late night digging sessions, waiting for you to find what is mine so I could take it back."

Matthew's eyes narrowed as another piece of the puzzle clicked into place. "You killed Tom Willstone."

Berwick shrugged again. "Unfortunately for him, he saw me in the woods that night. Threatened to tell you I was trespassing. I couldn't risk him doing so."

Keep him talking. Surely if they stayed out here long

enough someone would come looking for them. But Matthew feared it might be quite some time. After he'd arrived at the house and been told by Lady Wingate that Sarah was in the garden, he'd sent Daniel a meaningful look. There was no doubt in his mind that his friend understood that he wanted some privacy with Sarah. Therefore, Daniel would do his utmost to ensure that they weren't disturbed for as long as possible.

But Berwick didn't know that. If he kept him talking long enough, surely the bastard would make a mistake. And all Matthew needed was one tiny mistake.

"So your discovery that I was looking for the money is why you wished for an invitation to my house party," he said in a conversational tone.

"Yes. What better opportunity to observe your comings and goings? Thurston and Hartley provided convenient foils, extra bodies to keep anyone from observing me too closely." He chuckled. "I must say, it's been most entertaining. Especially watching you when you weren't digging, Langston. Clearly you meant to choose one of the beautiful heiresses present to be your wife, yet you saddled yourself with the homely spinster. But that is simply another bit of good fortune as far as I'm concerned." He smiled. "Lady Julianne will make *me* a very admirable wife."

A soft gasp came from Sarah, and Matthew prayed she'd remain quiet. Just as he was about to speak, he caught sight of a slight movement through the bushes behind Berwick, and hope raced through him. Seconds later a shadow inched into the opening in the hedges directly behind Berwick.

Determined to let whoever was there know what their situation was, he said, "There will be no more good fortune for you, Berwick, regardless of that pistol and knife you're holding. Even if you succeed in killing us in order to steal the money in the fountain, you'll never make it off this estate without being found out. You'll never see the outside of a jail cell again."

"On the contrary, it will appear that you used your knife against Miss Moorehouse—in self-defense after she threatened you—her lover who was abandoning her—with this pistol. I overheard your dreadful argument and tried to intervene, but alas I was too late. In the melee, the pistol went off and you were, regrettably, fatally wounded. And no one will know about the money because no one knows it exists." His cold smile could have chilled the air around them. "You see? A very tidy package. And now, sadly for you, the time has come to bid you both farewell."

"Julianne will never marry you," Sarah said, her voice perfectly calm.

Berwick flicked an annoyed glance her way. "I told you to be quiet."

"Yes. Or you'd shoot Matthew. But since it's clear you're going to do that anyway, I've no reason to remain silent." And with that she let loose with a bloodcurdling, ear-splitting scream.

Berwick, clearly furious and unnerved, swung the pistol toward Sarah. Matthew reached for her with one hand and the extra knife in his boot with the other hand just as a brown blur raced through the opening in the hedges. At the same instant Matthew jerked Sarah to the ground and let his knife fly, Danforth's teeth sank into the back of Berwick's thigh. Berwick cried out and a pistol shot exploded. Then the weapon fell from Berwick's hand and he crumpled to the ground, the knife buried to the hilt in his chest.

Matthew turned to Sarah and gathered her in his arms, his gaze anxiously scanning her pale face. "Are you all right?"

Her nod sent her spectacles sliding downward. "I'm fine. Are you hurt?"

"No." He gave a low whistle, and Danforth trotted over from where he'd been sniffing Berwick's motionless body. "Stay with Sarah," he said to the dog, who immediately sat on her shoe.

After quickly determining that Berwick was indeed dead, Matthew returned to Sarah and Danforth, the dog a tail-wagging mass of canine bliss from the behind-the-ear scratching he was receiving.

"Good boy," he said, patting Danforth's sturdy sides. By God, he really was one damn smart dog. "You quite saved the day." He glanced at Sarah. "Biting murderers on the arse—I taught him that."

"Nicely done. And you saved the day as well. Not only do you carry an extra knife, you know how to use it." She laid her hand on his and smiled. "A very handy talent in a husband."

He clasped her fingers and marveled at the sight of her. Bloody hell, how he'd ever thought her anything less than stunning, he'd never know. "A handy talent indeed. And one I hope never to have to display again. But I might not have had the chance to use the knife if not for your scream. Very effective. It quite raised the hairs on the back of my neck."

"Well, I certainly wasn't going to allow him to shoot you."

"For which I'm very appreciative." He rose and held out his hands to help her up. After she stood, he drew her into his arms. She rested her head against his chest and he buried his face in her hair. "Thank God he didn't hurt you," he whispered.

"Or you." A shudder ran through her, and he gathered her closer.

"You were very brave. Any other woman would have swooned."

"I nearly did." She leaned back in the circle of his arms and cradled his face in her palms. "But I wasn't about to let him hurt you. As you're one of my great passions, I'd prefer to keep you in one piece."

"*One* of your great passions? I believe I'm insulted."

Her lips twitched. "My *greatest* passion."

"Much better," he murmured just before his mouth covered hers.

"Matthew, Sarah, where are you? Are you all right?"

Daniel's voice, accompanied by the sound of running feet, had him lifting his head. "Here, by the fountain," he called.

Seconds later Daniel, along with Hartley and Thurston, as well as Logan Jennsen and Paul, all of whom held either a pistol or a knife, rushed into the small clearing.

Daniel scanned the scene, his jaw tight. "What happened?"

Matthew quickly explained, including the fortune supposedly in the base of the fountain, which had motivated Berwick's behavior, then looked at Hartley and Thurston. "Would you mind returning to the house and instructing Tildon to summon the magistrate?"

"Certainly," they agreed, appearing relieved to leave the scene.

After they left, Matthew turned to Paul. "Can you bring a tarp to cover the body?"

"Yes, my lord," he replied, then left as well.

"Unless there's something else you need for me to do, I'll explain the situation to the ladies," Logan Jennsen said. "We all heard the scream and the pistol shot, and they're very worried."

"Thank you," said Matthew, his jaw tightening at the lingering look Jennsen gave Sarah before departing.

"You're certain you're both all right?" Daniel asked.

"Positive," Matthew said.

"You're sure you didn't hit your head?"

"Of course I'm sure. Why do you ask?"

"Because you seem to have forgotten to look for the money in the base of the fountain."

Matthew shook his head. "I was so worried about Sarah I *did* forget."

Paul returned just then with a tarp and covered Berwick's body. After he left, Matthew looked at Sarah.

"Ready?"

"Absolutely."

He looked at Daniel. "Wish us luck."

Together he and Sarah knelt before the small opening. And slid their hands inside.

And felt nothing.

"It's . . . it's empty," Sarah said, her voice ringing with disappointment.

Matthew felt around the small space one more time, but there was no doubt it was empty. Daniel laid his hand on his shoulder. "I'm sorry, Matthew. I'll see you back at the house."

After Daniel's footfalls faded, Matthew rose and gently helped Sarah to her feet.

"I'm sorry, Matthew," she said, her eyes swimming with tears.

"As am I, but if you think about it, even without finding an actual cache of gold, the money has made me rich. Because without it, I never would have met you. And you are worth your weight in gold."

"No I'm—" She stopped abruptly and stared intently over Matthew's shoulder.

"What?" he asked, turning.

"The fountain. Berwick's shot hit Flora's urn."

He shook his head at the damage to the lip of the vase. "My mother loved this statue. My father had it made just for her."

Sarah looked at him. "Like the rose garden."

"Yes."

"Which would explain why he'd said 'fleur-de-lis.'"

She leaned forward and dipped her fingers in the water, then grabbed his arm. "Matthew. Look."

She was staring into the pool of water. Matthew followed her line of vision and froze. Reaching out, he slipped his hand under the water up to his elbow and scooped up the shiny gold disk. Then he pulled his hand from the water and opened his palm.

"A gold sovereign," Sarah said in an awed and excited voice.

They immediately started searching through the rest of the pool. After a few seconds, however, Matthew looked up. And a slow smile curved his lips.

"Sarah—I don't think my father said 'fern.'" When she looked up from her search of the water, he nodded toward the broken vase. "I think he said *urn.*"

With that, he hopped onto the waist-high edge of the pool and hoisted himself to his feet. Grabbing the lip of the urn, he peered inside.

"Well?" came Sarah's impatient voice. "Is there anything in there?"

Heedless of the trickling water, Matthew stuck his arm inside the deep, slightly tipped vase. As he withdrew his hand he said, "Remember what I said about you being worth your weight in gold? It would appear that we now actually do have your weight in gold."

He opened his fingers and a handful of gold coins spilled out, falling into the pool below.

Sarah gasped, then lifted stunned, shining eyes to him. "There's more?"

"Sweetheart, this huge urn is *full*."

With a whoop of joy, Matthew jumped to the ground, caught her up in his arms and hugged her to him.

"We found it," he said, punctuating each disbelieving word with a kiss. "I can't believe we found it."

"And how ironic that it was Berwick's wild shot that gave us the final clue," Sarah said.

"Yes, although I'm certain we would have found it anyway, seeing as how brilliant you are."

"You're the one who figured out *urn*."

"After you figured out the money was in the fountain."

"Which shows, I suppose, that we're very good together."

"Not just very good, sweetheart. Perfect."

She smiled. "I'm not surprised, seeing as how I'd already dubbed you the Perfect Man."

"Well now, I'd have to be pretty close to keep up with you—the Perfect Woman."

She shook her head and laughed. "I cannot fathom a single reason why you would say that."

He caught her in his arms and with a grin spun her around. "Don't worry, sweetheart. I can think of enough reasons for the both of us."

Epilogue

Two days after discovering the gold, Sarah hurried from her bedchamber at Langston Manor. Matthew had asked her to meet him in the front of the house at two in the afternoon, an invitation that piqued her curiosity, as he'd refused to offer any hint as to the reason.

The last two days had been busy, especially for Matthew. After dealing with the magistrate, he'd traveled to London to settle his father's debts, which were now not only paid in full, but with a substantial amount left over.

All the house party guests had departed except for Carolyn, who stayed on with Sarah in order to help her plan the small wedding that would take place in one week's time. When Matthew arrived home from London several hours ago, he'd surprised her with the best gift he could have given her when he opened the carriage door to reveal Desdemona—resplendent with a huge lavender bow around her neck. While she and her beloved pet were reunited amidst much laughter and tail wagging, he explained that he'd stopped at her home to pick up the dog.

When they introduced Desdemona to Danforth, the two dogs sniffed each other thoroughly. Desdemona then barked once and licked her chops. Danforth barked twice and licked his chops. And then promptly sat on Desdemona's tail. Desdemona grunted her approval.

Matthew laughed and said, "I taught him that."

And now it seemed he had another surprise for her, although she couldn't imagine what could be more wonderful than bringing Desdemona to her.

When she stepped outside a moment later, Matthew, holding the reins of his gelding Apollo, smiled in greeting. "Right on time."

She smiled in return, but eyed the horse warily. "Are you going somewhere, or returning?"

"Going. I was hoping you might join me."

"Where?"

"The village." He looked at her through serious eyes. "I thought if you came with me, and we went on horseback, we could help each other face down our bad memories. And make new, happy memories together."

Her gaze shifted from him to the horse and back. "Rather like killing two birds with one stone."

"Exactly."

She licked her suddenly dry lips. "I haven't been on a horse in a very long time."

"I haven't been to the village in a very long time." He held out his free hand to her. "My arms will be around you the entire time."

"That would help."

"Having you with me would help."

Sarah drew a deep breath, then slowly reached out her hand. "Let's make some new, happy memories together."

His smile warmed her to her soul. He mounted the horse with the ease of an expert rider, then held out his hand to her. After a bracing breath, she cautiously set her foot in the stirrup, and in the next second she was sitting sideways in front of him, one strong, masculine arm wrapped around her waist.

"Are you all right?" His quiet question blew past her ear, and she felt the brush of his lips against her temple.

"I'm . . . fine." And she realized she was. A bit nervous, but buoyed with the feel of him surrounding her, confident that she could do this. That he could do this. That they could do this. Together.

He set Apollo to a gentle walk, and they headed away from the house. "While we're in the village we can shop for a wedding gift," Matthew said.

"For each other?"

"No, for Paul. He's proposed to one of the upstairs maids, a young woman named Mary."

Sarah smiled. "Indeed? Mary is the maid who told me which bedchamber was yours the night I pilfered your shirt."

"Remind me to double her salary. Paul told me today of their plans. Seems I almost caught them together at his cottage the day I ordered all the lavender arrangements. Told me he decided then and there he didn't want to sneak around any longer."

"I'm happy for them." She snuggled closer against him. "You do realize that us traveling to the village on a single horse will set tongues wagging."

"No doubt we'll cause quite the stir. We can call it 'chaos in Kent.' And when we visit London, we'll set that town on its ear as well."

"And call it 'mayhem in Mayfair.'"

He laughed. "Precisely. You know, there's a small garden and conservatory at the London town house that have become rather run down due to my previous financial problems. They will require a great deal of tender loving care."

"I'm delighted to provide it."

"Excellent." He leaned forward and lightly nibbled her earlobe, sending a shiver of delight down her spine. "And I too shall require a great deal of tender, loving care."

She smiled into his beautiful eyes. "I'm delighted to provide it. I take it there are no roses in your London conservatory?"

He made a horrified face and she laughed. "God, no. I feel a sneeze coming on just thinking about it."

"Those sneezes *are* a handy way to know where you are," she teased.

His arm tightened around her, and the soft kiss he brushed against her lips made her heart skip a beat. "You never need wonder where I am, sweetheart. I'll always be right here. Next to you."

"Which makes you absolutely perfect."

*A*h, summertime. The kids are off from school and underfoot, the temperature may rise to an uncomfortable level, and your body can't believe it's already swimsuit season . . . but fortunately Avon Books has just the solution for the dog days of summer—escape into a sweeping, passion-filled romance.

Embrace the heat with these sizzling Romance Superleaders—so captivating they come with their own warning: You won't be satisfied until you read all four books.

Enjoy!

Not Quite A Lady
LORETTA CHASE
May 2007

Darius Carsington is the youngest of the Carsington brothers and divides his life into two parts: 1) studying animal behavior, especially mating habits, and 2) imitating these habits. His father challenges him to either bring one of their dilapidated estates back into shape within a year or get married. Having no interest in marriage, Darius moves to the country and—much to his father's despair—quickly begins to put things to rights. But his lifestyle is challenged when he meets the intriguing Lady Charlotte Hayward, a seemingly perfect lady with a past of her own.

"You put your hands on me." Charlotte's face was quite rosy now.

"I may have to do it again," Darius said, "if you continue to blunder about the place, alarming the wildlife."

He had not thought her blue eyes could open any wider but they did. *"Blunder about?"*

"I fear you have disturbed the dragonflies during an extremely delicate process," he said. "They were mating, poor things, and you frightened them out of their wits."

She stared at him. Her mouth opened, but nothing came out.

"Now I understand why none but the hardiest of the livestock remain," he said. "You must have either frightened them all away or permanently impaired their reproductive functions."

"Impaired their— I did *not*. I was . . ." Her gaze fell to the hat he still held. "Give me my hat."

He turned it in his hands and studied it. "This is the most frivolous hat I've ever seen." Perhaps it was and perhaps it wasn't. He had no idea. He never noticed women's clothes except as obstacles to be got out of the way as quickly as possible.

Still, he could see that the thing he held was an absurd bit of froth: a scrap of straw, scraps of lace, ribbons. "What does it do? It cannot keep off the sun or the rain."

"It's a *hat*," she said. "It isn't supposed to do anything."

"Then what do you wear it for?"

"For?" she said. "*For?* It's . . . It's . . ." Her brow knit.

He waited.

She bit her lip and thought hard. "Decoration. Give it back. I must go now."

"What, no 'please'?"

The blue eyes flashed up at him. "No," she said.

"I see I must set the example of manners," he said.

"Give me my hat." She reached for it.

He put the nonsensical headwear behind his back.

"I am Darius Carsington," he said. He bowed.

"I don't care," she said.

"Beechwood has been turned over to me," he said.

She turned away. "Never mind. Keep the hat if you want it so much. I've others."

She started to walk away.

That would not do. She was exceedingly pretty.

He followed her. "I collect you live nearby," he said.

"Apparently I do not live far enough away," she said.

"This place has been deserted for years," he said. "Perhaps you were unaware of the recent change."

"Papa told me. I . . . forgot."

"Papa," he said, and his good humor began to fade. "That would be . . . ?"

"Lord Lithby," she said tautly. "We came from London yesterday. The stream is our western border. I was always used to come here and . . . But it does not matter."

No, it didn't, not anymore.

Her accents, her dress, her manner, all told Darius this was a lady. He had no objections to ladies. Unlike some, he was not drawn exclusively to women of the lower orders. She seemed a trifle slow-witted and appeared to possess no sense of humor whatsoever, but this didn't signify. Women's brains or lack thereof had never mattered to him. What he wanted from them had nothing to do with their intellect or sense of humor.

What did matter was that the lady had referred to her *father's* property bordering Darius's. Not her husband's.

Ergo, she must be an unmarried daughter of the Marquess of Lithby.

It was odd—not to mention extremely annoying—that Darius had mistaken her. Usually he could spot a virgin at fifty paces. Had he realized this was a maiden, not a matron, he would have set her on her feet and sent her packing immediately. Though he had little use for Society's illogical rules, he drew the line at seducing innocents.

Since seduction was out of the question, he saw no reason to continue the conversation. He had wasted far too much time on her already.

He held out the hat.

With a wary look, she took it.

"I apologize for startling you or getting in your way or whatever I did," he said dismissively. "Certainly you are welcome to traipse about the property as you've always done. It is of no consequence to me. Good day."

Sins of a Duke
SUZANNE ENOCH
June 2007

Sebastian Griffin, Duke of Melbourne, is not pleased when the Prince Regent appoints him as cultural liaison to a tiny new kingdom. Sebastian is not entirely convinced that this kingdom is as great as its ruler claims it is—or if the kingdom actually exists! And the fact that Princess Josefina intrigues him far more than he wishes, makes the situation all the more complicated. Reluctant to lose Prinny's favor, but unwilling to allow England to be taken in, Sebastian settles on the only plan that makes sense: He will seduce the truth out of "the princess."

Princess Josefina, a maid and one of the black-uniformed men flanking her, faced him as he approached. Tonight she wore a rich yellow gown, low cut enough that the creamy mounds of her breasts heaved as she drew a breath. God, she was spectacular. Of course that didn't signify anyth—

She slapped him.

Sebastian blinked, clenching his rising hands against the immediate instinct to retaliate. The blow stung, but of more concern was the responding roar from the onlookers in the Elkins' ballroom. He looked directly into her dark brown eyes. "Never do that again," he murmured, curving his lips in a smile that felt more like a snarl.

"My father and your Regent made a very simple request of you," she snapped, no trace of the soft-spoken flirt of this afternoon in either her voice or her expression. "If you are incapable of meeting even such low expectations, I will see you relieved of your duties to Costa Habichuela immediately, before you can do any harm with your incompetence."

It took every ounce of his hard-earned self control to remain standing there, unmoving. No one—*no one*—had ever spoken to him like that. As for hitting him . . . He clenched his jaw. "If you would care to accompany me off the dance floor," he said in a low voice, unable to stop the slight shake of his words, "I believe I can correct your misapprehension."

"*My* misapprehension? I, sir, am a royal princess. You are only a duke. And I am most displeased."

The circle of the audience that surrounded them drew closer, the ranks swelling until it seemed that now people were coming in off the streets to gawk. Sebastian drew a deep breathe in through his nose. "Come with me," he repeated, no longer requesting, "and we will resolve our differences in a civilized manner."

"First you will apologize to me," the princess retorted, her chin lifting further.

All he needed to do was turn his back and walk away. The crowd would speculate, rumors would spread, but in the end his reputation and power would win the argument for him. As far as he was concerned, though, that would be cheating. And he wanted the victory here. He wanted *her* apology, *her* surrender, her mouth, her body. Slowly he straightened his fingers. "I apologize for upsetting you, Your Highness. Please join me in the library so we may converse." He reached for her wrist.

The princess drew back, turning her shoulder to him. "I did not give you permission to touch me."

At the moment he wanted to do so much more than touch her wrist. God. It was as though when she hit him, she'd seared his flesh down to the bone. "Then we are at an impasse," he returned, still keeping his voice low and even, not letting anyone see what coursed beneath his skin, "because I am not going to continue this conversation in the middle of a ballroom."

She looked directly into his eyes. Despite his anger, the analytical part of him noted that very few people ever met him straight on. Whatever she saw there, her expression eased a little. "Perhaps then instead of conversing, we should dance."

Dance. He wanted to strangle her, and she wanted to dance. It did admittedly provide the best way out of this with the fewest rumors flying. The rumors it *would* begin, though, he didn't like. Was she aware that she was making this look like some sort of lovers' quarrel? He couldn't very well ask her. Instead he turned his head to find Lord Elkins.

"Could you manage us a waltz, Thomas?" he

asked, giving an indulgent smile. "Princess Josefina would like to dance."

"Of course, Your Grace." The viscount waved at the orchestra hanging over the balcony to gawk at the scene below. "Play a waltz!"

Stumbling over one another, the players sat and after one false start, struck up a waltz.

That would solve the yelling, but not the spectacle. "May I?" Sebastian intoned, holding out his hand again.

After a deliberate hesitation, the princess reached out and placed her gloved fingers into his bare ones. "For this dance only."

With her now in his grasp, the urge to show her just who was in command nearly overpowered him. Mentally steeling himself, he slid a hand around her waist, in the same moment sending a glance over his shoulder at Shay. "Dance," he mouthed. Not for all of heaven and earth would he prance about the floor alone.

"Are you going to explain to me why you sent a carriage without bothering to attend me yourself?" Princess Josefina asked.

"Your English is surprisingly good for a foreigner," he said deliberately. "As a native, allow me to give you a little advice. No matter who—"

"I will not—"

"—you may be elsewhere," he continued in a low voice, tightening his grip on her as she tried to pull away, "you should consider that in England you do not strike a nobleman in public."

"For *your* information," she returned in the same

tone, "my English is perfect because until a year ago I *was* English, raised mostly in Jamaica. And I will strike anyone who insults me."

That settled it. She was a lunatic. "You're mad," he said aloud. "I can conceive of no other explanation as to why you would speak to me in such a manner."

She lifted an elegant eyebrow. "If I am the only one who tells you the truth, that does not make me mad. It makes everyone else around you cowards."

The muscles of his jaw were clenched so tightly they ached. "I should—"

"You should what, Melbourne?" she cut in, her gaze unexpectedly lowering to his mouth. "Arguing with me excites you, doesn't it?" She drew a breath closer in his arms. "And there is nothing you can do about it, is there?" she whispered.

Sleepless at Midnight
JACQUIE D'ALESSANDRO
July 2007

*Miss Sarah Moorehouse belongs to the Ladies Literary
Society of London, a group of young ladies who, rather
than read proper novels by Jane Austen, would much
rather read books they're not supposed to . . . Mary
Shelley's* Frankenstein, *for example. During a discussion, the women decide that they, too, would create the
perfect man—figuratively, of course. Each is assigned
a task, and Sarah's assignment is to pilfer clothing
from the host of a country party, the very attractive
and very broad-chested Matthew Devonport, Marquess Langston, who catches Sarah in his bedchamber,
his shirt in her hands.*

"Daffodil," Matthew murmured. "Very nice. You're
as talented with watercolors as you are at drawing."

"Thank you." Again she seemed surprised by his
compliment and he wondered why. Surely anyone
who looked at these pictures could see they were
excellent. "I've painted sketches of several hundred
different species."

"Another passion of yours?"

She smiled. "I'm afraid so."

"And what do you do with your sketches? Frame them for display in your home?"

"Oh, no. I keep them in their sketch pads while I add to my collection. Someday I intend to organize the group and see them published into a book on horticulture."

"Indeed? A lofty goal."

"I see no point in aspiring to any other sort."

He shifted his gaze from the sketch and their eyes met. "Why aim for the ground when you can shoot for the stars?" he murmured.

She blinked, then her smile bloomed again. "Exactly," she agreed.

Aware that he was once again staring, he forced his attention back to the sketch pad. He flipped through more pages, studying sketches of unfamiliar plants with unpronounceable Latin titles, along with several flowers he didn't recall the names of, but which he recognized thanks to his hours spent digging holes all around the grounds. One bloom he did recognize was the rose, and he forced himself not to shudder. For some reason the damn things made him sneeze. He avoided them whenever possible.

He flipped another page. And stared. At the detailed sketch of a man. A very naked man. A man who was . . . not ungenerously formed. A man, who based on the letters printed along the bottom of the page, was named Franklin N. St.—

She gasped and snatched the sketch pad from his hands and closed it. The sound of the pages snapping together seemed to echo in the air between them.

Matthew couldn't decide if he was more amused, surprised, or intrigued. Certainly he wouldn't have suspected such a drawing from this mousy woman. Clearly there was more to her than met the eye. Could *this* have been what she'd been up to last evening—drawing erotic sketches? Bloody hell, could this Franklin person who'd modeled for her sketch be someone from his own household? There *was* a young man named Frank on the grounds-keeping staff . . .

Yet surely not. She'd only just arrived! He tried to recall the man's features, but as best he could remember from his brief look, his face was shadowed and indistinct—the only part of him which was.

"Friend of yours?" he drawled.

She hoisted up her chin. "And if he is?"

Well, he had to give her points for standing her ground. "I'd say you'd captured him quite well. Although I'm certain your mama would be shocked."

"On the contrary, I'm certain she'd take no notice at all." She stepped away from him, then glanced in a pointed fashion at the opening in the hedges. "It was lovely chatting with you, my lord, but please don't let me keep you any longer from your morning walk."

"My walk, yes," he murmured, feeling an inexplicable urge to delay his departure. To look at more of her sketches to see if he could discover yet another layer of this woman whose personality, in such a short period of time, had presented such contrasts.

Ridiculous. It was time to leave, to continue with his mind-clearing walk. "Enjoy your morning, Miss

Moorehouse," he said. "I shall see you at dinner this evening." He made a formal bow, a gesture she responded to with a brief curtsy. Then, with a soft whistle to Danforth, Matthew departed the small clearing, with Danforth at his heels, and headed down the path leading toward the stables. Perhaps a ride would help clear his head.

Walking at a brisk pace, he reflected on his meeting with Miss Moorehouse and two things occurred to him: First, the woman's in-depth knowledge of horticulture might be of use to him, provided he could glean the information he wanted from her without her realizing his reasons for wanting it—a challenge, given her nosey nature. He'd attempted to get such information from Paul, but while his head gardener knew a great deal about plants, he did not possess a formal education such as Miss Moorehouse clearly did. In having her as a guest, he might have stumbled quite inadvertently upon the key to finding the missing piece to his quest.

And second, the woman very effectively, albeit very politely, dismissed him from his own bloody garden! As if she was a princess and he a lowly footman. He'd not made an issue of it as departing was precisely what he'd wanted to do. Bloody hell. He still couldn't decide if he was more annoyed or intrigued.

Both, he decided. Miss Sarah Moorehouse was one of those annoying spinster women who peered out windows when they should be sleeping, always turned up in spots where you didn't wish them to be, and tended to see and hear things they shouldn't.

Yet the dichotomy of her bookish, plain appearance and her erotic nude sketch fascinated him. As did her knowledge of plants. If she could prove to be of some use to him in his quest, well, he'd simply find a way to suffer her company.

For he'd do anything to end his mission and get his life back.

And if, by some chance, she'd followed him into the garden last night, he intended to see to it that she did not do so again.

Twice the Temptation
SUZANNE ENOCH
August 2007

*In two connected novellas, Suzanne Enoch will cap-
tivate her historical readers with a sparkling romance
and mystery about a cursed diamond necklace set in
Regency England, then catapult them to contempo-
rary times, where billionaire Richard Addison and re-
formed thief Samantha Jellicoe will solve the case.*

"It occurs to me, Miss Munroe," Connoll said, taking a half step after her, "that you might wish to give
me your Christian name."

She paused, looking over her shoulder at him.
"And why is that?"

"We have kissed, after all." And he abruptly desired to kiss her again. The rest of his observations
had been accurate; he wanted to know whether his
impression of her mouth was, as well. Soft lips and
a sharp tongue. Fascinating. He wondered whether
she know how few women ever spoke frankly to
him.

With what might have been a curse, she reached
out to close the morning room door. "We did not
kiss, my lord," she returned, her voice clipped as
she faced him directly again. "You fell on me, and

then you mistakenly mauled me. Do not pretend there was anything mutual about it."

This time he couldn't keep his lips from curving, watching as her gaze dropped to his mouth in response. "So you say. I myself don't entire recollect."

"I recollect quite clearly. Pray do not mention your . . . error in judgment again, for both of our sakes."

"I'm not convinced it was an error, but very well." He rocked back on his heels. "*If* you tell me your given name."

He couldn't read the expression that crossed her face, but he thought it might be surprise. Men probably threw themselves at her feet and worshipped the hems of her gowns.

"Oh, for heaven's . . ." she sputtered. "Fine. Evangeline."

"Evangeline," he repeated. "Very nice."

"Thank you. I'll tell my mother that you approve of her choice."

Connoll lifted an eyebrow. "You're not precisely a shrinking lily, are you?"

"You accosted me," she retorted, putting her hands on her hips. "I feel no desire to play pretty with you."

"But I like to play."

Her cheeks darkened. "No doubt. I suggest that next time you find someone more willing to reciprocate."

Connoll reached out to fluff the sleeve of her cream-colored muslin with his fingers. "You know,

I find myself rather relieved," he said, wondering how close he was to treading to the edge of disaster and still willing to career along at full speed. "There are women of my acquaintance who would use my . . . misstep of earlier to gain a husband and a title. You only seem to wish to be rid of me."

Evangeline Munroe pursed her lips, an expression he found both amusing and attractive. "You were blind drunk at nearly ten o'clock in the morning. In all honesty, my lord, I do not find that behavior . . . admirable, nor do I wish to associate myself with it on a permanent basis."

"Well, that stung," he admitted, not overly offended. "Suffice it to say that I am not generally tight at mid-morning. Say you'll dance with me tonight at the Graviston soiree, Evangeline. I assume you'll be attending."

"Are you mad? I have no intention of dancing with you." She took a step closer, lifting up on her toes to bring herself nearer to his height. "I have been attempting to convince you to leave since the moment you arrived. Why in God's name would that make you think me willing to dance with you? And I gave you no leave to call me by my given name. I only told you what it was under duress."

"I'll leave, but not until you say you'll dance with me tonight. Or kiss me again, immediately. I leave the choice up to you."

She sputtered. "If I were a man, I would call you out, sir."

"If I were a woman, I would kiss me again."

* * *

"What do you have there?"

"I don't know," Samantha said absently, brushing dust off the top of the box and stepping to the ground. Mahogany, polished and inlaid—and old. Not some child's treasure box.

"Goodness," Montgomery said, looking over her shoulder. "Open it."

She wanted to. Badly. She was in charge of security for this building, after all, so technically she needed to know about everything inside it. Even old, hidden things. Even when they were inside the stable walls of Rick's ancestral property.

And a closed box of all things—she'd spent the last ten months resisting temptation, but nobody could expect her to ignore a box that had literally fallen into her hands. Rick wouldn't.

Taking a deep breath, she opened the lid. A blue diamond the size of a walnut winked at her. Gasping, she snapped the box closed again. *Christ*.

Montgomery gaped. "That—"

"Excuse me for a minute, will you," she stammered, and headed for the door.

The box gripped hard in her hands, she crossed the temporary parking lot they'd put in for the exhibition, opened the low garden gate with her hip, and strode up to the massive house.

A diamond. A *fucking* diamond. That sneak. They'd been dating—hell, living together—since three days after they'd met, and he'd made it clear that he wanted her in his life for the rest of his life. But he also knew that she had an abysmal track record for staying in one place for very long and that she didn't work with partners.

If this was his way of giving her a gift without sending her running for the hills, well, it was pretty clever, really. He knew she liked puzzles—and a hidden box in a secret hold in a wall was a puzzle. But a diamond wasn't just a gift. Diamonds meant something.

"Rick!" she yelled as she reached the main foyer.

"What?" He leaned over the balcony above and behind her. "You didn't kill Montgomery, did you?"

"I like Montgomery."

For a heartbeat she just looked at him. Black hair, deep blue eyes, a professional soccer player's body— and all hers. The smart-ass remark she'd been ready to make about the diamond stuck in her throat.

"What is it?" he repeated in his deep, slightly faded British accent, and descended the stairs. He wore a loose gray t-shirt, and his feet were bare. Mmm, salty goodness.

Still clutching the box in one hand, she walked to the base of the stairs, grabbed his shoulder, and kissed him.

Rick slid his hands around her hips and pulled her closer. She sighed, leaning along his lean, muscular body. Out of the corner of her eye she saw Sykes the butler start through the foyer, see them, and turn around to head back out the way he'd come in.

Pulling away from her an inch or two, Rick tucked a piece of her hair back behind her ear. "What exactly

were you and Mr. Montgomery discussing?" he
asked. "Not that I'm going to complain about it."

She took another breath, her heart pounding all
over again. "I found it, Brit. It's . . . Thank you, but
. . . it's too much."

His brow furrowed. "What are you talking about,
Yank?"

Samantha moved the box around between them.
"This. When did you put it—"

Rick took it from her hands, glanced at her face,
then opened it. "Good God," he breathed, lifting
the sparkling orb out of the box by its silver chain.
"Where did this come fr—"

"You didn't put it there?"

Of course he hadn't. She was an idiot. Did that
mean she'd been hoping for a diamond? So much
for independent Sam Elizabeth Jellicoe. Great.